The Queen of Diamonds
J M Diggle

Also available by J M Diggle

ZAK

A mind-blowing, rollercoaster ride full of surprises that will keep you enthralled until the final page

Zak's day wasn't going exactly as planned.

Abducted from prison, he finds himself at the mercy of the enigmatic Ron Miller who is hellbent on experimenting on him with advanced technology and increasing danger.

Lost and confused in a practically deserted town, Zak teams up with Julie who seems to be having a worse day than him, and Randy – a bright but stroppy teenager who is trying to take on the world with a homemade spear.

Escaping Ron's army of guards and rodent-like robots won't be quite as easy as they first thought and when they finally discover Ron's goal and how their lives are inexplicably linked, the terrifying truth is far more unbelievable than any of them could have ever imagined.

Zak is available from Amazon books in paperback or for download as an E-book.

First Published May 2020

For my wife and children

(Sorry about Chapter 24)

Part 1
The Challenge

Intro – GreySpider

Wednesday 1st January.

He pressed the "Enter" key on his post on the GreySpider public forum at exactly midnight on 1st January 2020. He could hear a countdown to New Year's Day just starting in the apartment below. Idiots. They're ten seconds late. What's the point of counting in the New Year if you can't get it right? Punctuality was something that mattered, timing was everything – a trait that he had adopted from his overbearing father who had once grounded him for a week for coming home thirty seconds past his curfew.

He re-read the post, checking the spelling and grammar, making sure the punctuation was perfect. Then he did it again. He'd already made four drafts and read it umpteen times before he posted it. Measure twice, cut once - another pearl of wisdom from dear old daddy.

Most people wouldn't see it until long after the partying had finished and the hangovers had subsided, but it was done. It was out there. It was the beginning. He got up from the comfortable leather chair in his makeshift office, yawned, and stretched. Time for bed. As he made his way through the apartment to the master bedroom at the back, he paused in the kitchen to turn the calendar to January and pour himself a glass of mineral water from the bottle in the fridge. Glancing out the window he saw fireworks being let off over the city, the muted explosions followed by raucous cheers and drunken laughter. He raised his glass of water to the outside world.

"Happy New Year" he mumbled, taking a swig.

He lay in bed in the dark, staring up at the ceiling, and thought about the coming months and what might happen. He had taken a step into the unknown – something that didn't sit well with him but was necessary if he was going to achieve the impossible. He couldn't do it alone. He needed help. He needed expertise. And, if he was going to steal the most valuable diamond in the country then he needed others to pin the blame on. All the planning he had done so far was perfect. Meticulous. The one thing he couldn't fully plan was who would be joining him. How trustworthy would they be? Would they be loyal if things started to go wrong? One slight personality clash and it could all come tumbling down. As he struggled with this concept, an idea formed. He was too tired to pursue it fully, but sat up, switched the light on, and wrote it down on the pad he always kept by the side of the bed. He replaced the pen on the bedside table, ensuring it was laid perpendicular to the side.

He lay back and considered the new idea. Could he do it? It might work. It would take some additional planning, but that was what he was good at. "Be prepared." He'd never been a scout, but their motto was something he liked to always adhere to where possible.

Enough for now. He needed sleep. He had plenty of time to work the details out later, but he liked it. A small smile crept on his face as he pictured the diamond. The "Queen of Diamonds", estimated at fifty million – not a figure he would ever see, but he had a contact who knew a man who would give him twenty.

He reached for the light, checked his pen was straight and clicked it off.

Yes. It might be possible. He could use GreySpider.

****

GreySpider Public Forum

Date: 01-01-2020 00:00
From: AceOfDiamonds
Subject: A Challenge

Greetings fellow spiders. Happy New Year to you all.

A new year brings new prospects, new hopes, new ideas – and new challenges. Challenges that could lead to big changes. Changes that could lead to big rewards. Rewards I'd like to share with like-minded Spiders such as your good selves.
I'm looking for a team. A team that is worthy to join in something big. Huge. Life-changing. Never-having-to-work-again enormous.

Interested?

Then here is my challenge. Actually, let's not call it a challenge. An Interview – Or an induction if you will.

There are four diamonds scattered across museums in London. They have nominal value – about ten thousand each, but the value is of no significance at this time. This is merely a chance to prove yourself for something bigger. The diamonds are known as "The Four Feathers" – you can read all about them on Google. The challenge is to steal a diamond and post a picture in a private message to me. Pass my challenge and you join my team. Join my team, and the "Four Feathers" will seem like costume jewelry compared to what is coming.

Oh, and there's a deadline. Let's make it the 14th of February. I mean – Everyone wants a diamond for Valentine's Day.

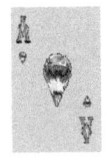

Chapter 1 – "The Wizard of Oz"

Friday 3rd January.

"Ladies and Gentlemen. As you can see, behind me is a glass tank in two sections. The bottom section contains two holes, one on either side. The top section..."

He removed the silk sheet that was covering the top of the tank with a flourish to reveal that it was filled with snakes.

"...contains ten. Yes - That's ten pythons. These snakes are highly poisonous and are liable to bite given half a chance. Now - I need a volunteer."

Oscar Zachery, aka "The Wizard of Oz" looked out to his audience hopefully. Not that there was much of an audience to consider. No one had any money in January, he mused. He'd been playing the circuit for a while now and had gained a following, but the small club was only about a third full. It was a far cry from the more prestigious talent spots available in places like "Everest" or "The Sunrise", but it gave him a chance to hone his act to perfection. And he got to spend some time with Brandy.

"Come on, I won't bite. The snakes might, but I'll do my best to keep them locked up."

The beautiful Brandy shimmied down the steps of the small stage into the audience to look for a likely candidate. She generally had better luck than Oscar at finding offers of help. Probably something to do with the red, skin-tight leatherette dress she was wearing that barely covered her ample bosom and showed off her bare-toned legs that went on forever. He was momentarily distracted as her bottom wiggled its way through the tables in front of him before stopping at a middle-aged, balding man who probably thought he stood a chance with this goddess and was staring at her hopefully.

She grabbed him by the wrist, and led him back to the stage, hips swinging provocatively with every step.

"Give the man a round of applause. Thank you, Sir. What's your name?"

"Bob. Bob Roberts" said the man, stealing a final glance at Brandy as she retreated behind him to the glass box.

"Bob Roberts? Seriously? Were your parents drunk when they named you?" Oscar earned himself a mild ripple of laughter from the thinning crowd. "I think I'll call you Bob Bob." Another ripple, slightly louder. Maybe he could win them over yet.

"OK, Bob Bob. I want you to make sure that I'm not cheating and that when I'm chained into the box it's all secure and fair. Is that OK?"

Bob Bob nodded and Oscar led him back to Brandy who had a smile fixed on her face like an air stewardess. Brandy helped Oscar into the box through a front panel and he crouched down thrusting his hand through the hole on the left while she danced provocatively around with a pair of handcuffs.

"Bob Bob, can you please check the handcuffs? Make sure there are no trapdoors, holes, or release mechanisms and that there is nothing out of the ordinary with them."

Bob Bob took them from Brandy and examined them.

"Looks fine to me," he said, looking directly at the girl as he said it. Who needed a good act when he had Brandy as the perfect distraction, mused Oscar?

Brandy retrieved the handcuffs and continued her dance around the stage. She spun around the back of the box, and with one swift, practiced move switched them for another pair that was hooked to the back of the box. Oscar continued his spiel while this was happening. It was hard to distract attention from the gorgeous blonde, but it had the desired effect, and no one spotted the switch.

"OK. Brandy will now strap my hand to the side of the box with the handcuffs so that I cannot pull it back through."

She obliged, slipping it around his wrist and through a metal loop and he tugged his hand a few times to show that it wouldn't come off.

"Are you paying attention, Bob Bob? To me, I mean. Are you happy that my hand is secure?"

Bob Bob reluctantly tore his eyes away and checked the cuff once more that was now holding Oscar's wrist in place.

"Yes. All good."

Brandy repeated her performance with a second cuff and secured Oscar's right hand.

"What a life," said Oscar. "She chains me up every night you know, and I only pay her twenty percent." A louder laugh from the audience. Things were going well.

"OK, Bob Bob. Before I let you go, I want you to close the lid of the box and lock it with the padlock."

Brandy handed him a strong brass padlock, that he checked thoroughly. This one had no need to be switched, so it looked more substantial on purpose. Bob Bob bent and closed the door shutting Oscar in, and secured the padlock through another metal loop, giving it a shake to confirm that it was indeed shut.

"Excellent. Thanks for your help, Bob Bob. Can you kindly return to your seat before I let the snakes out? Give him a round of applause."

Brandy led him reluctantly off the stage to a small smattering of applause.

"OK. Now watch closely."

Brandy continued her prancing to the back of the box and climbed up some steps that led her to the top, so she was standing above the snakes. She raised a black curtain up that surrounded the box, and Oscar slowly disappeared from view.

Time stood still for a moment and everything appeared to go silent, and suddenly Oscar heard a rush of air followed by a faraway voice in his head.

"It's not going to work Ozzy. Don't do it. It will never work."

He shook his head. Shit. Not now. Not while he was working. He'd missed his pill yesterday. Did he take one today? He always had problems if he skipped his medication. Get out of my head he screamed silently and knocked it on the side of the glass wall of the box. The rushing sound in his ears disappeared and he was back.

The curtain was just covering the lower box when he sprung to action, the voice forgotten. He had the handcuffs off in four well-rehearsed seconds. Brandy was gyrating sexily with the curtain while this occurred. Another two seconds and he was out of the back of the compartment. He pulled a lever and the snakes were released into the lower compartment and he gave a long piercing shriek while clipping the handcuffs to two loops on the upper box and pulling another lever which dropped a new base to the upper box, trapping the snakes below. The audience gasped as they saw the snakes drop. This was his favorite bit. He loved the drama. He'd seen similar tricks performed time and time again — but the snakes were his own addition and it was always a crowd-pleaser.

Brandy raised the sheet above her head, and he jumped up so they could swap places. He lowered the sheet half a second later to reveal just his head and shoulders and the audience applauded while Brandy was stripping off the outer layer of her costume, quick-change style into a snakeskin outfit. Before the applause subsided, she had clambered into the back of the upper box, thrust her hands through the holes, and into the open handcuffs that Oscar had left for her. A quick flick of the wrist and they snapped shut just as Oscar dropped the sheet, revealing Brandy in her new, even sexier attire, chained up in the top box.

The audience got to their feet as Oscar released Brandy, led her to the front of the stage and they took a bow.

"I've been the Wizard of Oz. Thanks for coming. Enjoy the rest of your night."

****

"What 'appened?" said Brandy.

They were in the tiny dressing room after the show, packing up their gear.

"What do you mean?" Oscar was preoccupied with the snakes, making sure they were well secured before he went back out front to have a drink, something he always liked to do with his audience. He thought it made him more personable and approachable.

"You paused. I saw ya stop and then bang yer 'ead on the side of the box. Are y' OK?"

As beautiful as Brandy was, she had the most common of common East end accents, something that didn't quite fit her look.

The memory of the voice returned. "Oh. Nothing. My mind wandered" he said evasively. "Good show tonight. You're getting quicker at that costume change, and the handcuffs worked perfectly tonight."

She winced. At the last show, she couldn't get the left handcuff to snap shut when she got into the upper box and it was left dangling. Oscar had removed it as quick as possible, but she was sure the people at the front had seen it.

"Bloody 'andcuffs. Fink they need oilin' or summink."

"I'll get them checked out. Don't worry. Let's go meet the punters. I think Bob Bob might be waiting for you" he said with a glint in his eye.

She cackled. "I'd fuckin' eat 'im alive."

Oscar winced. He loved being on stage with her, loved watching her, watching the effect she had on the audience, but five minutes chatting to her was enough to remind him that keeping things on a professional basis was a good idea. He still had fantasies about her when he was alone though.

"Come on. I'll buy you a rum and coke."

Chapter 2 – "Voices"

Oscar got home just before midnight. He had only had half a lager, while Brandy quickly finished off three rum and cokes and was working on a fourth. He had left her chatting to a young barman who was doubling up her drinks without her noticing as she got friendlier.

"Be careful" were his parting words.

"Where's the fuckin' fun in that" she replied and cackled.

He shook his head, gave her a peck on the cheek, and scarpered. He wasn't her dad and at twenty-three she was old enough to look after herself. In hindsight, he should have been warning the barman who, by now, was probably chained to a bed somewhere while she showed him her own brand of magic. Lucky bastard.

He grabbed himself some cheese and crackers – not the best snack before bed, but his stomach was calling him.

"Cheese at night will only make the voices worse" he heard Dr. Pullman, his shrink telling him. How ironic that the doc was treating him for his condition, and it was his voice that was often prominent in his mind.

"Fuck you doc" he mumbled, munching on a large hunk of smoked Applewood.

He sat at his desk and took his laptop out of standby, taking a bite on a cracker while he waited for the familiar Windows screen to appear. He checked his emails; one from his brother, two from Amazon, and a dozen or so junk messages from various online shopping companies. He deleted the junk, checked the Amazon orders – one for a new stage jacket, another for some silk handkerchiefs for the act, and then opened the one from his brother.

"Hey Oz, how's it hanging. Need your advice. Call me."

A man of few words, Ed was a part-time security guard, part-time dad to Benji, and part-time twin brother to Oz. They rarely spoke to each other on the phone, communicating more often in short sentences via emails such as this one.

Oscar glanced at his watch. It was a bit late. With any luck, he wouldn't answer, and the ball would be back in his court. He called Ed's number and was relieved when it went to voice mail.

"Hey, Ed. It's just gone midnight. Just got in from a show. Thought you might still be up. What's going on? I'm out a fair bit tomorrow, but you can leave me a message if I don't pick up."

He hung up and tossed the phone on the desk, returning to the laptop. Emails dealt with, he closed the Outlook app and clicked on the spider icon on his desktop. The GreySpider logon screen appeared and he entered his username, Ozzy92, followed by his password.

He had been a member for just over a year and used it as a forum to talk to others in his business. GreySpider connected people from all walks of life, but generally those leaning towards the darker, more sinister side of the web. Illegal software, movies, and music were prominent – but equally, there were just as many members looking for shady deals, dark magic, weapons, pornography, and it was rumored that there were even hit men available if you knew the right people to talk to. Oscar's interest lay at the whiter end of this very questionable site. He had made some good contacts and was currently picking up normally unaffordable magic paraphernalia at a fraction of the cost of other online stores. Was it legit? He never asked and they never told him, but money was tight, and keeping the show fresh wasn't cheap.

He checked his GreySpider messages hoping to find an update from TrickyDicky_09 but his "web" was empty. GreySpider's private messages went into what they called "webs". Then there were the open forums called "clusters". The clusters were listed in popularity order, with the ones getting the most hits at the top. Oscar rarely had much interest in clusters but tended to glance at the daily top five to see if there was anything that caught his eye. He once got interested in a discussion about voodoo and how DarkQueen69 claimed that she could make you feel her touch over the wi-fi waves. He thought there may be some content for his show, and her profile picture was hot with a capital H, but it had turned out to be a sales scam.

"For just £19.99, I can show you how this works, and demonstrate it, one-on-one in a private web chat."

Tempting? Not really. Her profile pic was probably fake anyway – as most of the members' photos were. GreySpider had a very anonymous clientele.

He scanned the top five clusters, seeing nothing of interest, and was about to close the page, when he noticed the number of posts. There was usually around a hundred if it was something vaguely interesting. Today though, he found the top cluster had over eight hundred – surely a record. He looked at the subject – "A Challenge" and, intrigued by the sheer amount of attention that the cluster had obtained, double-clicked to open it.

He read the message from someone calling himself the AceOfDiamonds. Pretty bold message, he thought. Most users of the site were hidden behind unbreakable firewalls but were still cautious when posting in clusters - especially due to the nature of some of the things that went on. He read it again and then started glancing through some of the comments. There was a real mix – some thought it was a joke, some thought it was funny, and others strongly condemned "Ace", as they were calling him, for bringing such illegalities to the forefront of their site. Who were they kidding?

01-01-2020 00:14, Squealer_21

Ace-dude, Love the post. HNY to u 2. Count me in. This could b FUN

01-01-2020 00:15, Bimbo123

Ten thousand – Nominal value? If it's nominal to u, then pls pass them my way honey

01-01-2020 00:22, WonderWoman1

Why not steal the crown Jewels while you're at it. Oh no, too late – I've beat you to it [Image attached]

01-01-2020 00:23, XavierTheGreat

What a dick

01-01-2020 00:24, VibratingRabbit

Hey Ace, look forward to joining your team on Valentine's Day.

It went on, pages and pages. He scrolled down a few:-

01-01-2020 14:01, BadgerBadger80

Do the police monitor this forum? These diamonds will be under lock and key by now

01-01-2020 14:02, LoonyToons88

Sounds like fun. Can I sell u my diamond when I get it? Cud do with 10 big ones right now

01-01-2020 14:03, JackHammer11

Gullible idiots. This guy's full of shit. If u get caught trying this, then u deserve all u get

Oscar chuckled. It had certainly sparked some interest. He'd never seen anything like it before. He added his own message before switching off.

03-01-2020 00:21, Ozzy92

I applaud you for livening up the clusters. The promise to join the 'team" sounds intriguing

He logged off. He'd have to keep his eye on the news to see if anyone actually tried to pull this off. There were enough desperate people out there who would attempt this and fail. He would also check in on the cluster from time to time to see if there were any updates about anyone joining Ace's team.

Twenty minutes later, as he lay in bed, his mind started wandering as he dozed. What exactly did Ace have in mind if he thought that ten-grand diamonds were just costume jewelry? Oscar's bank balance was more often in the red than the black right now. He would never get his show to Vegas on the poultry sums of money he was earning working the local circuit. He needed to get bigger and to get bigger he needed a big influx of cash.

A vision of Brandy in her red, leatherette dress filled his mind. He was on stage, cuffed to a chair and she was cavorting around him, a snake around her neck, her lips painted the same red as the dress that was slowly riding up over her thighs. She stopped in front of him and bent forward, her partly naked bottom inches from his face as she lowered the snake to the ground. It slithered away, forgotten as she turned around and straddled his legs, thrusting once, twice against him, holding his head between her huge breasts, preventing him from breathing.

Suddenly, a rush of air, a faraway voice.

"Do it, Oscar. Get the feather. One feather is all you need. Change your life."

Oscar woke with a start and banged his head on the pillow three times. Was that part of the dream? He knew immediately that it wasn't. The rush of air that preceded the voice was always a giveaway. He turned the light on and scrabbled in his bedside cabinet drawer for his tablets, wide awake now, the dream of Brandy long lost. He swallowed one down with a glass of water, hesitated, and then took another. His hands were shaking. It had been under control for quite a while, so hearing it twice in a day had really unnerved him. He reached for his wallet and thumbed through the various credit cards, a coffee loyalty card, and a condom that had been there longer than he would like to admit to anyone. He dragged out a business card for a "Dr. Pullman, Private Psychiatrist."

Well, he always said call at any time, thought Oscar. He tapped the number into his phone and waited as it rang three, four, five times.

"You've reached the voice mail of Dr. Aaron Pullman. I'm not available right now, but please leave a message and I will call you back."

"Erm. Hi Dr. Pullman. It's Oscar. Oscar Zachery. I've had a couple of episodes today. First time in ages. It's kinda spooked me a bit. I wanted to talk about the medication. I think I may have missed one, but I've done that before, and it's usually OK. I may need to up the dose a bit. Anyway, umm, sorry to call so late. Call me back tomorrow and let me know."

He hung up.

Sleep forgotten, he scrolled through his phone again and stopped at Brandy, the dream resurfacing. He typed her a quick message

"Hey. Just dozing off and thought I'd check you got home safely. Good show tonight. See you on the 15th. We're at the Lincoln. Bring the black sparkly leotard. We're doing the knife-wheel. Take care x"

Knife throwing was a recent addition to the act, but Oscar had practiced it to perfection. Brandy was OK with the knives but wasn't too keen on being spun upside down for over a minute.

He didn't expect a reply and was surprised and pleased when his phoned pinged. She'd sent him a throwing-up smiley and a kiss. Well, at least she was OK. He had mixed feelings for the girl. She was five years younger than him, annoying as hell to talk to, but he struggled to keep his eyes off her. Dreams like the one he'd just had were becoming more common. She'd joined the act six months ago, and the audience was definitely on the up, and definitely more male orientated.

He sent her a laughing/crying smiley, another kiss, and muted the phone.

He turned the light off again and tried to sleep, his mind switching between Brandy, his brother, and the GreySpider message from Ace. Maybe I'll check out one of the museums tomorrow he thought as he finally succumbed to sleep.

Chapter 3 – "Buddy"

Tuesday 7th January.

Buddy Barnes sat at the bar and peered over his fake Rayban sunglasses watching the couple by the window sipping their coffee. They were deep in conversation, blissfully unaware of what was going on around them, eyes locked on each other. First date? thought Buddy. Maybe the second. Either way, they were perfect. Buddy had watched the plates being cleared away, and the two bottles of expensive wine were nearly gone. Even better. The more wine, the less observant the mark in his experience.

The restaurant was crowded when he had entered twenty minutes before. He had no intention of eating and was drinking his pint of mud at the bar as slowly as possible, waiting for his moment.

"You want a pint of mud?" The barman had never heard of it, something that Buddy experienced a lot.

"Yes mud," said Buddy.

Still a blank look.

"Orange juice and coke," said Buddy.

"Together?" said the barman in disbelief. The name tag pinned to his smart white shirt informed Buddy that he was talking to "Ged".

"Yup. If you get it right, it should look just like mud."

Ged looked around to see if he was being pranked – not the first time since he had taken the job.

"You want orange juice and coke? In the same glass?"

"That would be nice."

Ged gave him an "I've seen it all now" look and turned to make the drink, then stopped and came back.

"What goes in first?"

"Ged my man, I'll let you decide. Just make sure you mix it well."

Buddy had been drinking it for years. Not as sharp as Orange Juice, and not as fizzy as coke, it was his drink of choice when he was working. The only downside was that it tended to attract attention, something he normally liked to avoid.

As he observed the couple at the window, he played his usual time-passing game of sizing up the mark. The guy was mid-thirties, good-looking in a clean-cut kind of way, smartly dressed, beige trousers, and a tight-fitting designer shirt. Expensive haircut – undoubtedly done today just for the date, and the watch on his wrist looked expensive too. Probably works in the city. A banker maybe? No, the mannerisms were all wrong. He was cocky, and he wasn't wearing socks. Probably a stockbroker. Probably called Rupert or something.

The girl was a gorgeous brunette, quite petite, around five-three he reckoned, also well dressed, but he could tell that she had done it on a budget. The jewelry was cheap, and the "designer" shoes were readily available down at Camden for fifteen pounds - he knew because he had bought a pair for his girlfriend Shanice for Christmas. If the brunette was trying to bag herself a rich, city-type boyfriend then she seemed to be getting it right though as "Rupert" was transfixed.

He watched her toss her long locks of hair, laughing at something inane that Rupert had just said, and finished off her coffee.

Ten minutes passed and Buddy thought that they were never going to leave. Just as he was about to buy another mud, he saw Rupert signal a passing waiter for the bill. That was his cue. He watched carefully, knowing that timing was off the essence. A few minutes passed, and the bill was presented to Rupert on a little silver tray and the waiter wandered off.

Too soon, and it would be suspicious. Too long, and the waiter would be back. Buddy had this part down to a fine art though. He took in the busy restaurant, the number of waiters, the lack of a queue – no one was waiting to nab their table, and he knew it would be a good five minutes before the waiter returned.

After four, he got up and grabbed a beer towel off the bar. The white shirt he was wearing was the same style as the guy behind the bar who had served him. He removed his sunglasses, tucking them away, and made his way to the couple. As he approached, he casually took a card reader from his pocket, dropping it on the table in front of Rupert when he got there.

"Sir, madam. I hope you had a pleasant meal" he said. He picked up the discarded coffee cups, took the beer towel, and wiped the coffee rings off the table.

"Oh, lovely thank you," said the girl, barely looking at him. "We must come again, Rupert."

Buddy nearly choked. Bloody hell, his name really is Rupert. He composed himself as Rupert passed him an American Express card. He stuck the card in the machine, checked the bill - £89.49, and typed in the amount, passing the keypad to Rupert.

Rupert was cautious and shielded the pad as he typed in his pin code. No matter, the machine didn't work anyway. It read the card, took all the details, and stored the pin, but didn't have any possible way of taking the payment.

He handed the card machine back to Buddy who took it and frowned. He held it in the air as if he was trying to get a signal, shook it, and then sighed exasperatedly. Taking a quick glance around, he noticed that the other waiters were at the far side of the restaurant, so thought he'd try his luck.

"I'm sorry Sir. I've been having trouble all night with American Express cards. The machine isn't connecting. Let me go and try another."

Jumping at the chance to impress, Rupert stopped him. "No worries, I have a Barclaycard. Shall we try that?"

They repeated the process with the Barclaycard, and not surprisingly, that one didn't work either.

"I'm so sorry," said Buddy. He handed the card back. "It must be my machine. I'll send my colleague over with the other one. He won't be long."

He carried the coffee cups towards the door, found an empty table, dropped them, wiped it with the beer towel as he glanced back to make sure Rupert wasn't watching, and casually exited the restaurant.

Two cards and no suspicions. Within the hour, he would have cloned the cards, and taken the maximum daily limit from the nearest cashpoint machine from both. If he was lucky, he could do the same tomorrow, and again each day, until Rupert checked his account and canceled the cards.

****

While Rupert and his new girlfriend were sharing their first kiss in his modern penthouse suite overlooking the Thames, Buddy was back home cloning his two cards. He'd also made a quick call on the way back home.

"Hi, Shanice. It's Bud. What you up to? Fancy a bite to eat? My treat. I'll be at Raphael's at...", he checked his watch. "Nine forty-five. I'll go ahead and order. Join me if you get this."

Their relationship, if you could call it that, had been more off than on since they had met three months ago, and part of him believed that she was only interested in his work. He had met her while pulling the same scam that he'd just done on Rupert. She had been sat on the table next to the mark and had watched the whole thing play out. She'd followed Buddy out of the restaurant and threatened to go back and spill the beans, demanding half the money. She had balls, a cute face, and a determination about her that he found appealing. And he just loved that Irish accent. He agreed but managed to persuade her to join him for dinner. They had met just four times since, twice at Raphael's and, although he enjoyed her company, he didn't really believe it was going anywhere.

The cloning unit spat out the second card and he was good to go. It was the best investment he'd made on GreySpider since he'd joined just over a year ago. He shut down his computer, grabbed a coat, and headed to the tube station. Trafalgar Square this time. He never liked to try a cloned card too close to home in case an alert had been placed on the account, so he was currently working his way around the Monopoly board to ensure he didn't visit the same place twice.

Twenty minutes later, he pulled an Arsenal cap down low over his face, aware that most city cash machines had cameras behind them, and inserted the first card into a machine at the subway station, typing in the pin number that he had acquired. He held his breath. Had Rupert got suspicious and already canceled the cards? Not tonight. It seemed that he had other things on his mind. Each card promptly gave up £300 in crisp twenties.

Result. He stuffed the notes into his wallet with the cards, removed the baseball cap, and dropped it in a nearby bin, congratulating himself on a job well done. He left the tube station and took a slow walk to Raphael's in Covent Garden, one of his favorite Italian restaurants. He was a few minutes early and Shanice hadn't replied. Looks like he could be dining alone.

Raphael's was only about half full, and he was lucky enough to bag a table by the window.

"Buona sera Raph. Quiet night?"

"Hello my friend," said Raphael embracing him. "It's January. It's always quiet. Even in central London, we get fewer people out in January. I think Christmas should be canceled."

"Ahh, but then you won't get the Christmas parties, the ladies dressed in their little black dresses, and the big tipping city boys." He thought of Rupert as he said it and smiled to himself. Poor Rupert had had an unexpectedly expensive night. At least he was with his girl, he thought glumly.

"December was a good month" admitted Raphael. "Should pay for my trip back home next week."

Raphael's elderly parents lived on the outskirts of Rome, and he tried to get back to see them once a year. He had moved to London over twenty years ago to study languages and cookery – a strange combination, but one that had been invaluable when he opened the restaurant in such a multi-cultural city. His English was better than Buddy's and he was also fluent in Spanish, French, and of course Italian.

"Are you on your own tonight? Where's the beautiful Shanice?"

"She's right behind you" came a strong Irish brogue. Right sounded more like "royt".

He spun round and threw his hands in the air. "Sei Bellissima," he said beaming, and grabbing her face in his hands, kissing her on both cheeks.

"Hey, hands-off. You get more action than me" said Buddy laughing, jumping up to pull her chair back for her. "You made it."

She kissed him, her flowing fire-red hair tickling his neck as she came close.

"I was on the tube when you called. The signal was awful. God, I need a drink. I've had a shocking day."

Shanice was twenty, very Irish, and very, very red-headed. She spent too much money on hair dye, something she admitted herself, but the look was very striking, and it certainly turned heads. She was a part-time personal trainer at a gym on the south of the Thames. The rest of her time was spent studying for a business degree - two more years and some hard saving and the plan was to set up on her own. "Shan's gym" was the unimaginative name she had come up with, something she had reminded Buddy each time they had met.

"You look great," said Buddy.

"I look like shite," said Shanice. "Two guys got into a punch up at the gym. One went sprawling and knocked this poor young lass flying. She starts crying, and I had to deal with the mess." She turned to Raph. "You got a gin 'n' tonic Raph. A double would be grand."

"I'll have a beer," said Buddy to Raph. "Get one for yourself."

"Jesus. You must have had a good day."

He quietly told her about his success with Rupert, being careful to leave out the fact that he'd scored two cards instead of one. He still didn't fully trust her after the way they had met, although she had seemed pretty genuine on their other dates.

"I think I need to change careers," she said. "Three hundred. Just like that? If you need any help, just give me a call."

"I might take you up on that. Most cons are easier with two people. We can…." He stopped as Raph trotted over with their drinks.

"You're a star, my man," said Buddy. "Are you eating?" he asked Shanice. She hadn't even glanced at the menu.

"Just some olives for me," said. "Got to watch my figure."

"Something I like to do all the time" muttered Buddy. "I'll have the Carbonara and some garlic bread," he said to Raph. "With mozzarella."

"So, what did you have in mind?" said Shanice, when Raph was gone, taking a large swig of her gin. "Awww, that's good"

"There are quite a few cons where two people are better than one," said Buddy. "But I've been considering a landlord scam. Basically, we find an abandoned flat, shove up a "To Let" sign and stick an ad in the paper. It's pretty easy to get some keys cut, and I can draw up a fake contract. What I'd need from you is to show the mark around the flat. Give him a price he can't refuse, flutter your eyelashes a bit. Basically, do a good sales pitch. Most people trust a woman more than a man when it comes to this. Once you get a bite, we send them the contracts, take a deposit, and the first month's rent. We can even hand over the keys."

"That's it?"

"Yep. We just disappear. If you're good, you can even sell the same place twice before we hand the keys over. You might have to do something with your hair though. You're very," he paused and took a sip of his beer. "noticeable". He grinned. "Believe me. That's a good thing, but not when you don't want to be remembered."

She stirred her gin and considered it.

"So where are you while I'm taking all the risks?"

Buddy laughed. "I'll be playing the part of the landlord. You're the agent. Once you agree on a deal, I'll be there insisting on cash only. This is where we may lose the mark. No one likes to hand over a grand plus in cash, so it's all about persuasion. It works well if you can befriend them. If they look like they're gonna run, I can always back down, pretend to take a card payment, and steal their card details instead. We probably won't get as much, but it's a fair backup plan."

"I could tell them I live in the flat above," said Shanice, thoughtfully.

"That would work. All helps with adding to the trust. You could tell them what a good landlord I am and that I don't give you any grief."

The food arrived, and they chatted some more, ironing out the details. Buddy ordered a second beer and began to relax. He found that he really liked this girl but kept warning himself not to get too close.

"So how do you get the keys for the flat?" she said while he was tucking into his pasta.

"Ahh, there's some pretty reasonably priced kit on GreySpider that I've been looking at. It can take a mold of the lock-in seconds, and then we make a set of keys to fit." He had told her about GreySpider on their second date and she had signed up straight away and downloaded a ton of music to play at the gym.

"Ah, have you seen that post about the diamonds?" she said, chasing an olive around the bowl with a cocktail stick.

"Diamonds?" He was intrigued.

"Yeh. Some idiot asking people to steal some diamonds. It's gone mental. Well over a thousand posts. Apparently, it's like an interview – for something bigger."

"I'll have to take a look," said Buddy. He'd scored some diamonds on a con a couple of years ago and made a killing.

"You can't miss it. It's been the top post all week."

After the meal, Buddy paid the bill, hugged Raph, and they said their goodbyes and took a walk to Leicester Square so she could pick up the Northern Line.

"Find that flat," she said, kissing him hard on the lips. "God knows I need the money right now. Call me."

He watched her bright red hair disappear down the steps, contemplating the evening. She had definitely seemed keener tonight. Was it just the lure of the con? Maybe it would be worth bringing her in from time to time just to keep her sweet. She turned and waved, blew him a kiss, and was gone.

Chapter 4 – "It's all in the Planning"

Buddy was home within the hour and logged onto his GreySpider account – Budster_007, one that he had chosen after watching Daniel Craig in the latest James Bond film. He ran a quick search for "key copying" and "lock moulding", and made a few notes, saving one device into his favorites. If the landlord con turned out to have legs, then he would need to spend some money first. It would take a chunk of money out of the first scam, but if it paid for the gear it would be a good investment.

He turned his attention to the top clusters, and sure enough, there it was – "A challenge" at number one. Nearly fifteen hundred people had left comments now. That's nuts, he thought. The second most popular, a forum about safe cracking that had sparked some interest a week or so ago, only had a hundred and two. He read the message from "Ace" twice and then fired up a browser to google "The Four Feathers".

"The Four Feathers are a set of pear-shaped purple-pink diamonds of half a carat each. They were commissioned in 1985 by Sir Tom Mathers for an exhibition celebrating the twenty-fifth anniversary of Mather's Diamonds and were subsequently donated to the Society of Jewellery Historians on the death of Sir Tom in 2012. They are now on show at four museums across London (See links below). As with all diamonds, valuations fluctuate wildly, but the latest suggestions predict them to be worth around ten to fifteen thousand pounds each. The stones....."

He scrolled down to the museum links and was surprised to see that all four were in lesser-known, smaller museums around the city. It seemed that Sir Tom was keen for his diamonds to be showpieces and didn't want them to be lost amongst the finer jewels found in the likes of the British Museum or the Tower of

London. Very clever Ace thought Buddy. No one would contemplate a diamond heist from the Tower of London. The security would make it impossible. However, by setting a modest challenge such as this, then it would definitely spark more interest, something that had clearly worked because he could already feel his own adrenaline pick up a notch.

When he was younger, he had dabbled in a spate of robberies but found he had more of a flair for small cons. They were easier to get away with, and harder for the police to trace him. Straight robberies always left clues - fingerprints, footprints, DNA, images on cameras. A con tended to happen on the streets, or in public spaces. A lot of people who fell for cons were too embarrassed to report them, something that had allowed him to stay under the radar for the last eight years.

He read about the four museums and picked the one furthest from where he lived. It was in Borehamwood - "Rhombus House", a three-story former townhouse with just six exhibition rooms, one of them dedicated to jewelry. He scribbled down the name and address and spent half an hour reading their website, learning as much as he could about the place. They even had an online interactive video where you could fly through the museum's rooms, and it didn't take him long to learn that one of the Four Feathers diamonds lived on the second floor.

Sounds like a visit could be in order, he thought. Should he take Shanice? It would be less conspicuous if he went with a girl, but then again this was something he wanted to do alone, even though she had brought it to his attention. He wanted to see how she worked on the landlord scam before he brought her into anything riskier. Maybe he would tell her later, show off the diamond – assuming he could pull off the robbery.

He started to make a hand-written list of things that he needed to consider, something he always did when planning a con. Always pen and paper. He didn't like to leave a digital trail on the PC:-

- Security
    - Camera
    - Guards
    - Locks
    - Alarms

- Access
    - Entrances
    - Exits
    - Windows
    - Roof?

- Personnel
    - Staff - Day
    - Staff – Night

- Location
    - Nearby Street cameras
    - Streetlamps / Visibility from the road

- Other
    - Opening times
    - Disguise
    - Purpose for Visit?

He stopped and pondered the last point. If he could come up with a story, he may be able to innocently ask more questions when he was casing the place. Then again, it would make him more memorable. As a con man, he was used to talking - it always worked as a distraction and tended to set people's minds at ease. He was very good and had often dreamt of being an actor, something he could probably have succeeded in given the opportunity. However, in this situation, inconspicuous would be a better way to play it, and an idea sprung to mind. He scribbled a note on the bottom.

"Short-sighted"

It was an act he'd played before. Pretending to be short-sighted allowed him to peer closely at things without raising too much attention. It would also allow him to wear dark glasses – perfect, as he would be able to glance around at the cameras, security staff and check out the windows and doors. The disguise would need to be a little better though if he was going alone. He added some more notes:-

"Moustache"

"Older"

"Eccentric"

Not many men of his age would visit a museum alone. However, an eccentric older man, maybe pensioned off early due to his sight, wouldn't look out of place. He considered the size of the place again. Only three floors. Unlikely to get many visitors in the week, so added a final note:-

"Saturday"

He would go at the weekend. He didn't want to be the only person in the room. Much easier to stay discreet in a crowd, even if the crowd was only three or four people.

He re-read his list, satisfied that he was ready for a visit. The top item – "camera" reminded him that he needed to take some pictures. He had purchased a spy camera from GreySpider last year, a button-sized digital miracle that would hold several thousand high-quality shots, or thirty minutes of video and could be pinned to a jacket or hat completely inconspicuously. He would prefer to take video. Would thirty minutes be enough? He thought so. He retrieved the camera from a drawer and plugged it into the USB socket on the laptop to charge it.

Buddy yawned and checked the time. 1am. Crikey. Where had the evening gone? He considered texting Shanice and was surprised and pleased to see that she had beat him to it. He hadn't heard the ping of the phone.

"Hey Bud. Gd 2 c u 2nite. Drinks Sat? Finish gym at 6"

He hated text speak, and he had to read it twice. Did it really take much longer to add two O's to the word "Good"? At twenty-six, he had somehow managed to sidestep the need to do every text, post, and note in shorthand on his phone.

It was usually three to four weeks before they saw each other. His spidey-sense told him again that she was more interested in his skills as a con-man, and the opportunity to make money, but he couldn't help texting back.

"Look forward to it. Where do you want to meet?"

If he went to the museum at lunchtime, he could grab a bite to eat at the café - the website promised "The best cream tea in Borehamwood", and then get home in time to remove his disguise and meet up with her in the evening.

She hadn't replied twenty minutes later after he had brushed the garlic from his teeth, so he took himself off to bed, contemplating a successful con, enjoyable evening, and a tempting diamond prospect. All in all, it had been a good day.

****

Saturday 11th January.

The old man shuffled down Shenley Road in Borehamwood, passing the Elstree Studios looking for Rhombus House. Google Maps had told him that it was a fifteen-minute walk, but Buddy needed to look the part, and briskly walking into the Museum would shatter the illusion. He had been hobbling along for twenty-five minutes, his tweed jacket pulled tightly around him, and the cold wind threatening to remove the handlebar mustache that he had thoroughly glued to his face a couple of hours ago, and pulling at the striped Fedora hat that had the tiny button camera pinned to the front underneath the trendy logo.

He saw the entrance in the distance and paused to sit on a bench, seemingly taking a rest, but actually checking out the surrounding area. The road wasn't manic but still busy, and three people, a dog, and a bike passed him on the pavement as he sat for a few minutes, the dog stopping to pee up the side of the bench where he sat, and the owner apologizing profusely as he jumped alarmingly out of the way. The museum was next to a church which might make a good entrance point. Lots of places to hide in a churchyard, and unlikely to have any CCTV. Also, the church would be very dark at night. Opposite was an Indian takeaway and he groaned. He could check it out later, but it was likely to be open until at least midnight. It would have to be a late one.

He got up from the bench, stretched, pulled his jacket tighter, and headed into the wind, glancing at the church as he passed it. As he approached, he retrieved a pair of sunglasses from his pocket and put them on. They were quite dark from the outside, but he could see quite clearly with them, perfect for this kind of work. He also muted his phone. He didn't want any interruptions, and his ring tone might cause suspicion as "Highway to Hell" by AC/DC didn't really fit his persona.

"Good afternoon young lady," he said to the girl on the door, a teen with blue streaks through her hair who was more interested in her phone than him.

"Hey. Donations in the bucket please." She didn't even look up.

He threw a handful of coins in the bucket which proclaimed, "Your donations allow us to keep the museum free and give you the best possible experience". Might want to invest in a new front-of-house girl, he thought. How many punters did she scare off each day?

He made a point to peer closely at the sign, muttering and playing the part. She glanced up, smirked, and returned to her phone.

Passing through into the first room, he noticed three people were looking at various sculptures around the room, and an older lady sitting on a chair knitting, likely to be one of the staff, he thought. He already knew from Google that this floor contained sculpture and bronze. The middle floor was dedicated to jewelry and the top one was art. He didn't want to arouse suspicion by going directly to the jewelry section, so he browsed the sculptures, paying particular interest to a bronze dragon sat upon a large stone - mainly because it stood proudly in the corner of the room and it allowed him to check out the CCTV camera mounted directly above it. He had also noted that the main front door in reception had a pull-down metal shutter that locked at the bottom, similar to what he'd seen in jewelry stores in the high street. He owned a portable metal cutting laser that would make short work of the lock on the shutter, but if he tripped an alarm, he would be on a short time scale. The CCTV wouldn't pose a great issue as his face would be covered. Its only real benefit was to keep an eye on things while the museum was open.

There was a high-level window with bars on it, and just above that was a PIR – an alarm sensor, with a flickering red light as it detected movement. Damn it. The place was alarmed too. However, seeing alarms, gates, and CCTV in the downstairs area might be a good thing. It was likely that there was no overnight security guard, so if he could work around the systems then at least he would be alone.

"Excuse me," he said to the knitter. She looked up over her spectacles and gave him a smile.

"Yes Sir. How can I help?"

"Sorry to trouble you, but could you point me to the bathroom?" He wanted to turn the spy camera on before he visited the jewelry section above.

"Up the stairs and through the jewelry section. There's a large sign. You won't miss it" she said helpfully. "Or there's a lift back in the foyer if it's easier."

"No trouble. The exercise will do me good. Thank you."

He headed up the stairs and walked casually through the jewelry section towards the toilet, making mental notes all the way. Two people, another knitter, another CCTV, and another PIR, and a glass case presenting the highlight of the museum's artifacts. One of the Four Feathers pink diamonds stood on its own plinth directly opposite the PIR. The corners of the room might not be in the range of the sensor, but there was no way that the diamond was not covered on all sides.

He continued to the bathroom without breaking stride and entered into a tiny room with two doors. One for men, one for women. A quick glance into the ladies showed him that they were identical. A small window, a toilet, a sink, and a hand dryer. Again, the windows had bars, but being upstairs, they weren't as substantial as the security on the ground floor. He stood on the toilet and looked out of the window. It overlooked the churchyard next door, about fifteen feet above the ground. The window was small, but he thought he could probably get through it if needed. Just the minor problem of getting up to the second floor from outside then, he thought.

He activated the tiny video camera, flushed the toilet, and left. He had about thirty minutes before the recording stopped.

Stepping back into the jewelry room, he made a point to look slowly around so that the video captured everything. There were four people now, and one of them was talking to the lady, who was working on what seemed to be the largest and bluest scarf he had ever seen. While she was distracted, he moved to the diamond and peered closely at it from all angles, trying to see if there were any obvious alarms on the glass case itself. There was a small yale lock at the back that locked the case, but nothing else of any concern. There could have been a pressure sensor inside, but he had no way of knowing until he lifted the diamond – not a job for today. He spun around and looked at the PIR, which was busy blinking away catching the activity in the room. He would need to find a way to deactivate the alarm system. It was probably set by the last person that left each day.

He did two circuits of the room, peering at the jewelry, and then headed upstairs. The art room was much like the others with two exceptions. Firstly, there was no staff in this room. The pictures were all secured to the wall, so no one would run off with anything anyway. Secondly, there was a door at the back, directly above the toilets that said "Private." Also, the room was empty, and the CCTV was above the door, pointing in the opposite direction. Time to take a chance.

Buddy headed straight for the door, pretending to look at the picture below the CCTV camera, and tried the handle. It opened. If anyone was in there, he would play the short-sighted old man act, and ask them where the toilet was, but it seemed that luck was on his side as the room beyond was empty. He closed the door gently and scanned the room. Not much to see. It seemed as if it was a store cupboard containing a couple of old paintings, a stepladder, a broom, a sink with mop and bucket, a coat hook with a couple of coats, and a small grey metal cabinet in the corner. The cabinet had the keys hanging from the lock. He pulled a glove on and turned the key. Inside, as he had anticipated was the keypad for the alarm and a computer running the CCTV system. He peered closely, making sure his camera got a good view of the model, did the same on the computer, and then closed the door, and exited the storeroom, just as he heard voices coming up the stairs.

He headed back down to the jewelry room, clocking another door on the left. There was no one around, so he quickly stuck his head in. It was a cleaner's cupboard, just big enough for a hoover, a roll of bin bags, and some toilet cleaner. A rota was stuck to the door with tick boxes. It seemed that the toilets were cleaned every four hours, and a cleaner also came in the evenings twice a week on Tuesday and Friday. He closed it and quickly turned back to take one last look at the diamond. As he stood admiring it, he heard a familiar voice behind him and instinctively turned to look at her.

"What time are you open until?"

Shanice. She was addressing the old lady knitting the scarf, her hair tied back, and a hat partly covering it but there was no mistaking the wisps of bright red sticking out everywhere and the accent. What the hell was she doing here? Same as me of course, he thought. But without the same precautions. She glanced over at him as he turned, and he managed to compose himself, put himself into character, and gave her a polite nod. She smiled and turned back to the lady, not recognizing him.

"We close at 5pm on weekdays, and 5:30 at weekends," she said. I have a leaflet somewhere."

Buddy strolled past while the lady started looking through her knitting bag for the museums' literature and headed down the steps twice as fast as he'd climbed them, and much faster than he should have. Luckily no one saw him. He exited past the teenage girl who still had her head buried in her phone, and past the tiny café and Museum shop where he had been hoping to indulge in a coffee and cake. He didn't breathe until he was back on the street.

Chapter 5 – "The Monument"

Tuesday 14th January.

"You have two new voicemails. First new voicemail…."

"Hey Oz. It's Ed. We keep missing each other. I'm gonna be down at Verdi's at 1pm if you're about and want to grab a coffee."

Oscar deleted the message. What was his brother doing over this side of town? He never called to meet up for coffee. He'd mentioned he'd needed advice in the email he'd sent, so something must be up. Did he really want to know?

"Message deleted. Second new voicemail…"

"Hello, Mr. Zachery. It's Doctor Pullman's office. Sorry we haven't got back to you. Doctor Pullman would like to have a short catch-up to discuss your medication. He's had a cancellation for 12:45 today if you can make it. I'll assume all is good. Please call back if you can't, and we'll rearrange. The number is….."

Bugger. Could he make both? It would be tight. It was gone 12:00 already. He messaged Ed.

"Hey bro. I got a docs appt across town at 12:45 so might be a bit late. I'll call you when I'm on my way."

He had been planning to go to the Monument – one of the museums that were home to the Four Feathers diamonds, but he'd have to push that back a couple of hours. He knew the Monument and had visited once a few years ago. It was a tiny converted chapel in Fulham that now housed a collection of jewelry, art, and precious stamps, most of them donated by wealthy lords and ladies from many years prior. He had chosen it on the basis that he knew the area quite well and if he was seen then he could make a getaway on the back streets with relative ease. He had no real plan at the moment and wasn't even sure whether he would go ahead with it. The lure of a ten-thousand-pound diamond was clearly tempting – the money would help him massively with the show, but it was the challenge that had really got him thinking. As a magician, he thrived on the challenge of doing the impossible. Fooling his audience. Making them believe that magic actually existed. Could he steal a diamond using sleight of hand, distraction, and smoke and mirrors? He didn't know, but it was a puzzle that he was keen to explore.

He grabbed his wallet and keys, checking he had his Oyster card, and headed for the underground. Dr. Pullman ran a private psychiatry practice, twenty minutes up the Piccadilly line. As he walked, the rain started to come down and he picked up his pace, pulling his coat up around his neck. He was two minutes from the station when the heavens opened and a waterfall of rain cascaded down, soaking him through.

"You got to be kidding" he mumbled, ducking into a shop doorway that didn't give him much shelter. People were running in all directions, and the doorway where he stood began to fill up with others seeking any kind of reprieve from the onslaught of rain. A small child got jostled over and fell in a pool of water and started to cry. Oscar bent down to assist the youngster, but he received an accidental shove from behind too and went sprawling.

He was soaked. He helped the small child up, nodded to the thankful mother, put his head down, and sprinted for the station. He was so wet now, that a little more rain wasn't going to hurt. He reached the tube, and trudged down two escalators, before reaching the station, just to see the train leaving.

He cursed loudly and dripped his way to a bench, checking his phone. 12:17. He considered calling ahead to warn Dr. Pullman that he may be a few minutes late, but the red icon on his phone told him that he had no signal.

It was 12:20 before the train rattled slowly into the station. He leaped on, found a seat, and picked up a discarded Evening Standard, thumbing through it casually. Two stops later, after reading a review about the latest Tom Cruise blockbuster and an article about global warming, he flicked the page and the headline jumped out at him.

"Black market web site lures diamond thieves".

Someone had been talking about the GreySpider post about Ace's challenge, and somehow the press had got wind. The report started with some background information about GreySpider, condemning the unethical practices it was known for, and then went on to give Ace's full post and a handful of some of the more interesting replies. It ended with a list of the museums where the Four Feathers lived, giving a short bio for each.

He read the article twice, wondering how much this would affect the security at the museums. Would they hide the diamonds away? Unlikely, thought Oscar. They were probably loving the free advertising that the article had unintentionally given them. It was possible that the Monument would be busier though, probably not a bad thing for his recce, as he would be lost amongst many others who would be looking at the now-famous diamond.

The train had stopped and was just pulling away again when he looked up from the article.

"You got to be kidding," he said for the second time. He'd missed his stop. He turned back frantically to check, and sure enough, the sign for "Earl's Court" was disappearing in the distance. It was 12:40.

"Damn it, Damn it. Damn it."

It was fifteen minutes before he reached the next stop, caught the train back, and surfaced from the underground. He tapped Doctor Pullman's number into his phone but got a busy signal, so started running through the rain. It wasn't as bad as earlier, but the puddles still splashed up to his knees. It was 1:05 before he reached the psychiatrist, and he nearly fell into the door in his haste to get in.

It was locked. A sign in the window informed him that the practice was closed from 1:00 to 2:00 for lunch.

****

Oscar cursed. He was soaked through, had missed the doctor, and would now be a half-hour late meeting Ed, something he wasn't particularly looking forward to anyway. He scrolled to Ed's number to call and cancel but chickened out and sent a text instead.

"Sorry, Ed. I was late getting to docs. Not gonna make it. I'll call you later."

Ed wouldn't be happy, but they were hardly close. He couldn't remember the last time they'd actually seen each other, and to be fair, Ed hadn't given him much notice.

He headed back to the station and contemplated whether to go home and get a change of clothing or go straight to the Monument. The trip home and back would take over an hour and he was only two stops from Fulham. Should he go to the museum without any form of disguise? Why not? It's not like he would be stealing it today and there would be plenty of others looking, especially after the article in the Standard.

Decision made, he turned to the District Line, stopping to grab a coffee from a kiosk at the station. At some point in the last fifteen years, the world of coffee seemed to have completely changed. No longer did you just go and grab a coffee and a biscuit for little more than a pound. The choice at the kiosk was limitless. Americano, Expresso, Latte, Cappuccino, Flat White, Macchiato, Caffe Mocha, Expresso Doppio. What on Earth is an Expresso Doppio? thought Oscar as he scanned the take-away menu, trying to find a plain black coffee. The list went on. There were shots that you could add for extra flavoring, caramel, ginger, spices. Then a whole host of different teas and hot chocolates.

"Do you do a black coffee?"

"Americano, Expresso or long black?" said the girl with the tongue piercing serving behind the counter. He noticed she had a cute butterfly tattoo just below her left ear, that was spoilt by an ear stretcher just above leaving a hole as big as his finger in her lobe.

He stuttered. "Ummm. Just a black coffee please." How can there be different types?

She laughed. "I'll do you an Americano," she said pushing buttons on a machine behind her. "Do you want chocolate sprinkles?"

He declined the sprinkles and grabbed a couple of pound coins.

"That's £3.50," she said handing over a small paper cup with a lid.

"For a black coffee? Are you kidding? I could buy a jar for less than that."

She shrugged. "I know. I wouldn't pay it. Seems that people do though, especially in this weather."

He grumbled, dropping the coins back in his wallet and pulling out a five-pound note. The bad morning had made him grouchy.

"Have a nice day?" said the girl brightly as she gave him his change.

The coffee wasn't even that good, but it warmed him up a bit. He exited Fulham station twenty minutes later to discover that the rain had subsided, and the sun was even trying to poke through the clouds. His mood brightened.

Five minutes later he entered the old chapel that was now the Monument. The building was a small but impressive late 19th-century Victorian conversion and was beautiful from the outside. The inside was just as stunning. Clean white high ceilings, pillars holding up a viewing mezzanine so that the art could be viewed from above, and marble floors. A security guard stood in the entrance, checking bags and generally looking menacing.

There was only one showroom, containing jewelry on one side, stamps on the other, and many different styles of art – Abstract, Baroque, surrealism, cubism, impressionism, and many other isms according to the literature that Oscar had never even heard of. His eyes were drawn to a particularly impressive oil painting of a girl, circa 1920's wearing a flapper dress and dancing with a small boy. The look on the girl's face reminded him of Brandy and the way she looked when she was performing on stage with him.

He tore himself away from the Brandy look-a-like and walked slowly around looking at the art on the walls, ignoring the stamps, but when he reached the side where the jewelry was, he started to pay more attention. There was a lot of vintage jewelry – mainly in silver - bracelets, rings, elaborate brooches, but he couldn't see any lone diamonds. He worked his way along, stopping occasionally and pretending to read about the various donations that had been made to the museum. He didn't want to look too conspicuous, but over a dozen people were looking around including two small children whose sticky fingers were leaving prints all over the glass cabinets, causing the security guard to get a bit twitchy. Oscar smiled. No one was paying any attention to him.

He was nearing the far end of the room when he spotted it. Two small steps were leading to a raised staging area with three individual plinths housing the more impressive museum pieces. On the first was a gold brooch, donated by the sister of Lady Anne from some town in the Isle of Man he'd never heard of. It was a gaudy thing in his opinion, but apparently, it was a one-off, commissioned by Lady Anne's late husband in the 1960's.

He moved on.

The second plinth held a pair of platinum earrings, each with a half-carat diamond. Pretty, but not what he was here for.

The third plinth had gained some interest and was currently surrounded by three people who were peering closely at the pink diamond. He waited patiently, taking in the surroundings. He gave a quick glance to the security guy who was now marching towards one of the small children who had taken it upon herself to play hopscotch in the stamp section, while the other one was running along and sliding on his knees. A security camera scanned the room from the middle panning left and right. Interesting that it was only covering the diamond half the time, thought Oscar, making a mental note. That might prove useful.

He looked back at the plinth itself just as a young couple moved away, leaving an older man with a bald head who was squinting and reading about the, now infamous Four Feathers Diamond. The diamond was under a glass bowl of about thirty centimeters – Almost like a see-through cake cover – He had seen one at the coffee shack earlier, and not dissimilar in shape to the old man's head. He chuckled at the thought and the man glanced at him and moved away. The cylinder didn't appear to have any form of lock, but a discrete nudge confirmed that it was completely solid. Probably a globe of glass secured from underneath the plinth. If the lock wasn't accessible, then it was harder to get to. The plinth itself contained its own lock too.

The diamond was sat on a velvet cushion inside the glass bowl and was gleaming as if it had just been polished. A white plaque was screwed to the plinth, informing him what he already knew about the diamond - that it was one of four, and that it was a kind donation from Sir Tom Mathers. It then went on to explain where the other three were housed. I wonder for how much longer, thought Oscar.

He moved away from the diamond and climbed a spiral staircase that sat just behind it that led to the mezzanine. The mezzanine ran the full length of the museum, with a staircase at either end, giving a birds-eye view of the art and artifacts below. He stopped halfway along and leaned on the side taking it all in. The camera was just beneath him, pointing downwards, a quiet hum emitting from it as it surveyed the room. Mental note, he thought. The mezzanine is a blind spot. He looked around. It was just a viewpoint - no valuables. It didn't need to be covered by the CCTV. This area would be perfect for the plan that was forming in his mind. He already knew how he could get the diamond out, and now he knew how he could disappear. The security guard was the concern though. The museum would be locked down instantly, and everyone would be searched as soon as they discovered the diamond was gone.

He continued along the mezzanine, stopping to use the toilet, and the rest of the idea sprung to mind as he was relieving himself. The whole plan had its risks, but with some practice, he thought it would be possible. It was Tuesday. He had a show on Wednesday and Friday, so decided that Saturday would be the day. It would be busier, and in this instance, more people would work in his favor. They would help to create a distraction.

He left the museum, and headed back to the station, a spring in his step that hadn't been there an hour before.

Chapter 6 – "Ace"

Wednesday 15th January.

Katy Adams knocked on the door of the apartment below and stood waiting, impatiently tapping her foot.

"Who's there?"

"Oh Hi. It's Katy. Katy from upstairs?"

"Hi, Katy. How can I help you?"

He didn't open the door, not the first time that she had stood trying to have a conversation with him like this. He was clearly a private person and didn't like to be bothered.

"Look. I'm sorry to bother you. I was having problems with my hot water and was wondering if yours is OK?"

"I think it's fine. Let me check."

She heard footsteps disappearing and a tap running. She couldn't work the guy out. They'd only met face to face twice, both times on the stairs and she'd tried to start a conversation, but he wasn't having any of it. Maybe he was just shy. He was quite good-looking in a rugged kind of way, but his personality didn't seem to match his looks.

"He's too guarded that one" she heard her mother say in her head. "You'll never be able to trust him".

No bother. Her love life was far too complicated as it was and starting anything up with her seemingly unfriendly neighbor was not on her list of priorities or any list for that matter. She generally got a fair bit of attention though, often being compared to the American singer and her namesake Katy Perry.

"Shame you can't sing like her." Thanks, mum. Always glad for your support.

Maybe he's gay, she pondered. Her thoughts were interrupted by his voice through the door.

"Mine seems fine. I'd call the landlord if I were you."

"Ah OK. Thanks. Do you have his number?"

"No."

More footsteps. I guess that's the end of the conversation! She headed to the apartment below where old-man-Maurice lived. Maybe she'd have more luck there.

****

Ace walked back to his computer, annoyed at the interruption, and straightened the pens on his desk. He had nothing personal against the girl, but she just didn't factor in the things that were important to him. Anything that wasn't important was just noise.

He was researching his "Queen", trying to establish a plan, working out how he was going to use his pawns in the upcoming game. The chess analogy appealed to him. Maybe he should've called himself the King rather than the Ace? It had been two weeks since he had laid down his challenge, and as of now, there had been no attempts to steal one of the Four Feathers diamonds. He was monitoring the museums closely, and so far, nothing.

His cluster was still gaining momentum – over two thousand posts now, and he had read every one of them, making a note of the usernames on some of the comments that looked promising.

04-01-2020 17:59, BobKnobber

Checked out the Monument today. Beautiful diamond. Pic to follow.

08-01-2020 19:22, BillyTheQid

Plan in place. Hitting the Rhombus tonight. Watch this space.

He already knew and expected that there would be a lot of spam and so far, Bob and Billy had not followed up with their promises. He wasn't sure that he wanted someone with the name "BobKnobber" working with him anyway.

He hadn't added anything to the cluster himself since the original post, but the lack of progress was frustrating him. He was hoping that one of his team would be in place by now, or at least that someone would have made an attempt. Perhaps he'd over-estimated the greed and caliber of the spiders on the forum. What would he do if he only got one or two? What if "BobKnobber" came through and turned out to be a bit of a twat?

He rubbed the back of his hand back and forth on his forehead, a tic that often materialized when he was anxious, and then leaned forward and straightened the pens on his desk again, picking them up and turning them over one hundred and eighty degrees, before replacing them in the same spot.

Some of the more recent posts had troubled him. Apparently, the news had gotten wind of his cluster and the reporter with the delightful name of Judy Writer - could that be real? – had gone to great lengths to describe his post and GreySpider, effectively warning the museums that they may be under attack. He had no concern that they could trace the post back to him. His "Phantom X" firewall was top-of-the-range and unbreakable but raising the profile like this may scare people off.

A memory from his father surfaced. "Worry is like a rocking chair. It gives you something to do but never gets you anywhere."

Where did his dad get this stuff from? His head was full of mindless proverbs and quotes. They must have had an impact though if he was still recalling them all these years later.

He returned his focus to the plan. He wouldn't post to the cluster today. Give it a few more days. Surely someone will make a move soon. He scratched his left elbow and got an instant urge to scratch the right one in the same place. He pushed his spectacles up onto his nose and straightened his pens.

****

Buddy stood under the hot stream of water, contemplating the upcoming heist. He had decided that he wanted a quieter day for the robbery itself and had chosen Thursday. After watching the video back, several times, he had found a hole in the security that he intended on exploiting. His plan did not involve going in at night as he'd first considered, but at about 4:30 pm just before they were closing. It was all about timing, bluffing, disguising, and, as with all things in the con-artists game, confidence. He had revisited the museum on two more occasions, watching from a distance at closing time, and then again when they opened, noting the order of events.

His last puzzle piece fell into place as he'd watched the young girl with the mobile phone and completely carefree attitude, open up at 8:45 yesterday. He had stepped through the plan about a dozen times since, to ensure that he'd not missed anything. He even had a backup plan to escape if something unexpected happened, although he didn't believe he would need to use it.

He washed his hair, his minding wandering to Shanice and his date last Saturday. They had both gotten quite drunk and talked and laughed for most of the evening. Neither of them brought up their trip to the Rhombus, and although Buddy was concerned that she was contemplating stealing the same diamond as him, he didn't want to let her know that he was there and that he'd seen her. The fact that she didn't mention it either meant that she was keeping secrets too. He was concerned that she was planning on her own raid and would most likely get caught, raising the security and scuppering his own plans.

The best thing he could do for all concerned was to get in there first.

She had spent much of the evening talking about the landlord scam again, and twice he had to tell her to lower her voice, as the volume of alcohol seemed to have a proportionate effect to the volume of her speech. They had hit the dancefloor of a small club at 1am, and she had thrown her arms around him, dancing provocatively up against him, receiving admiring looks from other guys – and even some of the girls at the bar. It had been an expensive night, but the bill was still being picked up by Rupert, who had left his bank cards at the mercy of Buddy for three days before he realized something was amiss.

They finally rolled out of the club at 2:30am, and Buddy had thought that tonight was going to be the night that she came back to his, but it wasn't to be. There had been a lot of kissing, and a promise to meet up soon, and then she was diving into the back of a taxi. Was she playing him? Only time would tell.

He shut off the shower and towel dried himself and contemplated his disguise.

Chapter 7 – "Heist #1"

Thursday 16th January.

Buddy had decided to go older, but with a completely different look than before. He had long dark hair that had more than a touch of grey in it, sunglasses, a cowboy hat, long boots, and a guitar slung over his shoulder. He had used the middle-aged rocker look on a con a couple of years ago where he blagged his way into a two thousand-seater music venue after a packed-out gig, claiming he was with the band. It was amazing what people believed if you looked and talked the part. He had gotten backstage and no one batted an eyelid and he had escaped with the takings from the merchandise on that particular night.

Today was a different target – far more valuable, but far more risks. He had considered the other jewelry at the museum but told himself not to be greedy and just go for the diamond. If he did things right, then it might be days before they even noticed it was missing. Days of other people treading over evidence and leaving fingerprints everywhere. If he had chosen to ransack the place and steal other items, then the police would be all over it which increased his chances of being caught.

He approached the museum at 4:25 as planned, and found the same young girl scrolling through the same phone as on his previous visit.

He adopted an American accent. "Hey honey. What time do you close?"

She glanced up, looking him up and down, and smiled. We shut at five, but you should be able to get around it in half-hour. It's pretty small in there.

"Thanks...," he looked at her nametag. "Angel. Hey, cute name. Love the hair too." He pushed his sunglasses up onto his head, gave her a smile, and moved on, throwing a handful of coins into the donation bucket. He wanted her to remember him, but not in detail. Funny how she was more receptive today. Everyone loves a musician, he mused.

"Have fun" said Angel, returning to her phone.

OK. Half hour. The timing had to be good. He spent some time browsing the first two floors, barely even looking at the diamond in the jewelry section. He knew where it was and didn't want to draw attention, although the place was almost deserted. He only saw two other people. There was a young college girl who spent most of her time with the sculptures, taking photos and making notes. Probably an art student. She gave him a nod and a smile but returned to a very life-like bronze of a man cuddling his wife, with a small child tugging at his hand, urging him to come and play.

He also saw the old knitter-lady who was packing up her bag for the day.

After fifteen minutes, he entered the toilet cubicle by the jewelry section and dropped his sunglasses on the side by the sink on the way out. Stage one complete, he mentally ticked off the well-rehearsed plan.

He continued up to the third floor which was empty – just as he'd hoped at this time of day. If there had been anyone there, he would have had to have waited until they called everyone out for closing, and things would have been very rushed. He went straight to the storeroom at the back of the room and approached the metal cabinet that housed the alarm keypad. He removed his tiny spy camera from his pocket and mounted it on the wall, high up opposite the cabinet so it was directed down. The wide-angle lens should be able to pick up any activity inside the metal cabinet. He started the camera and scarpered from the store cupboard as quick as he could, checking his watch – 4:52. Stage two complete.

He killed two more minutes and was back in the reception area at 4:55.

"Wow, there's come cool stuff in there. I'll have to come back when I have more time."

"You should. We're open till 5. 5:30 at weekends" said, Angel. "I'm here most days from nine am." She twirled one of her blue strands of hair as she spoke. Was she flirting with him? What was it with girls and long-haired musos?

"Thanks, honey. I'll remember that. Have a good day."

He tipped his cowboy hat at her and headed out, walking slowly up towards the church. The young art student was a couple of steps behind him, and the older lady with her knitting was just behind her, shouting goodbye to Angel on the way out. OK, so the place is empty. Would she close early? Probably not. She hadn't when he was watching her the other day, but she was unlikely to hang around past five o'clock with no one there.

At 4:59, he turned around and headed back quickly. He got to the door, just as she was locking it.

"Oh, hey there. Are you still open? I think I left my sunglasses in the bathroom."

"Oh. Hi. I was just closing up."

"I'm so sorry. Do you mind? I'll only be a minute."

"Sure. I'm just heading up to set the alarm. I'll walk with you."

They walked up the stairs.

"Are you in a band?"

"Not here in London. I've been doing a bit of busking but thought I'd take some time out to see some sights. I play a bit back home in LA."

"Oh Cool. I'd love to go to LA. Is that where you live?"

"Sure do honey. London's OK – It's great to see it, but the LA weather is waaaaaay better." He laughed, and she joined in, agreeing as they reached the first floor.

"Hey - I won't be a second. I put them down when I washed my hands, so I'm sure they'll still be there."

He walked to the toilets, retrieved his sunglasses, and headed back to Angel.

"Got them. Gee, thanks again for letting me back in. I gotta shoot. Need to be across town in….," he checked his watch, "Oh man, thirty minutes. Looks like I may be late." He rushed down the stairs, giving her a wave. "See you around."

"No problem. Bye. Come back soon." She looked disappointed.

Buddy kept moving, not looking back but preying that she wouldn't follow him. The plan relied on her going up and not down. If she was the owner, she would probably have seen him off the premises, locked the door, and then gone back to set the alarm. But she wasn't. She was the hired help, barely earning minimum wage, and the friendly American in a hurry to leave was not an issue. Buddy was counting on this, and his instincts were right. He heard her footsteps receding as she headed up to the top floor to set the alarm.

He opened the front door, and let it bang closed with him still inside. He sprinted back up the stairs as quietly as he could and dived into the cleaner's cupboard. As he silently pulled the door shut, he heard the distinct sound of beeps as Angel was setting the alarm, above him.

Stage three complete. He started counting.

He heard Angel's footsteps come down the stairs, past the cupboard, and on down to the reception. He figured that with the alarm panel so far away, there would be at least two minutes between her setting it and it actually being armed. Whoever installed the alarm must have been severely short of space when it came to the location of the panel, thought Buddy. Most alarms would be in the reception area, or at least on the ground floor where they were easily accessible. To be fair, it made it much harder for anyone breaking in. They had to find the alarm panel before they could disarm it, something that his planning and prep work had made possible.

He got to ninety when he heard the sound of the metal security shutter being pulled down by Angel. He had planned to move at one hundred seconds regardless, so the sound of the rumbling metal was a welcome bonus. She must be keen to get home. He ditched his guitar case in the cupboard, opened the door, and bolted up the stairs. The alarm was still beeping its warning, indicating that it wasn't activated yet. He had researched the alarm and knew that it could be set with a delay of either one, two, three, or four minutes, giving the operator plenty of time to lock up and get out of the armed zones. He suspected it was set to three but didn't want to risk setting it off.

He had reached one hundred and eight when he wrenched the store cupboard door open and pulled it closed behind him.

Stage four complete.

He waited breathlessly.

Twelve seconds later, the alarm tone changed, gave one long beep, and went silent. So, it was set to two minutes. If he had waited any longer, then right now he would be stuck in the art section with alarm bells clanging around him. He sat down, cross-legged, and breathed slowly for ten minutes. One thing he had now was plenty of time, and he wanted to make sure that Angel was long gone and didn't return for anything.

His mind returned to the day after his final visit. He was sat watching the video back, trying to find the best way to steal the diamond. His original idea was to come in at night and do a bit of "breaking and entering" but figured that were too many risks. Someone could easily have spotted him, even in the early hours of the morning. London was definitely a city that never slept, and that metal shutter wasn't going to be quick or easy, and it was in full view of the street. The windows were all solid too.

It was the combination of the alarm being upstairs and the location of the cleaner's cupboard that had given him the idea. He knew that it would require a spot of acting, and some split-second timing, but at this stage, he had nothing to lose. He couldn't be arrested for going back for his sunglasses. There were a few fail-points, and he counted himself lucky that they hadn't turned into problems.

Angel could've followed him down and locked him out.

She may not have been ready to leave for the day when he came back for his sunglasses.

There could have been more people around, meaning he couldn't get into the storeroom to set his camera up.

One thing he had relied on was that people were creatures of habit. He had observed Angel carefully. She wasn't exactly enamored with the job, and he figured she'd be out the door as soon as possible, something he had observed a couple of evenings before when he was sat across the road watching her. The one thing that surprised him was that she had been given the responsibility of locking up.

Also, for a museum so small, he had reckoned on it being empty at 5:00, another prediction that had paid off.

At any stage so far, he could've abandoned, and no one would have known. Yes – There would have been a camera in the storeroom that would eventually be found, but he had been very careful to ensure that it couldn't be traced and was wiped clean of prints.

Now he was locked in for the night, the risks had increased.

Buddy got up after fifteen minutes, stretched, and retrieved his camera. He blue-toothed it to his phone, and downloaded the latest video file, marveling at how easy it was to use and how far this kind of technology had come in recent years. He pressed play, and a picture of the grey cabinet appeared on his phone in full HD. He pressed fast-forward, and watched as nothing happened for a few minutes, and then – the light changed as Angel entered the cupboard. He pressed play again and saw her retrieve a coat from a peg on the wall, stuff her arms into it, and head for the cabinet. This was the moment of truth. If she obscured the alarm keypad, then he was stuck in the cupboard for the night and would have to move very fast to get back to the cleaner's cupboard in the morning when she came back in.

Her finger reached up as she pressed four keys. 2-5-8, and then her hair flicked just a fraction and obscured the last number.

Oh shit.

She closed the cabinet, turned away, and headed out the door.

Buddy wound the video back and watched it again.

And again.

The keypad ran from top to bottom with the numbers one, two, and three across the top, four, five, six in the middle, and seven, eight, nine beneath that. The bottom row had a "Clear" button, a zero, and an "Enter" key.

He could see the top two rows clearly, and she definitely didn't go back up. It was either seven eight, nine, or zero.

His mind raced back to the alarm manual that he had downloaded a few days before.

"If a wrong code is entered, the user has thirty seconds to make another attempt. If two wrong codes are entered, the alarm will sound, and can only be stopped by entering the correct code."

He had two attempts and four options. If he got it wrong twice, then he could still reset it, but the alarms would ring for a good few seconds. Would people come running? Was it tied into a local police station? Should he abandon and attempt an escape in the morning?

He watched the video twice more but couldn't be sure what the last digit was.

OK. Breathe. Think. People forget codes and passwords all the time. They use numbers that mean something or patterns they can remember. The logical fourth digit was a zero, as then the code was a straight line from top to bottom. 2587, 2588, 2589 were the other options, but these numbers couldn't be dates or years, or anything that meant anything.

He put his phone away, headed for the cabinet, held his breath, and typed it in.

2-5-8-0

The alarm gave a deep fart-type sound and started beeping rapidly.

Shit shit. He threw his hands in the air.

It had to be a zero. People always conformed to common sense and logic. Whoever set this must have had a warped sense of humor.

A few seconds passed before he realized that his time was counting down. Thirty seconds, more like twenty-five now.

Three choices. It was like choosing which wire to cut on a bomb.

His finger hovered over the keypad, as his other hand wiped a bead of sweat away. Seven, eight, or nine. What was the logical choice?

None of them.

Zero was the logical choice.

He didn't have time to look at the video again but knew it wouldn't help anyway.

The monotonous beeping continued as he struggled with which way to go. He lowered his hand.

OK, got to go with logic again. Most people would choose four different numbers. So, let's forget the eight. Seven or nine? Nine or seven? He reached up again, just as beeping intensified - getting faster and higher-pitched, making his heart pick up to a similar rate.

Seven or nine?

He committed, held his breath and typed 2-5....and stopped.

He stared in amazement and let out an incredulous laugh. Just below the keypad, out of view from the camera, was a sticker with the serial number and support phone number for the alarm company, and underneath that, someone had written four numbers. The penciled numbers were faded, and the first digit was smudged, but the other three were 588.

"It's a bloody eight," he said out loud, and quickly stabbed the eight-button twice.

The alarm beeped once more, and then gave a two-tone sound and went silent.

Buddy's knees went weak and he sunk to the ground, his heart returning to normal.

Stage five complete.

Chapter 8 – A rumbling in the night

The plan was to wait until dark, which would only be an hour or so, get the diamond, replace it with a fake, erase the CCTV, get some sleep, and then wake early, reset the alarm, and get back into the cleaner's cupboard. When Angel returned and opened the front door, she would have two minutes to turn the alarm off, giving Buddy about one minute to run down the stairs and disappear.

Stages six to ten.

The only issue he could see was if she locked the front door and took the keys with her. Logic suggested that she would leave the key in the lock while she dealt with the alarm, ready for opening ten or fifteen minutes later. He wouldn't be able to lock the door behind him, but she was unlikely to suspect any foul play if everything appeared to be undisturbed. More likely, she would believe that she'd not locked it properly while rushing upstairs to the alarm.

However, it seemed that logic had gone out the window, and as he sat, heart-thumping, contemplating his luck that someone had been stupid enough to write the alarm code down, he started thinking about the following morning. As was his nature, he had considered this option before and had a backup plan. If he couldn't get out, he would return to the cleaner's cupboard and wait for the museum to open. He had another disguise – and a backpack in the guitar case. He would get changed, fold up the guitar case into the backpack, and spend some time looking around before leaving, hoping that Angel wouldn't recognize him. It wasn't perfect, but as backup plans went it would suffice. The new disguise – A young blonde skateboarder, complete with low slung jeans, Tony Hawk board, and a backpack wasn't the typical person who visited the museum, but it was as far from the aging rocker as he could manage.

While he waited, he turned his attention to the CCTV system in the grey cabinet. It was a fairly modern, digital setup that had a PC that recorded the museums' antics onto a hard drive. The software – CC-Copy, was familiar to him, and he wasn't too concerned about it. He would just copy an old recording from a couple of weeks ago over the latest file.

Of course, he had to crack the CC-Copy login first. If that wasn't possible, his backup plan was a little more brutal – Take out the hard drive, smash it very hard on the floor a few times, and put it back in. He should be able to damage the drive without damaging the case, and the hard drive would just be replaced, under the assumption that it had failed. Again – it relied on him escaping without leaving any trace. If they suspected the diamond was missing, then it was always possible to recover data – even if the drive was severely damaged.

He wiggled the mouse on the computer and the screen sprung to life, requesting the password. He had a few options. All software had a default admin password when it was installed, with a recommendation to change it when the software was first run. Few ever did, and his plan was to try "CCADMIN", the password that he had found in the user manual that he had downloaded a few days before. If that failed, he would work through the top ten passwords that everyone used. "123456" was a favorite, as was "password" followed by "qwerty". The stupidity of some people amazed him. He could then move on to other obvious options such as "rhombus" and now "Angel".

However, he didn't think that any of that would be necessary now, and as expected, it took him less than two minutes to find the password stuck to the bottom of the keyboard. He chuckled as he typed it in – "CCTV" in "CAPITAL LETTERS" the piece of paper kindly told him.

It took him less than five minutes to turn the cameras off and change the files. He wouldn't turn them back on until later. As he worked, he stopped suddenly, the blood draining from his face. How was he going to get back to the cleaner's cupboard when the cameras were on again? He'd missed it. How could he have missed something so obvious? Maybe he'd have to destroy the hard drive after all.

He spent twenty minutes watching the video footage back. The only camera that would be a problem was the one on this floor. Simple solution – move it. Just enough so that he could get out without being seen.

He peeked out of the storeroom, checking that he couldn't be seen from the windows, and looked up at the camera that was above him. He returned with the stepladder from the storeroom and nudged the camera up an inch. Not enough to be instantly noticed he figured, but enough for him to crawl along the floor without it spotting him. He turned the cameras back on, and did a practice run, wriggling commando style across the room in both directions.

The camera just caught the top of his head a couple of times. He was about to move it a bit further up when he had a better idea. He went downstairs and retrieved his guitar case and took the skateboard out. Repeating the process while lying flat on the skateboard did the trick, and he mentally patted himself on the back for choosing the disguise.

Fifteen minutes later, the CCTV was all off and reset again, and he was happy that it was dark enough for stage – what was he on now – seven? He made his way downstairs to the jewelry section and stood in front of the glass case that held his prize, his small torch glowing and throwing sparkles back at him as it caught the facets in the fine cut diamond.

He shone the torch around the case and focused on the lock around the back. It was nothing special. No more than what you would find in a jewelry store. Not surprising really as it only had to prevent people from making a quick grab for it. He had already overcome the real security.

In his pocket, he had a set of picks, something he'd not used for some time, but he knew the lock wouldn't pose any great problem for him. He had the glass case open in a matter of minutes. He shone the torch around the inside, looking for any wires or other signs of a localized alarm, but he didn't find anything. He held his breath and reached for the diamond. If the sirens started to wail now, then he would be testing his lock picking skills again on the metal shutter at very high speed.

He lifted it.

Nothing happened, so he let his breath out, retrieved it, and stared at it under the torchlight. It really was a stunning piece, and his eyes shone back at the diamond and his heart picked up its pace with the exhilaration of what he had achieved.

Don't celebrate too soon. You're not out yet.

Wise words, he thought, snapping out of the trance that the diamond had momentarily put him in. He reached into his pocket, and retrieved the fake, comparing the two. It wasn't nearly as impressive, but the size and color were almost identical, something that "Jake the Fake", as he liked to be known, prided himself on. It was worth about fifty pounds but had cost Buddy five hundred, about double what he wanted to spend, but Jake had heard about the GreySpider diamonds and had inflated his price. Five hundred was the haggled price, so he hadn't done too badly – and Jake had a contact who might be able to get a good price for the real one.

Most importantly, Jake was discrete, something that was worth far more than the extra couple of hundred.

He took out his phone and snapped a couple of pictures of the two diamonds, and one of the open glass case, ensuring that the "Four Feathers" plaque was in view. He had to have proof to send to Ace if he wanted to be on his team.

He placed the fake onto the stand, closed the case, locked it with the pick, and checked it from above. He was no expert, but under the torchlight, he was hard pushed to tell the difference. He took out a velvet bag, took one last look at the diamond, and dropped it inside, zipping it securely into an inside jacket pocket.

****

Twenty minutes later, Buddy was stood looking in the mirror in the restroom, dressed as the young skateboarder. He barely recognized himself and figured that it was one of his better disguises. The short spiky blonde hair and backward cap really changed the shape of his face. It may not be necessary, he thought, but at least he was ready if needed.

He checked his watch. Nearly 7pm. Angel would be back at about 8:45am. It would be a long night, but if he wanted to escape without leaving any trace it was his best option. He retraced his steps, checking that he'd left no evidence anywhere, and returned to the storeroom, turning the CCTV cameras back on. He had loaded his phone with a couple of films, and he settled down to watch Leonardo DiCaprio in one of his favorite movies – Inception.

The small screen wasn't ideal, but he loved the dream-within-a-dream action sequences and the mind-bending story. It also had the added advantage of being nearly two and a half hours long.

Around 10pm, after a quick snack, he settled down for the night, retrieving a sleeping bag from the guitar case. He ensured that everything was packed up and prepared for the morning, skateboard at the ready to transport him across the room to get to the cleaner's cupboard below. He set an alarm on his phone for 8:15, a good half hour before Angel was due, but he figured he'd be awake long before then. His morning would consist of setting the museums alarm again, skateboarding across the room, and jumping into the cleaner's cupboard for an uncomfortable half-hour wait, and then a quick dash out the front while Angel turned the alarm off.

As he dozed off, he considered the evening. Had he missed anything? No. He was convinced it had gone like clockwork so far, and he had high hopes for the morning.

He didn't expect to be awoken at 2:23 am by the deep rumble of the metal shutter being lifted.

Chapter 9 – "Danny Diamond"

Buddy sat bolt upright, immediately alert, and checked the time. What the hell? His mind started racing as lots of thoughts hit him at the same time.

Is my watch right? He checked his phone, but it confirmed that it was definitely the middle of the night.

It's unlikely to be any of the staff coming in at this time.

So, who?

The challenge from Ace. It had to be someone else attempting to steal the diamond.

Shanice? A feeling of dread hit him. Surely not?

The rumbling stopped. Panicking, Buddy realized that in a few seconds, whoever it was would be coming through the main door, and the alarm would start to beep, giving them two minutes to turn it off.

Another bunch of rapid thoughts.

Can I hide?

Do I turn the alarm off?

Do I attack whoever comes in and scarper?

How can I keep this covered up now?

A quick glance around told him that there was nowhere to hide in the cupboard, and if he went out, he would set the alarm off – and be seen by the camera.

He was running out of time, so he did the only thing that made sense. He threw himself towards the alarm and deactivated it – and then immediately set it again, giving him two minutes to get downstairs. He grabbed his backpack, quickly checked that he'd left no evidence, opened the cupboard door, and lay as flat as possible on the skateboard, giving himself a push to propel himself across the room. He reached the stairwell, rolled off the skateboard, and scooped it up, just as he heard the door below opening.

As quietly as possible, he ran down the flight of stairs to the middle floor, and jumped back into the cleaner's cupboard, pulling it closed as he heard footsteps ascending. The beeping of the alarm continued. The would-be robber would assume that he had two minutes to turn it off, not realizing that it had just been set. The beeping was the same and entering the code would have the same effect and disarm it.

Breathing heavily, he considered his next steps. The obvious one was to wait for the robber to deactivate the alarm upstairs, and then just leave. The front door and metal shutter were open. He could go home and have a comfortable night's sleep in his own bed. However, that raised two immediate problems. Firstly, whoever had broken in would steal the fake diamond, leaving the glass case empty and the police would be called, and everything would be closely scrutinized leaving him at risk of being caught. Secondly, wandering around in the early hours of the morning was likely to leave his face on every CCTV in the area, which – again, raised the risk of him being caught.

All of his preparation, scoping and backup plans, had not considered this scenario for one moment. His safest bet was to stay put, wait for the robber to steal the fake diamond, and leave in the morning. He'd have to stay in the cupboard for a few hours, but he could then escape as he had originally planned. But what if

Angel chose not to come in when she saw the broken metal shutter? What if she called the police while he was sat in the cupboard? That train of thought led him straight to prison.

He tried to put himself in the mind of the robber. Would he spend some time with the CCTV system before coming back downstairs, just as Buddy had? If so, then he had one possible option that may just work. If it failed, then he'd have to lump the unsuspecting thief with the full force of the flat end of his skateboard.

It's surprising how many thoughts the brain can process in such a small amount of time. The alarm was still beeping, which meant that whoever it was hadn't switched it off yet. If they failed to do it, and the alarm rang, he'd have to come up with a new plan, but as this thought flashed across his mind, he heard the deactivation sound, and then it went quiet.

Buddy moved quick. He grabbed his set of picks, the torch, and the skateboard, and dashed across the corridor and into the jewelry section of the museum, aware that the cameras were probably recording him. He'd have to deal with that later. He dropped down behind the Four Feathers diamond cabinet and started on the lock again. His hastily thrown-together plan consisted of taking out the fake diamond, leaving the cabinet open, and retreating back into the cleaner's cupboard so that the new robber would rightly believe that someone had beaten him to it. Hopefully, they would disappear, leaving him to put the fake back, sort out the CCTV, metal shutter, and front door, and with a bit of luck, he might just be able to leave everything as he had originally planned.

As he worked on the lock on the cabinet, he realized just how many flaws and risks this new idea had. The lock on the metal shutter was on the outside for starters. He wouldn't be able to lock it from inside. The guy upstairs could appear at any moment – and he was an unknown element. He could be armed. Being shot was not high up on Buddy's to-do list today. What if the intruder decided to steal something else instead? Another door that led to the police being called.

Buddy considered plan B or was it C? Walloping the guy with his skateboard was an option, but he wasn't a violent man, and the thought of knocking him out sickened him, and leaving an unconscious robber in the museum would also lead to the police being called.

Just as this thought crossed his mind, two things happened at once.

There was a click as the lock on the cabinet opened.

He heard footsteps coming from the stairwell.

Oh shit.

He grabbed the fake diamond, seized the skateboard, killed his torch light, and ran for the toilets. There was no way he could get back to the cleaner's cupboard now.

He glanced back, and as the toilet door closed, he saw a torch light bobbing up and down, and the shadow of a large camouflaged figure wearing a balaclava entered the room.

****

The large torch in the robber's hand scanned the room and settled very quickly on the glass case that held the Four Feather Diamonds. He approached it and gasped in disbelief.

"You got to be fucking kidding me."

His name was Danny Simpson or "Danny Diamond" as his friends liked to call him, a name that stuck due to his quite lucrative pastime of successfully relieving diamonds from jewelry shops all across the city. He had bigger plans though, and when he saw the proposal from Ace on GreySpider, he knew he had to get one of the diamonds.

He went around the back and saw that the case was open, and the diamond was most definitely missing. This was not part of the plan. He checked the other glass cabinets nearby but knew he had the right one. The torch picked out the plaque confirming that this was where the diamond should be.

"Fuck. Fuck. Fuck."

What now? He had taken too many risks to leave empty-handed. For a thief like Danny, it was obvious. Steal what he could and plan again for one of the other three. The fact that there were four diamonds, meant that he had many more opportunities to do this again.

He approached a wide glass cabinet that had a decent selection of sparkling gems and raised the heavy torch high above his head, just as he felt a pistol dig him in the ribs.

"Hands up. Pass me the torch, and don't turn around." Buddy was improvising. This guy was going to leave a mess, and he couldn't let that happen. His deep menacing voice and the gun pushing into his side had the desired effect.

"Whoa. Steady. It's cool man" said the robber, lowering the torch.

"I said hands up" Buddy shouted and dug the end of the toilet brush harder into the man's back.

"OK. OK." He raised his hands, and slowly lowered the torch backward over his head.

Buddy grabbed it and considered his options.

"OK. It's your lucky night. If you do as I say, you can just walk away. Have you left anything upstairs?"

"No. I've got everything I need."

Buddy shone the torch down and saw that the camouflaged pants had many pockets.

"OK. Very slowly, start walking."

"Did you steal the diamond?"

"No talking. Just move."

How long could Buddy convince this guy that a toilet brush was a gun? He didn't like his chances.

"I'm not going to hurt you if you don't turn around. If you see my face, then that may have to change. I'm going to take the gun out of your back, but if you try anything, I will use it."

He moved the toilet brush away and switched the torch to his right hand. It would make a better weapon if he had to use it. He hoped to hell that the smell of the disinfectant dripping off the brush didn't tip the guy off.

They moved out of the room, and onto the stairs, the robber looking straight forwards, and stumbling slightly on the bottom step.

"That's good. We're nearly there" said Buddy. "This is very easy. All you need to do is disappear. Tonight didn't happen. What you do tomorrow is up to you, but I wouldn't come back here for a while."

They had reached the front door, and the man opened it. Buddy had one thing more he wanted to do.

"Just a second. Don't move." He reached up, and lifted the man's balaclava an inch, and plucked a hair off of his head.

"Ow. Hey."

"Just a bit of insurance. Go. Pull the shutter back down behind you. If you turn back, it will be the last thing you see."

The man hesitated, and Buddy stuck the toilet brush in his back again, so he obliged. The shutter was raised and dropped, and he heard the sound of footsteps running away.

Buddy sank to the ground. Did that really work? What was he thinking? He was lucky that the robber hadn't smelt a rat. The guy was a good four inches taller and three stone heavier than him. He wouldn't have come off well in a fight.

Time to leave. He would have to take shelter elsewhere for the night. The only way to lock the metal shutter was from the outside, assuming that the guy hadn't broken it.

He had a few things to finish up before he left.

Return the toilet brush – Now there's a story to tell the grandkids one day, he thought chuckling.

Put the fake diamond back. He dropped the robber's hair into the cabinet behind the diamond. If someone discovered that it was a fake, then the DNA on the hair would focus the police's attention on the wrong man.

Lock the cabinet.

Pack everything into his rucksack.

Check that everything looked undisturbed – The cleaner's cupboard, the jewelry room, the toilet, and the storeroom.

Sort out the CCTV again.

Set the alarm.

Buddy took a final look around, and skateboarded himself across the room, as he had done just a short time ago. He took the stairs two at a time, the beeping alarm growing more distant at each step, and looked outside to confirm the streets were empty. He turned back and spent a minute locking the front door with his lock picks. The metal shutter took a bit longer, but thankfully it wasn't damaged, and no one was around.

Buddy turned his cap forwards and lowered it over his face, put his head down, dropped the skateboard on the ground, and pushed off heading for the church next door. It would be a cold night, but he was less likely to be seen by anyone if he laid low. In the morning, he would head to the tube at rush hour and disappear into the crowds.

He didn't spot Danny Diamond crouched in the shadows snapping a few photos with his phone as Buddy passed under a streetlamp.

Chapter 10 – "Half a Brandy"

Friday 17th January.

Ace logged into his GreySpider account and caught up with the messages being left on his cluster. They were beginning to thin out, and he was concerned that interest in the challenge was dying. As he scrolled through, he noticed he had a private message in his web. He clicked into it and saw it was from someone called Budster_007. There were just two words "Challenge completed" accompanied by a photo. He held his breath in anticipation and double-clicked the photo link.

The first of the Four Feather's diamonds stared back at him, along with a similar one which he deduced was a fake. In the background was the plaque describing the diamond, and the open case in the museum.

He gasped, leaned back, and spun his chair three hundred and sixty degrees in delight, which was short-lived, as he knocked his neatly arranged pens flying when he came to a stop.

He gasped again, this time in dismay, and dropped to the floor grasping around until he had retrieved them all, and then replaced them one at a time carefully on his desk.

"Lids to left" he muttered over and over like a mantra while he performed this regular ritual.

When he was happy that his pens were in order, he returned to the computer and zoomed into the picture that Budster had sent. It certainly looked genuine. If he had replaced the diamond with a fake and left no traces, then it wouldn't be hitting the news anytime soon. How could he be sure that this guy was for real?

His father's words rang in his ears – "You can only trust yourself... and barely that".

Good one dad. What does it even mean? He pondered it for a second, then shook his head to dismiss it.

He clicked the "reply" icon and started typing a message back. Thirty minutes and five attempts later, he re-read the message for the third time as his mouse hovered over the send button.

Budster.

Thank you for accepting my challenge, and congratulations on being the first to succeed. I would like to invite you to join my team, but first, I require a few things from you to ensure that you are genuine. I apologize in advance, but as you can imagine, I have had many empty promises and fake messages from fraudsters and charlatans. I need full trust in my team going forwards, so I am sure you will understand the need for such measures.

- Which museum did you steal the diamond from?
- What steps have to taken to ensure that you won't be caught?
- Did anybody see you?
- Does anyone else know that you have the diamond?
- What skills did you use to complete the challenge? This is important as I need to understand my team better in order to give them the correct roles in my future plans.

I will be in touch shortly and will let you know as the team grows.

He finally hit send and then spent another ten minutes on a one-liner for his cluster.

Greetings fellow spiders. Tick-tock. Tick tock. Time is running out, and only three spaces left on my team.

He didn't want to give too much information away about Budster's success but wanted to raise the profile of his challenge again. The timing of Budster's message couldn't have been better. This should provoke some action he thought.

He checked the time. Just after 11:00. He'd check back again later, see what the Spiders had to say, and see if he had a reply from Budster. A grin spread across his face for the first time in days. He finally had someone for his team and was looking forward to finding out more from his new friend.

He reached out to straighten his pens – but no. They were perfect. Things are looking up, he thought.

****

"You're on in fifteen Oz."

"Thanks, Mick."

Oscar was waiting to go on stage at the Mirage Lounge, cursing Brandy because she hadn't turned up yet, and scrolling through GreySpider reading the messages. It had gone mental since Ace had re-posted. Someone had actually done it. One down, three to go. Where did he steal it from, he wondered? His plans for the Monument tomorrow would be completely scuppered if he got there and found that the diamond was gone.

As he scrolled, he noticed that he had a missed call. Dr. Pullman again. Oscar had called back, leaving a message and apologizing profusely about missing the appointment. It seemed almost impossible to actually talk to someone in the medical world these days. He clicked into his voicemail.

"Hello, Mr. Zachery. It's Doctor Pullman's office. Don't worry about the missed appointment. We had a few that day because of the weather. Dr. Pullman has reviewed your notes and has agreed to up the dosage for your tablets. They will be ready to pick up from your pharmacy on Monday 20th. Please read the bottle carefully. It's one tablet, twice a day now. Any questions, or if you really need to see Doctor Pullman, please call back."

He hadn't had a repeat of the strange voice in his head, but he was still pleased to be able to double up on his tablets. He was distracted as Brandy came rushing in.

"Sorry I'm late. I've 'ad a proper shitty day." She pecked him on the cheek and proceeded to strip to her underwear in front of him. "How long have I got?"

"About ten minutes," said Oscar, blushing, trying not to look at her, but at the same time transfixed. It wasn't the first time she had done this, and he wondered if she did it on purpose to embarrass him, or she just liked to flaunt her body.

"Fuck. Can you help me with this?"

She dragged a sexy black and gold strapless number out of her bag that looked like it was two sizes too small for her boobs.

"Erm. What can I do?"

"Just grab the left side and pull upwards," she said climbing into it. She grabbed the right side and they pulled upwards together, her breasts jiggling with the effort.

"It's no good. Me tits are too fuckin' big." She laughed. "'ang on. I'll take me bra off."

Oscar looked horrified as she turned away, and whipped her bra off, and hoisted the dress up, pushing and pulling herself into it.

"Got it. Zip me up."

Oscar grabbed at the zip, and it took a whole lot more pulling and squeezing before he finally managed to complete the task.

She spun around beaming.

"Fanks. How do I look?"

Her boobs looked like they were going to escape at any minute. Good job they weren't knife-throwing tonight, or the audience would have got more than they bargained for.

"You look amazing. Do you think you'll be able to stay in it?"

She cackled. "Let's find out. If these babies escape, I'll take out the front row."

****

The show was going well, and the front row had remained unscathed so far, and Oscar was enjoying himself.

"In 1921, Horace Goldin was the first magician to saw a lady in half, something that all magicians perform in various different ways. Sometimes it's a saw, sometimes a sword or guillotine. I've even seen a magician in Las Vegas use fire to burn through the middle of his poor assistant before welding her back together."

A slight chuckle from the audience.

"But today, I'm going to do something that you wouldn't have seen anywhere else. My own take on this amazing illusion. I will be cutting the beautiful Brandy in half…..lengthways."

The lights dimmed slightly, as Brandy shimmied onto the stage, her boobs leading the way, and the Mission Impossible theme tune was cranked up loud. Oscar took her hand and led her to a coffin-sized box, which he helped her into. She laid down and pushed her hands through holes in the sides, and he gave her a silk handkerchief to hold in each. He clipped the box closed concealing her completely, except for the hands, that gently waved the silks up and down, and her head which was stuck out of the top of the box.

He spun the box around dramatically, so that her head was closest to the front of the stage, and grabbed a chainsaw, spinning it around his head as he danced around to the music. He stopped at her feet end, and lowered the chainsaw, inserting it into a groove in the center of the box, and started cutting as if he was sawing between her legs. About halfway, the music stopped suddenly, and the lights went out, plunging the whole room into an eerie silence and blackness for half a second.

Brandy bit into a blood capsule, gave a piercing scream and a strobe light kicked in, showing blood dripping down her face, and she started thrashing her head back and forwards as Oscar continued to saw. The music returned and intensified as he kept sawing.

The showmanship and effects were all there to hide the illusion. In the split second that the lights went out, Brandy triggered a lever with her foot that rolled her body to the left side of the box. She removed her right hand, and a fake one popped up that had a mechanical hand that continued to move and wave a similar silk handkerchief. When the strobe light came on, all focus was on the thrashing Brandy and the blood and there were many gasps from the audience. Oscar continued to saw right up to where her neck should have been. He removed the saw and waved it around in the air, cackling wildly - playing the part of a deranged murderer.

He dropped the chainsaw to the floor, grabbed the ends of the box, and separated the two halves into a V-shape. Brandy's head went limp at the apex of the box, and her hands dropped the silks.

Oscar spun the box around again, showing it from all angles, before pushing the two halves back together. Two more spins of the box for effect, which actually gave Brandy a chance to roll back and remove the fake hand when it was out of sight at the back of the stage and replace it with her own. She came back to life and started thrashing again as he unclipped the box, and helped her out, blood now dripping down her chest. They both walked to the front of the stage to thunderous applause.

"I've been the Wizard of Oz. Thanks for coming. Enjoy the rest of your night."

****

Brandy was stripped to her underwear again, cleaning the fake blood and chattering about the show when it happened.

The familiar rush of air and the faraway voice. This time though the voice was shouting, and Oscar sank to his knees clutching his head, his vision blurring.

"What the hell do you think you're doing Ozzy? Don't go there. It's too risky."

He didn't quite blackout, but it was close. The room swam for a few seconds and then slowly returned to focus. He could hear Brandy's voice trying to get through, but his brain felt like it was wading through syrup.

"...you OK Osc? What's wrong? Fuck. Someone call an ambulance. Mick. Micky." The last word was a scream, her voice rising in panic.

"I'm OK. It's fine. I don't need an ambulance." He sat up, shaking the fog from his head. "Just get me some water."

Brandy grabbed a bottle of water as Micky, who booked the acts for the venue rushed in. Micky was a barrel. At just five feet tall and almost as round, a fast-moving Micky was in danger of tripping and rolling straight on by.

"What's up, guys? Oscar. Are you OK?" He realized that Brandy was half-naked and gawped at her and she grabbed for a towel.

"I'm fine. Just a shooting pain in my head. It's passed now." He sipped the water gratefully and the color returned to his face. He carefully stood up with Brandy's help and she led him to a chair. "See. I'm all good."

"You scared the shit outta me," said Brandy punching his arm. I fort you were a goner."

"I've got a friend in the audience who's a nurse," said Micky. "I can get her if you like. She won't mind."

"No. Seriously, I'm OK. I've seen the doc already." Well, not quite he thought, but at least I've got some more tablets coming. "Thanks anyway, Mick."

Mick waddled back out, glancing back once to try and get another glimpse of Brandy.

"You just sit there for a bit," she said, returning to the fake blood that she seemed to be smearing further over her chest rather than wiping off. "Fuck this blood's everywhere. Gimme some of that water back."

Oscar passed her the water and she poured a generous amount over her chest, making the skimpy outfit see-through. She squealed, dabbing at it with the towel.

"Fuck. That's fuckin' cold. I'm glad we don't use this stuff in every fuckin' show."

"It looked good," said Oscar laughing, amazed that anyone could get the word "fuck" three times into one sentence. He stood up, feeling better, and forced his eyes away from her. "I better pack the gear up."

"If you keel over again, I won't be very fuckin' 'appy."

"I'm fine. Don't worry. Get yourself dressed. We'll go get a drink."

Chapter 11 – "Heist #2"

Saturday 18th January.

Oscar woke early, his brain in override as he went over his plan for the diamond, mentally mapping out the Monument, and tracing the steps that he would need to take.

He needed to take some things into the museum and had spent much of the previous day trying to find a bag that had a hidden compartment – something that he used to use in his show with Daisy, his now-deceased white Vienna rabbit. He smiled at the irony that his bag with the hidden compartment was proving to be very well hidden itself. It turned up at the back of a closet that he never used, behind an ironing board, that he also never used. He had discovered long ago that good quality shirts and body heat meant that creases were something he never had to deal with. It was worth paying the extra for the shirts if he could avoid picking up an iron.

Why was the ironing board even there? Something he bought when he moved in, threw in the cupboard, and there it remained, gathering dust, and providing a good hiding place for his magic bag.

He had opened the bag, and the smell of rabbit hit him hard. Not that Daisy had died in the bag. No – she had met with an unfortunate electrocution accident involving a toaster cable that had dried jam on it, something that it seemed she couldn't resist. Sadly, her teeth were a little on the sharp side, and the cable a little on the worn side.

Oscar had never replaced her. Or the toaster

After his breakfast, he cleaned the musty bag and checked that the secret compartment at the bottom operated OK. It wasn't very big but should be good enough to hide the items that he needed. He loaded the compartment, clipped it shut, and added a camera, a jumper, a bottle of water, and a magazine on top so that it wouldn't look suspicious if searched.

He fired up GreySpider and checked the messages again. The cluster had started gathering interest now that one of the diamonds had been stolen. He still hadn't seen anything on the news though, so wondered if it was true, or whether Ace was just trying to attract attention to his post. If Oscar managed to pull off the robbery today, then the cluster posts would surely go ballistic tomorrow.

He finished his coffee, rinsed it under the tap, checked the bag again, and was about to go out when he remembered Ed. They still hadn't managed to talk to each other. He got the impression that his brother was sulking after he had let him down in the week. Should he call? Not today. He didn't want to be distracted from the job at hand. He could call him later.

****

As he rode the tube, his mind returned to the episode he'd had after the show the night before - probably his worse one ever. He wasn't happy that Brandy had witnessed it and was concerned that it could jeopardize further work at the club. He had made a point to buy Micky a drink afterward, and Micky hadn't canceled his show next month, so he thought he'd be OK – for a while at least. He needed to get his extra tablets and get this thing under control.

The one positive benefit from the incident was that Brandy had seemed very concerned about him. She kept on looking over at him and asking if he was OK and had made him promise to call her if it happened again. She had texted him when he got home too. Could he go out with her? Mixing business and pleasure was never a good idea and although her looks and body made every man in the vicinity do a double-take, her potty mouth was something that he knew he could never get used to. She was just being friendly anyway, he convinced himself. Probably worried about losing work.

The tube train slowed to a stop and he gathered his bag and made his way up to the sunshine. It was a lovely bright wintery day, although a bit cold. Good day to visit a museum, he thought. Hopefully, the place will be busy.

It was. There was even a small queue standing outside the old chapel. The security guard only gave a cursory glance at his bag when he opened it, more concerned about trying to get people through the door. There was already another six people behind him by the time he got to the front. I wonder if the security would have been tighter if the news of the other diamond theft had hit the papers, thought Oscar.

The showroom was teaming with people and a glance up to the mezzanine showed him that that too was packed, people leaning over the side admiring the fine art on the opposite wall. He slowly made his way around the room, looking at the art, reading the various plaques, and generally blending in, doing his best to be a visitor. When he reached the three plinths at the end of the room, he heaved a sigh of relief to see that they were all intact. If a diamond really has been stolen, then it wasn't from here, he thought. A dozen people were milling around the plinths, so he walked past, and headed up the spiral steps to the mezzanine. He stopped halfway to use the toilet and with the cubicle door closed, opened his bag and transferred the items from the secret compartment to the top of the bag. He also put four small items into his pocket.

Heading back out and down the same steps, he approached the Four Feathers diamond which was being viewed and admired by a young couple.

"That's what I want darling. One just like that." The cute blonde girl with the pixie haircut smiled up at her future fiancé hopefully and fluttered her eyelashes.

"Sure. I think I saw one just like it in Argos" teased the young lad – a beanpole of a man with floppy blonde hair and a small scar above his left eye. He snapped a photo of the diamond with his phone.

"You get me an Argos ring and you can keep it your bloody self," said the girl indignantly. "I love the purple in that one. I want a purple diamond."

Spoilt brat thought Oscar stepping behind the plinth. The couple moved on arguing about their engagement ring and Oscar had the plinth to himself for a few seconds. He reached into his pocket and extracted one of the four items. It was about the size of a matchbox and had a magnetic back to it. He glanced over at the CCTV camera and saw that it was turning away from his direction. When he was sure that he couldn't be seen he pushed it against the plinth under a small rim and it stuck solid with a quiet snick sound. He had spray painted it to be the same color as the plinth and at a glance, it appeared to be part of the box that it was stuck to. He stayed for a few moments admiring the diamond and then swapped places with an elderly couple who were just finishing with the middle plinth.

Less than five minutes later he had repeated the process with all three plinths - a box stuck just behind each one. He had made similar boxes before in his show but these he had modified to fit his purposes. Each one contained a chemical that when activated would produce smoke. A lot of smoke. And very quickly. He had added a remote electromagnet so that he could stick them to the plinths. In the bag he had a transmitter that could send a signal to the boxes, release the magnets and activate the smoke bombs.

Oscar casually moved away from the diamond and perused the other jewelry on the way back up toward the front door. He glanced at the security guard who was still busy searching bags as people continued to flood in. When he was near the front, he climbed the mezzanine steps at the opposite end from the diamond, stopping halfway up the steps to stick the fourth box on the back side of the metal balustrade of the staircase. He continued up without breaking stride and strolled across the mezzanine, stopping three-quarters of the way along to look down at the art.

It was now a matter of picking his moment. He needed enough people to cause a distraction but not too many that they got in the way. He watched the staff, the security guard, the other people, and the CCTV camera. If he waited too long someone might spot one of the boxes, or he may look suspicious.

Five minutes later the perfect moment arose. He started walking along the mezzanine towards the diamond, reaching into his bag his heart climbing ten, twenty beats per minute. The camera was turning away, and he was at the top of the spiral staircase when he pressed the button on the transmitter. There was an audible pop, not as loud as a gun, but loud enough to make people look round.

The smoke bomb on the far side of the museum near the entrance dropped to the floor and activated and smoke began to pour out. A shout could be heard from someone nearby followed by fragments of voices in quick succession.

"What was that?"

"Is there a fire?"

"...Lots of smoke."

"Did someone say fire?"

The security guard looked over, left his post, and headed towards the smoke.

While the distraction began to build, Oscar descended the stairs and pressed the button again. This time, three were three pops – much harder to hear because of the commotion, and then much more smoke, coming from the plinths. Cries from beneath him could be heard and he saw people moving hurriedly away. By the time he reached the plinth, the whole area was shrouded in smoke concealing him completely. He couldn't see the camera, which was now turning back towards him, but equally the camera couldn't see him.

He guessed he had about five seconds before the security guard left the smoke at the far end of the room and waded through the crowds of people moving away from where Oscar stood now, and maybe another ten before he got to him. Fifteen seconds in total. He held his breath.

He already had the bag open and had removed a device that was the size of and looked like a runner's baton. He pushed a button on the top and it made a quiet whirring noise as the glass cutters in the bottom started spinning frantically. He placed the baton on top of the glass dome directly above the diamond and pushed down hard. The glass started to squeal as the cutters dug in, making short work of the dome. Less than three seconds later a small round piece of glass dropped down, clipped the diamond, and fell to the bottom of the dome. Oscar had visions of the security guard running his way but calmly pressed another button on the baton. The glass cutters stopped, and a powerful vacuum replaced them. He lowered the baton slightly and the diamond was sucked instantly inside. He was already turning away and heading back to the stairs when he pressed the button to stop the vacuum. The staircase was now completely shrouded in smoke too as he ran up them three at a time. He forced himself to stop running and walked casually along the mezzanine, a quick glance telling him that no one was looking up. The security guard had just arrived at the smoke that was beginning to subside. The smoke bombs had used up their supply.

He ducked into the toilets as the security guard grabbed his walkie-talkie and ordered the doors to be locked. No one was to be allowed out.

Oscar dived into a cubicle and locked the door. He grabbed his phone and took a quick photo of the diamond before wrapping it in a waterproof bag with the baton. He stood on the toilet seat and lifted the lid on the high-level cistern and dropped the bag into the water.

He jumped down, exited the cubicle, and washed his hands in the sink, removing the ten clear plastic tips that covered his fingertips. He collected them together, flushed them down the toilet, and left the restroom, doing his best impression of looking bemused, acting as if he had been in the toilet for the last five minutes and missed all the commotion.

****

It took over two hours before Oscar was able to leave and everyone had been searched and identified. He silently cursed as they never discovered the compartment in his bag.

He could have taken the diamond with him.

Chapter 12 – "Madison Monroe"

Sunday 19th January

Greetings fellow spiders. Two in two days. Only two spaces left on my team.

Ace was ecstatic. Just the other day he was worrying that no one was going to accept his challenge, and now there had been two successful robberies. He had received a message from "Ozzy92" with a picture of the Monument diamond and it had been all over the news that morning, pictures and video footage taken from inside the museum on shaky handheld phones. He had marveled at the audacious attempt to steal the diamond with so many people around. It seemed that Ozzy may be a good addition to his team – assuming that was, that he didn't get caught.

The news broadcast had mentioned GreySpider and the diamond challenge and there had been lobbying and debates about shutting the underground website down. Easier said than done. As soon as sites like this were closed, another three would spring up overnight. Sometimes it was best to know where the enemy lived and keep an eye on them. One thing was for certain. GreySpider's membership was likely to rocket in the coming weeks with all the extra publicity.

The broadcast had also picked up on Ace's previous message – that a diamond had been stolen the day before. The museums were being contacted to check that their "Four Feathers" were intact. It won't be long before the fake is discovered, he thought. Assuming that Budster was genuine, and he had indeed managed to steal the real one.

Ace dunked a digestive biscuit into his tea as he watched the latest bulletin and cursed as it broke off and sunk to the bottom. He grabbed his teaspoon and fished the soggy remains out, looking for a bin to throw them into, finally giving up and spoon-feeding them to himself. He winced at the mushy texture and took a large swig of the tea to wash it down but burnt the roof of his mouth.

"Shit."

He jumped up and rushed to the kitchen to grab some mineral water from the fridge. Bottled and chilled, just how he liked it. He couldn't believe how people could drink water from a tap. Water that had passed through dozens of other bodies and been cleaned with chemicals God knows how many times.

As he returned to the lounge, there was some breaking news.

"Rhombus House, one of the four museums who hold the diamonds have just admitted that their Four Feathers diamond has been stolen too - and replaced with a fake. Both Rhombus House and the Monument will be closed while police investigate. No further details are available at this time, but we'll have more on this story in our lunchtime bulletin".

Ace smiled as he placed his bottle of water on a coaster, which in turn was set centrally on a patterned circle on his desk. So, Budster is for real. Two diamonds down. The next two would prove far more difficult. He settled down to compose a response to Ozzy and to invite him to join the team. He was looking forward to finding out what skills he had.

He reached for his keyboard, pausing on the way to check his coaster was centered correctly, and took another swig of his water.

****

"Monroe? Where are you?" bellowed Inspector Adrian Simpson striding across the incident room. "We need to be at the Monument, like ten minutes ago."

Simpson bellowed a lot. He was old-school, nearing retirement, and as he'd got older, he'd got more cantankerous. He was also a touch eccentric, at least with his dress sense, rarely seen without his tweed waistcoat and a gaudy selection of bow ties – today's being a fluorescent tangerine color. His appearance was often likened to Sherlock Holmes – He even smoked a pipe when he had the chance, but not in the station. Not anymore. Oh no, that pleasure was taken away from him long ago when everyone got all "politically correct" about passive smoking. He had to go to the "designated smoking area" about a hundred yards away in a flimsy bus-shelter-type construction and freeze his arse off, huddled with all the other outcasts. It was nuts.

"Monroe." He managed an even louder bellow making officer Dickson jump about three feet in the air.

Madison Monroe rushed in, phone to her ear and struggling to carry a stack of files. She wore the standard police uniform, her blonde hair tied into a neat ponytail, green Versace glasses perched on her nose, and a frown on her face.

"What do you mean it's turned up? Yesterday it was stolen." She listened to the other end as she dumped the files on a desk and gave an exasperated look to Simpson who stood impatiently glancing at his watch.

"So, you want us to drop the case?" Another few precious seconds ticked by. Simpson was getting antsy.

"OK. Thanks for calling." She hung up and sighed. "You're never gonna believe this. You remember that painting that was stolen from…"

"Tell me on the way," said Simpson interrupting and striding to the door. He strode almost as much as he bellowed.

She looked bemused. "Where are we going?"

"Monument" he bellowed back at her. "Move. We haven't got all day."

"It's 10am" she muttered, running behind him. "Actually. We have."

****

"So, what have you found out?"

Simpson was stood outside the Monument smoking his pipe and glancing at the dark clouds forming in the sky, threatening rain. He had taken a quick look around, spoken to the manager, and retreated to the street, leaving Monroe to do the leg work.

"So, it seems that smoke bombs were set off at 12:22pm yesterday," she said consulting the shorthand she'd made in her notebook. "One on the stairs – apparently as a distraction, and then three down the far end where the diamond was. The security guard, Olek Kaminski, reached the plinth no more than twenty seconds after the smoke was triggered. He found that the glass dome had been cut from above with some kind of glass cutter. Must've been fast. The diamond was taken out through the hole."

"Any witnesses?"

"None. The smoke was causing some panic. Kaminski barged a kid out of the way and knocked them flying in his rush to get there. Parents kicked off and are talking about suing."

"Not relevant," said Simpson. "And not our problem. Do we know the source of the smoke?"

"Four small canisters. Really small. Matchbox-sized, maybe slightly bigger. I've got them bagged, but I'll be surprised if they give up any fingerprints. We might be able to trace where they've come from. They're unusual. Not something I've seen before."

Simpson grunted and took a puff on his pipe. "Anything else?"

"The hole in the glass dome was small. Too small to put a hand in. They must have fished it with some long tweezers or something. Tough job to do at speed. Whoever it was, was in and out and disappeared in about twenty seconds."

"Cameras?"

One CCTV covering the whole room. I've got a copy of the footage so that might throw something up. Oh, and we've probably got the guy's name."

Simpson had been concentrating on re-lighting his pipe but looked up when she said this.

"They locked the doors, checked everyone's ID to get a list of names, and searched them too. We've got seventy-two names. Was really busy for a small place."

"We'll run them when we get back. See if anyone's got any previous. Did anyone get out before they locked down?"

"Maybe a few. But the diamond was a long way from the door. There's no way he could've got across the room and out in time. Kaminski radioed to shut it down pretty quickly."

"OK. Good job. Any ideas how he did it? How he got away?"

"Difficult to say without checking the cameras. Apparently, it was a bit manic when the smoke started. Whoever it was left a good distraction. Probably just joined the panicking crowds."

"But they didn't find the diamond?"

"No. But they hardly did a strip search. Would've been pretty easy to conceal. Probably stuffed it down his pants."

Simpson smirked. "Why did they wait until today to call it in?"

"The manager was away. Kaminski spoke to him and convinced him he had it in hand. He got the names, closed the place down, and searched them all. Quite thorough really. Thing is, they've still got a diamond missing, so they called it in today."

Simpson shrugged, reaching for his phone that was ringing. "Works for me. If we can't find it, we can blame them for not calling us sooner."

He put the phone to his ear. "Simpson" he bellowed loudly. It was as if he didn't even need it.

He listened for about twenty seconds.

"And why are we only hearing about this now?" he said impatiently. Another ten seconds.

"How do you spell that?" He signaled to Monroe to hand her the pad and scribbled an illegible word on it.

"OK. Send me the postcode. We're just finishing up here. We'll swing by straight after. Have you got someone checking out this spider thing?" He handed the pad back and started striding, signaling her to follow.

"Keep me posted." He cut the call off, never one for the pleasantries of hellos or goodbyes.

Madison was trotting to keep up while trying to read what he'd written on his pad. How the hell did he get to be an inspector with writing worse than a four-year-old, she thought.

"Have you heard of Grace Spider?" he said as they got in the car.

She looked puzzled. "Do you mean GreySpider? Part of the Dark Web?"

"What's a dark web?"

"Porn, drugs, guns, bootleg software, music..." she said. "GreySpider's been about for a few years. I think it's flavor of the month at the moment."

"That must be it. Fire it up. Apparently, there's a message on there, telling people to steal diamonds."

She tapped on her phone and brought up the GreySpider logon screen.

"Looks like we'll need an account." She had one but didn't want to admit it. She hadn't used it for over a year. Pirating music and films wasn't something she was proud of and as a police officer, she could easily lose her job, or worse if she was found out.

"Get on to Dickson. He's the computer whizz. Let him check it out. Tell him to get us a password."

She dialed the number as he pulled out in front of a BMW, narrowly missing it causing a cacophony of horn blowing from the young suit in the car and the one behind it as they both slammed their brakes on.

"Dickhead" muttered Simpson.

"Where are we going anyway?" asked Madison, grappling for her seatbelt. Simpson's driving was erratic on a good day and downright dangerous when he was in a hurry.

"Rhombus. It's written on the pad.

She glanced back at her pad but still couldn't make it out.

"What's that?"

He almost cracked a smile. "Another museum. Another diamond missing. Looks like we've got ourselves a serial robber."

Chapter 13 – "Investigation"

They arrived at the Rhombus in less than half an hour, mainly thanks to the siren and some driving that a rally car driver would have been impressed with. Madison's knuckles were a little white and she climbed gratefully out of the car when it pulled up outside.

Dickson had provided them with a GreySpider account, and she had spent the last ten minutes scrolling through the comments.

"There's over three thousand of them. That's gonna take some reading through" she said, stopping and chuckling at a comment from "LoobeeLou" suggesting that Ace could stick his diamond where the sun doesn't shine.

"There's a good chance that our guy would have left a message though," said Simpson. "We may be able to cross-check against the names from the Monument."

Simpson was a bit of a Luddite when it came to anything techie and she had patiently explained that on GreySpider people had an alias and didn't generally use their own names – and after reading the challenge, it was more likely they were looking for two different robbers, not one.

"Can we trace their real names through the website provider?"

Madison looked up over the rim of her glasses, impressed that he knew what a provider was.

"Unlikely," she said. People using sites like this hide behind a firewall. The forums will be difficult to trace. Even if we could, any user could easily set up a bogus email address for their account.

Tracing an individual is almost impossible if they know what they're doing. We could get Dickson to see what he can find though."

Simpson grunted. She'd lost him at 'firewall'.

They banged on the door of the Rhombus, which had a hastily hand-written sign in the window proclaiming that they were "Closed for refurbishments".

Madison scanned the area. "It's pretty open," she said. "I wonder if there are any street cameras?"

They'd struck out at the Monument. The nearest street camera was half a mile away, and not even on the same road. They'd asked Dickson to get a copy anyway.

"Might be more promising" said Simpson, following her gaze. "The Indian takeaway over there might have something. It's the sort of place that gets grief when the pubs close. I'd have a camera if I were them."

He banged on the door again, and it was abruptly opened by a fifty-something creepy-looking man who had "Museum curator" written all over him. He introduced himself as the manager, Thomas Cruz.

"Like the actor but with a Z."

Nothing like the actor, thought Madison as he looked her up and down with piggy eyes that were too close together.

He took them past a young girl who glanced up from her phone nervously and gave them a nod. They climbed the stairs to the middle floor, and he presented them with the diamond.

"Except it's a fake. A pretty good one, granted but the cut and clarity are nowhere near as good, and it's a little smaller. We've had our expert check it over, and it's only worth about two hundred pounds."

"It's been handled?" said Simpson abruptly. "Did he wear gloves?"

"I'm afraid not. You see. We didn't really believe that it had been stolen. When we were notified that the Four Feathers were being targeted...well," he looked a bit sheepish, "our diamond was there and at first glance, you really wouldn't know it was different."

Simpson resisted the urge to give a lecture and settled for rolling his eyes.

"We'll need to fingerprint your expert to remove him from investigations," said Simpson. "Monroe, bag the diamond. Maybe we can find out where it came from." He turned back to Cruz. "So, do you have any idea when the real one might have been taken?"

"Absolutely none," said Cruz with a shrug. We run a very small staff here, only Angel our receptionist – you saw her on the way in, and then there's Maggie and Molly. They're sisters – upstairs getting coffee. Maggie sits on this floor nearly all day, assisting with any queries. I've spoken to all of them and they've not noticed anything suspicious. I mean, look at the case. It's intact. Someone managed to swap it out without us noticing."

"Have you checked the camera?" said Madison, indicating the CCTV looking down at them.

"No. Not yet. We called you as soon as we confirmed it had been stolen. We didn't want to touch anything else."

"OK," said Simpson. "We'll need to talk to the three girls, and we'll take a copy of the footage. We'll dust the case for prints, but to be honest the whole scene has been compromised. You could have had hundreds of people through here since it was taken. I think the camera is our best bet."

Cruz gave them the phone number for the expert that he used to check the diamond, Robert French, explaining that he wasn't on the payroll. They just used him as required and paid him per job. He then took Simpson upstairs to get copies of the CCTV videos and introduce him to the sisters while Madison looked around trying to piece together how someone could've swapped the diamond out without being noticed. She deduced very quickly that it was unlikely to have happened in the daytime. More likely someone broke in at night. She noticed the metal shutter above the door. Pretty secure, but not impossible.

She asked Cruz about it when he came back downstairs, and he explained that they had a large padlock that secured the shutter. She gave him a pair of gloves and he took it out of a drawer in reception and offered it to her.

"Angel usually opens and closes, but I came in early today, so it will have both our prints on it," said Cruz.

She peered closely at the padlock. "There's a few scratches around the lock. Could have been picked. Is it old?"

"At least a few years. It was here when I came" said Cruz.

"Could be just wear and tear" said Madison. "Can we take this?"

"Sure. We have a spare up in the storeroom."

Madison bagged the padlock.

"I'm going out for a smoke," said Simpson. "Get a statement from the girl. Ask her about the alarm."

Cruz introduced Madison to Angel and left them to chat while he went upstairs for his coffee.

Angel didn't have a great deal to offer. She opened up most mornings at 8:45 and closed at 5:00, 5:30 at weekends unless the cleaner was in.

"Shaz comes in twice a week. Gets here just before we close and spends an hour running a mop and a vacuum around. She locks up on Tuesdays and Fridays."

Madison took her number.

Angel's routine consisted of checking that the museum was empty, setting the alarm, locking the door on the way out, and fixing the padlock through the loop in the shutter.

"Have you all got keys for the door and the padlock?" asked Madison.

"Just me, Shaz, and Mr. Cruz," said Angel. "Molly and Maggie wait for one of us to open up if they're here first."

"And the alarm?"

"Same. Mr. Cruz doesn't like too many people to know the code."

Madison established that the alarm was on the top floor and that Angel had two minutes to get out before it was triggered. They walked the stairs and Madison checked out the alarm cabinet.

"We'll have to get this dusted for prints too," she said, making notes. "We'll send a guy over when we're finished here."

They headed back to reception.

"Have you seen anyone suspicious in the last couple of weeks? Anything out of the ordinary? I guess most days are the same here, so if anything comes to mind it may be relevant"

Angel frowned. "I don't think so," she said. "I mean, it's pretty quiet on a weekday and I only work every other weekend. I've been here a year, and this is the most excitement we've had since I started."

"No one taking pictures or anything?" pushed Madison.

"Lots of people take pictures. It's a museum" Angel shrugged.

"And you make sure that everyone's out before you lock up each night?"

"Yes. I walk each floor on the way up to the alarm and check the loos too." She stopped; a look of concern on her face.

"What is it?" Madison had picked up on the subtle change in her expression.

"Probably nothing," said Angel. "There was a guy. A couple of days ago. I was just locking up when he came running back. Left his glasses in the toilets."

"Something unusual about him?"

"Not unusual. He was really nice, chatty. American. It was Thursday. I was in a hurry to leave as I was meeting a friend. He went into the loo, grabbed his glasses, and then left. I didn't check the loo."

"But you saw him leave?"

"Yes. Well. Kind of. We chatted for a bit, and then I went up and he went down." She looked worried. "God. Mr. Cruz will kill me if I left someone in the loo when I locked up."

Madison was more interested in the man that came back. "Could the guy have hidden somewhere when you went upstairs?" She looked around the reception area, but there were no obvious hiding places. It was fairly open.

Angel considered it. "He was in a hurry to leave. I heard the door slam behind him. If he came back..." she shrugged. "You can see for yourself. There's nowhere here, and if he went into the exhibition rooms, he would have triggered the alarm when I left."

"Anywhere upstairs?"

They walked back up and Madison spotted the cleaner's cupboard. She wrenched it open. Small but big enough to hide.

"I'm going to need a full description. Hopefully, we can find him on the CCTV."

****

"Middle-aged. Long hair, guitar case. Should be easy to spot on the CCTV." Madison was bringing Simpson up to speed on her chat with Angel as he swerved around a bicycle on their way back to the station.

"Bloody bikes. Shouldn't be allowed on the road" he fumed.

Madison nearly pointed out that he was in a cycle lane and it was Simpson who was in the wrong place, but she refrained.

"Did you get anything from Molly and Maggie?"

"Waste of bloody time. They're both older than God. Topping up their pensions by knitting and drinking coffee by the sounds of it."

"Let's hope the CCTV will help. Whoever did it wasn't stupid though" said Madison. "I've put in a call to Dusty to dust for prints, but I doubt he'll come up with anything."

Dusty was the affectionate nickname for the appropriately named Dustin Banks who worked in forensics.

"That place has been trampled like a subway station" moaned Simpson. "He won't find anything. He'd be better spending his time at the Monument. Send him there to dust the case, and make sure he gets those smoke box thingies. See if he can track down where they came from."

"I'll tell him to swing by the Monument after. There could be prints on the alarm at the Rhombus. Or the cleaner's cupboard?"

Simpson grunted. He wasn't optimistic, and he wasn't feeling too charitable towards Mr. Cruz at the Rhombus. He was still struggling to believe that no one had noticed the diamond had been switched.

They screeched into the station and Madison thankfully got out of the car.

"I'll go sit with Dickson and we'll start on the CCTV footage," she said. "We'll concentrate on the Thursday. See if we can spot the rocker dude."

"Get Jones looking at that diamond first. It's likely it was custom-made for purpose. He can talk to that expert too. What was his name?"

"French." Madison checked her notes. "Robert French. Will do. Anything else?"

"I'm gonna grab some lunch, and then call the other two museums. I think they need a lesson in vigilance."

Chapter 14 – "Gambling Man"

Wednesday 22nd January

"Hit me."

Owen Kelly looked down miserably at his two cards. The nine of hearts and five of clubs. Fourteen. He was having another bad run. He took a large gulp of his double whiskey as the dealer, a spotty teen in a badly fitted suit, flipped over the jack of clubs.

"Twenty-four. Bust." He swept the chips away in a flourish and Owen promptly replaced them with two more.

His rapidly decreasing pile told the ever-familiar story. When was he going to learn that it was OK to get up and walk away? An hour ago, he'd doubled the two hundred pounds he'd walked in with and could've called it a night. It would have fed him for the week, paid back part of the debt he owed Johnny "four fingers" Caine, and still given him some play money for the rest of the week. Now he was concerned that he might end up like Caine if his luck didn't turn around soon. He was quite attached to his fingers and needed them to run the till at the bookies he worked at part-time.

Two more cards landed in front of him. A seven and a four. That's more like it. He tapped the table, and the dealer flipped a three and his moment of joy was replaced with more despair. He already knew what the next card would be before it landed, and true to form, the ten of hearts was revealed and the spotty little snot dragged his chips away.

He downed the whiskey.

"Where's Estelle tonight?"

"She's on the roulette," said the teen. He leaned in. "Had a bit of a run-in with a high roller, so they've stuck her over in the corner."

"She deals better cards than you" he slurred, waving his hand at a passing waitress to top up his drink. "And her tits are nicer." He laughed out loud at his own joke, and the guy playing next to him grabbed his chips and hastily moved on.

"Again?"

Owen looked at his chips.

"Fuck it. Why not. He pushed two more forward, and within thirty seconds they were whisked away.

His drink arrived, and he scooped the remaining chips into his hand. The fact that fit in one hand said it all.

"I wish you well and hope to never receive your shitty cards again," he said with a mock bow as he lumbered off in search of Estelle.

"Have a good evening Sir."

****

Estelle Rose-Price sat alone behind the roulette table filing a perfectly manicured nail. She wore the casino's standard uniform of black trousers, a white blouse, and black waistcoat, but somehow made it look good. As Owen lumbered drunkenly toward her, she reminded him, not for the first time of Uma Thurman, her jet-black hair and fringe modeled on Mia Wallace from his favorite Tarantino film. She had an air of composure and quiet self-assurance about her, and her plummy accent completed the upper-class look.

She suddenly twitched, her head flicking violently to the right and slightly upwards. "Drunken Fucktard" she blurted out.

Estelle had Tourette's syndrome. Her looks, poise, and upbringing should have led her to greater things, but the unfortunate disorder had struck when she was twelve, and it had affected her teenage years, causing her to drop out of her five-thousand pound-a-term private school. After some successful home-schooling, she tried college but dropped out after a month of not fitting in and being ridiculed by her peers. Since then, she had bounced from one job to another, finally finding herself in this grubby little casino - Not because she wasn't clever, but because the symptoms caused by the Tourette's didn't allow her the opportunities that she should have had.

Owen laughed at her outburst. He had struck up quite a rapport with the girl during the many nights they'd spent together in the casino, him throwing his money at her, and her sympathizing as she sadly took it from him. He was one of the few who wasn't worried about what she said and made a point to see her whenever he visited.

"Stuck in the corner again?" he said sadly. "You should be front and center sweetheart. Standing proud, screaming a big fuck you to the management."

"Bunch of arseholes," she said quietly.

Owen loved it when posh people swore. The way she said the word "arse" almost made him spit his drink out.

"They knew about my condition when I started" she continued. "Said it wouldn't be a problem, and now they stick me in the corner and make me wear this." She indicated the lanyard around her neck with the words. "I have Tourette's Syndrome. Please forgive me if I say something offensive".

"It's embarrassing." She twitched, whistled, and tried to suppress herself before uttering "Dick-munchers."

"Dick munchers" agreed Owen. "Every last one of them." He swigged his whiskey. "No one playing with you tonight?"

"Not for a while. I don't actually mind working here when I've got something to do. Sitting doing nothing is soul-destroying though. I even spin the wheel occasionally and try to guess the number it lands on. I think I'm going out of my mind."

"Are you winning?"

"Never. You should know by now that roulette is a mug's game. But you still come back for more."

"I just love seeing your pretty little eyes sweetheart." Owen dumped his meager stash of chips on the table, about a dozen. "Let's see if I can make it last until the next drink at least."

The drinks at the casino were free as long as you were spending money. Owen had long since realized that if you didn't keep giving your money away, the waitresses kept a wide berth - and if you did finally catch their eye, the drink you were going to receive would be heavily watered down.

He stuck two chips on the second twelve and Estelle spun the wheel. He watched mesmerized as the small metal ball rolled rapidly in the opposite direction, clattered around the numbers before coming to a stop on seventeen.

"Seventeen. Good start" said Estelle, adding four chips to the two that he had bet, twitching and proclaiming "Lucky-fucker."

"I told that spotty twat earlier that I have more luck with you," said Owen smiling for the first time in about an hour. He downed his drink and waved it in the air to a waitress who completely blanked him as she headed to a table of businessmen in suits, playing Craps and throwing their money around like confetti.

"Come on. I'm spending money here." Owen gesticulated to the roulette table, caught the edge of his empty glass, and sent it tumbling to the floor. The last whiskey was taking effect and he was getting louder. The waitress gave him a nervous glance and her eyes flicked to the burly security guard – Jonno, who gave her an imperceptible nod. He was watching.

Owen clambered from his stool and retrieved his glass.

"Maybe you should ask for some water," said Estelle quietly. "You don't want to be thrown out again."

Owen had been ejected on numerous occasions for his drunken behavior, and even had a two-week ban on that occasion where he had fallen off his stool, grabbed hastily at the dress of the girl next to him, and almost torn it off her back. The girl had screamed the place down suggesting he was trying to grope her, and her fiancé had gone mental, landing a couple of good kicks in Owen's ribs before Jonno had dragged him away. Luckily the security cameras had caught everything, and he got away with just the ban.

"Fucking water is for fish," said Owen trying to get back on his stool and missing. "Let's play. Let 'em ride." He indicated the six chips that now sat on the second twelve. Estelle grabbed the ball, glanced at Jonno, and gave a look to say, "Everything's OK – for now" and span the wheel.

"Thirteen" she exclaimed brightly. "You're on a roll."

She added twelve more chips and Owen gleefully pulled them all back towards him, counting his stash. He had a total of twenty-eight now. He glanced towards the waitress again but earned a serious stare from Jonno who had moved a little closer.

"They're a bit tetchy tonight," he said, turning back to Estelle. I only want one more.

"Arse bandit. Dick cheese." She whistled, twitched, and tried to carry on as if nothing had happened. "Again?"

Owen snorted back a laugh. "Dick cheese? Where did that come from?"

Estelle was used to Owen calling her on her outbursts, and she quite liked it. It was better than the odd looks that most customers gave her. If only he wasn't such a drunken bum. She needed to meet someone who understood her condition rather than condemning her for what she couldn't control. Owen was a nice guy when he was sober. She'd gone out to dinner with him once but soon realized that he had a drinking problem. An alcoholic gambler who worked at the bookies was hardly the type of man she wanted to spend her life with.

"Let's switch," said Owen. He dropped six chips on "Even" and the ball span. The waitress approached and dropped a glass of water on the table next to him without a word and wandered off.

"Is there a whiskey in there sweetheart?"

She ignored him and he watched her bottom all the way back to the bar, stealing a glance at Jonno who stood grimly watching him. He grinned, shrugged, and turned back to Estelle who had just swept his chips away.

"Eleven. Sorry Owen."

"Fuck it." He grabbed the water and sniffed it. "It's fucking water" he announced, a bit disgusted.

Estelle laughed. "Drink it. It won't hurt. You never know, they may bring you something stronger if you play ball."

Owen turned, raised the glass to Jonno, and downed the half-pint of water in one. Jonno ignored him.

"How's work?" said Estelle, doing her best to save Owen from a humiliating exit from the premises.

"Shit. Always shit" said Owen glumly. "I spend half my wages before I even get out the door. They should pay me extra for keeping their profits up." He stuck two chips on twenty-eight, knowing that betting on a single number was never a good idea, and losing them instantly when the ball dropped into three.

"Maybe you should find something else. Working in a bookie isn't the best vocation for someone with a gambling habit." She twitched and added "Prick-loser" and flushed a deep red that matched her lipstick.

Owen ignored the insult, knowing it wasn't really directed at him. "Maybe you're right. I need to be earning more. I still owe Caine four hundred, and God knows where the rent's coming from this month."

"I know that feeling" she sympathized. She rented a studio, and city prices were crazy. Her parents were always there to help out, but she was adamant that she was going to stand on her own two feet.

"Fuck it," said Owen again, and pushed his remaining chips onto black. If I can't get a drink I might as well go all in.

Estelle spun the wheel. She knew he'd regret it if he lost, but if he won, then the whole lot would be gone on the next bet. Or the next. She'd seen it time and time again.

"Sorry Owen. Number thirty. Red."

His head dropped and he stumbled from his stool. "Good to see you, Estelle. Don't let the bastards get you down." He lumbered past Jonno and held his hand up for a high-five which was promptly ignored.

"Take care Owen" she called back, before twitching. "Cock-sucking man-whore."

Chapter 15 – "Bones"

Owen stumbled out of the casino into light rain and attempted the half-mile stagger home, something that he could normally do in ten minutes while sober but would likely take at least twice that in his current state.

It took even longer when he rounded a corner and came face to face with Marky Bowers, or "Bones" to his friends, not that he had many. Bones was about six stone in a rainstorm and just over five feet tall. The nickname was two-fold. One, he was literally skin and bones. It looked like a strong gust would knock him off his feet, and two, he was a hired goon for "Four-Fingers" Caine and was notorious for breaking the bones of Caine's unfortunate clientele who didn't pay their debts. People like Owen Kelly. His diminutive size caused many to assume that he was harmless, but the hammer he carried in his pocket and the psychotic look in his eye soon made people realize that he wasn't one to be messed with.

A drunken Owen was a lot braver than maybe he should've been in the circumstances.

"Boney. How's it hanging, dude? High-five. Or maybe that should be low-five." He chuckled and swayed a bit.

He held his hand at waist level for the "low-five", which Bones promptly grabbed by the little finger and twisted fast and hard. Owen squealed like a pig and found himself on the floor with his arm up behind his back, and his finger almost dislocated.

"Hey Kelly. Long-time no see." Bones had a nasally voice that was nearly an octave higher than Owen's due to a damaged throat he'd received in a knife fight that nearly cost him his life several years before.

"Ow. Shit. You're gonna break my finger you fucker" he screamed breathlessly.

Bones smiled, grabbed the finger next to it, and twisted again, receiving a glorious squeal from Owen, louder than before. Two young girls turned the corner towards them, and Bones look around menacingly. They took one look at what was going on, another at the look in his eyes, and promptly turned back and scarpered.

"Boss wants his money, Kelly. Five hundred. It's due today."

"Five? I only owe him four."

"Well, he had to pay me to come and remind you, so it's five now."

"Come on Bones. Four hundred is nothing to Caine. He knows I'm good for it. I always pay him back."

"Then why the fuck am I stood here in this shitty weather partaking in chit-chat with a drunken twat like you? Give me the money. You. Useless. Prick." He emphasized each of the last three words with a twist on Owen's fingers, bringing tears to his eyes.

"I haven't got it," said Owen miserably. "But give me a few days. I get paid on Friday. I can probably pay half."

"What the fuck good is half?"

"Maybe three quarters," said Owen desperately. "Come on man. I'll get the rest next week."

"Maybe I'll leave you with half a fucking finger seeing as you think that half isn't a problem." Bones looked over his shoulder, checked that no one was around, and pulled out a knife.

Owen's eyes opened wide in alarm. Things had suddenly got very real. "Jesus. OK. I'll get the full four hundred. Friday night. I'll take it straight to Caine."

Another twist on his already excruciating fingers. "It's five hundred, and it goes up by fifty a day. I'll do the maths for you. That's six-hundred by Friday night."

Owen went white. How the hell was he supposed to find that kind of money in two days?

"Six it is. I've got a friend who can help me. I'll bring it." Right now, his main concern was to get as far away as possible from this skinny psycho.

Bones let go of his fingers and wiped his hand on his raincoat.

"Jesus, you stink. I'm gonna be smelling you for the rest of the fucking night." He smiled down at Owen who had fallen to the wet ground clutching his fingers and breathing heavily. "Have a pleasant evening Mr. Kelly. I guess we'll be seeing you on Friday. I trust that you won't try and disappear. If you do, then I may just have to make that a reality."

The threat hung in the air as Bones pulled his raincoat up around his neck and sauntered off.

Owen leaned over and vomited up most of the whiskey he'd consumed in the previous two hours. Five seconds later, the rest followed.

****

He got home, threw his clothes in the washing machine, and had a quick shower, trying to rid himself of the sticky remains of the sick on his hands. As he stood under the hot flowing water he thought about Bones and Caine and the problem at hand. He was due to be paid two hundred on Friday morning. How can he turn that into six in less than a day? Actually, he'd need more than six. He had rent and bills to pay too. He needed more like a grand.

As always, his prime solution turned to gambling. A horse at five to one would do it? Or a few lucky spins on the roulette wheel. It all sounded so simple. Double the money three times and he'd have plenty.

But what if he lost? His encounter with Bones was not something he wanted to repeat.

He dressed, made some pasta, and sat on the sofa scrolling through his phone while he ate slowly in a bid to keep it down. His fingers were throbbing but by some miracle, they didn't appear to be broken. He signed into his GreySpider account to see if there were any good tips on the racing forum. He mainly used GreySpider for online Poker games, but his last session had emptied his account when he dropped over a hundred and fifty pounds holding three Kings. Some lucky bastard calling himself "MisterTwister" had pulled a flush on the river and prematurely ended what was looking like a good run.

He nearly missed it. He was in autopilot, opening his "Favourites" page to find the racing forums when he did a double-take. There were three thousand, eight hundred posts on one of the clusters. Intrigued he clicked into it and read about the challenge from Ace. Scrolling down through the most recent messages he realized that two of the diamonds had already been stolen. Hang on, he'd seen something on the news. He hadn't really been paying attention, but the reporter had been stood outside of the Monument, and she'd caught his eye because she was cute.

A ten-grand diamond? That's all my problems solved right there, he thought. He googled the museums and was surprised to find that one of them — "The Tempest" was only a mile away. He'd never heard of it. Museums weren't really his bag.

What am I thinking? A robbery? I may be desperate, but I'm not a thief.

He closed the cluster, connected to the horse racing forum, and posted a message.

22-01-2020 22:45, GreenZero

Any gd tips 4 Friday? Need 2 make some fast dosh

He had picked "GreenZero" as his GreySpider name as a nod to the roulette table. The day he had joined he had stuck a bet on the Zero, a moment of madness, and it had paid off at 35-1. He had tried to repeat this feat several times since only to see his chips swept away.

As he finished his pasta, his phone pinged twice - Two quick replies to his post.

22-01-2020 22:48, RonMcDon

Hey Green. Dead cert — "Olivetti", running at Kempton on Friday at 2pm

22-01-2020 22:50, MissPiggy

"RollEmOver" is on a winning streak. Odds may not be much, but worth a bet if she's running

He pulled up a racing page. RollEmOver had won three of her last five races and pulled a second too. Looked very promising but probably wouldn't give him the 5-1 he needed. Olivetti was a wild card. Two wins last month but hadn't even placed since. The race on Friday was a higher class though, so it could be a good shout.

He grabbed a pen and scribbled the horse names on a scrap of paper and put a reminder on his phone to check the odds on Friday morning. Shame he didn't have the money for a trip. He loved a day at the races, and Kempton was one of his favorite racecourses. Could he warrant spending some of his stake money on a train ticket and entry to the races? Would depend on the odds. If he failed to make the money he needed, at least he'd have a good day out before Bones broke all of his fingers. He checked the train times and added another note to the pad.

As he lay in bed an hour later, he thought about the diamond sitting just a mile away at the Tempest. Could he use it as a backup plan? He wouldn't have much time after the races if he went, and he could hardly pay Caine with the stone. He flexed his bruised fingers. Anything would be better than having to endure another visit from that skinny freak Bones though.

Let's see what Friday brings. It will all come down to one or two horses.

Story of my life, he thought.

Chapter 16 – "A Trap"

Thursday 23rd January

"Tell me what we've got" bellowed Simpson. He didn't beat about the bush.

Madison had collected information regarding both robberies from the other officers and had it all written down in her neat, orderly handwriting on a flip chart in the Incident room.

"OK. Let's start with the Rhombus" she said. At the top of the flip chart she'd written "Rhombus" and beneath that were various bullet points.

"Fingerprints," she said, pointing to the first bullet point. "Dusty has been over the padlock, the metal shutter, the glass case, the fake diamond, and the alarm system. Lots of prints and partials matching Angel, Cruz, Shaz the cleaner, and Robert French the diamond expert, but nothing else. Looks like the guy wore gloves."

She moved to her next bullet point – "Fake Diamond".

"French has suggested that the diamond was probably made in a lab. Most synthetic diamonds are done this way. Due to the similarity in color and size to the Four Feathers diamond, he thinks it was likely made to order. Jones has contacted the usual suspects, but no one knows anything or they're not talking if they do."

Simpson grunted. Most of the low-life contacts that they used were untrustworthy, and only in it to get something for themselves. The information they got rarely led anywhere.

"However, he believes it was made in a hurry" she went on. "On closer inspection, the finish is pretty poor. Good enough to fool most, but anyone who knows anything about diamonds can clearly see that it's fake."

"It did its job" pointed out Simpson. "Fooled the staff there for a couple of days. Sounds like a dead-end too. Move on.

"OK. The CCTV doesn't show anything as such, but it was tampered with in the early hours of Friday 17th. The time stamp on the files shows that an old video file was copied over the file for Thursday night/Friday morning. We've confirmed that the file was from two weeks prior. The copy was done at 2:50am."

"Was that the day that the musician guy – the American, went back for his sunglasses?"

"Yes. Looks like he may have doubled back, hid somewhere, cracked the alarm, and spent the evening there. Obviously, he's not on the CCTV so it's all speculation. Not sure why he spent ten hours in there though."

"Maybe he struggled with the alarm."

"Unlikely." She produced a photo. "Dusty found this in the cabinet."

Simpson squinted at the picture and his eyes opened wide in amazement. "Is that the code?" he asked incredulously.

"Yep. We've told them that they may want to change it and that writing it down is probably not a good idea."

Simpson threw his hands in the air. "Can we move on to the Monument? I've got better things to do than waste my time with these idiots."

Madison laughed. "Hang on. We did get something. Dusty found a hair in the glass case. At a glance, it doesn't match any of the staff. We've sent it for DNA testing. If our perps got previous, then we may get a hit. Gonna take a couple of days though."

"Good spot." Simpson turned around. "Well done Dusty."

Dusty looked up from his nearby desk and gave him a nod. Simpson could be a bit of a bear, but at least he gave credit when it was due.

"Anything else?"

"Just one thing that we can't explain. I told you that the CCTV recording was overwritten. Well, after the Thursday night, the camera on the top floor has moved. It's only a couple of inches. We missed it at first but for some reason, he nudged the camera up."

"He'd have to. To get out of the room without being seen after he reset the cameras."

"That's what we first thought, but it's not high enough. I went back with Dickson and we tried to get out of the room without being seen. It's impossible. Even crawling along the floor, his head would be in view. We tried it. We've watched the video closely from 2:50am when he copied the file until the museum was opened up in the morning. No one left that room."

Simpson pondered it for a second but came up blank. "OK. Good one. Leave it on the board. Not sure if it'll help us though."

Madison moved on to the Monument.

"OK. The Monument. We must've watched the CCTV twenty times. It's quite something. I'll show you."

She pressed a few buttons on a nearby laptop, and the image of the museum sprang to life on a large TV screen on the wall next to the flipchart.

"We've watched the footage leading up to the point that the smoke bombs were set off. Fifty-one people approached the diamond case and looked at it in the preceding two hours. It must've been one of them that planted the smoke bombs, although the camera didn't catch anyone doing anything suspicious. It's unlikely that he could've placed all of them in the time that the camera swung away and back, so he's probably one of the fifty-one."

When the clock on the corner of the screen hit 12:22, Madison said. "OK. Keep your eye on the front of the room. The camera catches the first smoke bomb going off."

Ten seconds ticked by, and then smoke suddenly appeared and started to fill the front of the Museum. There was no audio on the recording, but it was easy to see people backing away startled.

The camera panned slowly towards the back of the room and showed people hurrying from the back towards the main entrance. As it swung all the way round Simpson saw that the whole end of the room was shrouded in dense smoke. People were covering their eyes and mouths and panic was beginning to ensue. As it swung away again, he saw the security guard, Kaminski barging through the crowd, knocking a small child over in his haste to get there. Kaminski disappeared into the smoke as the camera turned all the way back towards the front. When it swung back, most of the smoke had cleared and Kaminski was striding back up the room covering his mouth and coughing while talking into his radio.

Madison stopped the video.

"Fast isn't it. We've tried enhancing, zooming in, and even watching frame by frame. We can't see anything through that smoke, and the camera turns away again before Kaminski comes back through. It's possible that someone skirted around him and emerged when the camera wasn't looking, but it's a bit risky. My bet is that he escaped up the stairs and over the mezzanine. The camera doesn't cover it."

"Did you discover where those smoke canisters came from?" Simpson scratched his head, reset the video, and watched it again while she spoke.

"They're homemade. Small metal box with three sections for different chemicals, separated by thin glass. There's a small amount of trace chemical left – Sodium bicarbonate, ammonia, and hydrochloric acid. He added an electromagnet on the side so that he could stick them to the metal plinth, and a receiver so that he could activate them. They were found on the floor, so we believe that he had some kind of trigger unit that sends a signal to the boxes. The signal kills the magnet, the metal boxes drop to the floor and the impact breaks the glass and mixes the chemicals. Voila. Instant smoke. Very clever."

"Are the chemicals readily available?"

"Everywhere. You can even get them from Amazon" said Madison.

"Shit. What about the boxes? Can you buy them with the glass panels in place?"

"Not seen them. We think they're homemade too. Seems likely our guy is quite handy."

"Any prints on them?" Simpson wasn't hopeful.

"None. Dusty checked around the cabinet too and we've got over thirty different prints. The guy was too careful though. If the boxes were clean, he's not going to leave anything on the case."

Simpson grunted an agreement. "So, what have we got left? The seventy-odd names. We'll have to canvass them all. One of them must be our guy."

"We're on it, but it's slow going, and I'm not hopeful. They took names and numbers, but why would he leave a real name? Not everyone had ID, so they may not be genuine. We may find someone who saw something though."

"Two diamonds stolen, and we've got diddly-squat," said Simpson exasperated. "What now? Wait for the next one? See if we can find a pattern?"

"I'd like to go back to the Monument," said Madison. "I've spoken to Kaminski again, and he claimed to have a done a pretty thorough search on the customers, and he didn't come up with the diamond. It's a long shot, but if our guy went over the mezzanine to escape, it's just possible that he hid the diamond up there somewhere."

"Real long shot," agreed Simpson. "But nothing to lose. I'll come with you. I could do with some air."

****

"I don't bloody believe it." Simpson looked amazed as Madison pulled the see-through bag from the toilet cistern.

Neither of them really believed they would find anything. Most police work consisted of dead ends and wasted time, traipsing down one lead after another and coming up empty-handed. Her expectations had been low, but as it happened it hadn't taken long at all. The mezzanine was literally just a walkway with the toilets in the middle. The walkway had offered no hiding places so they had ordered the toilets to be cleared and within three minutes she had reached into the cistern and her hand landed on something that really shouldn't have been there.

"Sometimes the long shots pay off." She grinned and jumped down from the toilet bowl that she was precariously balanced on clutching the bag.

"What's that? Next to the diamond?" said Simpson, peering through the plastic.

"Probably the glass cutter. We'll get it back to Dusty. I doubt he'll find anything on it, but then again, we seem to have luck on our side. I didn't think this trip would prove so productive."

They headed along the mezzanine and down the staircase.

"I guess we should speak to the manager and give him the good news," said Madison. "I doubt he'll be too happy about us taking it away."

"Tough shit," said Simpson brusquely. "We're still doing an investigation here. He'll do as we tell him."

Five minutes later they were sipping coffee in the manager's office. Raj Amin, a middle-aged, smartly dressed Indian was delighted that they'd found the diamond.

"So, it's been on the premises all the time?" he asked, amazed.

"Seems like it," said Simpson. "I hope you understand that we need to take it away now though for our forensics team to check it out."

Raj's face dropped. "Why is there a need for that?" he said. "I'd like to put it back on display and tell everyone we've recovered it."

"If it's OK with you, I'd rather you keep it to yourself for now." Simpson scratched his chin. "You see, as long as our robber friend thinks that it's still in the toilet, then he's gonna come back and collect it. Once he puts his hands on it, then we can nab him."

"How's that going to work?" asked Madison thoughtfully. "Are we going to plant someone in the museum until he turns up? He might wait weeks."

Simpson considered this for a moment. "Unlikely to be weeks, but you're right. We don't have the resources for that. I wonder if Dickson can put a tracker on the bag. We could put it back, and once the diamond starts moving, we can follow him."

"Yes. We've used them before. That could work." Madison sounded excited at the plan.

"Give him a call. I want this in place today if possible."

"Just a minute Inspector Simpson," said Raj. He had been looking back and forth from Simpson to Monroe like a spectator at a tennis match, listening to their exchange and looked very perturbed. "Are you seriously suggesting that we put the diamond back where it was hidden, and let this man come back and steal it again?"

"Oh no. I forgot to mention" said Simpson with a smile. "We have a fake."

Chapter 17 – "A day at the races"

Friday 24th January

Owen woke early, grabbed his phone, and checked the horse racing pages. Olivetti was in an eight-horse race at 2pm, and the current odds were 5/1. He was the second favorite to Chantilly who had won her last two races and was getting heavy betting at 9/4. An each-way bet would be more sensible, but the odds would be quartered, not giving him nearly enough if he came in second or third.

He checked on RollEmOver and was pleased to see that she was also running at Kempton in the first race at 1:30. As expected, she was the clear favorite and had odds of 2/1.

He did some quick maths. He could get to Kempton for a tenner. The entrance fee would be another tenner. If he went, he'd want some beer money and a bite to eat. Let's call that thirty pounds, leaving him one hundred and fifty to bet with. If he stuck the lot on RollEmOver and she came in, he'd have four hundred and fifty for Olivetti. An each-way would only give him a tad over five hundred pounds if it came in second or third. If it came first on the each-way bet, however, he'd clear over eighteen hundred pounds. If he went for the straight win, it would be more than two and a half thousand.

Of course, if RollEmOver failed to win, he'd have nothing left for Olivetti.

After much deliberating, he decided he had no choice. The only way that he could make the thousand pounds he needed, was for Olivetti to win. Forget the each-way bet. It gave him the cushion if the horse didn't win, but the numbers didn't work. The only other option was to stay at home and put the full two hundred pounds on Olivetti.

The sensible call would have been to stay at home and only rely on one horse to win, but Owen Kelly was not a sensible man when it came to gambling. He was thinking beyond the 2 o'clock race. If they both won, he could pocket fifteen hundred pounds and still have plenty of money for a good day out.

Decision made, he jumped out of bed and got his arse in gear.

An hour later, he was stood at the cashpoint staring unbelievably at his bank balance. His wages hadn't gone in. Owen sagged and pressed the "Balance" button again, assuming the machine had made a mistake. No, the screen clearly stated that he was ninety-eight pounds overdrawn, and his overdraft was only one hundred.

He grabbed at his phone and called his manager.

"Where's my money Col?"

Colin Freemantle was at work and wasn't aware that there was a problem. "What do you mean Owen? Oh, just a sec. We got customers. I'll call you back."

He hung up, and Owen paced back and forth for ten minutes, staring at his phone getting more agitated by the minute. When it rang in his hand, he almost dropped it in shock.

"Colin. What's going on?"

"What do you mean?"

"I've not been paid. I need my money."

"It's Friday. It should be in. Hang on." Another customer, lots of talking that Owen didn't catch. "Sorry. You know what it's like on a Friday. Big meet at Kempton today too."

"I know. I'm on my way, but my money's not in. I keep telling you."

"Are you sure?"

"No. I just like fucking phoning you for the shits and giggles." Owen was getting stressed.

"OK. I'll look into it. I'll put a call in to head office. They probably fucked up the payroll again. Wouldn't be the first time."

"But I need my money today. I'm catching a train to Kempton in an hour."

More talking in the background and two minutes passed before Colin came back. "Sorry. It's mental today mate. Look. I'll call it in, but I'm not sure how fast they can sort it. Gotta go. I'll call you later."

"Can I borrow it from the till?"

There was a click. Colin had gone.

"Fuck."

A young mum was walking past with a toddler and gave him a filthy look, taking a wide berth.

Now what? Owen ran his fingers through his hair and checked his watch. It was nearly eleven o'clock. He had to be on the train for twelve if he wanted to get there for the first race.

Estelle. Would she be able to help? He was only five minutes from the casino and she normally worked the early shift on a Friday. Worth a shot. He hurried down the road, nodded to Jonno on the way in, spotted Estelle, still in isolation in the quiet corner on the roulette table, and dashed over.

"Hey Owen. Early one for you." She smiled, but the smile turned to a frown when she saw the anxious look on his face. "What's up?"

"Hey Estelle. The bookies have fucked up my wages and I'm in a spot. I don't suppose you could sub me something until tomorrow. Couple of hundred?"

"I don't have that sort of money spare Owen. You know that." She twitched and exclaimed "Wanker."

"I'm really sorry to have to ask you. You know I wouldn't if it wasn't urgent. I don't have anyone else I can turn to. I'll pay you back as soon as my wages are in. It may even be later today."

His desperate look made her pause. He'd never asked her before, but she knew what his gambling and drinking habits were like. If she gave him money would she ever see it again?

"Please Estelle. One day, I promise. You'll have it back tomorrow."

It was against her better judgment, but she took pity on him. He was always there with a kind word and always listened to her bitching about the management at the casino. Now his management had let him down, she could sympathize. She reached for her purse.

"I've only got a hundred. Don't even think about asking for more. She looked him in the eye. "Don't let me down on this Owen. I seriously need this money."

He took the money, grabbed her face in his hands, and kissed her on her forehead.

"Thanks. You're a lifesaver. Literally. I'll have it back before tomorrow."

"Yes, you will." She gave him a glare as he retreated.

"You're a princess Estelle. Don't let anyone tell you different."

"More like a mug", she muttered to herself before twitching and adding "Twat. Bastard"

****

Owen was sat on the train re-doing the maths. Following his train ticket and entrance fee, he only had eighty pounds stake money. He'd have to forgo a beer until after the first race and hope that RollEmOver came in. He could turn the eighty pounds into two hundred and forty, have a couple of beers, and then put two hundred and twenty on Olivetti, still clearing thirteen hundred pounds if he won.

If he was going all in, he should really put the full two hundred and forty on the second race but knew he couldn't face it without a drink to calm the nerves.

As he entered the racecourse, the sun was shining. Even for January, it was a beautiful clear day and the crowds were beginning to gather. He found a spring in his step and a buzz of anticipation that he always got when he got near the racetrack.

At 1:10, he checked the odds and was pleased to see that RollEmOver was still favorite in the 1:30 at 2/1. He opened his wallet and handed over eighty pounds to the man in the flat cap who scrawled the bet on a piece of paper and handed it back to him. That piece of paper was the only thing that mattered in the next twenty minutes. If the horse failed, then his day would be over. Not even enough for a beer. He would be heading home with his tail between his legs, pondering how he would be evading Bones in the near future.

At 1:15, the horses started entering the parade ring, and he stood admiring Number three RollEmOver, who had come out looking every bit the winner. She was poised and calm, and her coat was gleaming. She was led around the ring twice before the jockeys came out. He looked for the young lad with the red and white stripes and spotted him talking to the trainer, getting some last-minute advice. As the jockey approached RollEmOver, the horse chose his moment to dump manure all over the grass.

Good sign thought Owen. He knew a guy who waited for the horses in the parade ring to do their business. He placed his bets on the one that dropped the most.

"Less weight" was his logical explanation.

Owen wasn't sure if a pound of poo would make that much difference, but always remembered it, and considered that if he was going to have to run for eight furlongs, he'd feel better doing it after a good shit.

The jockeys jumped aboard, and they cantered off to the starting line. Owen headed for his favorite spot near the finish, his nerves beginning to jangle.

"And they're off," the voice of the commentator could be heard over the tannoy as the race started. "RollEmOver, the favorite had a terrible start. She almost fell out of the box and is a good few lengths behind the pack while Dark Night takes an early lead."

Owen groaned. It couldn't be a worse start. He had watched it on the giant screen, and the horse was clearly at the back. As the race progressed, the jockey spurred her on, and she began to slowly make ground.

"And as they approach the halfway mark, it's still Dark Night leading by a head from Prince of Persia, Uncle Bob, and Eighth Wonder, closely followed by Arc Royal. RollEmOver is making ground at the back but is still in last place at this stage."

"Come on," said Owen exasperated. Half a mile and it would all be over. He watched as RollEmOver, with plenty of room at the back had a sudden surge of pace and passed a couple of horses putting her into sixth place. A roar erupted from the crowd. He wasn't the only one with money on her.

"Uncle Bob now moves up to take the lead from Dark Night, Prince of Persia, and Eighth Wonder. Magic Mike moves into fifth and RollEmOver the favorite making ground, now in sixth place. Two furlongs to go."

Owen looked down the racecourse as the horses turned the last corner and came into view.

"It's the final furlong. Uncle Bob still has it, with Eighth Wonder on the inside rail just nudging into second place from Prince of Persia. Magic Mike is coming through fast and RollEmOver. RollEmOver is flying. RollEmOver and Magic Mike move forwards but Uncle Bob is still holding."

The crowd was going wild. Owen was leaning over the rail screaming, completely lost in the race.

"RollEmOver is coming through. She's in the lead. Magic Mike is with her. It's going to be a photo. On the line. Magic Mike and RollEmOver with Uncle Bob taking third, Eighth Wonder in fourth and Prince of Persia fifth."

Owen was sweating. He couldn't call it. The replay was showing on the giant screen in slow motion. The two horses were neck and neck, the footage being scrutinized by the experts, keeping everyone on edge, especially Owen who, unlike most people had everything on the line.

It took nearly two minutes.

"And the winner of the first race. RollEmOver with Magic Mike in second and Uncle Bob third."

The roar and groans from the crowd came in equal measures. Owen was vaguely aware of people around him tearing up their tickets in disgust while others celebrated their wins.

He grasped onto his betting slip tightly and headed to collect his winnings. He needed a drink.

****

"Two ten, two-twenty, Two-thirty. Two-forty."

The bookmaker counted the notes into Owen's hands. He checked the board for the next race and saw that Olivetti had dropped to third favorite and was now at 6/1.

"Two hundred to win. Olivetti" he said, handing back most of the cash. He grabbed his slip. The odds dropping gave him a bit more beer money, and he really needed it. He headed for the bar, ordered a double whiskey which he downed in one, and a beer which he took over to the parade ring to wait for Olivetti.

By the time the race started, most of his beer was gone and the booze was kicking in. The same feeling of excitement and dread came over him as the horses flew out of their traps and started thundering down the course. Unlike RollEmOver, Olivetti led from the front, taking a three-length lead in the early stages. The favorite Chantilly was mid-field and looked keen. When they rounded the final bend, Olivetti was four lengths clear and showed no signs of tiring. Chantilly made her move. The horse seemed to glide smoothly, gaining ground with every stride. In the final stages, Olivetti clearly flagged and dropped to third.

"And the winner is Chantilly, ridden by Laura Jayne. Second FlashInThePan and third Olivetti."

Owen stood stunned as he watched the replay, willing his horse to do something different, even though he knew that it wouldn't. He sunk to a bench and checked his money. He had thirty pounds and change. He found a discarded racing card and flipped through, looking for a possible outsider bet. Twenty pounds at fifty to one would do it, with a tenner for two more drinks. He found two options in the next race. Digestive at 50/1 and the Terminator at 75/1. He liked the name, and it meant that he could put fifteen pounds on and have an extra drink.

He ordered another double whiskey, downed it, and headed back to place the bet.

"Fifteen pounds on The Terminator." He was already slurring his words, but flat cap didn't bat an eyelid as he wrote the bet out. He'd seen it all before.

He was hungry but chose to spend the last of his money on another drink. He missed the start of the third race and by the time he got to the finishing post, the horses were already on the home stretch. He watched them run past at a blur, and barely heard the commentator announcing the winner as his horse came trotting through eight lengths behind the rest.

It was 2:45pm. He had until 8pm before Bones would come looking for him. He was skint, and he was wasted. Heading for the train, he considered getting back to Waterloo, jumping a mainline train, and heading south, but he had nowhere to go.

As the tube train rattled along, stopping at the station after station, a grey cloud came over him like never before. This was bad. He had to run. But where? He glanced up as the train slowed. Two more stops. A poster came into view stuck on the station wall advertising Shakespeare's "The Tempest" at the Royal Theatre. He wasn't a fan of the performing arts, and Shakespeare was the last thing he needed. It did however remind him of the diamond.

It was 3:40. The Tempest Museum would be open until at least 5pm. He had time to go home and pick up his gun.

Chapter 18 – Heist #3

    The gun was a cheap American import, a Cobra that he'd picked up on a second-hand sales forum on GreySpider for less than a hundred pounds just over a year ago. He had got it for protection following a spate of burglaries in and around his apartment block after returning from a successful night at the casino with nearly a thousand pounds in his pocket and found the police knocking on doors asking questions about whether people had seen anything. He had slept with the money under his pillow that night and bought the gun the next day. For months, he kept it in his bedside drawer but had since relocated it to a small safe in the back of his wardrobe.

    It had a five-round magazine and was very small weighing in at just seventeen ounces, perfect for concealing. Even in his drunken and desperate state, he had no intention of actually shooting anyone. He just needed it for persuasion. It made a loud noise, and he was relying on that to convince the staff at the Tempest to be cooperative.

    He checked the safety was on, tucked the gun in his belt behind his back, and pulled his raincoat over it. He rooted around the same cupboard looking for some stockings. He knew that an old girlfriend had left a pair here a long time ago. He always meant to throw them out but was ever hopeful that she might return one day. The stockings were a bit musty, and when he pulled one over his head, it didn't distort his features much. He pulled the second one over too. Much better, but now he was struggling to see. He grabbed some scissors from the kitchen to make two small eye holes, but the stocking split, making a large gash.

    "Fuck it."

Luckily, he'd only done one. He put the split stocking on first and covered it with the good one. It did the trick and at least he could partially see. Hopefully, it wouldn't split further.

What else? He'd not been to the museum before, so he was completely winging it here, but decided to grab a hammer. Might need to break something. The hammer tucked into his belt next to the gun.

While looking for the hammer, he found a half-empty bottle of vodka at the back of the cupboard that had been long forgotten. Result. He took two large swigs and decided that the bottle was just as important as the hammer. It tucked neatly into his inside coat pocket. He also found an old pair of gloves.

The museum was a mile away and closed at 5pm. He decided to leave it as late as possible so there would be fewer people around. He finished the vodka while he waited, and at 4:20 he stumbled out the door.

The walk should have taken twenty minutes, but due to much swaying, it took him closer to thirty. The remains of the vodka had really kicked in, and his vision was blurring even before he pulled the two stockings over his head. He had found an old abandoned red telephone box just up the street from the museum and decided to use this to put his disguise on, feeling a bit like Superman, emerging as a different character, and chuckling at the thought.

"Shit. Where's my gloves" he mumbled aloud.

The gloves were on the table at home, next to the empty vodka bottle. He didn't have time to go back so decided to improvise. Returning to the phone box he sat on the floor, pulled his boots off, took off his socks, and pulled them over his hands.

"Ha. Perfect."

He spent another two minutes trying to put his boots back on but couldn't do the laces with the socks on his hands and the stockings hampering his vision.

"Fuck. Fuck."

He finally emerged from the phone box at 4:58, stockings askew, and socks pulled up over his hands and sleeves of the jacket. The sun had dropped, and it was getting dark as he stumbled to the Tempest drawing some odd glances from passers-by.

He carefully climbed the four small steps, fell into the door, and found himself in the lobby.

"Sorry, we're just closing." The lady was in her fifties, a petite blonde with more grey hair than she would have liked. She would have been cute twenty years earlier, thought Owen distractedly. Her eyes widened as she realized he had a stocking over his head.

Owen, reached under his coat, grasping for the gun, but struggling with the sock-gloves. He grabbed the hammer by mistake and pointed it at her.

"Don't move and you won't get hurt." He realized his mistake. "Oh shit. Hang on." He struggled with his coat and finally pulled out the pistol just as a younger man stepped into the lobby.

"Exhibition rooms are clear Angie. We can…." He stopped when he saw Owen. "Can we help you?"

"He's got a gun Ash." Angie had gone pale.

Owen was fiddling with the safety catch when the gun slipped from his hand, landing at his feet. The guy took a step forward, but Owen screamed at him and wielded the hammer.

"Stay back. I don't want to hurt you." He grappled for the gun, got the safety off, and stood up pointing it, but promptly dropping the hammer.

Ash jumped back in alarm. This guy was unhinged, drunk, and armed. He wasn't about to get himself shot.

"It's cool man. Take it easy."

Owen was on the floor scrabbling around, trying to keep one eye on Ash, one looking down for the hammer, and one on the lady. Hang on that's three eyes. No wonder I'm struggling he thought through his drunken haze. He finally managed to scoop the hammer up and returned his attention back to the man.

"I need some cash, and the diamond," he said.

"Which diamond?" said Ash. The police had been in touch telling them about the Four Feathers diamonds being stolen, so he assumed he meant that one.

"I don't fucking know. The diamond diamond." Owen was waving the gun precariously about, and Angie was backing away, trying to get behind the counter. "Don't move. Stay together."

"It's OK Angie. Let's just give him what he wants" said Ash, clearly the one in charge. "Can you lower the gun? We won't try anything."

Ash led him through some double doors to the exhibition room with the terrified Angie and took him to a display cabinet.

"Is that it?" Owen peered at the diamond through two layers of stockings, two double whiskeys, half a bottle of vodka, and several beers. "It doesn't look much." There was a placard next to it describing the diamond, but Owen could barely see it.

"You" he waggled the gun at Angie. "Read what it says".

Angie was trying to hide behind Ash, but tentatively crept forward and started to read. "This striking purple diamond is one of the Four Feathers diamonds, kindly donated by Sir Tom Mathers in 2012. Part of a set of four..."

"OK. That's the one. Back away."

Angie retreated back behind Ash as Owen stepped forward, raised the hammer, stuck his tongue out the side of his mouth in concentration, and prepared to smash the glass.

"Hang on. I can find a key" said Ash, anticipating the mess. If this guy was going to take it, he'd rather he didn't leave the place smashed up."

Owen considered this for a second, hammer in the air. He wanted out as quick as possible.

"That's too slow" he slurred and brought the hammer down hard.

The glass shattered, splinters bouncing in all directions and Angie let out a squeal as a small piece struck her on the face leaving a tiny cut. Owen used the hammer to break away the sharp shards that were sticking up, dropped the hammer into his pocket, but missed and it bounced on the floor again. He reached into the cabinet with his sock-covered hand to grab the diamond.

Ash made his move. He lunged for Owen's right hand that held the gun and both men toppled to the floor. Amazingly, Owen managed to keep hold of it, but the diamond went flying when they hit the ground and rolled away. Angie screamed and ran for the door.

Ash was heavier and sober and was doing a good job of overpowering him. The sock on his left hand came off in the struggle and Owen panicked and done the only thing he could think of that might give him an advantage. He pulled the trigger. Whether it was bad luck or a complete fluke, he never knew but the bullet caught Angie in the leg as she neared the entrance to the room. She screamed and fell and gave Owen the distraction he needed. Ash had gone pale, realizing that his actions had caused Angie to be shot and Owen pushed him off fired again, at the ceiling this time, and regained control.

"What the fuck did you fucking do that for. You've gone and got her fucking shot now. I said I wouldn't fucking hurt you." Owen was losing it, screaming at Ash. He really hadn't wanted to shoot anyone.

Angie was screaming and clutching at her leg and Ash went to her.

"Don't move. Fuck's sake." He plucked the diamond off the floor with his free hand and dropped it into a pocket and looked around for the sock, struggling to find it.

"Shit" he screamed and lumbered towards them, a pain in his head materializing making him feel even worse.

"He shot me. The bastard shot me. It hurts like hell."

"I'm so sorry Angie. I thought I could stop him." Ash looked miserably down at her. "I'll call an ambulance."

"No phones. You'll get me the cash first" growled Owen from behind them. It looked like the bullet had only clipped her, but Owen – even in his drunken stupor, was mortified. "I'm sorry I shot you. This prick jumped me. I wasn't aiming."

"We haven't got much cash. We're a museum. We don't charge" said Ash.

"What about the shop? Come on. She's not gonna bleed out." He had to finish what he started and get out of here as quick as possible.

Ash led him to the shop and opened the register. There was about a hundred and fifty pounds and change.

"Is that it?"

"It's a museum shop," said Ash as if that was explanation enough.

Owen switched the gun to his uncovered hand, grabbed at the notes, and stuffed them in his pockets but gave up on the coins. The sock was really hindering him now and he was getting impatient. He didn't want to risk touching anything and leaving prints.

"I need more. Scoop the pound coins up." He leveled the gun at Ash.

"OK. OK. Come on man. You've already shot Angie. I'm not gonna try anything else." He grabbed at the pound coins and shoved them into Owen's raincoat pocket, amazed that this guy was worried about loose change when he'd just stolen the diamond.

"I still need more. Where else do you hold cash?"

"There's a coffee shop on the other side of the foyer. There's more in there."

Owen shoved him, and Ash led him through the foyer to the coffee shop. The till faired a little better and he grabbed a wad of twenties and tens and got Ash to repeat the process with the coins.

Owen was sobering up. Shooting the girl had been a mistake and it had sharpened his senses. How the hell had he got himself into this situation.

"Right. Back to the girl and I'll leave you in peace."

They returned to Angie who had pulled out a mobile phone and had her finger on the nine.

Owen roared and ran towards her, managing to trip over his own feet. He nearly righted himself but crashed to the ground next to her, pound coins spilling from his pocket and rolling away. He batted the phone away from her, lurched after it, and brought his boot down three times smashing it.

Angie was crying. "I'm sorry. I need an ambulance" she wailed. "I'm bleeding. It hurts so bad." Ash was bending over trying to calm her down, telling her that everything was going to be OK.

Owen held his hands to his head. What a mess. He took a quick glance around for his sock, gave up, and fled. He had the diamond and maybe enough cash, but things really hadn't panned out the way he'd hoped. Less than five minutes later, he exited the phone box, stockings, and a solitary sock stuffed in his pocket to stop the remaining coins from jangling.

Chapter 19 – "Three down. One to go"

Owen arrived home at 6pm and just wanted to crawl into bed, but knew he had to pay Caine if he wanted to keep Bones off his back.

He locked the gun back in his safe, burnt the stockings and the sock in his fireplace, pondering where the hell the other one had gone, and realized that the hammer was missing too. He didn't even remember dropping it.

"Shit." Did it have his prints on? Was he still wearing the sock when he wielded it? He thought so but couldn't be sure.

He counted the money. He had five hundred and fifty pounds in notes and seventy-five-pound coins. Just enough to pay Caine his six hundred, but he also had his wages when the bastards at work sorted it out. That meant that he could pay back Estelle and he would have just over a hundred for the week. His rent was due tomorrow, and he predicted an argument with his landlord but figured that that was more preferable to letting Caine down again.

He also had the diamond.

He looked at it lovingly. It was quite something and would hopefully make him a tidy sum. He didn't know anyone who dealt with diamonds though and knew that he could hardly take it to the local pawn shop. It was hot as hell. He took a photo and uploaded it to GreySpider in a private message to Ace.

Date: 24-01-2020 18:19

From: GreenZero

Subject: A Challenge

Ace. How much are you gonna pay me for it? (Pic attached)

He put the diamond in the safe with his gun, packed the notes into an envelope, dropped fifty of the pound coins in his pocket, and headed straight out to see Caine.

****

"Hey Caine. I've got your money." He was too tired for pleasantries. He wanted to pay his debt and get out. It had been a stressful day.

"Your two days late Kelly" growled Caine turning away from the huge television in his lock-up.

Caine was huge. At least twenty stone, six foot two with tattoos on his arms and neck – if you could call it a neck. His head sat perched on his shoulders with very little in-between. There was another tattoo of a large skull and crossbones on the top of his bald head. Owen always wondered why the hell he needed skinny Bones to do his dirty work. This guy looked like he could tear your arms out with his bare hands and eat them.

"The delightful Bones reminded me," said Owen grimly. "Bookies fucked up my wages." He dropped the envelope on the table and reached in his pocket, splashing the coins on top. "It's all there."

Caine arched his eyebrows. "Are you fucking serious? Pound coins?"

"They paid me from the till. It's all they had."

"What the fuck do I want with all this shrapnel?" said Caine eyeing the pound coins in disgust. "Take this shit away."

"It's all I've got Caine. Bones told me you needed six hundred. That's six hundred. With the coins."

Caine grabbed the envelope with a sigh, knocking some of the coins to the floor, flicked through the notes counting them, and stuffed it into his pocket.

"Looks like we're starting a new debt. You owe me fifty. Usual interest."

"Come on man. The fifty's all there. You've wiped me out with the extra two hundred."

"Well, that's good news for you then. You've got fifty for the week now." He turned back to his tele. "I'll see you next week. Take your chocolate coins and fuck off."

****

While Owen was burning his stockings, Madison and Simpson were hurtling towards the Tempest, clearing a path with their blue flashing light.

Simpson had picked Madison up en-route and filled her in.

"Diamond number three is gone. You won't believe this one. Apparently, some guy waltzed in at closing time with a gun, stocking on his head, pissed as a fart, and fired a couple of rounds and managed to hit one of the staff. Ambulance is on its way too. I want to talk to her before she gets carted off."

"Any witnesses?"

"Only the duty manager. Ash someone or other. The girl that got shot was Angie Cummings. Shit." He slammed on the brakes as an old man in a Fiat turned from a side road in front of them. Simpson expertly steered around the car, cutting him up. He glanced in his mirror to make sure that the old guy was alright.

"Jesus. He looks like he's about a hundred. Shouldn't be on the bleeding road."

Madison had adopted her usual position of clinging on for dear life, her nails digging into the bottom of the seat and silently praying. She wouldn't miss this part of the job when Simpson finally decided to take retirement.

"Over there," she said pointing to the museum as it approached on the left. "Looks like the ambulance beat us."

"Shit." He skidded to a halt in front of the ambulance, and they jumped out. "These bloody museums all look the same. I'm getting a real sense of déjà vu."

They climbed the steps, went through the double doors, and found themselves in the exhibition room with two paramedics who were fussing over a blonde lady, and a younger guy who was standing over them looking concerned.

"Inspector Simpson. Constable Monroe" said Simpson, holding up his badge. "Are you Ash?"

"Hi Inspector. Thanks for coming so quickly" said Ash. His eyes flitted about nervously and he looked a little pale.

"Is she going to be OK?" asked Madison, indicating the girl on the floor. There seemed to be quite a bit of blood.

"She's stable," said one of the paramedics, a young girl with a streak of green through her hair and more freckles than Madison had ever seen on one face. "Lost a bit of blood but looks like the bullet only nicked her. It's not hit any major arteries. She'll need a couple of stitches. We'll take her in, but she'll be home in a few hours bragging about it" she grinned.

"Can I have a few minutes with her?" barked Simpson. It was more of an order than a request.

"As long as you can talk while we're cleaning her up," said the guy bent over her, not looking up.

Madison took Ash out to the foyer to get his story while Simpson stayed with Angie. It was always better to work like this to ensure that their stories were corroborated.

"Jesus. I need a drink" said Ash as he slumped into a chair. "It's my fault she got shot. I tried to take the guy down." He leaned forwards and put his head in his hands.

"Hold on. One step at a time" said Madison, pulling out her notebook. "Tell me from the beginning."

****

Forty minutes later, they'd taken statements from Ash and Angie and bagged the hammer, the remains of the phone, and the sock which Ash had managed to keep hold of during the struggle. They even took the stray pound coins that had scattered when the drunken robber had tripped over his own feet. The museum had a far better CCTV system than the previous two, with cameras covering all rooms and the foyer. They had taken copies of everything and Simpson was keen to watch it back.

"Let's grab some takeaway and run through this now," he said in the car on the way back to the station. "You don't have plans tonight do you?"

"Nothing that can't wait," said Madison. She was keen to see the video too and it wasn't like she had a hot date lined up or anything. The long, relaxing soak in the bath with candles, music, and wine would have to happen another day.

"Chinese or Pizza?"

"Oh, God! If you want Chinese, I'll pass. The place we used last time was shocking. It went through me and out the other side within an hour."

Simpson grimaced. "Nice image Monroe. Pizza's fine by me."

****

"Jesus. Look at the state of him." Simpson stared in disbelief as they watched the guy with socks on his hands pull a hammer out of his belt to threaten Angie with. "He's off his face."

"He had the sense to cover it though," said Madison. "And wear gloves. Well. Socks. What's that all about?"

"Probably a last-minute thing. Thought he better cover his hands, and that's all he had. I think we can safely say that there wasn't much planning involved with this."

"But he went for the diamond," said Madison. "If he was just passing and wanted to make a quick buck, he would've smashed other cabinets and grabbed a pile of jewelry. But he didn't. The only thing he took was the diamond and some cash. He knew what he wanted."

They watched as he grabbed the diamond and Ash jumped him.

"Christ, he was lucky he didn't get himself killed," said Simpson, throwing his hands in the air. "If that shot had got him at that range, we'd have been bagging him up. Pillock."

"She was unlucky" pointed out Madison. "What are the odds that that bullet clipped her from that distance. She was over about fifteen meters away."

"What's that in English?" said Simpson calculating. "Forty-foot? I don't get this metric bollocks."

"More like fifty," said Madison. "Look. That's when he dropped the hammer. And he's down to one sock."

They kept watching. "I wonder why he took the pound coins" wondered Madison as they saw him stumble and a bunch of coins fell out of his pocket. Seems a bit, I don't know. Cheap. He's got a bunch of twenties, a ten-grand diamond, but makes a point to take the coins too."

"Wait. Stop. Wind that back." Simpson had spotted something.

Madison clicked stop with the mouse and took it back ten seconds. "What did you see?"

"Watch. He knocks the phone out of her hand."

They watched him stumble again, pick himself up and take a swipe at the phone. The gun was in the hand with the sock on it. Madison paused the video.

"He used his other hand," she said.

"It was a swipe, but we might get lucky. A partial at least" said Simpson.

She pressed play and they watched him smash the phone.

"The print would be on the back. The phone landed face up. His boot won't affect it. Call Dusty. Let's see if we can get ahead of this." Simpson clapped his hands together. "Finally, some good news. All we need now is for that other prick to pick the fake diamond up from the Monument. Did Dickson get that tracker working?"

Dickson had been having problems. He couldn't attach the tracker to the diamond and was worried it might be spotted if he just put it loose in the bag.

"He cut open that diamond cutter device in the end. Planted the tracker inside, and then glued it back together again. He dropped it back in the cistern this morning. We're good to go."

"Good work," said Simpson, stuffing a slice of pepperoni pizza into his mouth. "With any luck, we'll bag two of these bastards before the end of the week."

****

Saturday 25th January

Ace read the short message from GreenZero again. He had woken up in a bad mood with a headache having had a sleepless night, tossing and turning and trying to work out some of the problems in his master plan. He carefully cut an aspirin in two and swallowed it with his mineral water and then repeated it with a second, a procedure that he'd done since he was a kid and wasn't able to swallow a whole one.

He sat down and composed his standard reply, asking his questions about the details of the robbery. He added a sentence that he'd not included before to address GreenZero's question.

"The diamond is yours to do with as you please. I have no interest in such a menial item. Once our team is complete and you see my plans, then you will agree that your diamond is of no consequence".

Again, he added a message to the public forum.

Greetings fellow spiders. My team is nearly full. One more feather and the nest will be complete

He opened the two replies that he'd received from Ozzy and Budster who had both gone to great lengths explaining how they had stolen the diamonds and what specific skills they had. Budster's art of disguise, gift of the gab, and ability to blend in would be very useful, and Ozzy had suggested that he had sleight of hand skills as well as being able to build devices such as the smoke bombs that he'd used in the Monument robbery. Ace was building up a picture of how he could best use them in his future plans. He was looking forward to seeing what GreenZero had to offer.

He opened a notebook where he had detailed all of his plans, grabbed a pencil, and jotted down a couple of thoughts.

He heard music thumping from the apartment above. Katy was playing a song he liked from Florence and the Machine, but it wasn't helping his concentration. The music faded, but then started up as the next song began and he gritted his teeth.

The pencil lead snapped as he pushed hard in his frustration, and he stuck it into the pencil sharpener he had attached to his desk, one of those with the rotary handle that could be found in most schools. He sharpened it back to a point, measured it against his other three pencils, and added them one a time to the sharpener until they were all the same length.

He needed to know more about GreenZero. He switched the television on. Maybe the latest robbery would be on the news.

It was, and he watched horrified when he heard the report. A robbery at gunpoint, a shooting, and a suspect who was considered to be drunk, armed, and dangerous. Was this the man who had just joined his team? That is, he thought, in the unlikely event that he didn't get caught and arrested.

He switched off again, rubbed the back of his hand back and forth on his head, and grabbed his pencils again, inserting them one at a time into the sharpener, not even aware that he was obliterating them into stumps.

Chapter 20 – "A close call"

"Hi Brandy. It's Oz. It's 11:30 am. Saturday. We've been offered a last-minute show tonight at the Cumberland, 9pm. Sorry for the short notice. I can do it without you if you can't make it but let me know so I can plan the show. Hope to see you later."

He had no plans for the evening anyway. The extra cash would certainly come in handy and he hadn't seen Brandy all week. He hoped that she could make it. In the meantime, he was planning on returning to the Monument which he had purposely left for a week to give the police time to crawl all over it. He was fairly optimistic that the diamond would still be in the cistern where he had left it. They had no reason to suspect that it was still on the premises and he'd not seen anything on the news.

He grabbed the same bag that he'd used for the heist a week ago and threw in a water bottle and a jumper. He didn't think they'd search it on the way out, but he wanted to ensure that he could hide the diamond in the base of the bag just in case. He contemplated a disguise. Three visits in two weeks might look suspicious if anyone recognized him. As a magician, he had plenty of sparkly stage outfits, but nothing really that he could wear to change his appearance and look discreet. Should he get a wig? A fake mustache maybe?

He'd worn a fake mustache once before, many years ago when he'd attended a fancy dress party as a Mexican. He had met a French girl with the unfortunate name of Lucille Lasteek "call me Lucy." He was egged on by some friends to do some table magic and she had been impressed when he had made her ring disappear from her finger and reappear at the bottom of the wine glass she was drinking from. They had got chatting and he'd discovered that she was a dancer and that they had performed at some of the same venues in the city. They'd spent most of the evening dancing, talking, and drinking, and all was going well until they kissed at the end of the night. The fake mustache had started to slip in the heat, and in an over-zealous moment of drunken French passion, she bit his mustache and managed to rip it off his face.

No fake mustache he thought with a shudder, remembering the incident. Lucy had run off mortified and refused to answer when he called her the following day. He saw her a couple of years later at a show doing backing dancing for a Madonna tribute. If she recognized him, she didn't say anything and had disappeared with one of the other dancers as soon as they had come off stage. Strangely, he had a mustache too. Funny what little details the brain remembers.

Oscar snapped back to the present, looking in the mirror wondering what he could do. Haircut, he decided. He had been growing it for six months in an attempt to look more mysterious on stage, but in reality, it was just getting more bouffant. If I add a mustache now, I'd look like a seventies porn star, he thought. He grabbed a flat cap that used to belong to his brother Ed and pulled on a smart suit complete with a waistcoat. With the haircut, it would be a very different look. He was aiming for a sophisticated English gentleman guise, but in reality, he wasn't a million miles from London gangster. Either way, he looked nothing like he had on his previous visits.

He checked GreySpider before he left and saw Ace's post regarding the third diamond being taken. He had sent Ace the details of his own robbery and Ace had said that he would be in touch when the team was complete. That might be sooner rather than later, he thought.

By 1pm, he was on the way to the Monument having stopped off at his local barber's. The barber had shaved the back and sides to number two but left a bit of floppy hair on top. With the cap and the smart suit, he thought even Brandy would pass him in the street.

The museum was busier than his previous visit. Looks like the news coverage had raised the profile of the place, he thought. He was in no hurry. He figured that diving straight into the bathroom and running out the door would look suspicious. He worked his way around the museum, noting the empty glass dome where the Four Feathers diamond once sat. A new dome had replaced the one that he made the hole in and a hastily added sign stated that the diamond had recently been "misplaced" and that they hoped to have it back on display very soon.

He smirked at the audacity of the management. Everyone knew that it hadn't been "misplaced". The robbery had been extensively covered on every news channel and in every newspaper for the past week. One of the tabloids had run with the awful attempt at a rhyming headline - "Crime and Diamond", while another hadn't got it much better with "Monumental Feather Filch". With the Tempest diamond being stolen too, the story would be resurrected and replayed all over again.

After half an hour of browsing and a quick look around the museum shop, he headed up to the mezzanine and into the bathroom. The cubicle he needed was occupied, the noises coming from within suggesting that its occupant had probably had a rather dodgy kebab the night before. He groaned. This sort of thing never happens in the movies, he thought. A few minutes later, a young guy exited the cubicle and left without washing his hands. Grim. Oscar held his breath and entered, locking the door behind him. He didn't waste much time and within two minutes had opened the cistern and retrieved the clear plastic bag containing the diamond and his glass cutter. He tipped the contents into his secret compartment in the bag he carried, flushed the plastic bag down the toilet, and exited the bathroom as quickly as possible.

Five minutes later he was striding towards the tube station, congratulating himself on a job well done.

****

"He's on the move."

Five miles away, the movement of the tracker caused an alert on Robbie Dickson's laptop. He pushed a few buttons, and a map appeared centered on the Monument showing a small red dot moving slowly away from it.

"Any teams nearby?" bellowed Simpson, appearing at his side.

"Monroe's the closest. She's about three miles away, following up on the Francombe case."

"Call her. This takes precedence. Who's she with?"

"She's on her own," said Dickson calling the number. "We're thin on the ground today. Jones is on holiday and Jackson's come down with the flu."

"Bloody lightweight" muttered Simpson, who hadn't taken a day off sick in his thirty-five years with the force. "Patch me into the call." He grabbed a headset as Monroe answered.

"Monroe. Hi Robbie."

There was a loud squeal on the phone line and both Dickson and Simpson grappled with the headsets to remove them from their ears.

"Shit. What the fuck...." Said Dickson.

There was more commotion on the line, and finally, Monroe came back.

"Sorry. I'm at the Francombe factory" she shouted. "They just fired up the machine next to me. What's up?"

"The diamond's on the move. Start heading for the Monument. We'll give you updates as you go. Right now, he's heading to the station."

"The station? Erm, maybe it's a bit late in the day to ask this, but will the tracker work if he's underground?"

Simpson opened his mouth to speak, and snapped it shut again, glaring at Dickson. "Well?"

"We've never tried," said Dickson meekly. "But if it doesn't, we should be able to pick it up when he resurfaces. Unless...."

"Unless what?"

"Unless he's out of range. The tracker's good for six, maybe seven miles as the crow flies"

"You got to be fucking kidding me." Simpson threw his hands in the air. "Monroe. Fulham station. How long?"

"With the blues – about seven or eight minutes. I'm on my way. Stay on the line."

"Shit."

A minute later they heard the wail of a police siren and a squeal of tires as Monroe started moving.

"Just a second. He's stopped" said Dickson excitedly, pointing to the screen. The red dot had stopped just short of the station and slowly blinked on the screen motionless. Dickson zoomed in to the map. "Looks like a coffee shop."

"Stay there you bastard," said Simpson. "Just a few minutes."

****

"Black coffee, please. No sprinkles, no foam, no trimmings. Just a plain black coffee." Oscar was learning.

He sat at a table in the tiny café by the station and sipped his coffee. He'd done it. The diamond was safely in the bottom of his bag, and no one had stopped him or chased him down the road. He sat contemplating how he was going to turn the diamond into cash. Maybe there was someone on GreySpider who could point him in the right direction. Maybe Ace. He wasn't convinced he'd get full value for it, but a few thousand would allow him to get some much-needed gear for the act, with maybe a bit spare for a short break abroad. He had always wanted to go to Venice. Would Brandy come with him? He shook that idea from his head. No, business only. Got to keep it business only.

He grabbed his phone to see if she had messaged him back, but the screen was distorted. Weird. He pushed a few buttons, but nothing changed. He turned it off and on, waited about a minute for it to power up, but it was no different.

"Oh, come on," he said. The last thing he needed was a broken phone. He sipped his coffee and tried holding his phone up in the air. It got a little better. He stood up. Better still. He sat down again, and the interference returned. What the hell's causing that?

It hit him immediately. He lowered the phone to his bag and the picture completely disintegrated. In the distance, he could hear a siren.

****

"I'm a minute away. Is he still in the café?"

"Yes. He's….no wait. Shit. He's moving. Fast. Towards the underground."

Monroe hit the steering wheel in frustration and floored the accelerator. She had been driving at "Simpson-speed" already and had received more than one angry horn on her dash across town.

She skidded to a stop by the station, leaped out of the car, and sprinted in.

"Where is he?"

"Still moving. District Line by the looks of it. Can't tell which way yet though."

She ran towards the District line, flashing her badge and hurdling the barrier to take her to the escalator. She ran down the moving steps shouting at people to move to the right.

Dickson was talking. "He's going….." The phone broke up.

"Where?" she screamed. "Which way?" She was stood at the intersection at the bottom of the stairs. Left was North, right was South.

An unintelligible crackle of Dickson's voice on her phone.

"Shit." She made a decision and headed for the North platform.

****

Oscar was sat on a bench at the far end of the platform, trying not to breathe too heavily when the policewoman turned the corner. He quickly turned away from her as the train rushed in. Come on. Come on. He could hear her footsteps getting closer as the train came to a stop. Every bone in his body urged him to sprint for the train, but he managed to restrain himself. He took his time, glanced towards the policewoman who had turned away and was walking back the way she had come. He picked up his bag and casually walked to the train.

****

Monroe was back outside when she got a signal. She had considered boarding the train, but with no contact with Dickson and Simpson, she had no way of knowing who to arrest, where to get off, or even if she was heading the right way.

"He went North" screamed an exasperated Simpson. "Where's your police radio? It would've worked underground."

"Shit. Shit. Shit" yelled Monroe. "It's in the car. I jumped out and sprinted for the station. I didn't stop to grab it. I was on the North platform too. Can we get him when he gets off?"

"It's all we have, but he moved fast from that café. He might have discovered the tracker."

"Surely he would have ditched it if he did," said Monroe. What's the next stop? I'll have to follow the line until he surfaces."

"West Brompton, and then Earl's Court. He could change at either though" said Dickson "At least the tracker works underground" he added.

"I don't believe it" fumed Simpson. "We had him. We were right on top of him."

Monroe was back at her car. "I'll head for Brompton. Let me know if he exits the network. Don't worry boss. It's not over yet."

****

Oscar made his way to the quietest carriage he could find. He had seen the policewoman walking away from the platform when the train started moving, so he knew she hadn't boarded. He couldn't believe how close she had come though. He sat at one end of the carriage, away from the other passengers, and reached into the secret compartment at the bottom of his bag. He felt around and could only find the diamond and his glass cutter. No tracker. He retrieved the cutter and inspected it. It was a very fine line, but he spotted it around the base where it had been cut and glued.

"Bastards" he muttered, knowing that they had rumbled him. The diamond was unlikely to be real.

He quickly looked at the diamond to check that there was no bug on it but could tell that it was intact, so dropped it back. Probably worthless, but he could confirm that later. He had a more pressing issue to deal with.

He wiped the glass cutter thoroughly with his jacket to remove any prints as the train pulled into West Brompton. He jumped from the train, deposited the cutter in a nearby bin, and jumped straight back on again. It had been a good five minutes since he had got on the train at Fulham, and his heart rate was still way over one hundred.

****

"He's stopped at Brompton," said Dickson over the radio. Madison had switched from her mobile phone. "Confirm. He's at West Brompton, one-stop up."

"Almost there," said Madison.

"He's ditched it," said Simpson resignedly. "Look. It's not moving. What a complete and utter fuck up."

This was confirmed five minutes later when Madison fished the glass cutter carefully from the bin.

"I'll bag it and bring it in for prints," she said miserably.

Simpson punched the desk in frustration. "Get back to that café at Fulham. See if they have a camera. I want all the cameras checked from that fucking museum to the station. We should be able to spot him running for that train."

He stormed from the station. "I need a smoke."

Chapter 21 – "The Hacker"

Monday 27th January

Amy Ross had been watching the GreySpider activity with interest since the challenge was posted at the beginning of the year. The latest post from Ace a couple of days ago prompted her to take action. Three diamonds down, only one to go. The last one would be a real hot potato. If the museum had any sense, it would be locked down in a vault with day and night security. Number four was always going to be the hardest one to steal, and Amy had been waiting for this moment. Ace's challenge was too easy in her mind. She wanted number four – the difficult one. She wanted to be tested.

Amy was twenty-five, single, never wore makeup or nice clothes, and barely left the house. Her short-cropped blonde hair rarely saw a brush. She saw no need. She didn't like people. She didn't need the material items that others spent all their hard-earned wages on. She had just one thing that was of importance to her - her laptop.

For a dozen hours a day, she sat in front of it, speed scanning thousands of lines of code, digesting sub-routines, absorbing SQL queries, switching between Java, HTML, and C with seemingly no effort at all. Most of what she looked at was like a foreign language for most, and in some ways, it was, but for Amy, it was like breathing. A slightly upturned smile was always present when she was in this state. She was in the zone. She was like Keanu Reeves in her favorite film from the Wachowski's - The Matrix. She was Neo.

The doorbell rang three times before she noticed. She looked up in frustration, annoyed at the interruption. She opened the door to a pizza delivery service. Had she ordered pizza? Probably. She realized she was hungry, so somewhere during her marathon session in front of the laptop, she must've placed an order. Ham, cheese, and pineapple on a thick crust. At least she'd had the foresight to get her favorite. She returned to the computer, pulled the box open, and stuffed a slice in her mouth as she returned to the code.

Amy was a hacker, and not just your average whizz-kid college dropout who had managed to break the security on a social media account. No. Amy was at a whole different level. Corporate systems, road traffic systems, security cameras – any security camera anywhere. She'd not found one that had beaten her yet. Government institutions, some of the smaller banks, she had even managed to connect to the air traffic control system for an airport in Croatia. It scared the life out of her, knowing that people like her could do this stuff. If she had been inclined, she could have manipulated the location of a plane and crashed it into another. Terrorists would kill for some of the skills she had. On that particular day, she'd left a detailed explanation of how she had connected to their systems and suggested that they may want to upgrade their less-than-adequate security.

For Amy, it was about the thrill. The challenge. Most of the time, she had no need to do what she did. No end goal, except the knowledge that she'd succeeded in breaking in. Occasionally, she would do things for personal gain though. The pizza she was devouring had been the result of an online order, placed directly in the back end of "Mr. Pizza's" aging software. She'd marked the transaction as "Paid" in the system, and even added a generous tip for the delivery boy, although she wasn't convinced that any money actually got back to the poor sod who had driven through the rain on a moped on a cold January evening to get it to her.

She never paid for groceries either, always picking on the big supermarkets, the ones that could afford to lose seventy-five pounds a week and were buried in so many transactions that they failed to notice that the books didn't quite balance to the penny, and if they did, they could just write off the discrepancy. If someone decided to dig deeper, they wouldn't be able to trace it back to her. Her order was legitimate. According to the system, it was paid for.

Amy generally ate well.

She was currently connected to the corporate system of the Society of Jewellery Historians – or SJH as the spinning logo told her at the login screen that she had just cracked. She had read about the Four Feathers diamonds and discovered that they had been donated by SJH many years before, who subsequently housed them to the four museums across London. The final diamond resided in a quaint little jewelry museum in Islington called "Sparkles." It had taken her fifteen minutes to connect to Sparkles' computer systems and CCTV. She had even managed to take control of the lone camera and pan around the room, zooming in on the diamond that was proudly displayed behind a floor-to-ceiling glass window. The only way to access this particular diamond was from behind that window.

She could have disconnected the camera, changed the recordings, overridden the electronic security locks and alarm, and broken in at night. She'd have the diamond in her possession in less than twelve hours. Amy didn't operate like that though. Why go out in the rain when it wasn't necessary? Why go out at all, when it was just as easy to steal it from here.

She had found an email from the manager of Sparkles to one of the directors of SJH – a Colin Rhames, discussing the diamond. It seemed that they were horrified at the recent break-in at the

Tempest and were concerned that their diamond might be next, and that their staff could potentially be in danger. They were requesting that the diamond be moved back to SJH, which had far more secure premises in many different locations around the country.

SJH had replied in agreement and said that they would be in touch shortly with arrangements.

"Time to make some arrangements," said Amy aloud, stretching her back and clapping her hands together. She could manipulate people just as well as a computer given the right circumstances.

From SJH's system, she sent an email back to the manager of the museum from Colin Rhames.

To: ray.boyden@sparklesmuseum.com

From: colin.rhames@sjh.co.uk

Subject: Four Feathers diamond collection

Dear Mr. Boyden,

Following your recent request regarding our "Four Feathers Diamond", I have arranged for our courier company "Star Runner" to collect the diamond from you on Tuesday 28th January at midday. Star Runner provides a packaging service and will do everything necessary to ensure that it is securely returned to us. Your only requirement will be to allow them access to the diamond.

When the diamond is back in our possession, and in our secure vault, I will release a statement to the press to let them know that we have moved the diamond in a bid to keep both it, and the staff at Sparkles safe, and to prevent a repeat of the unfortunate incident at the Tempest.

We hope to return the diamond to you later in the year when the circumstances have changed.

Many Thanks

Colin Rhames
Business Director
Society of Jewellery Historians

Amy had read through Colin's other emails and discovered that SJH used Star Runner for courier and packaging work. She had also found a contact – Felix Radcliffe. It seemed that Colin's emails to Felix were a little less formal. She composed another email from Colin's mailbox.

To:	felix_radcliffe@starrunner.co.uk
From:	colin.rhames@sjh.com
Subject:	Four Feathers diamond collection

Hi Felix,

How's things? Need to catch up for a beer at some point. January's a wipe-out for me, but hopefully sometime in February.

Got a job for you. You probably heard about the Four Feathers diamonds in the news. We need to move the last one – protect the museum and the diamond. Can you pick up tomorrow at midday? Usual packing service required. It's at Sparkles museum in Islington. You better take an extra guy for security. It's quite hot at the moment so we don't want it on our local premises. Can you deliver to:-

EZ-Store Services
121 Marshwood Lane
Croyden
CRO1JJ

I have arranged a secure vault there as a holding place before we move it out of the city. The code for the facility is "A63try", and the vault code is "422537".

Thanks, speak soon

Colin

Colin Rhames
Business Director
Society of Jewellery Historians

    Amy had used EZ-Store before. It was a 24-7 secure storage facility that allowed entry at any time. When you purchased a box, their system emailed you a code to get access into the facility, and another for your specific deposit box. On-site security was minimal, but the boxes themselves were very strong. The only way to get into a box was with the appropriate code.

    The best thing about EZ-Store in Amy's opinion was the fact that their systems were all cloud-based, meaning that for someone like Amy, accessing them was a breeze. She had "purchased" a box for two days, and she was now in possession of the required security codes to access her box. When the Star Runner courier delivered to EZ-Store, they would enter the gate code to get into the vaults, and then enter their box code on a touch screen in the unmanned reception area. This would be verified against the system and direct the courier to the appropriate box. The box would be opened, ready to deposit the diamond. The courier would close the box and it would electronically lock.

Pick-up was similar, but in reverse and with a time delay. The user could enter their code, and the system would direct the user to the correct box. It would open one hundred and twenty seconds later. EZ-Store was used by many online delivery companies for small value items, as well as room-sized vaults for banks and other similar institutions.

They had over one thousand boxes of varying shapes and sizes. Amy had ordered their smallest box, not much bigger than a bread bin. It was only two pounds a day, but she hadn't paid. She wasn't concerned about the money but paying would leave a trace. The record she added directly into their system couldn't be traced back to her, and once it had served its purpose, she would log in and again and delete it. It would be as if the transaction had not even occurred. She had even picked her own code – 422537, a code she'd used before as it spelled out HACKER when she typed it into her phone. Little touches like that always made her smile inwardly, even though no one would ever pick up on it.

She sat back, munching on a slice of pizza. Had she covered everything? At this point, the diamond would be neatly packaged up tomorrow by Felix and his team and dropped into EZ-Store just after midday using the code that she had emailed him. She could go down at any time and collect the diamond, and then erase the EZ-Store transaction. The diamond would be gone, and there would be no record of it ever being delivered to the storage facility. She would wipe any CCTV too – just in case.

She still had to go out and collect the diamond though, something that didn't appeal to her. She turned back to her laptop and logged on to a local taxi firm that had computerized their setup the previous year. Five minutes later, she had added a taxi pick-up from the EZ-Store Vault for 6pm tomorrow. She had asked for it to be delivered to the apartment two floors above hers. The building she lived in had its own electronic boxes for each apartment. The taxi company would use the video-call facility when they arrived to call the unsuspecting owner of apartment 306. Amy had hacked her building's system long ago and routing the call to her own room would take her seconds. She would take the call, open up room 306's box from her laptop for the taxi driver to deposit the package, and wish him a good day.

    Amy considered the fact that she would have to walk down a whole flight of stairs to retrieve the diamond. She grabbed the last slice of pizza.

    "I guess the exercise will do me good."

Interlude

Chapter 22 – "Interlude"

Wednesday 29th January 2020

Oscar was working through three dilemmas.

Firstly, he had discovered that his diamond was fake and was contemplating what to do next. He had kept an eye on the news, and so far, there hadn't been any mention that the Monument diamond had been found and returned, and he certainly didn't want to risk another trip back to check. Maybe they were keeping things quiet until they either found the other diamond thieves or until the fourth one was safe. At least this bought him some time. Right now, Ace had no idea that Oscar had failed the challenge. Would he be able to bluff if it was reported on the news? He had a diamond, and unless Ace expected it to be sent to him, then he would never know the real truth. Keep your head down, he thought. See what happens next.

His second dilemma occurred in the aftermath of Saturday night. Brandy had messaged him back and agreed to do the Cumberland show with him. All was going well until they performed the levitation illusion. Brandy was suspended on a table with a silk sheet covering her and balanced between two chairs. Oscar had removed one chair with a flourish leaving Brandy floating horizontally, seemingly suspended from one end only. The trick was to remove the other chair, but as he had grabbed it, he encountered a voice in his head like never before. It literally made him sink to his knees and grasp his head in agony. The voice was relentless.

"Why did you leave the diamond in the museum?"

"They're on to you."

"They've got CCTV footage."

"The policewoman saw you in the station."

"She's coming for you."

"You gotta run man."

"Get out of town."

Somehow, he managed to compose himself and finish the act. He had run backstage afterward in a sweat, swallowed one of his tablets, and sat breathing heavily for a good five minutes. He had been double dosing for over a week, and things had been OK. The unexpected onslaught from within had really scared him. Maybe he needed a proper psychological evaluation. He had managed to get a telephone appointment with Dr. Pullman for Friday, and it couldn't come soon enough.

He should have seen the third dilemma coming. Brandy would not leave his side following the incident. She was so concerned about him that she had insisted on taking him home and staying the night on his sofa to keep an eye on him. They had had a couple of drinks, and just like in all good movies, one thing had led to another.

He had had the most memorable sex of his life. Brandy was hot, uninhibited, and seemingly insatiable. After the third "fuckin' amazin' shag" as she had put it, they had both fallen asleep. He was woken just two hours later to the sound of music. He had found himself cuffed to his own bed, while she was dancing around the room provocatively to a Pussycat Dolls song, slowly removing her clothes, while brandishing a leather whip.

Where she got the whip from, he had no idea, but he could still feel the after-effects of the session every time he sat down. She was hot as hell but frankly scared the life out of him. If it was possible to kill someone with sex, then Brandy would be the girl for the job.

Oscar's mind was reeling.

Was he attracted to her? God yes.

Did he want a repeat performance? Probably, although he would quite like to keep the skin on his left buttock intact.

Was it a good idea? Absolutely not. If things went south, then he'd never find an assistant as good as her.

She had stayed the weekend and left him with a kiss and a warning to "conserve your energy for Friday night darlin'. I've got fuckin' plans for you." It probably shouldn't have come across as a warning, but Oscar couldn't see it any other way. He was terrified.

****

Following his escape at the Rhombus, Buddy had hunkered down in the covered entrance of the church next door and had a very chilly night, keeping an eye out for the intruder that he'd somehow managed to outwit with the toilet brush. At around 5am, his mind and ears started playing tricks on him, hearing eerie sounds from the nearby graveyard, and he had nearly bolted. Common sense prevailed though. After a successful robbery, he didn't want to be caught by being picked up by a street camera at such an early hour. He had managed to wait until the commuter traffic started to build up at 7:45am, going over the robbery in his head and ensuring that he hadn't missed anything that would get him caught. He had finally made his way to the busy train station on his skateboard just before 8am, cap pulled down low and an "I don't give a fuck" attitude that he knew was in fitting with his character and would not get him noticed.

That was ten days ago, and no one had come knocking. He had made contact with Ace who had welcomed him to his team and seemed delighted to have someone with Buddy's skills on board. He had answered Ace's questions, and purposely left out the part about the intruder who had nearly screwed it all up for him.

He had spent the following few days looking into the "landlord scam", more for Shanice than himself. He could make more money on street and restaurant hustles, but a call from the beautiful redhead had made his brain stop doing the thinking. She was coming to his for dinner on Thursday and said she couldn't wait to see him again and had casually dropped the landlord scam into the conversation. He didn't want to let her down and had managed to find a suitable property in a quiet street in Brent Cross – a one-bedroom garden flat that would normally fetch well over a thousand a month. He would only be charging nine hundred to make a quick "sale" but would require a one-thousand-pound deposit. If Shanice could help seal the deal, they could still make a tidy sum.

There were two downfalls with this type of scam though. Firstly, it could take a while before they got someone to bite, and secondly, it was quite high risk. You had to be friendly and helpful but completely forgettable - something he wasn't sure that she would be able to pull off with her striking looks and strong Irish accent.

By Thursday, he had all the details worked out and had a perfect evening planned with her. Wine, flowers, candles, and a new white linen shirt that he'd spent half an hour trying to iron the creases out of. He'd even gone to the chemist to get some condoms. Best to be prepared. He wasn't going to get caught short if the evening went the way he hoped it would.

At 6:30pm he was browsing through his music collection, trying to decide between George Michael or Michael Buble to set the mood, and wandering not for the first time how the hell he had ended up with these particular CDs in his collection.

She had called. She was really sorry. A work thing. Rain check. Sometime next week. Sorry again.

He had blown out the candles, swapped the George Michael CD for Joy Division, and spent the evening drinking the wine and sinking into depression. Bloody women weren't worth it. They caused more grief and heartache anyway.

****

Owen had spent his time since the Tempest break-in lying low. After he'd sobered up, he'd watched himself with alarm on all the news channels, the reporter's highlighting that if anyone recognized this dangerous, armed criminal then to get in touch with the police urgently. They had focused on the poor lady, Angie who had been shot, and she had given a tearful interview. Luckily, the stockings had done their job and it was pretty hard to make out any of his features, but the report suggested that police were checking out nearby CCTV and were following up on leads.

He had panicked and nearly fled but had nowhere to go and no money. His company had come through with his wages, but after paying back Estelle and Caine and buying some pasta and vodka (with more emphasis on the vodka) he was left with nothing.

His second visit to Caine in as many days had been pretty uneventful, and he hadn't even argued when Caine had insisted on a full week's interest. He was just glad to be out of debt with the thug and his psychotic sidekick Bones, who had stood menacingly nearby wielding his hammer. Hopefully, it would be the last he would see of them.

He had seen Estelle in a rare sober moment and given her her money back, thanking her again and reminding her that she'd literally saved his life. She was grateful that he'd returned the money so quickly, and was pleased to help him, but she'd still managed to call him a wanker twice and a "mother-fucking-inbred" in the ten minutes that he was with her.

Ace had been in contact with a list of questions regarding the robbery, which he had replied with a one-liner – "Fucked if I know. I was completely off my face. Do you know anyone else who will buy the diamond?" He was still awaiting a response.

By Wednesday evening he was bored. He had no money, the vodka was almost gone, the pasta was bland, and he'd spent most of the day hiding from the landlord who was screaming for his money and threatening eviction. He was sat browsing through GreySpider twiddling the ten-thousand-pound diamond in his fingers wondering how the hell he could convert it into real money. It was ironic that he was so skint yet was holding something in his hands that was more valuable than anything he had ever owned. He snapped a picture of the diamond with his phone and added a post to the forum.

19-01-2020 21:11, GreenZero

Diamond for Sale. Sensible offers please.

He poured the rest of the vodka into his glass, stirred in some ice, and fell asleep waiting for a response.

****

Amy looked at the diamond in distaste. It was a bit gaudy for her. The real pleasure came in the fact that she had managed to steal it with little to no effort on her part.

The taxi driver had rung the intercom for apartment 306 at 6:30pm the day before and she had intercepted the call, opening up the appropriate security box for him to deposit the parcel. Five minutes later she had collected the diamond and barely glanced at it, more interested in wiping her electronic fingerprints from Star Runners systems and the taxi company. She even went back into Sparkles and SJH's emails and removed them. If the police were called, they would literally have nothing to go on.

She had composed a reply to Ace and also sent him details of the robbery when he requested it, using one of her many GreySpider Aliases, "Pandora". She wondered what would happen next. All four diamonds stolen meant that Ace had his team. What were his plans? Would she help? Maybe. *If it means I can be tested then count me in*, she thought.

Her thoughts turned to her fellow teammates, and she fired up GreySpider to see if she could find them. GreySpider's security was some of the best she'd ever seen, but she'd accessed it long ago, leaving a tracer that informed her when they made any password changes. She connected as "Admin" and accessed the back-end dataset with an SQL query, searching for Ace's cluster. She found the information and ran a second query on Ace himself, which gave her his unique GreySpider ID. A few minutes later she was accessing his "web" where his private messages were kept.

She smiled as she pieced together the information from the messages that had been passed between Ace and each of the diamond thieves. The team looked good.

Budster had divulged that he was a small-time con artist with aspirations for something bigger. He had gone on to talk about the heist in detail with some meticulous preparation, disguises, and acting which in turn led to a smooth robbery and a well-thought-out plan. This guy was way too good for small-time cons, she thought.

Ozzy was a bit more mysterious, but it seemed like he could build some useful stuff. The gadgets he had used in his robbery proved he was capable of making bespoke tools fit for purpose. The way he had stolen the diamond also showed that he had balls of steel and a sense of timing that was faultless.

GreenZero was the weak link, but an interesting prospect. Amy had seen him on the news, so she already knew that he was a bit of a live wire. His short one-track responses in his messages to Ace confirmed that he was definitely in it for the money and nothing else. However, if they needed some muscle, he seemed like he wouldn't be afraid to be the thug of the team.

Ace was an enigma. His messages gave very little away, but they were well written and eloquent. She was intrigued by him and spent some time trying to dig further into the GreySpider files. She came up empty. He was either very good at covering his tracks or was really careful at what he posted. She believed it was the latter. If there was something to be found, Amy was good enough to find it.

She considered reaching out to the team but refrained. Let's see what Ace says first. He might not trust her if he knew that she was spying on them all.

She realized she was hungry and considered cooking something but really couldn't be bothered. Two minutes later, she had ordered some sweet and sour chicken and prawn toast from Wong's Chinese take-away chain. She hadn't used them for a while, but the passwords that she had kept that gave her direct access to their order and delivery system still worked. It was only ten pounds. Mr. Wong could afford it.

****

"Where's Monroe" bellowed Simpson, striding into the incident room. "We need an update on the evidence. All four diamonds gone, and we still haven't caught any of the bastards."

"She's on her way in," said Dickson looking up from his computer. "Maybe five minutes away."

"We'll start without her. Tell me what we've got. Anything new?"

"We'll start at the Rhombus," said Dickson. "As you know, the diamond was replaced with the fake, and the crime scene was trampled…"

"Bunch of morons" interrupted Simpson and proclaiming his contempt for about the hundredth time since they'd got the call about the Rhombus diamond.

"So, the fake diamond didn't reveal anything" continued Dickson. "But we did find that stray hair in the case. We ran the

DNA and got a hit. Daniel Simpson." He looked up from his notes. "No relation I presume?" he said with a grin, passing a picture to his boss.

"Daniel Simpson," said Simpson knowingly. "Absolutely no relation. Affectionately known in these parts as Danny Diamond. He's shady but never got into anything serious. Never gone down. So, where is he?"

"We've not been able to find him," said Dickson. "Last known address was in Brixton. It's boarded up. Landlady said she hasn't seen him in months, and he left the place in a right state."

"He must be somewhere near here if his hair turned up inside that bloody case," said Simpson, his voice rising. "Keep digging. At least we've got a name for one of them. Have we checked the cameras in the area?"

"A couple. Some places aren't being as forthcoming as others."

"Forthcoming? Tell me who's not being forthcoming, and I'll go down there and ask myself." He almost spat it out. "Lean on them. We need a recent picture of him. This one's years old. If we can get a new one, we'll splash it over the news and smoke him out." Simpson was getting red in the face. "OK. Anything else?"

"The camera on the third floor," said Dickson. "If you remember, Monroe noticed it had been moved slightly. We've got an idea. It's a bit speculative though."

Simpson grunted. He couldn't work Dickson out, He was a geeky, techie whizz-kid but used words like "speculative" in his everyday speech. No one says "speculative" he thought.

"Go on."

"Well, we said before that we tried to get out of the room crawling along the floor, but the camera got us every time. We couldn't work out how he left the room. Well, we got to thinking. What if he used a low trolley? Something on wheels. It would keep him below the camera." He dug out another photo and handed it to Simpson. "Then we found this."

"What am I looking at?" said Simpson looking at a photo of a busy station entrance.

"That's the station at Borehamwood. It's the nearest one to the museum. This was taken from the CCTV the morning after the robbery. We were thinking that maybe our guy laid low all night and headed for the station the next day. He pointed to a kid on a skateboard. Long shot" he shrugged, "but this kid came from the direction of the museum at about 8am." He pointed at the skateboard. "He's got wheels."

"Very long shot," agreed Simpson. "And the photo's not all that. Have we not got anything better?"

"No. From the angle, that's the best we can do. Might be worth showing it to the girl on the reception." He checked his notes. "Erm, Angel."

"Worth a try. The American guy was apparently older and long-haired, but it could've been a disguise. Follow it up, even if it's just to eliminate it."

"OK. The Monument. We've been over the CCTV for the café near the station and we've got this." Dickson pressed a button on his laptop and a video played on the large screen. "He's on-screen for nearly two minutes, but the camera is high. It's the smartly dressed guy with the cap. Unfortunately, the cap covers most of his face. He looked quite relaxed to start with, but watch."

They watched the guy in the smart suit and cap stand up and hold his phone in the air and sit down again. A few seconds later he leaped up and literally sprinted from the café leaving his coffee cup.

"We think the bug interfered with his phone and tipped him off. By the time Monroe got back, the cup had been cleared away. We've got their trash, but it's a minefield. No way of knowing which cup was his."

"Any more footage from the station camera."

"Nothing as good as this."

"Shit."

"We've checked against the CCTV at the Monument, but not found a match. There's a couple of possibles, but really hard to be sure. We're taking this picture back in later today. See if anyone recognizes him."

"OK. What about the new place? What's it called again?" said Simpson

"Sparkles. Silly name. This one's odd" said Dickson. I was speaking to the manager this morning, a Ray Boyden. It seems they wanted the diamond off their premises after they saw what happened at the Tempest. They contacted the Society of Jewellery Historians. Bit of a mouthful, so I'll just call them SJH. Well, SJH owns the diamonds - they're on loan to the museums. They agreed that it would be better to get the last diamond off the premises and said they'd be in touch."

"So, the diamond was stolen in transit?" said Simpson.

"No. Well, we don't think so. It was picked up by a courier service called Star Runner. Very reliable apparently. They've used them before. Star Runner collected the diamond and dropped it as requested to a storage facility called EZ-Store in Croyden."

"I know EZ-Store," said Simpson. "I've used them myself. So, what happened?"

"This is where it gets weird. The manager, Boyden emailed the director of SJH and thanked him for organizing the diamond removal so quickly, but it seems that SJH hadn't organized anything yet. They were still considering the best plan. We've spoken to the courier service, who swore blind that they had an email, but they can't find any records."

Simpson scratched his head. "No email sent, and nothing received? Sounds like someone at Star Runner's swiped it."

"Well, that's what I thought, buy the guy who collected it is a personal friend of the director of SJH. A Felix Radcliffe. He had the necessary security clearance to drop it at EZ-Store. The code for both the facility and the box."

"Let me guess. It's not in the box."

"Nope. No diamond, and no sign of Felix going in or out on the EZ-Store CCTV. We're still going through it. There will have been several other people dropping off and collecting stuff at the same time as Felix claims he was there. They may have seen something. We're trying to get a list of names from the EZ-Store people, but they're not being too helpful. Claiming that as far as they're concerned, their facility can't be broken into. They've got no record of the transaction and nothing on camera – so they're suggesting that Felix never went there.

"Sounds like the most likely explanation," said Simpson. "Has the CCTV been tampered with?"

"If it has, it's been done well. No obvious time jumps or gaps. The time stamps on the files are all OK too." Dickson shrugged. "This one's got me stumped. We'll keep checking. The fact that there are no records, and Felix is so adamant, I was thinking that maybe the systems were hacked by someone who knows what they're doing."

"You're the techie. Do your thing. If you can't prove that the systems were hacked, then pull Felix in for more questioning.

"Will do boss."

"OK. The Tempest?" Simpson was getting weary. The lack of progress was frustrating the hell out of him. "Tell me you got something on the drunk guy."

"So, we've been all over the sock that he dropped. No clues sadly. Hard to get a fingerprint on it, and it's nothing out of the ordinary. Came from a high street chain store, and pretty old by the looks of it. Maybe useful if we find a suspect and find the matching one in his sock drawer, but that's about it."

"I bet the other one's long gone. It's not like he can use it. Anything else?"

"Pretty much the same story with the hammer. Bog-standard. No prints. Dead end."

"Do we have any good news today?" Simpson's depression was gathering by the moment.

"Well, I've saved the best for last. We've pulled a partial fingerprint off the phone that he knocked out of the lady's hand. Angie Cummings?"

Simpson's ears pricked up. "And we've got a match?" he said excitedly.

"Um, no. The good news was the partial. It doesn't match any records, but again – we could use it if we get a suspect."

Simpson threw his hands in the air.

"How the hell are we going to find a suspect with no bloody clues" he bellowed. "Four robberies and all we've got is a partial print, some pretty sketchy CCTV footage, and a smelly sock. The only suspect we have is Danny fucking Diamond and he could be in Timbuctoo by now."

Dickson opened his mouth. Closed it again because he didn't know what to say, tried again but was saved by a commotion at the entrance to the incident room. Madison walked in, manhandling a scruffy, heavyset man, wrists handcuffed behind his back and looking really pissed off.

"Bagged me a diamond thief," said Madison with a grin.

Simpson looked up and smiled for the first time all day. "Hello Danny."

Part 2
The Heist

Chapter 23 – "The Team"

Thursday 30th January

Ace read his message again while eating his cereal. His team was complete, and he was reaching out to them, and true to form he was worrying over the content in his post. He was also worrying about GreenZero. The guy looked like he could be a liability and he needed to know more about him. There must be some skill he possessed that could be an asset to his otherwise strong team. Despite his concerns, GreenZero had not been caught and he did have the diamond, so maybe he was more resourceful than Ace gave him credit for.

He made a final change to his post and hit send. Done. Too late to change it now. It was out there. Let's see how they respond.

GreySpider Private Cluster #371238

Date: 30-01-2020 11:22
From: AceOfDiamonds
To: {Private List}
Subject: Welcome

Greetings fellow team members. I am delighted to finally address you all together.

In the last month, you have all proven yourselves to be worthy contenders of my little challenge, and I thank you for partaking in the fun. However, as I alluded to you previously, this is just the beginning. A far greater reward awaits us all on the

31st March. We have just over two months to prepare. A little longer than I previously anticipated due to your speedy and successful response to my task.

I will not be divulging full details of the plan at this stage, but I have a little taster to whet your appetites. As you may have gathered already, my desires lie with diamonds, but most certainly not the throw-away museum trinkets that you have already acquired.

Think bigger. Much bigger.

At the end of March, one of the world's most valuable diamonds, the "Queen of Diamonds" is being shipped into the country from Tahiti where it currently resides with a private collector. It will be transferred to a bank vault in London for two days, before being relocated to the Tower of London where it is supposed to live for the foreseeable future.

Ladies and gentlemen. We have those two days to make a rather special withdrawal from that bank. Once it reaches the Tower of London, it will be forever safe, and our opportunity will have passed.

The diamond is valued at approximately fifty million pounds.

I trust this has piqued your interest.

One final consideration. You will notice that I have kept your names private on this post and I'd like to keep it this way. As you know, I like a challenge, so we will be stealing the "Queen of Diamonds" without any of us ever meeting. If anything goes awry, and one of us gets caught, then the others will be fully protected. This condition is absolute and any attempts to reach out to each other will result in instant dismissal from my team.

I will be in touch with further details, but for now, please take a couple of days to relax and consider my proposal. If you feel this is something that you wish no part of, then I will bid you farewell with no hard feelings.

Ace calmly stood up from his computer and took a deep breath. Attempting to steal a diamond with a team that would never see each other had been troubling him for a long time. Was it possible? Was it really necessary? His biggest concern was trust. Who can you trust when you are working with people that you don't know? He believed it could be done, but the whole plan was fluid. He may have to break his golden rule if problems arose along the way, but for now, keeping the team anonymous felt like the right thing to do.

He paced across the room, turned a sharp one hundred and eighty degrees at the end, and paced back again, quietly mumbling as he counted the steps.

"One, two, three, four, five, six, seven, eight, nine." Turn.

His thoughts returned to GreenZero, and he rubbed the back of his hand against his forehead as he paced, trying to decide what to do. Four lengths of the room later, he settled back into his chair and composed a private message to him, reiterating the need to understand a bit more about him and where his skills lie. If he proved to be useful, then he would use him. If not, then he'd have to adjust his plans and see if it was possible to steal the diamond with just Ozzy, Budster, and Pandora.

He smiled as he thought of Pandora. If he could've hand-picked someone for his team, an experienced hacker would have been top of his list. She was going to make parts of the plan much easier to deal with and he had already adjusted certain elements to use her skills. He needed her from the start. Getting eyes on the bank vault was his number one priority, and despite the fact he'd promised them a few days, he couldn't resist sending her a private message to get the ball rolling.

Pandora,

Apologies for contacting you so soon after promising you a couple of days to consider. If you are indeed interested in my proposal, then your unique set of skills are required as soon as possible in order for me to plan out some finer details of the heist.

We need access to the cameras in the bank. I have a way to do this, but I believe that you could achieve this far quicker and with much less risk than my own idea. This is the reason why I build a team. Use individual strengths, lower the risks.

The bank in question is Larkins Bank of London on the King's Road in Chelsea. Anything you need to help access the cameras, don't hesitate to ask and I'll make it happen.

I am very much looking forward to working with you on this venture.

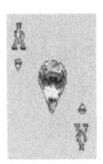

Ace stood and resumed his routine of wearing down the carpet, back and forth, counting the steps quietly.

"One, two, three, four, five, six, seven, eight, nine." Turn.

He was still performing this fretful ritual ten minutes later when his computer pinged with a reply from Pandora.

Ace,

I'm in. As long as I can work from home. I don't like to go out much.

I have a modified wireless repeater that will need to be placed in a safe place in the bank for me to remotely connect to their systems. It runs on a high-powered lithium battery that is good for three months on standby. As long as we are not permanently connected, it will work fine. Oh, and it's untraceable if it does get found. I will drop the repeater at the same EZ-Store site I mentioned to you before and send you the access codes. Let me know when it reaches the bank.

Pandora

He read the message twice, a nerve twitching at the first line. "As long as I can work from home."

As it happened, her skills required her to work in front of the computer. He could use the others for any legwork, but it irked him that she was calling the shots. At the same time, the most useful person on the team was on board, and he didn't want to upset the apple cart. He sent a reply.

Pandora,

For you, homeworking is an essential part of the plan so this will not pose a problem. Thank you for your support. I will organize the collection and relocation of your wireless repeater as soon as I have the details.

He wanted her to think that her staying at home was already in his thoughts and that he was in control. He was delighted that she was in though. He pushed back from his desk, made sure he was well clear, and done a double celebratory spin in his chair.

****

Simpson and Madison sat opposite Danny Diamond and his lawyer - a weaselly little man called Billy Truman. Danny had clamped up as soon as he had arrived and demanded to see his lawyer. It had taken nearly twenty-four hours to locate him and get him to visit the station, and they were running out of time to charge Danny with anything. They had spent their time collating the evidence and preparing their questions.

Madison started a video camera to record the interview

"Thursday 30th January, 14:30," she said. "Present are Inspector Adrian Simpson, Constable Madison Monroe, Daniel Simpson, and his lawyer Billy Truman."

She nodded to Simpson who was drinking a strong black coffee from a giant mug that read "Number One Inspector," a gift from his wife many years before. The mug was so stained inside that Madison thought he could just pour hot water in and still get a passable cup of coffee out of it.

Simpson lowered the mug and dropped it on the table. "Where's the diamond, Danny?" He wasn't messing with any preamble.

Danny looked at his brief who nodded and mumbled something. He turned back to Simpson and said, "no comment."

"Where were you overnight from the sixteenth to the seventeenth of January?"

Another look, another nod. "No comment."

Simpson pushed a photo of the entrance to the Rhombus museum in front of them. "Recognise this place?"

Danny was looking Simpson directly in the eyes and didn't even flicker at the picture. After another nod from his brief, he repeated in his monotone voice, "no comment."

Simpson sighed. "Do you really need approval from him to say nothing before you say nothing?"

The lawyer nodded again, and Danny started to open his mouth.

"I got it. No comment," Simpson said exasperatedly. He stood up. "You see, the thing is Danny, we've had our eye on you for a long time. We know you're up to no good, and up until now, you've been lucky. Luck can only get you so far my friend, and right now that's all changed. Because this time, you got sloppy."

He pushed another photo in front of the two men and glared at Danny.

"What you're looking at is a picture of a hair. A hair that was found inside a locked glass cabinet inside a locked museum. This museum." He pointed back to the other photo and then dropped a third on the table. "And this cabinet."

The new photo was a stock picture of the Four Feather's Diamond that they had obtained from the museum.

"Of course, the diamond isn't there anymore. All we found was the hair." He leaned menacingly over the table and loomed over Danny. "And the hair is yours, Danny. We have a DNA match. So, I'll ask you again. Where is the diamond?"

Truman spoke for the first time in a clear, slightly bored voice. "For the benefit of the record, I'd like to state that Inspector Simpson is questioning my client in an intimidating manner and I request that he refrains immediately, or we will consider pressing harassment charges."

Simpson glared at the lawyer and opened his mouth to let rip, but Madison put a restraining hand on his arm.

"Mister Simpson," she said politely, turning to Danny. "I'm not sure if you know how this works, but I can assure you that mister Truman here most certainly does. We have DNA. That's hard evidence that places you at the scene of the crime. That gives us enough to hold you here for as long as we like while we obtain more evidence. It's enough for a warrant to search your premises and your car. There is absolutely no reason that your hair can be in that case unless you were there. Also, a valuable diamond is missing from that same case, and you have a known reputation for, how can I put this politely, acquiring diamonds to order."

"Nuffin' illegal about havin' a reputation," said Danny gruffly. His lawyer raised a finger.

"I'd like a minute with my client?" he said.

Madison glanced at Simpson who nodded. "Interview suspended at 14:34," she said and stopped the recording. They left the room without a word and closed the door.

"What do you think?" said Madison.

"Oh, he's guilty as hell. We all know it, even the lawyer. They'll call us back in a minute and try and offer us something. Try and make a deal to get him off. Wouldn't be the first time with this clown."

"Truman's good, but if he's guilty, then what can they offer us?" said Madison. "Unless he has any knowledge of the other diamond robberies."

Simpson raised his eyebrows. "However much I'd like to see Danny go down, we need a result. If he's got info on the others, then we'll have to consider it."

The door opened and Truman beckoned them back in.

"Interview resuming at 14:36," said Madison after they had settled back in their chairs. "Do you have something to tell us, Danny?"

Danny took a photo of his own out of his pocket and pushed it across the table. Madison and Simpson leaned forward in unison and stared at the photo.

"That's the guy who stole the diamond," said Danny. "I was framed."

Simpson had heard the "I was framed" plea hundreds of times in his career and he would normally have ripped the suggestion to shreds. On this occasion though, the words caught in his throat. The photo showed a guy with a cap pulled down over his face, and the guy was under a streetlamp outside the Rhombus museum.

On a skateboard.

Chapter 24 – "Brandy for dinner"

Friday 31st January

Oscar paced up and down in his apartment, stopping in the hallway every couple of laps to check himself in the mirror. He looked at his watch for the fifth time in as many minutes. Nearly seven-thirty. She would be arriving in five minutes and his nerves were jangling. After six months working the circuit together, practicing their routines, and sharing many drinks in the bar after their shows, he was always relaxed around Brandy, although sometimes a little embarrassed at her brashness.

That had all changed. A vision of their previous encounter burned in his mind; him face down, tied to the bedposts, her straddling him, beating him with the whip screaming "Who's my bitch. Who's my fuckin' little bitch." When he hadn't answered quickly enough, she'd turned the whip around and threatened to shove it up his arse.

"I'm your bitch. It's me. Jesus. No."

She had cackled and put the whip between his teeth.

"Bite down on this bitch. I'm gonna ride ya 'till ya balls are black and blue."

There was a sharp knock on the door that physically made him jump and brought him back to the present. He looked in the mirror one last time, took a deep breath, and opened the door.

"Hey baby," said Brandy, giving him a full-on snog and smearing bright red lipstick on his face.

"Hey. Come in" said Oscar nervously. "Get you a drink? Rum and coke?"

"I bought wine," she said, brandishing a bottle of Pinot. "Makes me horny." She cackled and handed him the bottle, dropping a large bag in the hallway. He eyed the bag nervously, wandering what delights it might contain.

"Err. Great." He took the bottle and they headed for the kitchen. "Let me take your coat."

She unbuttoned her coat, dropped it to the floor, and stood before him completely naked. Oscar's jaw dropped and she cackled again.

"Pour the wine lover" she whispered sexily in his ear and then bit it. Hard.

"Ow. Shit. Easy Brandy."

She gave her braying cackle again, released him, and jumped up onto the kitchen counter, legs splayed, and started fondling her nipples.

"Let's start in here. How many rooms you got in this place again? I think they all need the Brandy treatment tonight."

He uncorked the wine, the pop making him jump again. His nerves were completely frazzled. He mentally counted. Lounge, kitchen, bathroom, two bedrooms, hallway. Jesus. Six. Would she count the cupboard in the hall too?

"More than I can cope with I think," he said, mustering up a brave smile. He grabbed two glasses and started pouring. "Shall I put some music on? What do you like?"

She took the glass of wine, swallowed it in one large gulp, and gripped the back of his neck, forcing him down between her legs.

"Forget the music, I'll sing. You just get busy." Another cackle. She grabbed the bottle from him and took a large swig and started a really bad rendition of Whitney Houston.

He could barely breathe as she forced him down harder and started twitching underneath him, proclaiming loudly and very untunefully that she would always love him.

She grabbed his ears and pulled them up and down rhythmically and attempted the key change. Oscar was almost glad that he couldn't hear her very well with his head sandwiched between her thighs.

"Oh, God. Yes. Keep going" she screamed "Don't stop. Fuck. Yes."

She released his ears, leaned back, and scooped a wooden spoon off the kitchen counter, and slapped the top of his head with it.

"Faster" she yelled. "Oh, God. Faster." Another slap on the head.

He tried to protest but couldn't get the words out. He made a mental note to talk to her about a safe word, not that he could use one right now.

She suddenly screamed, threw her head back, and clamped her legs together, crushing his head and making the blood pound in his ears. She hurled the wooden spoon across the room, and it bounced off the wall, narrowly missing the clock and it landed on Oscar's head giving him another slap.

"Fuck yeh" she screamed again. She plucked the bottle of wine off the side and took another hefty gulp and finally released him.

He gasped a lungful of oxygen as she jumped down from the counter and grabbed his hand.

"Kitchen done" she cackled. "One-nil to me. Let me grab my bag. I've brought some toys."

She pulled him back into the hallway and Oscar followed obediently like a frightened puppy as she plucked her bag off the floor. She'd been there less than five minutes and he was a blubbering mess already.

One thing's for sure, he thought. I'll never listen to Whitney Houston in the same way again.

****

An hour later, they were sat on the sofa talking and tucking into a large pizza that Oscar had thrown in the oven between their hallway and bathroom sessions.

Not long before, Brandy had delved into her bag and retrieved what she called a "Triple Whipple butt plug" and shown him in no uncertain terms how it worked while they showered together. She had also invented what she called her own magic trick - "Hide the loofah" and asked if they could make it part of their act. He had laughed but wasn't sure if she was serious or not. Either way, he would need to buy a new one next time he went shopping.

"So, what did the doc say?" she said, taking a large bite of pizza and wrapping her tongue around the stringy cheese that refused to let go of the crusty top. "Can he fix you?"

They had opened a second bottle of wine, and Oscar was feeling quite light-headed. Brandy, on the other hand, was like a machine. She had gotten a little tipsy, but it had barely affected her, other than making her randier.

"He's going to run some more tests," said Oscar, relieved to be having a breather and on safer ground. "Told me to stick to the double dose of tablets and he'll book me in as soon as possible. You know what it's like though. It will be a fortnight before I get a letter and another four to six weeks before anyone will see me." She'll probably have killed me by then anyway, he thought to himself.

"That's shit. What if it 'appens again? What if it 'appens while you're driving or summink?"

He shrugged. "I use the tubes mainly. I only need to drive for the shows."

She pondered it for a second. "I'll do the driving" she said. "For the shows I mean. You can use tubes the rest of the time."

He smiled. This is the Brandy that he liked. The Brandy that he enjoyed spending time with. The Brandy that worried about him. The caring Brandy.

"Then I can stay over and fuck ya brains out after" she cackled, and a piece of cheese shot out of her mouth and landed on his bare chest. His smile turned into a grimace.

"Oops. Sorry. Let me get that."

Before he could protest, she was on him and sucking the cheese off his chest, biting his nipple in the process.

"Owww. Where do you get your energy from?" he marveled. "I need more than just pizza and wine to keep me going all night."

"I can score ya some cheap Viagra if ya like," she said taking another large gulp of the wine and sitting astride him. "At your age, it'll keep you up for hours." She gave him a sexy smile and ground herself into him, her huge bare breasts jiggling up and down in the process.

"Um. Doc says not to mix tablets at the moment" said Oscar, thinking quickly. "There might be side effects." He picked up the last slice of pizza, but she took it from him and placed it between her boobs.

"You can eat it off me," she said and grabbed his head, shoving it between her boobs and placing his hands on her nipples. She shook violently back and forth, and most of the pizza went up his nose while her boobs smacked him about the head a bit.

"Jesus Brandy. You're gonna put my eye out" he said, laughing nervously, coming up for air.

She cackled again, turned around so she was sat facing outwards, and bent over to retrieve something from her bag. Oscar was picking pepperoni out of his eyebrows and couldn't see what she was doing but feared the worst.

"Close your eyes," she said playfully.

Oh my God. He started to protest, but she insisted.

"I'm not gonna hurt you silly. Close your eyes. Trust me."

He realized that she'd grabbed a couple of candles out of her bag and relaxed a little. She was just going to set the mood. Some nice romantic candles, maybe some music and a massage. He could do with that right now following the traumatic bathroom scenes with the butt plug. He closed his eyes, and she got off his lap.

"Keep them closed lover boy. No peeking or I'll have to punish you."

Not knowing where she was and what she was doing was terrifying, but the threat of punishment was even more disconcerting. He heard a click as the lights were turned out, and then a match strike. OK, she's lighting the candles. That's cool.

Suddenly she was back and whispered gently in his ear. "Lay down."

He did as she said, laying back on the sofa. She took his hands and stretched them out over his head and quickly handcuffed them to the coffee table leg. His eyes sprung open in horror and he saw shadows bouncing around the room from the flickering candles. She loomed over him with her hands on her hips.

"You peeked. You know what that means?"

He snapped them shut again. "No, I didn't. I didn't see a thing. Honest."

She laughed, reached into her bag, and took out a blindfold, snapping it around his head. He moaned.

"Just relax. You're gonna love this."

Oscar lay in the dark trying to relax but failing, as she got up again. This girl was crazy, and he was chained up and blindfolded. What did she have planned?

He soon found out. There was a sudden burning sensation on his chest, and he screamed like a girl.

"What the fuck was that?"

He kicked out with his feet, but she straddled him again, pinning him down.

"Just a little candle wax. Shhh. Stop being a baby."

More burning wax dropped - on his belly this time and he bucked and squealed again.

"Oh yes baby. Squeal for me" she yelled riding him as he bucked beneath her.

More wax, more screaming……

….He wasn't sure how long it went on for, but she eventually rolled off him, exhausted, removed his blindfold, and used her long pink polished nail to scrape the hardened wax off his body, a contented smile on her face.

"You were fuckin' amazin'," she said smiling.

"Brandy I'm not sure….."

"Shh." She kissed him gently. A loving kiss. A tender kiss. He closed his eyes and enjoyed it.

It was like being with two different girls. One minute she was gentle and affectionate like now, and the next she was dripping hot wax on his balls and moaning with pleasure like a crazed banshee.

"That's nice," he said, kissing her back. "That's really nice. Let's do this for a while."

She kissed him again and carefully ran her nails down his chest making him moan.

"Mmmm. So nice."

She kissed him yet again, as her nails went lower, and then slowly caressed back up again, over his belly, his chest, and up to his throat.

Suddenly she pinned him down by the neck and his eyes flew open in alarm, bulging.

"Two more rooms to go little bitch" she said in a sexy, but slightly menacing voice. "Let's get the real toys out."

Chapter 25 – "EZ-Store"

Saturday 1st Feb

Buddy had messaged Ace within an hour of receiving his message and agreed to be part of the team. When he realized what they were trying to steal, his head started to spin. A fifty-million-pound diamond? It made his small-time cons, which scored him a few thousand at best, seem completely insignificant. If they managed to pull this off, his biggest worry would be working out how to fill his day knowing that he would be set for life. He had had a sleepless night dreaming of how he would spend his share of the money. Chartering a yacht around the Mediterranean would be his first choice, closely followed by a Maserati MC20 – his dream supercar.

He woke up with a headful of happy thoughts and saw that Ace had sent him a private message.

Budster

Thank you for agreeing to proceed. Our team is strong and having you on board will be a massive benefit to the successful conclusion of our mission.

In the great words of Sherlock Holmes, the game is afoot, and I have a task for you.

We will be using a storage facility to pass objects back and forth. Have you heard of EZ-Store? I would like you to collect an item from box number 37. The object will allow one of our team to access the cameras in the bank. It needs to be placed somewhere safe inside the bank and remain undetected there until after we have procured our prize. I would like you to place it in a safety deposit box in the bank's secure vault for ten weeks. This is the same area where our diamond will be housed in a couple of months' time. While you are there, I would also like you to record as much video as possible on the approach to the vault, and the inside of the vault itself. The bank's cameras will only allow us to see certain angles and certain rooms. I don't believe they will allow us to see the actual vault itself as it would be a massive breach of privacy to the people using the deposit boxes, so we need to understand the layout and working of this area the best we can.

There is also some money in box 37 for you to rent the security box at the bank and anything else that is required. I trust that you will return any change as it will be needed throughout our task.

Please let me know when this job is complete.

Pick up from:-
EZ-Store Services
121 Marshwood Lane
Croyden
CRO1JJ

Box No: 37
Site Code: A21JMD
Box Code: 422537

We're starting already? Buddy hadn't expected the ball to be rolling for at least a week but guessed that having eyes on the bank was pretty critical to the plan, and he was pleased that he was being entrusted with a task so soon. He wondered, not for the first time, about the other team members. He had no clue about any of them except for the drunken guy with the gun that had been all over the news in the last week. Ace had suggested in his message that the team was strong, so he guessed that whoever this guy was, he had managed to convince him that he was capable.

Buddy had a concern over trust but wasn't sure how to approach it. He was happiest working alone, but now he was getting into bed with four people he didn't know, and all of them were essentially liars and thieves. He was one himself. Why would he trust four people like him on a job such as this?

He composed a message back to Ace. I can't be the only one worrying about this he thought. Let's put it out there before we start.

Ace,

Consider it done. I will sort out a suitable disguise and collect the items from EZ-Store later today. I may need a little of the extra money to sort out a fake ID for the bank. I know a guy, and I've used him recently, so I'll get a reasonable price.

I have one concern and I hope you don't mind me raising it.

I don't know you - and I don't know the other team members. I fully understand why you want to keep it like this, but I find it hard to trust these people who are essentially crooks — myself included. What's to stop you, me, or any of the team from spinning off their own plan and stealing the diamond away from us all? We could invest time and money and put ourselves at risk for no reward. I am assuming that you have considered this already and I would expect the other team members to be thinking the same. Please can you reply to all on the central forum to alleviate this concern?

In the meantime, I have a bank to visit...

Budster

Buddy congratulated himself on the use of the word "alleviate". It's not a word he would normally use, but he was trying to impress, and Ace seemed to like his big words. He'd even had to google a couple of the words in Ace's earlier messages to understand what he meant – Who the hell uses "piqued" in their everyday speech?

He started to think about his upcoming task and grabbed a pen. The pickup from EZ-Store was easy, but he didn't want to be recognized. The drop-off at the bank would need a bit more thought.

- EZ-Store
    - Disguise
    - Bag
    - How to get there

- Bank
    - Disguise (same one as EZ-Store?)
    - How much is the deposit box?
    - Will I need ID?
        - What ID required
        - Call Bank
    - False ID (If needed)
        - Contact Jake.
    - Camera to record layout of the bank/vault

- - Can use the same one used at Rhombus
  - When to go?
  - Bag for the item
    - What size?

He pondered on this last point. He guessed that the item he was depositing in the bank was some kind of transmitter or Bluetooth gizmo that would connect into the cameras. He could hardly walk into the bank with it under his arm. He would need a suitable bag, preferably something that wouldn't attract attention. A briefcase maybe? He put an asterisk next to the "Bag" on his list. Let's see how big it is first.

He had a couple of phone calls to make but figured that he could get them out the way and be over at EZ-Store just after lunch. Then he could plan the trip to the bank properly.

He phoned the bank to check what ID was needed to rent a box, and how much it would cost for ten weeks. Sally was very helpful and informed him that if he didn't have an account with them, then a photo ID would be needed to drop off and pick up the item. Their new system was digitally controlled, so he would be able to choose his own six-digit pin number to close and open the box. No one else would know his number which ensured that the box was secure. Boxes were normally rented out by the year, but she could do him a three-month rental starting from £100 for a small box, rising to £250 for a larger one.

He thanked her and immediately dialed Jake the Fake to sort out his ID. He haggled for a bit, agreed on a price and Jake told him that he could sort something out for Monday, but would need a photo.

"I'll swing by later today. I presume you have a camera."

Jake scoffed. "I'd be pretty shit at my job if I didn't."

Buddy turned his mind to his disguise. He decided to use the same one for both EZ-Store and the bank so that he could drop by Jake's later while he was still dressed up - he needed the photo ID to match. He dug out a short blonde wig that he hated but it had a startling effect on the shape of his face. He guessed a hat wouldn't go down well in the bank, so decided on a mustache – another pet hate, but it would do the job. The trick with a fake mustache was trying to make it not look fake, something that was actually very hard to do. He had a very good one though that matched the wig, and within twenty minutes he was looking at himself in the mirror, pleased with the result. Some trendy chinos and a crisp blue shirt made him look a bit like Rupert, the guy who he had ripped off a few weeks before. Poor Rupert. He wondered if he was still with the petite brunette. At least it would be a consolation for his expensive night out.

He grabbed a sports bag, so he had something to carry the gizmo in. It was always going to be a gizmo in his mind, at least until he saw what it was.

He was about to leave when his phone rang. Shanice. After letting him down on their date in the week, he was tempted to ignore it, considered it for a second, but then punched the green phone icon.

"Hey Buddy. How are ya?"

"Hi Shanice, I'm good thanks. I was just off out. What you up to?"

"Work," she said miserably. "They've dragged me in for a few hours. At least I get paid overtime. Just grabbing a coffee. Are ya around tonight? I promise I won't let ya down again. I'll bring Chinese if you can supply the wine."

She's still interested thought Buddy. Maybe he'd been too harsh on his assessment of her when she'd canceled on him. His day just got a little brighter.

"Sounds great. Red or white?"

"You choose. I'll be round at eight. Text me what food you want. Gotta run. Take care."

"See ya later." Buddy hung up and stared at his phone. After the last-minute letdown before, he thought she'd gone cold on him. Maybe the condoms he'd bought would see some action after all.

He left with a spring in his step and headed for EZ-Store.

****

The EZ-Store facility was a pain to get to. The nearest tube station, Balham on the Northern line was about six miles from it, and he had to get a mainline train or two buses, to get anywhere near it. He made a mental note to talk to Ace about possibly using something closer. After an hour's traveling, he reached East Croyden station and his phone told him that it was just a three-minute walk. After getting lost twice and asking a grumpy traffic warden for directions, he finally found the place fifteen minutes later, tucked away behind a grubby car sales garage advertising "The best value cars in South London".

From the outside, it wasn't very impressive; a high wall with a heavy steel door with the EZ-Store logo printed just above and a small sign which read "Please enter site code." Under the sign was a keypad.

Buddy opened his phone, found the code that Ace had sent him, and keyed it in.

A21JMD

Nothing happened for a second, and then there was a click and the door swung inwards. He entered a small unmanned reception area where he found a touch screen computer, similar to the one at his doctor's surgery. The screen was asking for his box number and box code and had a large numeric keypad on it. He entered "37" and "422537" and pressed Enter. He wasn't sure if it was the confined space, the watchful camera high up on the wall, or the fact that he was about to collect something that was considered unlawful, but he felt a bead of sweat run down his neck as he waited for the system to verify him.

A second ticked by and there was a loud click behind him as the steel door he had entered, closed and locked making him jump.

After another two seconds that felt like twenty, the screen changed.

Welcome, Mr. Diamond. Please follow the yellow arrows to your box. It will open in two minutes. Please ensure you close the box when you have finished and follow the red arrows to the Exit.

Mr. Diamond? It seemed that Ace had a sense of humor. Or was it one of the others on the team? Another click and a second door to his right swung open. It led to a dimly lit corridor with bright yellow arrows every ten feet or so indicating which way to go. It led him round a few turns, passing some large locked rooms until he came to a smaller room that had about two hundred small deposit boxes in it. Number thirty-seven was on the middle row on the wall in front of him, and the number was flashing above, also in yellow.

Neat system, he thought. Another camera monitored this room, a red flashing LED reminding him that he was under surveillance. He thought it best to grab whatever was in the box and open it when he wasn't being watched. Even though he had done nothing illegal, his years of hustling on the streets had made him cautious.

A click in front of him and box thirty-seven swung open. He peered inside and wondered for a minute whether he had the wrong box. He reached in and took out a small cube, no bigger than the Rubik's cube that he used to play with in his childhood. Well, the bag certainly wasn't required. The cube fit in his coat pocket.

He peered into the box again and found an envelope with some money in it. He took just enough to pay for the fake ID and the safety deposit box at the bank, and then paused and added a twenty to cover his traveling expenses and stuffed the notes into his wallet.

Technology is just getting smaller all the time, he thought as he closed the box. He took a final glance at the camera and started following the red arrows to the exit.

****

Several miles away, hunched over her computer, Amy Ross watched Budster through EZ-Store's CCTV. She had already intercepted Ace's messages so knew that Budster would be visiting today at some point to collect her package. A quick subroutine that she'd added to the EZ-Store surveillance software, and her phone pinged whenever there was movement in the reception area. It was all so easy.

She spent two minutes erasing the CCTV footage of his visit, as she had done with Ace's earlier. She hadn't needed to visit the place herself. Why bother when she had taxis and courier services that could do it for her. All of the drop-off and pick-up transactions had also been removed. As far as the system knew, the box had been reserved for three months for a Mr. A. Diamond and, as yet it had not been used.

Before deleting the CCTV, she snapped a screenshot of Budster as he had looked up at the camera. She printed it out and stuck it on the wall. Next to one of Ace.

Chapter 26 – "Jake the Fake"

"Hi Jake. Good to see you."

Jake the Fake peered over his glasses but couldn't place the blonde man standing in front of him. He took them off, squinted, and scratched his bald head.

"Do I know you?"

"Jeez, Jake. It's only been about three weeks." Buddy knew that Jake was getting old, but they'd known each other for years. Jake was still looking at him bemused, and then Buddy remembered he was wearing the wig. Looks like the disguise was really working.

"It's Buddy," he said. "I've come to have my picture taken."

"Buddy? Fuck me sideways, so it is. Are you on the run? You look like an albino fucked a caterpillar. What the hell's that thing on your lip?"

Jake wasn't a man to mince his words. He was born and bred in East London on a shabby council estate nearly sixty years before. Beaten as a child, he'd escaped from his abusive father and had to stand on his own two feet from the age of fourteen, stealing scraps on the street in his teenage years, and somehow avoiding both the welfare system and the police. A lot of kids in similar circumstances had turned to drugs, or in the case of the girls - prostitution, but despite his traumatic upbringing, Jake had "the smarts" as he put it, and at the age of twenty found himself working for Brad McCarthy, a shrewd, although somewhat dodgy businessman, who mentored Jake in some questionable practices for the next five years. Jake flourished, and with Brad's contacts, eventually found his vocation in life – "Faking shit" as he'd liked to put it.

McCarthy had died from a hammer to the skull on a bad deal down by the docks twenty years earlier, but Jake had managed to carefully juggle being a law-abiding citizen when he needed to, with being a loyal friend to the criminal underworld in the city. People tended to like him. Buddy always thought that the fact that he looked like the actor Danny DeVito didn't hurt.

"Disguise," said Buddy, unnecessarily as Jake led him through a narrow passage to his office.

Jake's office looked like a bombsite. How this man had ever run a business for thirty-five years, Buddy could never understand.

"Get you a coffee?" said Jake, grabbing a pile of documents from the only chair in the room and offering it to Buddy. Buddy sat as Jake looked for somewhere to put the documents. After turning three-hundred and sixty degrees, he dropped them back on Buddy's lap.

"You actually have a kettle in here?" said Buddy looking around at the devastation. "It probably electrocuted itself to put itself out of its misery."

"Fuck you, tash man. Screw your coffee. You can go without. You got my money?"

Buddy passed him an envelope and Jake threw it in a drawer without checking. He'd worked with Buddy enough times to know that he was trustworthy. They had an odd "honor amongst thieves" friendship that somehow seemed to work.

"You sure you want an ID looking like that? You look like the shifty one from Abba."

"Abba? Who are they you old bastard" said Buddy with a grin. "I think you forget that I'm way under half your age."

"Wise ass. Can you see my camera?"

"Probably gone the same way as the kettle."

Jake grunted and then spotted the camera balanced precariously on a half-finished painting of an old balding man sat on a chair with his head in his hands.

"Self-portrait?" asked Buddy indicating the picture. "You've made him way too skinny."

"That's a Van Gogh you ignoramus. Look it up. I'm getting a fortune for that." He grabbed the camera. "And fuck you again. I've lost two pounds this week."

Where from? Buddy thought looking at his rotund companion but bit his tongue.

"Where do you want me?" he said instead. "The tidy part of the room?" He looked around but failed to find one.

"Up against the door," said Jake, closing it, "...and please don't smile. You look scary as hell."

Jake snapped a few pictures and uploaded them to a laptop that was buried under a pile of magazines.

"They'll do," he said. "Give me a couple of days. I'll try and make you look a bit less like a pedophile."

"Funny. You're funny man." Buddy turned to leave, and then remembered Shanice. "While I'm here, have you got anything that looks like an authentic landlords' contract? I could knock my own up, but if you've got something handy, I'm sure it would be better."

Jake clicked his mouse a few times, and a printer whirred to life somewhere in the room. After a few minutes of searching for it, he handed him a contract on headed paper from a fictitious company called "Roberts & Co".

"Just fill in the gaps and get them to sign. There's two copies there."

Buddy looked over the legal jargon in the document. It looked perfect, probably because it was an exact replica of a real one with a new name and logo.

"You're a star," said Buddy. How much?"

"To you? Thirty.

"Thirty quid? It took you two minutes."

Jake shrugged. "Suit yourself. Make your own." He took the forms back and threw them in the bin.

"I'll give you twenty. Surely I get a discount with all the work I'm bringing you."

"That *is* the discounted price, tight-wad. Take it or leave it."

Buddy grumbled but handed him the money and Jake fished the documents out the bin, rubbed the banana skin off with his sleeve, handed them to him, and ushered Buddy out.

"See you Monday," he said. "Call first. I'm bringing a lady friend back Sunday night. She may still be here if you're too early and I don't want you scaring her off."

"I'll take her guide dog for a walk if you like," said Buddy, laughing at the angry glare he received from Jake. "Take care, my man."

"Fuck you."

****

Buddy repeated his ritual from a couple of nights before making sure everything was ready for Shanice. He'd decided that if she let him down again, then he'd give up on her, but she was there bang on eight o'clock, complete with chicken chow mein, egg fried rice, and prawn crackers. She wore a simple black elegant dress and looked amazing.

"Wow," said Buddy looking her up and down. "You look incredible"

"Thanks. You scrub up pretty well yourself," she said leaning in to give him a kiss.

They dished the food out and Buddy poured the wine and turned the music on. They sat up at a table that was lit with candles and some fresh flowers. Buddy had pulled out all the stops.

"This is lovely," she said, sipping the wine. "I'm so sorry about the other night. The boss is being a right idiot at the mo." Her strong accent made it sound like "eejit". "That place is getting right on my tits. I might look elsewhere."

"It's fine" lied Buddy, thinking back to his depressing night alone just two days before when he had drained a bottle of wine and fallen asleep on the sofa in front of some mind-numbing reality show. "These things happen."

"What you been up to? Must be nice not having to report to anyone."

"This and that," said Buddy, not wanting to talk about the diamonds. "I think we're nearly ready to go on the landlord thing. I got the paperwork sorted. Just got to get a key made and stick an advert out. I've taken a mold of the lock already, so can hopefully sort that tomorrow."

"That's great," said Shanice, stuffing a prawn cracker into her mouth and crunching. "I can sort the ad out if you like. Should be pretty easy."

"We need to use a burner phone. One that can't be traced. I think I've got one somewhere. I'll dig it out later and give you the number."

"How much are we going to ask….." She stopped. "Jesus. What the hell is this music you got playing?"

His fork stopped midway to his mouth. "It's Michael Buble. Don't you like it?" He thought that all women liked a bit of Buble.

"It's really shite," she said laughing. "Is this what you play when you bring all your lady friends back? No wonder you've been single for so long."

He laughed. "It's been a while since I've brought anyone back here," he said. "That's reserved for the special people."

"Ah, so I'm special, am I?" She looked at him with a flirtatious glint in her eye.

"Clearly more special than Michael Buble," he said getting up and grabbing his Ipad. "What do you like?"

"You got any Guns 'n' Roses?"

"You like Guns 'n' Roses?" he said, surprised. "You weren't even born when they were around."

"Ah. They're great. Stick on November Rain. I love that."

He frantically scrolled through his music trying to find the track. He looked up mournfully. "I've not got that one. How about Paradise City?" It was a bit heavy for a romantic meal.

"Ah. Go for it" she said, putting down her fork on the empty plate.

"Do you want more?"

"No. I'm stuffed. You were telling me how much the scam was gonna make us."

Axl Rose started singing as Buddy cleared the plates away.

"Well, other flats go for over a grand a month, so I was thinking nine hundred. We want the first people through the door to buy it so we're not traipsing in and out. The neighbors might get suspicious. We should be able to swing a thousand deposit though on top and clear nineteen hundred."

He topped up their wine and passed her the legal contracts that he'd got from Jake.

"Here, I got these today. We may have a couple of hundred in expenses but should make nearly eight hundred each."

"That's grand," said Shanice, looking over the documents. "These are good. I'll put the ad together tomorrow. Let me know when it's ready to go."

"We need to do something about your hair," he said. I've got some disguises, but nothing that would work for you."

"Leave that to me. I've done some fancy dress before and got a couple of good wigs. Even you won't recognize me by the time I'm done."

"Looks like we're set then," he said with a smile as they left the table and settled on the sofa. "Once you get someone interested, you just need to do your sales pitch and convince them it's a hot property. The low price should help. As long as they're genuine buyers, it should go. It's a lovely place."

She leaned over and kissed him unexpectedly.

"This is great Buddy," she said. "I needed this after my bad day at work." She took a sip of her wine and sighed contentedly.

He kissed her back, a little more passionately and she moaned.

His hand found her neck and rubbed gently, and slowly worked its way down as they kissed. As it reached her right breast she froze.

"Hey steady now" she whispered. "Not too fast."

He removed the hand, mumbling "sorry" and they kissed some more.

After a couple of minutes, they came up for air and more wine.

"That's nice," she said. "I could do this all evening."

"Well if you insist," said Buddy. He couldn't believe his luck. This girl was way out of his league.

The kissing continued, and they lay back on the sofa, Buddy's hand finding her bare leg and slowly sliding upwards underneath the black dress. She gasped as it rose higher and again stopped him.

"Buddy. I can't."

She kept kissing him though and within a few minutes, Buddy's urges got the better of him. Shanice was making him horny as hell, and he started kissing her neck, working down, his hands cupping her breasts again. She moaned with pleasure, but pushed him away, sitting up.

"I'm sorry Buddy."

"What's wrong?"

"I. Well. I've not mentioned it before, but I'm Catholic. Irish Catholics take their religion seriously. I really like you and as I said, I could do this all night, but I can't go further. It wouldn't be right. Not until I'm married."

The blood drained from Buddy's face, and his penis didn't fare much better. He took a large sip of his wine. He hadn't seen that one coming.

"It's fine" he choked out. "It's fine. Really. Don't worry." He kissed her again.

"Are you sure Buddy? Most men run for the hills when I bring this up. I know it's a bit old-fashioned, but it's the way my ma brought me up." She was welling up.

He kissed her gently. "Shhh. It's fine. We can work this out."

She sniffed and nuzzled into his neck.

"Thanks, Buddy. That really means a lot to me."

He finished his wine as they cuddled on the sofa. She lay there thinking that Buddy was the nicest guy she'd met in a long while.

He was thinking how much he liked her too but wondered just how the hell he was going to keep his hands off her. He made a mental note to return to the chemist. He hoped they gave refunds. The dozen condoms in the bedside cabinet certainly wouldn't be required for a while.

Chapter 27 – "Larkins Bank"

Monday 3rd February

"But they're unopened. I only got them on Thursday. The seal isn't even broken?"

The young girl with the ponytail and the zits in the chemist was patiently explaining that condoms were part of their no-returns policy, and it was clearly stated on the shelf when he'd bought them.

"Well they're hardly used, are they?" said Buddy sarcastically, getting agitated, "and I don't think I can exactly stick them on eBay."

"I'm sorry sir," said the girl. "I don't make the rules."

He sighed. A queue was forming behind him. He would normally be hugely embarrassed at this scene, but he had his blonde wig and mustache on, ready for the trip to the bank.

"Is there nothing you can do?"

The young girl looked over her shoulder to make sure her manager wasn't nearby and leaned in.

"I'll buy them from you for half price" she whispered. "My boyfriend uses these ones. We're going through them faster than a junkie popping E's at a rave. Costing us a fortune."

Buddy's mouth dropped open. The girl looked about fifteen and was clearly getting far more action than he was right now. Before he could answer, she grabbed some money out of the till and thrust it at him.

"Pleasure doing business with you," she said with a smile and grabbing the box off him. "Why don't you lose the creepy tash. You might have more use for these."

"Who's next" she yelled.

****

He approached the bank and switched on the spy camera that was pinned to his coat. He had decided on a briefcase as it fit the professional look. The small cube was tucked inside it underneath a pile of documents. Anyone looking at him would see a smart, well-to-do young businessman, probably coming to organize a business loan with the bank. Buddy had decided that an arrogant persona would also fit well, and he strutted confidently to the Information desk and rang the bell.

After a moment, a middle-aged man wearing the most hideous glasses Buddy had ever seen, appeared. They were yellow. Sickly yellow and they had a string clipped to them that was sickly green. They also looked to be about an inch thick. Why the guy had a string connected he couldn't work out. Glasses that thick weren't made to be taken off. The guy would be blind as a bat if he tried.

"Good morning Sir. How can I help you?"

"Good day," said Buddy, adopting a plummy self-assured voice. "I have some important papers that I'd like to store in one of your safety deposit boxes. I have spoken to a young lady called Sally, and she has informed me that I can purchase said box for one hundred pounds for the duration of three months." He gave a curt smile.

"That shouldn't be a problem, Sir," said the guy with the coke-bottle glasses – Robert Marsden was the name on his badge. "I just need to take a few details. Please follow me."

Marsden led him into a small, glass-fronted office just behind the reception desk.

"Do you have an account with the bank?"

"No, but I'm considering moving my business account here. It's been recommended to me by a colleague. I thought I'd start with the box and see how things go." Buddy thought he might get preferential treatment if the guy thought that he could attract a young successful businessman.

"Of course, Sir. I'd be more than happy to assist with that when you are ready. Let me take a few details for the safety deposit box. As you don't have an account with us, I'm afraid I will need to see some form of photo identification. I trust that Ms. Mcnally made that clear to you on the phone."

Sally McNally? Poor girl thought Buddy. "Of course," he said, passing over a driver's license that he had picked up from Jake that morning.

Jake had come through with flying colors. The credit card driver's license looked exactly the same as his real one, other than the fact that the picture was new, and it sported the rather grandiose name of "Douglas Iford-King." It would be a few days before he realized that Jake had given him the initials "DIK."

"That's fine Mr. King," said Marsden, passing the license back, and tapping away on the keyboard.

He filled in a few screens of information and printed off a four-page document which Buddy signed with his hastily practiced new signature. He passed the hundred pounds over and Marsden made a quick phone call.

"OK. Our secure vault is downstairs. Please follow me."

They descended two floors in a lift, and the door opened out onto a corridor. Buddy kept his eyes peeled while trying not to look like he was paying any attention. He walked behind Marsden and twisted his body slowly left to right so that the camera would pick up the details of the corridor. Three doors on one side, two on the other. A large metal shutter at the end that looked like a loading bay. As he walked, he grilled Marsden innocently about the security.

"I trust that your safety deposit boxes are secure," he said pompously.

"Oh, our new system is state of the art," said Marsden. Fully electronic. The only person that can get into your box is you. You will choose your own code and it will be stored in a fully encrypted computer system. I don't know the ins and outs, but I have been told that it uses 512-bit encryption." He smiled and shrugged. "I don't know if that means anything to you, but I've been assured that it's unbreakable. The boxes themselves are inside the vault, and the vault security is even better. Here we are."

He stopped at a large metal door with a bored-looking security guard sat on a chair.

"Morning Aseem."

The security guard struggled to get out of the chair and nodded a polite hello. He was a large man who looked like he was carrying nearly twenty stone. Getting out of the chair was the most exercise he'd had all morning.

"Is Steve not here yet?" said Marsden looking around.

As he spoke, a man in a smart grey suit stepped out of a nearby office.

"Hi Bob. Aseem." The newcomer reached a hand out to Buddy and shook it. "Good morning. I'm Stephen Briars, the manager. Thank you for using our services today Mr….," he left the sentence hanging.

Buddy went blank. Shit. What was his name? He hadn't considered that he might have to introduce himself. He had been concentrating on the surroundings and ensuring that the camera was picking everything up. He hesitated a beat and bought himself some time.

"Mr. Briars. Good to meet you. I didn't expect to have to bother you on such a trivial matter."

Marsden rescued him. "Mr. Briars is needed to open the vault. He has one of the two keys that are needed to allow access" he said. "Aseem, our head of security here has the other. As I said. It's very secure." He turned to the manager. "Mr. King here has rented one of our security boxes."

Buddy's heart returned to a normal rhythm.

"We pride ourselves on this new system," said Briars, continuing with Marsden's explanation about how secure the vault was. It was designed especially for the Larkins group and is state of the art. Look."

Buddy wondered if "state of the art" was in the sales literature. They all seemed to be banging on about it.

Briars walked about ten feet up the corridor and stopped in front of a card reader that was stuck to the wall. The security guard walked the other way and did the same. They both had a swipe card.

"Three, two, one," said Briars, and nodded to Aseem.

The two men swiped their cards at the same time.

"That's how you open the vault?" said Buddy amazed. "It looks like something you see in the movies when they arm a nuclear weapon."

Marsden laughed politely. "Both cards are required at once" he explained. "Oh, and we're not in yet."

Briars took his phone out of his pocket and approached a keypad next to the door, typing in a long number.

"Once we have swiped, Aseem and I both receive a text with a security code," he said. "It changes every time. If we get it wrong, then we have to swipe again. Three mistakes and the system locks down for half an hour and alarms start ringing at the security firm."

The door made a loud clink sound as the bolts were electronically drawn open.

"Luckily, we've not managed to do that yet. It would be a tad embarrassing."

He put his phone away and shook Buddy's hand again. "Good to meet you, Mr. King. I hope we can do more business in the future."

"Sure thanks," said Buddy. His mind was reeling. Getting through the swipe system was bad enough, but how the hell would they get a code from one of the designated phones.

Briars departed and headed back to his office as Marsden opened the vault door and Aseem dropped his heavy bulk back into the chair with a grunt.

"I have to say, that's pretty impressive," said Buddy, following Marsden into the vault. "Good to know that my items are going to be secure. Do you have 24-7 security? Is there always a guard here?"

"No. It's not covered overnight. Not necessary. The insurance company was happy that no one can get in with this new system. You may have noticed that there were cameras and motion detectors everywhere too, so if anyone got this far the silent alarms would be triggered."

Marsden stepped in front of a computer terminal that was hidden behind a plinth and touched the screen in a couple of places.

"OK. We have reserved you box number six. We need you to enter a passcode. Six digits, please. It's touchscreen." He moved away from the terminal and Buddy took his place.

The screen had a privacy filter so that it could only be seen if you were stood directly in front of it, but Marsden walked to the other side of the room anyway.

"You need to enter it twice and press 'Confirm'" said Marsden.

Buddy tapped in a code twice and pressed the "Confirm" button.

There was a click as a door swung open on his left.

"All yours," said Marsden. "Close the door behind you. It won't lock. Take as long as you need."

Buddy entered the door to a room that was just ten-foot square and almost empty. There was a table in the middle of the room, and twenty-five heavy-duty steel boxes in a five by five formation opposite the door. Each box was two-foot wide and a foot tall, so they ran from wall to wall and from the floor up to Buddy's neck. He closed the door and paced slowly around the room, ensuring that the camera picked up everything.

Box number six was on the second row and it was open. He put his briefcase on the table, clicked the latches, and removed a bunch of documents and the strange cube. He had inspected it at home and discovered that there was a button on one side that switched the box on. He pressed it now, and a green LED lit up. Good to go.

He placed the cube into box six, ensuring that the camera got a good look inside first, not that there was much to see. It was an empty metal box. He pushed the door closed and heard a whirring sound as the bolts moved into place. He gave the door a tug to confirm that it was locked tight.

Buddy gathered up his documents and returned them to the briefcase, took another walk around the room for the sake of the camera, and then left.

He thanked Marsden and nodded to Aseem on the way out.

Back in reception, Marsden shook his hand and passed him a business card.

"If you would like to transfer your business accounts to our bank, please do give me a call," he said.

"Thank you for your help. I am most impressed with what I've seen today and will certainly give it some thought. Your vault is very impressive. It's good to know that my articles are safe.

****

A few miles away, Amy Ross tapped away on her keyboard. Her box had connected to the bank's public wi-fi when it had been switched on and pinged her a message to tell her it was online. She now had three levels of security to get through.

First, she had to get into the bank's private network - their VPN, in order for her to access their systems.

Second, she had to crack the admin passwords on the CCTV system so she could get control of the cameras.

The third task, and the one that was likely to cause the most problems, was to access the system that controlled the vault. She had already warned Ace that this one was likely to be impossible. She was good, but the vault security would be something else. Ace hadn't seemed concerned. If she did manage to access the vault's security system, then the rest of the team wouldn't even be needed. If he could get access to the cameras, then he could deal with the vault later.

She set a timer running on her computer. Her record for connecting to a business VPN was just twelve minutes. She expected the bank to take a bit longer but liked to challenge herself.

A familiar smile appeared on her face as she was presented with the login screen.

"Go get 'em, Amy," she said to herself.

Chapter 28 – "Return to the Rhombus"

Tuesday 4th February

"Let's go Monroe" bellowed Simpson, striding past her desk and heading for the door. "Rhombus. Let's see if anyone recognizes our skateboarder friend."

Madison skipped behind him, trying to keep up.

"Have you got that photo of Danny we took? I still don't trust him. We can show that one too."

She ran back to her desk, scooped a photo from under a pile of paperwork, and trotted after him, not relishing the journey across town."

"How's Jackson getting on with the coffee shop trash?" he said, wheel-spinning out of the station car park and turning left in front of a Toyota. "That's our Monument guy, right? I'm losing track of which evidence goes with which diamond."

Madison held her breath and braced for the impact as the Toyota driver slammed the brakes on. Simpson had floored it though, and the police car sped away leaving the furious driver leaning on his horn in a cloud of dust.

"Yes. The Monument. He's bagging and tagging" she said, releasing her breath and glancing in the wing mirror. "Some of it's been destroyed with coffee dregs, but he's building up a bunch of fingerprints. It could be a while."

"We bloody had him," said Simpson banging the steering wheel. You must've been on that platform at the same time as him.

Madison had taken a good look at the CCTV that they had of the guy at the coffee shop but couldn't be one hundred percent sure if she had seen him on the platform or not.

"At least we got the diamond back," she said. "Looks like they did as we said and kept it out of the press."

Simpson grunted as he overtook a row of parked cars on a narrow street as a motorbike was coming towards them. Madison let out a squeal and grasped the seat as they passed each other with a fraction of an inch to spare. Simpson glared at her.

"Would you like to drive?" he said sarcastically.

"God, yes please," she said. "We might get there in one piece."

"Talk to me about the Tempest. Any progress there?" he said, ignoring her.

"We've picked up some CCTV from the surrounding streets. That's on Dickson's to-do pile. The drunken guy should be easy to pick out. We might get a shot of him without the stocking on his head."

"Probably see him rolling out of a pub," said Simpson smirking. "OK. Good. Did he get anywhere with the computer systems on the Sparkles case? He was looking for traces of hacking."

"Nothing yet."

"Shit. We need to lean on the courier. Felix something-or-other.

"Radcliffe. Like the actor."

"There's an actor called Felix Radcliffe?"

"No. Daniel."

"But his name's Felix."

"But he spells Radcliffe the same as Daniel."

Simpson was looking at her confused and started to veer towards a parked car, making her squeal again.

"Car" she yelled in a high-pitched voice, adopting her all too familiar crash position.

He wrenched the steering wheel to the right, and the car lurched and snaked down the road for a bit. He finally got the car under control.

"Felix Radcliffe" he continued as if nothing had happened. "I think we should pull him in."

Madison was still holding her breath and let it out slowly.

"Yes. Good plan" she said weakly. If we live to see another day, she thought.

****

"Hello again," said Angel, looking up from her phone. The blue strands in her hair were now bright pink. "Have you got some news?"

"Sadly, no arrests yet," said Madison, happy to be out of Simpson's car and on solid ground. "I've got some photos for you to look at though. People of interest in the investigation."

Madison took out the photo of Danny Diamond and showed it to the young girl, but she shook her head.

"Don't recognize him. He doesn't look like the sort of person we get in here."

Not in the daytime, thought Madison, fishing out the second photo.

"What about this one?" The photo that Danny had given them of Buddy on the skateboard was quite sharp considering it was taken at night on a mobile phone.

Angel paused. "There's something about the shape of his face. I don't remember a kid on a skateboard in here though. Difficult to be sure with the cap."

Madison pushed. "It could be a disguise. Take away the clothes and the skateboard. Could it be anyone you saw on the day of the robbery? Or just before."

She squinted a little closer. "The American guy," she said slowly. "With the guitar. Well, it could be. Put some hair and glasses on him. It's the same cute face." She handed the photo back. "Not one hundred percent sure. If it is, he's pretty good at disguises."

Madison was thrilled. As a positive identification it may not stand up in court, but the girl had linked the skateboarder and the American unprompted. It may give them another angle to follow.

"That's great, thanks. I don't suppose you've seen him since?"

Angel shook her head.

"OK. No worries. Thanks for your help. If you see him again, can you give me a call?" She handed her a business card.

"Sure. I kinda hope it wasn't him. He was nice."

Madison returned to the street where Simpson was puffing on his pipe.

"Dead end?" he said.

"Actually no. She thinks it might be the same guy. The American."

Simpson's eyebrows shot up. "No shit? Did you prompt her?"

"Nope. She made the connection herself. Looks like Dickson's bit of surmising might actually be right."

"Good lad," said Simpson, tucking his pipe away. "So, we have a new lead. Let's focus on the skateboarder at the station and any CCTV that we've got on him. Get Dickson to pull the video from the train network too. We might be able to see where he gets off."

They headed back to the car, a feeling of dread rising in the pit of Madison's stomach.

"Do you want me to drive back?" she asked hopefully. "You can smoke if you're a passenger." She figured that she'd rather die of passive smoking than by hitting a lamppost sideways at high speed.

"Not a chance," said Simpson, jumping in the driver's seat. "But good to know that you don't mind me smoking."

He pulled his pipe out, lit up, and spun out into the road one-handed, letting go of the steering wheel to change gear and nearly taking out a young boy with a dog.

"Chop chop, Monroe. Get on the blower. I can feel us closing in on the bastard."

****

Wednesday 5th February

Amy was in. The bank's VPN had taken her a couple of hours to crack. Once she'd connected to their servers, she fired up the software that ran the CCTV and alarm systems. It had taken her most of Monday evening, but she'd persevered and just before midnight the feed from the video cameras sprung up on her laptop and she punched the air with delight. She added an additional app to the software that allowed her to log in and out unnoticed, and even download recordings back to her laptop.

She had reported her findings back to Ace, and was now tackling the bank's other systems, and specifically the software that managed the vault. She'd never seen anything like it before. She'd expected it to be tough, but this had failsafe's all over it. If she stayed connected for too long, it would report an alert. If she entered a wrong password, it would report an alert. Every keystroke she did while in the vault software was recorded and stored, buried in the database where it could only be removed once she got access. She was leaving electronic fingerprints and she didn't like it.

Too many attempts and the bank might get suspicious. Nothing could be traced back to her, but a continuous attack may prompt them into action. If they thought their systems could be compromised, then they might consider a different branch for the diamond when it came into the country.

She had messaged Ace and he had agreed.

Pandora

Alerting the bank at this stage is too risky. We have eyes inside, and I am formulating the next part of the plan. We can get into the vault the old-fashioned way. Thanks for your help. Good job. I will be in touch.

She had spent many hours studying the cameras that she now had access to. The reception, the main bank lobby, the lift, the corridor outside the vault, the underground car park. As expected, there were no cameras in the vault itself. She had seen the vault open just once for a customer and had watched the two guys with their swipe cards. At first, she hadn't picked up on the additional security on the mobile phone, but after watching a recording of it back, she realized that one of the guys was copying the code from his phone.

Good luck cracking that one Ace, she thought. Maybe he would be calling her back to have another go.

The one ray of light was that the vault swipe card system was separate from the bank's other security entry system. After a few hours, she cracked that one too. Opening and closing the various doors and deactivating the alarms and motion sensors could now be done from the safety of her own home.

****

Ace was facing the same mobile phone dilemma that Amy had picked up on.

Buddy had uploaded the camera footage from his spy camera to GreySpider and Ace had pored over it meticulously. The quality was good, and the tiny built-in microphone allowed him to pick up most of the conversations that were going on.

Thanks to Pandora, he also had access to the bank's CCTV. This meant that he had full visibility of everything he needed. It didn't make it any easier to get into that vault though. The swipe cards might be manageable, but the mobile phone security was a real unexpected kick in the nuts. He really didn't want to have to kidnap anyone in order to do this. Stealing it without anyone knowing was always the plan. It made it harder for the authorities to know where to look.

By the time a sketchy idea started to come together, his carpet was nearly worn out and his pens were the straightest they'd been all year.

He started to compose another message to Pandora. He needed more information about the security guard, Aseem, and the bank manager Stephen Briars. She had already informed him that she couldn't override their swipe cards, and he couldn't steal them as they would be canceled and replaced. That left one solution. Borrow them, make a copy and return them without them knowing they'd gone missing.

Could he do the same with the phones? Surely the mobile phone security would be far lesser than the bank. If the bank manager's swipe card could be cloned, then maybe his phone sim could too.

He added to his message, spell-checked it, read it again, rubbed his forehead, got a bottle of mineral water from the fridge, and read it once more, finally hitting send. There was a moment of panic where he thought he'd sent it to the wrong person. Did he check that? A further check set his mind at rest, but he read the message once more while he was there.

His attention turned to the message that he had received at the weekend regarding trust within the team. He had wondered which one of them would bring this up first and was surprised that it was Budster. He thought it would be GreenZero. All four had replied to him and agreed to be part of the heist, but none of the others had mentioned it.

Ace retrieved a message that he had composed a while ago, but he still read it three times before hitting send.

Greetings fellow team members,

I hope you are all well and are looking forward to our endeavors. The plan is coming together, and I will shortly be sending you further instructions. In the meantime, I would like to set your minds at rest on the question of trust.

Please let it be known that I am very much a team player and have no interest in trying to cheat any of you out of your share of the rewards. However, I understand that words alone are unlikely to be enough in this vital matter. Therefore, I would like to inform you that I have no intention of being the one that collects the diamond from the bank. It will be one of you.

I will not even see the diamond until long after it is in our possession. I will add though, that I have a buyer for the diamond who has offered twenty million for it. This buyer has not come to me easily — if anything it has been the hardest part of the plan, so for us to succeed, I will need to be involved at the closing stages to collect our prize.

This is the part where I *will* invite you all to join me so we can each take our twenty percent share.

If you still have concerns, please let me know now. This is not something that we need to be worrying about later.

Chapter 29 – "Planning and discovery"

Wednesday 12th February

A week had passed, and Ace had spent much of it sending private messages back and forth with Pandora and had formulated the next part of his plan. He had also messaged GreenZero to try and find out a bit more about the drunken burglar. The guy claimed to be good at cards and roulette and apparently knew everything about racing, studied it religiously, and knew how to pick a winner. Ace wasn't impressed. The picture that he had put together was one of a drunken gambler who was trying to big himself up.

Pandora had done some digging on the bank manager Briars and the security guard Aseem. She had hacked their personnel records at the bank and their social media accounts. She had discovered names, addresses, phone numbers, salaries, credit information, family information and even managed to get into their internet service provider records to read their personal emails.

Aseem, it turned out was a poker freak. He lived alone, and online gambling was his favorite evening pastime – that and eating an inordinate amount of take-away pizza. He regularly joined online poker games and played till the early hours of the morning, generally making a decent profit. However, it seemed that it was his Monday night poker league down the local pub that he lived for. He constantly posted online about his wins, his losses, and his comebacks. He had even posted a photo of his cards that time he pulled the three of spades on the river making a straight flush and taking down the landlord for two hundred pounds who had trip Aces.

Ace still had his doubts about GreenZero, but at least he had a job for him. It would give him a chance to prove himself. He tasked him to get close to Aseem and relieve him of his bank vault swipe card. He had to clone it and return it without the security guard knowing it had gone.

Budster was given the same task for Stephen Briars. Ace sent him the details that Pandora had collected about the bank manager. Budster sent Ace back the details of his card cloning device as GreenZero was going to need one too.

Ace bought a second cloning machine and dropped it at EZ-Store, explaining to GreenZero that all he had to do was scan Aseem's card. A new card could be created by Budster later from the details collected.

It was Pandora who came to the rescue with the mobile phone problem. She spent a day writing a phone app and uploaded it to a private web portal. All they had to do was get their hands on one of the phones, download the app from the portal and install it. It would allow Pandora to intercept the text messages and forward them to another phone. She could activate the app at the appropriate time, read the text message with the vault code, and then delete it from the original phone so they didn't know that the vault had been accessed.

Ace was ecstatic. Pandora was coming up with solutions that even Ace himself had struggled with. He had pointed out that they would need to install the app on both phones though. The vault code would be sent to them both and if either Aseem or Briars received a text, they would know that the vault has been compromised.

GreenZero and Budster were given their instructions. They had a little over six weeks.

Ace had saved the most important job for Ozzy. It would be Ozzy that would be going to collect the diamond – but he would need to build something first. Ozzy had been sent the video footage from Budster's camera and he'd spent many hours studying the inside of the vault. He believed he could build what was required, but it was going to take some time. He informed Ace, that he should be able to do it but would likely need some help getting it inside.

Ace wrestled with this problem for three days. It broke his golden rule of keeping the team apart, but he finally agreed. The need to swipe both cards at the same time was causing him headaches too. A second person in the bank would resolve both problems. He told Ozzy to start work and that he'd get back to him. Maybe he could come up with an alternative solution before the end of March.

****

Friday 14th February

Madison was leaving for the day when Dickson called her over.

"What's up Robbie? I'm off out for a hot date tonight."

"Who's the lucky man?" said Dickson. "Going somewhere nice?"

"Italian in the West End and a show. Sadly, it's not a man though. Girly night out with my bestie Kate. Who needs a man on Valentine's day? We're off to see Magic Mike.

"Me and Tony saw that last month. It's great."

Tony was Dickson's boyfriend of two years. He tended to keep his private life to himself at work, mainly as he couldn't see Simpson and his old-fashioned ways totally understanding that he spent his evenings and weekends with a cross-dressing transsexual who used to be called Toni. Madison was a bit more understanding and he had confided in her when they had worked closely on a murder case earlier that year. If he was happy, then in her eyes, that's what was important.

Madison glanced at her watch. She was already running late.

"Sorry. I won't keep you" said Dickson quickly, turning back to his computer. "Take a look at this. I've finally found some time to take another look at the GreySpider forum. It's died down a bit, but there are over seven thousand messages there now."

"What you got?" she said, dropping her handbag on the floor and sitting down next to him.

"Well, I spent all my time looking at Ace's message, trying to see where it had come from. Complete dead end. His firewall is impenetrable, and the IP is private. There's no way to trace it back to him."

"English please Robbie. We're not all Mark Zuckerberg remember."

"Every computer is given a unique IP address when it connects to a network. Most people install a firewall to stop malicious attacks on their computer, but it can also allow a private IP to be used so that your unique number is not routed over the internet. You can't be traced."

"OK. Almost English, but I think I follow you."

"Well, Ace is protected. I tried everything, but I can't trace him. What I didn't do before was look at everyone else. I didn't see what we could gain. What can we do with several thousand IPs?"

"Makes sense. But I presume you have now." Madison looked at her watch again. Where was he going with this?

"Yes, and it's odd." He opened up a spreadsheet.

"So, we have 7,122 messages posted to the forum. There's a lot of people that posted multiple times, but we still have a total of 2,903 IP addresses of different people that have added something to the forum at some point."

"Sounds reasonable."

"This list shows them all with their IP addresses. Day one was quite busy. We have about four hundred different people who posted a message. That's fine. What's weird is if we remove the day one entries." He filtered the data so that it only showed messages from the 2nd January onwards.

"They're all the same," said Madison peering closer, intrigued now. "How can they all have the same IP address? They're different names. Different people."

"Almost the same," said Dickson. "Four of them are different."

"That doesn't make sense. What are you suggesting?"

"It's not a suggestion. It's a fact. The rest of the messages from the 2nd January onwards were posted from the same computer. Someone has been posting constantly under different names to make it look like a genuine forum." He paused. "And they've done it openly. It's not secure. It's almost like they wanted us to find out."

Madison scratched her head puzzled. "So, what about the other four?"

He changed the filter, and it left four names.

"GreenZero. Budster_007, Pandora and Ozzy92. They've all expressed an interest in the challenge in their posts. Nothing that gives anything away, but I'd lay good money on the fact that these might be our robbers."

Madison's jaw dropped. "Can you trace them?"

"Unfortunately, not. That's when I start to hit firewall issues again. These guys are protected the same way as Ace."

"What about the one we can trace? The one who's posted all the messages?"

"I'm on it now. Seems to me like someone wanted this hidden from the general GreySpider public. It's like they were directing the challenge to these four individuals. They were a day late though. Four hundred people saw it, including Danny Diamond and I guess a reporter picked up on it somehow." He smirked. "I'd bet half my wages that all these reporters are using these underground websites to look for stories."

"This is good Robbie. Look, I've really got to run. Have you told Simpson?"

"Not yet. I wanted to cross the T's. You know what he's like. If I can trace the sender, then we might be on to something. On its own, it's intriguing, but doesn't really bring us any closer to the robbers."

He's right, thought Madison. "Stick with it. Tell him in the morning regardless. He'll be just as pissed if he's the last to know. You can't win. Can you check other GreySpider forums for these four names? We might be able to see what other activities they've been up to."

"Good shout. I'll take a look. Go. Enjoy the show. I'll catch up with you tomorrow."

"I'll probably be pondering this all night. Leave me a message if you find anything. I won't sleep if not."

She grabbed her bag, gave him a wave, and called her friend Kate, leaving her a message to tell her she was already running late.

"Sorry honey. I'm only just leaving work. I haven't got time for pre-drinks. Can I meet you there?"

She almost ran to her car and performed a Simpsonesque maneuver as she screeched out of the police station car park, her mind thinking about Robbie's discovery.

Chapter 30 – "Poker Night"

Monday 17th February

Owen Kelly pushed the door open to the Royal Oak pub in Putney at 7:30pm. He was focused and surprisingly sober. He knew he had a task to do and had read Ace's instructions several times, but at the same time was looking forward to a night of poker. He had studied the video footage that had been passed to him and was fairly certain that he wouldn't have any trouble recognizing the security guard. There couldn't be many twenty-stone guys in the pub, and sure enough, he spotted him immediately as he approached the bar. Aseem was sat on a stool that was threatening to collapse under the strain at any moment. A banner had been strung up over the bar proclaiming, "Monday Night Poker League – Everyone welcome", and the tables were beginning to fill up. Aseem was gesticulating wildly as he relayed a story to the barman and as Owen was about to speak, they both laughed hysterically and Aseem banged the bar with his fist, his booming laughter reverberating around the small lounge bar.

"Hi," said Owen to Aseem and the barman with a smile. "Sorry to interrupt. I was hoping to join in tonight. Can you tell me how it works?"

"Hi," said Aseem brightly clambering off the stool. Owen could almost hear it sigh with relief. "You're more than welcome. I look forward to taking your money." He laughed and stuck a hand out. "I'm Aseem."

Owen took his hand and the squeeze he received from the man nearly broke his fingers. Aseem wasn't what he had expected. The video footage from the bank of the surly, uninterested security guard was a million miles away from the outgoing, friendly guy that stood in front of him. He was clearly in his comfort zone.

"Hi Aseem. I'm Owen. I've been meaning to come and join for weeks. I used to play in my local league, but it fell apart years ago, and I've never got around to starting again."

"Ah. A pro" said Aseem with a grin, "Where did you play?"

Owen had prepared a back story with minimal details and figured he could wing it if anyone got too interested.

"Oh, it wasn't around here. I used to live in Slough. Real shitty place though. The Red Lion. This looks a lot nicer."

"Yeh? I got a brother in Slough. The Red Lion? Is that the one on the High street in town or the one next door to the bookies?"

Oh shit, he thought. I could've picked any town but somehow managed to pick an area that the guy knew.

"The bookies. Crap location for me. Whatever I won at the poker got spent on the nags and vice versa. I rarely had much left by the end of the bloody week."

"I know that feeling brother. I try my best to keep my pot of money within these four walls. We just pass it back and forth week after week." He let out a hearty laugh again. "Not working in my favor at the moment though. These bastards keep taking it from me."

He had led Owen to one of the three round tables that were set up for the game and introduced the guys that were already sat down.

"Karl, Chris, Julius, Joe, and Buzz. This is Owen. He wants to give us his money."

Owen nodded to them and took a seat next to Aseem.

"Good to meet you," he said. "I hope he's wrong, but based on previous experience, I usually leave with a lot less than I started with. What's the buy-in here?"

"It's not too rich you'll be pleased to hear," said a short muscular guy with a crew-cut – probably Buzz, he thought. "We play Texas Hold'em. Twenty quid will get you a hundred chips but Romesh the landlord chucks a couple of pizzas on each table, so we get to eat too. Blinds start at one chip and double every half hour. There's normally twenty of us. When we get down to nine or ten, we take a break and bring everyone on to a final table. Last three standing split the take. Fifty percent to the winner, thirty percent for second, and twenty percent for third. The winners normally chuck a tip to the dealers though."

Owen did some quick maths. Twenty people paying twenty pounds each meant that the pot was four hundred. If he could beat this lot, he'd walk away with about two hundred pounds and have a good night out too. Why had he not found this place before? Even if he could only scrape third place, he'd get eighty and still be sixty pounds up. Certainly enough to pay for his drinks. The fact that he managed to convince Ace that he needed some "play money" and wasn't even using his own cash was a bonus. He'd taken fifty pounds from the envelope in the EZ-Store "heist" fund.

He fished a twenty out of his wallet and threw it on the table.

"Fuck it. Count me in" he said. "Who do I have to screw around here to get a beer?"

"That would be me my love, but you'll have to be quick coz we start in twenty minutes."

Owen spun around and came face to breast with a lady of about forty with bright orange hair and tattoos covering her neck, shoulders, and huge upper arms. Standing at about six foot two, she looked like she could've been a Russian weightlifter. He went red as the guys at the table let out a hearty cheer and Aseem thumped him on the back.

"Go easy on him Annie. It's his first time."

"Make sure you bring him back in one piece."

"Twenty minutes? You could do him twice and still have time to serve us all drinks."

The last quip came from a string bean of a guy with a goatee beard and dark sunglasses. Annie glared at him.

"And that's still twice as long as you normally last Julius," she said with her hands on her hips. "Maybe you want to watch. You might learn a thing or two." She winked at Owen who looked horrified.

She took their drinks orders and sauntered off.

Owen settled down and pulled out a pair of sunglasses. He had played a fair bit of poker before and the eyes could always give you away. Sunglasses were a common sight at poker matches, and in the next ten minutes, each player around the table did the same. Anyone walking in would have thought they'd entered a convention for the blind.

Just before 8pm, the drinks arrived, and the dealer sat at the head of the table, a pretty nineteen-year-old who they introduced as "Manda."

"Manda? Is that short for Amanda?" asked Owen.

"Nope, just Manda," she said with a smile. "I think my parents thought they were being cool. I kinda like it though."

She had a short, pixie-style haircut and the smile showed off cute dimples. He tore his eyes away from her. She was a distraction he could do without.

A bell rang at the bar - 8pm, and the game started.

Karl was sat to the left of Manda and he threw in the small blind – one chip, and Chris – to his left added the big blind – two chips. Each player was dealt two cards and the first round of betting began.

Owen was pleased to be sat next to Aseem. If the opportunity arose to grab his phone undetected, then at least he was close by. He also needed to find out if he kept the vault swipe card on him at all times, or whether he dropped it at home. The video footage clearly showed that Aseem had taken the swipe card out of his wallet when he'd swiped it to open the vault. There was a good chance that he kept it there all the time.

He glanced at his cards, Nine of spades and two of clubs. He promptly folded when the betting came around to him. Aseem threw in a chip to match Chris, Julius, and Buzz and Manda placed three cards face up – The Flop.

Texas Hold'em is the most popular poker game in the world. Each player has two cards that no one else can see. There is a round of betting, and then the Flop is produced - three new cards from the top of the deck. The idea is to make the best five-card poker hand out of the cards on display and the hidden cards in your hand. Another round of betting and another card is turned face up – known as the Turn. More betting and the final card – the River, is turned up. At this point, each player has seven cards that they can use to make their best five-card hand. A final round of betting for those players who haven't folded and the cards are revealed. The highest hand takes the pot. Each new round starts with two bets - the "small blind" and the "big blind". These bets are rotated around the table each round so that each player gets a chance to contribute.

Owen glanced at the Flop that Manda had dealt to the table.

QH, 10S, 2H

He was out of this round, but as with all good poker players, the game was to watch how the others reacted. Chris tapped the table – a sign that he wanted to bet nothing at this stage, but he was still in. Chances are the flop hadn't helped him, but it could mean that it had helped, but he didn't want to bet big and scare the other players off.

Julius surreptitiously looked at his cards again and threw a chip in the pot.

Buzz folded.

Aseem was looking straight at Julius, trying to read him. He picked up a chip without looking and threw it in the pot.

"I'm with you brother," he said with a grin.

Manda looked at Chris. He had to match the bet if he wanted to stay in. He didn't check his cards, but causally reached down and threw a chip into the pot.

"You got competition, my friend," said Aseem from across the table. It seemed as if Aseem was the talker of the table. There was always one.

Manda flipped over another card – The Turn and added it to the others.

QH, 10S, 2H, 10D

"Oooh hoo hoo. We have some tens" said Aseem. "You got any tens hidden in there Chrissy boy?" He was smiling as he said it but watching him for a reaction.

Chris smirked and threw three chips in the pot. Aseem's face dropped.

Julius pondered for a few seconds but folded. It was just Aseem and Chris.

Aseem leaned forwards and studied Chris closely.

"It's too early to be bluffing me boy," he said with a grin and matched the three chips.

Manda turned the final card – The River.

QH, 10S, 2H, 10D, 9H

Chris played with his chips, lifting up four or five at a time and dropping them back down again. Owen watched closely, taking it all in, looking for any little sign that could give away what the man was thinking.

He pushed five chips forwards.

Aseem puffed his cheeks out and blew air. "First hand and he's betting big already. What you hiding over there brother?" He took a swig of his beer and matched the bet. "I'm calling you. Show me what you got."

Chris flipped his cards over.

10H, AC

He had three tens.

"That's pretty good for a white man," said Aseem roaring with laughter. He flipped his own cards

AH, JH

"I got me a flush," he said with a whoop, dragging the chips towards him. Chris shook his head in dismay. Aseem had nothing until the nine of hearts had turned over.

"Jammy fucker" he mumbled.

Owen smiled. Aseem had played the odds. That last card could've been any heart or any king and he'd have taken the pot. A lot of the time though, the cards didn't matter. It was all about the players. Watching them, understanding when they bet big and why. Owen was thinking back to the round of betting following the Flop. Chris had pulled a pair of tens and hadn't placed a bet. Aseem had nothing but had bet on the promise of a heart or a king. There different approaches to play were logged in Owen's brain, along with the dialogue and the small twitches and gestures they made - Chris playing with his chips, Aseem sipping his beer. By the end of the night, Owen would have clocked several similar motions from each player on the table.

Manda had dragged the cards back and was dealing again while Aseem chatted inanely away.

"Keep 'em coming my lovely. We gonna take Chrissy boy down early this week."

At 8:30pm, the bell rang again to signify that the blinds were being doubled, and the pizzas arrived. Owen was down, but only by about ten chips. He was playing cautiously, losing a few chips here and there, but had taken a small pot with a pair of jacks. At this stage, he wanted to suss out the competition. He'd already decided that he wasn't going to worry about the security guard's swipe card and phone tonight. He had six weeks. He could get to know the man and pick his moment. Tonight, he would enjoy himself at Ace's expense.

The next hand was dealt, and he peered down at the Ace and King of hearts. The best hand he'd had by far. After a round of betting, the Flop came out.

AC, 4D, KD

He had two high pairs, Carl, Chris, and Julius had already folded. Joe bet three chips and Buzz matched them. Owen raised the bet to five.

"You raising brother? Hey – The new boys gone and got himself a hand." Aseem chortled and threw his cards in. "Too rich for me. I need another beer."

He got up and headed to the bar, leaving his mobile phone on the table less than a foot from Owen's hand. Owen's eyes flicked toward the phone. It might as well have been a mile away with six pairs of eyes watching him.

Joe and Buzz topped up the chips and Manda dealt the Turn. The King of Clubs.

AC, 4D, KD, KC

He'd just pulled a full house with Aces and Kings, almost unbeatable with the cards in play. He didn't register any emotion, even though he was silently celebrating, especially when Buzz bet high with ten chips. Joe had already folded, leaving just Owen and Buzz.

Owen spent a moment looking at his cards, pretending to contemplate his next move. He knew what his cards were without checking and already knew that he was going to push the ten chips forward. He scratched his chin and looked over towards Buzz who sat coolly staring down at his chips – about fifty of them. He'd had a bad run.

Owen matched the bet and turned to Manda for the River. She flipped over the four of hearts.

AC, 4D, KD, KC, 4H

Buzz didn't hesitate. He pushed his whole stack of chips forward. "I'm all in."

Owen's heart leaped. The only way that Buzz could beat him was with two Aces. He looked at his cards once more as Aseem came back.

"Shit. I miss all the fun. Look at that stack. You gone all in Buzzy-boy?"

Buzz was looking nervous. He'd expected the big bet to scare off Owen, but Owen was calmly pushing his stack of chips into the pile.

"Call," he said.

"The new boy is here to p-lay" screamed a delighted Aseem. Show them cards Buzzy. What you hiding?"

Buzz turned his cards. King of spades and four of clubs.

Owen let out his breath, flipped his cards, and took the pot. He had almost doubled his stash in one hand and was now the clear leader on the table.

"And Buzzy boy is out" yelled Aseem, clapping Owen on the back. "Have a slice of pizza as a consolation prize, my friend." He lobbed a slice to a dazed Buzz who picked up his pint and sat back mournfully.

"Nice hand," he said graciously. "I thought I had you."

****

At 9:30, the bell rang, and play was suspended while the remaining players moved to one table. Owen, Aseem, and Julius were still playing and they were joined by Alex, Frank, and the landlady Gina from table two, and Roley, Dave, and Dave from table three.

Owen did a double-take.

"Are you two brothers?" he said to Dave.

"Twins" replied Dave. I'm two minutes older."

"And your both called Dave?"

Dave looked at him as if he couldn't understand why this would be a problem.

"Yes."

"Your parents called you both Dave?"

"Still yes."

"Doesn't it get confusing?"

"No."

As he said it, the landlord called over "Oi Dave. Are you still playing?" and they both looked up.

"Yes," they said in unison.

Aseem was shaking his head laughing. "You'll get used to this lot," he said, beginning to slur his words a little. "Their dad's called Dave too. Think it's a tradition. They've got a sister called Davina too."

"No shit?" said Owen. "I used to know a Davina. Nice girl. Wonder if it's the same one."

"You talking about my sister?" Dave two glared at Owen intimidatingly. He'd been knocking back whiskeys all evening and was getting a bit punchy.

"Hey, cool it Davey the second. Owen's cool. Well, he is when he's not pulling Aces out of his arse." He snorted in his pint and beer shot out of his nose and hit an unsuspecting Roley.

"Shit. Really? Come on man" said Roley, dabbing at the mucus with a napkin. "You snotted on me."

That set Aseem off again and his laughter turned into a cough. He went bright red and Owen had to whack him on the back several times. He eventually stopped and clutched at the table, breathing heavily.

"You OK man?" said Owen. "Thought we were gonna lose you."

"I'm good," he said breathlessly. He took another large gulp of his beer. "Shall we play?"

Owen had just finished his beer and called for another as Manda dealt the cards. It was his fifth, and he was beginning to feel the effects. He was relaxed and enjoying himself though.

For the next half an hour, he watched his stash of chips diminish rapidly. Aseem was having a run of luck and he was sat with the largest pile. The next closest was Gina. Owen was about fifth. The two Dave's had both crashed and burned one hand after another.

Another half-hour and another beer and Owen was struggling. Frank and Julius had fallen, and Owen was down to his last twenty-five chips. Another ten minutes and he wouldn't be able to afford the blinds to play. At ten-thirty when the bell rang again, Owen pulled a rabbit out of the hat and doubled his chips with a bluff on a pair of sixes. Roley bowed out, leaving Owen, Aseem, Gina, and Alex.

If he could hold on for one more place, then he'd win a prize. Gina had taken the lead, with Aseem a close second. Alex had about seventy-five chips, and Owen just over fifty. Owen had about two hands to survive before the blinds came around and would finish him off. He looked at his cards and groaned out loud.

"Fuck's sake," he said under his breath.

The beer had taken away his focus. He wouldn't have let a sound out an hour ago.

"And the new boy's on the ropes," said Aseem enthusiastically.

Despite his drunken appearance, Aseem had managed to stay well in the game. Owen wondered if it was an act. He was a large guy and could probably sink twice as many pints as the average guy. Owen had lost count, but he must be on nine or ten he thought.

He folded his nine of diamonds, two of clubs combo, and prayed for a better last hand.

His prayers came true early though. Alex had been dealt a pair of queens and bet big. Aseem pulled a lucky straight on the River and put Alex out of the game.

Aseem got out of his chair and started wiggling his massive butt and singing "Another one bites the dust."

Owen couldn't believe it. He was out the next hand, but he'd managed a third place. He was going to leave with more money than he started with. The last order bell rang, and he grabbed himself and Aseem another pint.

Gina and Aseem battled it out for another twenty minutes before Aseem went all-in on the Flop when he'd pulled three tens. Gina stayed with him, holding a pair of queens, but the cards went against her and she bowed out.

"Thank you, my friends," said Aseem, bowing low and nearly falling on his pile of chips as the remaining punters clapped, some genuine, some jeering the big guy. Despite his brashness and drunkenness, it seemed he was popular.

They finished their pints together, took their prizes, and were booted out of the pub at 11:20, holding on to each other for support.

"Which way you heading?" slurred Owen.

"Tube my man" Aseem slurred back.

They weaved their way up to the District line, discussing their evening and various hands, and navigated their way through the barriers and escalators, and finally collapsed onto the train.

Owen was nearly asleep when Aseem jumped up.

"Good to meet you, my friend," said Aseem giving him a bear hug. "Same time next week?"

"I'll be there. Was a good evening. Glad I finally came down."

They swapped phone numbers and Aseem lurched to the doors as they opened.

"Hey, wait. You dropped something" said Owen, trying to focus on the object on the seat where Aseem had been sitting. Aseem turned, wobbled, and nearly fell over, grasping at the handrail.

"Ah thanks, brother. I'd have been in trouble if I lost that."

He turned and picked up his wallet from the seat.

"...and not just the winnings. My boss woulda killed me." The doors slid shut leaving him swaying on the platform. "Take care, my man. See you next week."

Chapter 31 – "The Landlord scam – A walk in the park"

Thu 20th February

"And this is the bedroom," said Shanice, escorting the young couple into a large bright, tastefully decorated room. "It's a bit bigger than a lot of flats on our books and has built-in wardrobes. Oh, and it looks out over the garden too. Lovely to wake up to."

It had taken a bit longer than Buddy had hoped to get a bite, but Shanice had taken the call yesterday and was showing James and Chloe the flat.

"This is really nice hun," said Chloe, looking up at him through her trendy sunglasses. Why she was wearing them on such a grey day, Shanice couldn't figure.

"It's the best one we've seen so far" admitted James. Shame it's only got one bedroom though.

"You know we can't afford a second bedroom in this area," said Chloe. "I'd rather sacrifice the second bedroom and be at work in twenty minutes."

"True," he said. "But we're stuck for a year if it doesn't work out. I want to make sure we get the right place."

Shanice sidled over. "Don't tell anyone you got it from me, but the landlord might take a six-month rental. He did it for me on my flat. I live upstairs."

James brightened at this news. "Do you think he might? I'd be happier with a six-month lease." Shanice wasn't sure if his change of heart was due to the six-month lease or the fact that she lived in the same block. He had been a bit leery as she'd shown them around.

"He'd still want the deposit and the first month in advance. I wasn't sure he was going to go for it when I asked, but I offered to pay him in cash and that swung it." Shanice had practiced her lines with Buddy a few nights before. She leaned in and whispered, "guess he doesn't put it through the books that way."

"I really like this," said Chloe. "The location is perfect, and we get the garden too. It's not going to hang about."

"True enough," said Shanice. "I have another viewing just after lunch. It's a second viewing too."

"If we can get the deposit to you before lunch, will you cancel the second viewing?"

"Let me call the landlord and see. You want me to push for the six-month lease?"

Chloe was nodding her head profusely at James.

"Sure. If that's OK? We can get the cash" said James.

Shanice punched Buddy's number into her phone.

"Hey sexy," said Buddy. "Have they turned up yet?"

"Hi Mr. Carter. I'm at the garden flat with Mr. Jonas and Miss Parker. They're interested, but they're not sure if they can commit for a year and were hoping for a six-month lease, and they want to know if you'll take it off immediately if they pay the deposit this morning."

"Cheap bastards," said Buddy laughing. 'That's a killer accent - good job. Go for it. We're not seeing any money after today. They can have a three-month lease for all I care."

"Two months upfront?" said Shanice doubtfully, frowning at the young couple. "I'll ask but that might be a stretch."

Buddy nearly choked. Shanice was going off-script.

"Don't push it. You don't want to lose them" he warned.

"Let me ask. Can you hold?"

"Go careful," said Buddy.

"Well, he's not said no," said Shanice turning to the couple. "As I suspected, he wants cash, but he'd like the deposit and two months upfront instead of one. That's two-thousand eight hundred now, but your next payment won't be until May. He did say that as the flat's been cleaned, I can leave the keys with you today and he'll give you the rest of February for free too."

"We could break into the wedding fund," said James thoughtfully, his brow furrowing at the thought. "What do you think? We can pay it back if we've got no rent for two months".

"As long as we do," said Chloe looking worried. "It's taken us a year to save that up."

Shanice nearly bailed. How could she take the savings from this young couple? They seemed really nice. Buddy had warned her that you couldn't get emotionally attached to anyone in this game, and now she could see why he had felt the need to tell her.

"There are a few banks up the high street," she said helpfully, suppressing the wave of guilt they swept over her.

"I don't know," said Chloe. "It's the wedding fund. Maybe we should go for the twelve months and only pay one upfront."

Buddy was listening in and yelling down the phone for Shanice. She put the phone to her ear.

"They're not gonna go for it. Tell them that I'll drop the deposit to nine hundred too" he said frantically.

Shanice held her nerve. "Why don't you go in the garden and talk about it," she said. "It's a pretty good deal with the free week and a half."

They left Shanice and headed into the garden.

"I'll call you back," said Shanice to Buddy and hung up before he could say anything."

****

Two hours later, Shanice was sat on Buddy's sofa wrestling with the cork on a bottle of champagne.

"I can't believe you got away with that," he said for the third time.

"If I lowered the price it would've looked desperate," she said. "I did feel bad though. The guy convinced the girl that they'd have the wedding fund topped up by the end of April. I feel like I've stolen more than just their money. It's their wedding. Every girl's dream. When they find out they've lost it, it will destroy her."

"And you being such a good catholic girl too," said Buddy, shaking his head in mock dismay. "Do you want a hand with that?"

He took the champagne from her. "It's not even midday. You're starting early."

"It's not every day I make over a grand in a morning," she said as the cork popped out. "I could get used to this."

"Not feeling so bad now then?" he said. "Seriously though, I hope the disguise was as good as you say. You don't ever want them finding you."

Shanice pulled a blonde wig out of her bag, tied her red hair up and plopped it on her head, and put on a pair of wide-rimmed glasses.

"Good morning Mr. Barnes," she said in the posh voice she had adopted earlier. "Please can you pass me a glass of fizz?" She sounded like one of the girls from that dreadful television show "Made in Chelsea".

"OK. That's pretty good" admitted Buddy. "I'm not sure I would have recognized you."

They clinked glasses and Shanice downed her drink in one. She dropped the glass on the table, pushed him back on the sofa, and kissed him passionately.

"Mmmm. I like posh Shanice" he said, kissing her back. "Does she have the same rules about sex as catholic Shanice?"

They had spent two evenings together in the last week and despite lots of kissing and the occasional sneaky grope, Shanice had stood her ground. Buddy was as horny as a teenager at an end-of-term school prom.

She pulled back, laughing, and removed the wig. "Posh Shanice is going back in the box," she said topping up her drink. "Thanks for letting me join in with this Buddy. The money's really gonna come in handy. If you've got anything else I could help with...".

Buddy sat up. How should he approach this without telling her the full story?

"Well there is something, but the pay-off may not be for a while. It's part of something bigger. I can't say too much at the moment – mainly because I don't know the details myself, but I've got a job that you could help with."

"I think I owe you after today," she said. "What do you need?"

"I need you to lose your dog."

****

Buddy had gone over the plan with Shanice, and she had agreed without asking too many questions. He had promised that if things went as planned, they would be getting a lot more than the money that she had made on the landlord scam.

He had spent many hours looking at the information that Ace had given him about Stephen Briars, the bank manager, and had found out three things that would help get what he needed.

Firstly, the guy was a dog fanatic. He had two Labradors – one black, one chocolate - that he completely doted on. His social media was full of pictures of them with captions like "Marmaduke eating his own tail" and "Marmite chasing the ducks." It was embarrassing for a middle-aged man. He even had a dog sitter when he was working at the bank so they wouldn't be left alone for too long. Maybe it helped him with the ladies, thought Buddy. The black one was pretty cute.

Secondly, he had discovered that Briars lived alone. Buddy had spent three early mornings watching him and had found a pattern. Briars walked the dogs at his local park before work each day. At 7am on the dot, he would leave the house, walk the same five-minute route to the park entrance, and spend half an hour doing a circular route around the lake with the dogs playing at his heels.

Finally, and most crucially, amongst Briar's emails, Buddy had found that he was signed up to a service called "SecuraDoor."

SecuraDoor allowed him to operate his home from his phone. Initially, they started out as a security company, allowing doors and windows to be opened remotely, but they had branched out to heating systems, music, security cameras, curtains, lighting, and any other number of appliances.

He could just imagine Briars switching music and television on for his prized pooches at different times of the day. Truth was, Briars even owned a video screen so that he could video call the dogs to make sure they were OK.

With Shanice's help, Buddy could hopefully get access to the phone and the swipe card at the same time.

It was 7am and he was sat in his car watching Briars' house as he had done previously. Almost to the second, the front door opened, and the bank manager came out to a bright morning with his dogs in toe. They turned left at the end of his driveway and headed for the park. Buddy called Shanice.

"He's on his way. Five minutes before he enters the park. Probably fifteen to twenty before he reaches the far side of the lake."

"I'm ready," she said. "What's he wearing?"

"Same as usual," said Buddy. "Jogging bottoms and blue Reebok sweatshirt. You should be able to spot him by the labs. One black, one brown."

Shanice had pictures of the dogs from his Facebook account.

"You got my Skype name memorized?" said Buddy.

"Budster_007. So childish" she said laughing.

"Hey. I was a Bond fan when I was younger" he said defensively. "Still am actually. What do you expect?"

"I expect you to die Mr. Bond." She did a pretty passable impression of Blofeld, the villain from some of the early James Bond films.

"Haha. That's pretty good. I didn't know you were a fan. We'll have to have a marathon session. You can dress up as Miss Moneypenny."

"You just like me in a wig," said Shanice laughing. "I'll call you shortly. I've got a dog to find." She hung up.

****

"Buddy" called Shanice loudly. "Buuuuuuddy. Where are you, you stupid mutt."

She had a dog lead in her hand and was walking by the lake, frantically looking left and right when Briars came towards her.

"Buddy." She whistled. "Come on Buddy," annoyed now.

"Everything OK?" said Briars, stopping and making sure his dogs were nearby. Marmaduke was having a pee and Marmite was trying his hardest to sniff the older dog's bottom. "Marmite. No."

"It's my dog," said Shanice tearfully. "He ran after a squirrel about fifteen minutes ago. I can't find him anywhere." She had the blonde wig on again, and at Buddy's request had worn a sexy pair of tight white jeans that accentuated her figure. She looked hot.

"What kind of dog is he?" said Briars, looking her up and down as he spoke to her.

"He's a Dalmatian. Easy to spot. I can't believe I've not found him yet. My mum's gonna kill me."

Buddy had suggested using "mum" rather than boyfriend or husband. It might make Briars more pliable.

"Buddy" she yelled again.

"Is there anything I can do to help?" said Briars. "I know what it's like. I lost Duke over here once. I was beside myself for about half an hour. Turned out that he'd made his way back home and was waiting in the garden. Have you called your mum to see?"

"My phone's dead," said Shanice mournfully. "Bloody charger's being playing up."

Briars took his phone out and unlocked it. "Here, use mine. I'll take a look over by the pavilion. Don't worry. We'll find him."

"You're a lifesaver. Thank you so much" she said, taking the phone and putting a grateful hand on his arm.

When he was a few steps away, she fired up the Skype app on the phone and called Buddy.

"Barnes. Buddy Barnes" he said in his best Sean Connery impression.

"I've probably got two minutes tops" she whispered.

"OK. Go to the web and type in "www.filesharez.co.uk/535771." It will ask you for a password.

Shanice's fingers flew over the touchscreen phone. She glanced up and saw Briars was still walking away from her calling loudly for the fictitious Buddy.

"You called the dog Buddy?" he said incredulously.

"Yep. He's cute and always trying to hump me" said Shanice. "OK. What's the password?"

He laughed "Pepperoni. With a capital P"

Jesus. Couldn't you have something easier to spell?"

"P E P....."

"Don't worry, I'm way ahead of ya. OK. It's downloading."

"Good job. Can you fire up the SecuraDoor app and open his front door?"

Shanice glanced up "Will do. He's coming back. I'll stall him as long as possible and call you when he's on his way home."

She hung up, turned away from Briars, and started calling for Buddy while frantically searching for the SecuraDoor app. She found it, pushed the door icon, and selected "Open."

She half expected it to ask her for a password, but it seemed that Briars hadn't set one. The phone lock was good enough she guessed.

"Any luck?" said Briars approaching her from behind.

The phone pinged as the download completed and the program started to install.

Come on. Come on.

"It was engaged," she said. "I called my friend who lives nearby, but he's already on his way to work. I hope you don't mind."

"No, it's fine. Why don't you try your mum again?"

This guy was making this too easy.

"Thanks. I take it you didn't see him over there." She nodded to the pavilion.

"Afraid not."

She called her works number, and it went through to the answerphone, as she knew it would.

"Oh, Hi mum. It's me. I've lost Buddy." Her voice cracked as if she was upset. "He's not come home has he?"

She heard another ping as the program finished installing.

"He is? Oh, thank God. I've been searching for ages. I've got this really nice guy helping me too."

Briars smiled at her and mouthed "You've found him?"

She nodded.

"OK. I'm so glad he's safe. I'll be back in a bit."

She hung up. How was she going to close down the web browser without him getting suspicious? She looked at him.

"He's at home," she said relieved. "Thanks so much. She started to hand the phone back but stopped. "Look, this is probably a bit forward, but do you mind if I put my phone number in here? I'd like to take you for a coffee to say thanks when you've got some time." She flushed, embarrassed.

"I'd like that. Maybe we could have a doggy date. I could meet Buddy."

Oh, God. This guy was a real dog freak.

She laughed. "Sounds good." She turned back to the phone, closed the web, and even deleted the skype call log to Buddy. She opened the contacts list and added "Billie," considered making up a phone number, but then entered her own. If Buddy couldn't find what he needed, then she'd be able to get Briars out of the house again.

She smiled. "I'm Billie with an IE" she said.

"Good to meet you Billie with an IE. I'm Stephen. Which way are you walking? I'll walk with you."

She picked the longest route to the park entrance and started walking as slow as she could get away with and chatting inanely. I hope you're in Buddy, she thought to herself.

Chapter 32 – "Break-In"

Buddy was waiting by Briars' front door when he heard a click, and it popped open. You beauty Shanice, he thought, smiling. Don't you just love technology? He glanced over his shoulder, checking no one was around, slipped inside, and closed the door.

He found himself in a bright hallway that led down to a modern kitchen. A large lounge/diner was on the left, and a staircase ran up to the bedrooms. He didn't have much time to waste, so took the stairs two at a time. Starting upstairs made sense for two reasons. The swipe card was most likely to be in the bedroom – maybe hung up with his suit. Also, if Briars came home without warning, it would be harder to make a quick escape from the upper floor. The bank manager was likely to come in and go straight upstairs to get changed for work.

He found three bedrooms on the first floor and started in the largest of the three. The bed had clothes laid out on it – the same grey suit he had worn at the bank when Buddy had met him, and an expensive, crisp white shirt with dog-head cufflinks. It seemed that the doggy passion even spread to his dress sense. He could imagine finding some novelty dog head slippers when he looked in the wardrobe.

He didn't. He did find four more suits though – all grey, and shirts that were varying shades of blue and white. It seemed that the cuff links were the most frivolous item he owned. Everything else fitted the persona of a dull forty-something bank manager. He checked all the suits in the cupboard, and carefully lifted the one off the bed. No swipe card.

He opened drawers, bedside cabinets and even checked the dressing gown hanging on the back of the door. No swipe card.

The time ticked away.

He looked into the second bedroom but didn't stay long. Why would he keep the bank vault swipe card in a bedroom that he didn't use? The third bedroom had a desk with a computer and was being used as a home office. He checked the desk thoroughly, finding pictures of his dogs and a picture of an older lady that he presumed would be Briars' mother. No swipe card though.

A quick look in the bathroom revealed nothing, so he headed downstairs to the kitchen. He was very aware that time was running out. Maybe he would keep it by the kettle?

The only thing he found of interest in the kitchen was a key hook with a set of car keys on it. He grabbed them and used the car key fob to unlock the BMW parked outside. It would make a lot of sense to keep the swipe card in the glove box, even though it would be easier to steal. He could check the car on the way out.

He returned the keys to the hook and was checking the lounge when his phone rang making him jump.

"He's just left the park" whispered Shanice anxiously. "If you're still inside, get out."

"I can't bloody find it," said Buddy, heading for the door. "I need to check his car. Do you think I have time?"

"He's got about a hundred yards and then he's turning left onto his street. He'll see you come out of the driveway if you're not gone in about thirty seconds."

"Shit. OK."

He hung up, sprinted for the front door, closed it behind him, and opened the BMW's passenger door. A quick look on the seat and the glove box revealed nothing. He checked the side pockets on the doors and the central console. He even looked over the headrests and scanned the back seat. No swipe card.

"Shit. Shit."

Could he stay ducked down behind the car and look properly while Briars was getting dressed? He considered it but then remembered the dogs. They'd sniff him out in seconds. He closed the car door, and casually strolled out of the driveway, walking away from Briars, and also away from his own car. It would be less suspicious. He could double back when Briars was inside. He couldn't lock the BMW, but Briars would assume he'd forgotten the night before.

Buddy was pissed off. He'd blown his chance. He wouldn't be able to pull the same stunt with the phone again. He was pretty certain that the card wasn't in the house or car though. He'd only had fifteen minutes, but he'd checked all the places that Briars was likely to put something that he took to work each day.

He turned a corner, stopped, and peered back around the hedge. In the distance, he could see Briars walking towards his house. He called Shanice.

"I'm out. I struck out though" he said miserably. "Give me five minutes and I'll come get you. How did you get on with the download?"

"All good I think," said Shanice. "I had to promise him a date though."

"You what?"

She laughed. "I'll tell you later. Come and get me. I'm freezing my tits off."

****

Buddy and Shanice were back in the car and sat opposite Briars' driveway.

"And there was nothing hanging up by his keys?" Shanice was getting Buddy to retrace his steps.

"No. It wasn't there. Unless he keeps it inside his cornflakes packet or something. I checked everywhere."

"Not in the car?"

"No. Well, I didn't have long, but again – it would be in the glove box or the door pockets. It wasn't there."

"Boot?" suggested Shanice.

"Possibly. But why would he keep it in the boot?"

"I don't know." She frowned. "Did he have a briefcase in the house?"

"I didn't see one."

"Maybe he keeps it in the boot and the swipe card is in the briefcase."

"Shit. I didn't think of that." He checked his watch. "He's only been in ten minutes. I might have time."

"Are you kidding?" yelled Shanice. "What if he catches you?"

"Let's find out," said Buddy with a grin.

He jumped out of the car. "If he comes out, stay low," he said. "He might recognize you."

"What if he recognizes you? You only spoke to him a few weeks ago."

"I was blonde then, and I had dodgy facial hair. Don't worry. I'll be quick."

"Buddy. No."

He was gone. She watched him dash across the road and into the driveway, ducking down behind the BMW. She glanced at the upstairs windows, praying that Briars wasn't looking out. She couldn't see him. Buddy opened the driver's door and pulled the catch to open the boot. He closed the door again and walked to the back. Thank God it's reversed in, thought Shanice. At least he's out of sight.

The boot lid lifted.

Ten seconds passed.

Twenty.

Come on Buddy. What the hell is taking so long?

The front door opened, and Briars clicked his key fob. The lights on the car blipped and Shanice threw herself down out of sight so he wouldn't see her.

****

Buddy had found the briefcase and was searching it when Briars came out and opened the car.

"Fuck."

He had already realized that the swipe card wasn't there. He closed the briefcase and reached up, pulling the boot lid down as quickly and quietly as he could. A glance to the right and he saw Briars talking on his phone. He couldn't close the boot fully without it making a noise, so he left it resting on the catch, about a quarter of an inch open. Hopefully, he wouldn't notice.

He dived down and scooted under the car feet first, staying as low as possible.

"I'm just getting in the car now" Briars was saying. "Will probably be about twenty minutes."

Buddy heard the car door close, and the engine started. The car moved a couple of feet forwards, revealing Buddy's head and torso, and stopped again.

The door opened. What Briars would think when he reached the boot and found a man lying under his car, Buddy had no idea. He didn't want to give him the chance. Scoot back under or roll away? He had a split second to make a decision and went for the roll. He ducked down behind the passenger side of the car and stayed as low as possible. Briars was lifting the boot, puzzled. He clicked it shut. Leaned on it to check it was closed and returned to his seat. Buddy eased slowly back to the rear as the car drive off.

Please don't look back. Please don't look back.

He didn't. The car bumped off the driveway and onto the road leaving Buddy laying on the gravel, his heart pumping out of his chest.

He waited for a minute, and then got up, brushed himself down, and returned to his car.

"You idiot." Shanice punched him on the arm. "I nearly had a heart attack when he came out."

"You and me both" Buddy chuckled. "Good job he was distracted by the phone."

"You get it?"

"No. Found his briefcase, but no swipe card. Just had some paperwork in it."

"You mean you did all that for nothing?" said Shanice in disbelief.

"Looks like it."

"So, what now?"

"I have no idea."

He started the car and headed home.

****

"So, are you going to tell me who he was?" Shanice sipped her coffee back at Buddy's. She had told him how the encounter in the park had gone.

Buddy hesitated. He didn't like lying to her, but at the same time, he wasn't about to tell her about the bank heist.

"He's just a means to get into a secure place. That's all I know at this stage." Buddy was wondering whether or not she knew that he was a bank manager. They'd been talking for a good fifteen minutes on the walk back from the park and she'd soon put two and two together. She hadn't said anything though.

"Have I got to go on a date with the guy so you can take another look?"

Buddy laughed. "Hopefully not. I wouldn't fancy going in when the dogs are in there, and I'd have to break in. He might get suspicious if you try and take his phone again."

"Thank God for that. He was a bit smarmy. I gave him my bloody phone number too. I'll have to make my excuses. What you gonna do next?"

"Go back to the drawing board I guess."

Buddy did have one idea, but he didn't want to check it out while Shanice was there. If the swipe card wasn't in Briars' house or car, then there was only one place it could be. In his office. It made sense. The office was secure, and the card was independent of the rest of the security.

He wanted to watch the footage that he got from the bank again.

Chapter 33 – "Deadline"

Tuesday 25th February

Oscar eased himself into the bath and groaned when the hot water touched the welts on his buttocks. Brandy had stayed over on Saturday night, and he was still feeling the after-effects of the table tennis bat that she had vigorously employed to his butt cheeks. It had been bearable until she uttered the words "Let's try the stipple side" and gave her infamous cackle. She'd asked him to spank her too, but despite the pain she'd bestowed upon him, he couldn't bring himself to put too much force behind it. Her words rang in his ears.

"Harder you pussy. Come on. Is that all you've got? Spank. Me. Harder."

How long could he keep this up for? Every weekend was becoming a marathon of pleasure and pain, with more emphasis on the pain as time passed. He was beginning to dread Saturdays.

He turned his mind back to the heist and to the project that Ace had him working on. He had had to hire a lock-up nearby to do the work as he didn't have enough room in his apartment. Ace had provided the necessary rent money for the garage-office combo, and also for the materials, and Oscar was nearly halfway through the build. He had added a Bluetooth connection to the item so that it could be operated remotely. Ace had passed this information to Pandora and she had confirmed that she would be able to connect to it once it was inside the bank.

Not for the first time, he thought about the team. Ace had so far managed to keep them apart, giving each of them individual tasks, being the go-between for messages, but not allowing them to connect or communicate with each other. He understood why

Ace had done this – it kept him in control as he was the only one who knew the full plan, but he found it frustrating. Oscar had been told that it would be him going in to steal the diamond, but as yet had not been given any further info.

"Full details will be divulged imminently" was all he had managed to receive from Ace when he had asked.

He stretched in the water, easing his sore backside and the ever-present throb that he now had in his over-used groin area.

His phone pinged and he grabbed it. A message from Brandy.

"Gd morning hot stuff. What u up 2? Thanks 4 having me on Sat – multiple times". She'd left a crying-laughing emoji. "I just can't get enough of u. We should do a weekend away 2gether. I really let myself go when I stay in a hotel. CU on Friday night lover xxx".

God. A whole weekend away with Brandy? Normally the idea of going away with his girlfriend wouldn't be quite so disconcerting. It would be good to get away before the end of March and the pressures of the heist though. Maybe he could take her somewhere nice. Paris or maybe Amsterdam? He wondered whether that would just be a waste. Knowing her, they were highly unlikely to leave the hotel room.

He messaged her back.

"Sat in bath easing my poorly butt cheeks. I need to take a cheese grater to that table tennis bat. Would love to. How about Paris or Amsterdam? xxx"

While he waited for her to reply, he fired up GreySpider to see if there were any updates from Ace.

There was….and the subject read "*** URGENT PLAN UPDATE ***." This didn't sound promising.

GreySpider Private Cluster #371238

Date: 25-02-2020 09:00

From: AceOfDiamonds

To: {Private List}

Subject: *** URGENT ***

Team,

We have a slight change of plan.

Our private collector from Tahiti has brought the date forward. Unfortunately, this was unforeseen and totally out of my control.

The diamond will now reach the bank on Tuesday 10th March where it will reside for just forty-eight hours.

We need to be ready by the 9th March. I understand that this time pressure will cause some concerns to you and your individual tasks, but it is unavoidable.

Please confirm that you will have your tasks completed in good time.

    Oscar sat up in the bath in shock and re-read the message. The 9th March was less than two weeks away. He'd just lost three weeks on his project, and he wasn't even sure that he was mentally prepared to enter the bank yet. He did some quick calculations. He'd have to double the hours that he was currently spending on the task each day to get it finished in time. He had a show planned with Brandy on Friday night back at the Mirage. Maybe he could cancel that. It might give him some breathing room, but he really needed the money. Saying that, if they managed to get away with the diamond, then money issues would be a thing of the past. Letting Brandy down was more of an imminent problem though. It might result in him being punished — something that his backside would never forgive him for.

He fired a quick message back to Ace.

Ace,

This is going to be extremely tight, but it's doable. As mentioned previously, I will need help setting up in the bank though. It will not be possible to do this on my own. Please let me know who will be assisting.

Ozzy

Time to get to work. He lifted himself up in the bath, but he came over dizzy and promptly sat back again. There was a rush of air and the faraway voice was back. Something that he'd not experienced for many weeks.

"13 days Oscar. Tick Tock. Time is running out."

His vision came back into focus and he found that he had slipped down in the bath, his head nearly underwater. He sat up gasping and breathed slowly for five minutes before easing himself out. He thought it had gone. The extra tablets were doing their job. Maybe it was the stress; the additional pressure from Ace's message.

He dried himself, took his tablets, and had a coffee and some toast before heading to the nearby lock-up to continue work. If he could get through the next two weeks he could relax — either in prison or on a beach in the Caribbean, depending on how things turned out. Looks like the trip away with Brandy would have to wait until after.

His phone pinged as he arrived.

"Hey - I've got a cheese grater. Great plan. I'll bring it round at the weekend. It's not 4 the table tennis bat tho". Another crying-laughing emoji. "I'd love 2 go 2 Amsterdam. The girls in the red-light district will do ANYTHING there and it's all legal. We could have a 3-some xxx".

He groaned. He had visions of them being arrested in Holland for cheese-grating a Dutch prostitute. It wasn't quite what he had in mind. Why had he mentioned Amsterdam?

He sent a quick reply "Ha ha. We'll talk at the weekend. Gotta run xxx".

****

Wednesday 26th February

Madison entered the incident room looking tired and drawn.

"You OK Monroe?" bellowed Simpson. "You look like shit."

"Thanks for that boss. You know how to make a girl feel good." She poured herself a strong coffee and plonked herself down on a chair. Starting that second bottle of wine last night had been a bad idea.

Dickson was there too for their weekly mid-week catch-up.

"OK. Talk to me" said Simpson. "It's been six weeks since the first diamond got nicked and we really need some results. What's new?"

Dickson glanced at Madison, who was focusing on her coffee, so he took that as a cue to take the lead.

"So, I told you about the GreySpider names – that most of them are bogus, but we have the four that look legitimate. Budster_007, Ozzy92, Pandora and GreenZero. I've done some digging. Budster is a dead end. I can't find any mention of it anywhere else. Same with Pandora. I've had a hit on Ozzy92 though."

He pushed a button on his laptop and the large screen on the wall sprang to life with a Facebook profile.

"This is Oscar Zachery. His Facebook profile is Ozzy92 too. It's an old account and he barely posts anything, but there are some pictures." He brought up a picture of Oscar dressed up in his stage outfit under the headline "The Wizard of Oz".

"He's a magician. The Monument robbery used smoke pellets to distract everyone. It's the kind of thing a magician might use on stage."

Simpson peered closely at the photo. "Where's that CCTV picture of the guy at the café. Could it be him?"

Dickson brought up the photo, so they were side by side on the screen and they all peered at them.

"Possibly," said Dickson. "The Facebook photo is dated 2014. Six years ago. Difficult to say for sure."

"It's enough to bring him in though," said Simpson, a hint of satisfaction in his voice. "A magician with the same username, with a legit comment on the GreySpider post. It's worth finding out where he was when the museum was robbed. Have we got an address for him?

"Nothing on social media that I can find, and I've checked the usual databases. The name's not ringing any alarm bells. If he is our Monument robber, then it's a first offense.

"Was he on the list of names taken at the Monument?" said Simpson.

"No. But as we said before, he could have left any name."

"So how do we find him?"

"Entertainments circuit" Madison piped up, and they both looked at her questioningly.

"If he was a magician then he might still be doing the rounds. Magic is rising in popularity. There are venues all over London that might employ him."

"Good shout," said Simpson. "Glad you're still with us."

She grimaced and took another sip of her coffee.

Dickson's fingers flew over the keyboard as he ran "The Wizard of Oz" through a couple of city entertainment websites.

"Found him," he said triumphantly. "He's playing at the Mirage Lounge in Paddington on Friday night."

"I've been there," said Madison. "Nice place, and quite a decent size. He must be doing well for himself."

"We could go and check him out and talk to him after the show," said Simpson. He liked a bit of magic.

Madison groaned. "A magic show? Really? Can't we just go and see the manager and get an address. I've got better ways to spend my Friday nights."

Simpson looked at her, almost with concern. She wasn't her usual cheery self and was acting very out of character. It wasn't in his nature to be sympathetic though.

"Jeez Monroe. Which side of the bed did you get out of this morning?" he said scornfully. "Don't worry. We can do it without you. I'd rather spend the evening with Dickson here if you're gonna have a face like a slapped arse all night anyway."

Madison turned red and drank more coffee.

"Right. Good job. What else?" said Simpson.

"Nothing concrete – but just a thought," said Dickson. "The GreenZero name. I thought it might be related to roulette. Maybe we could show some of the CCTV pictures to the local casinos. See if we get a hit."

"Worth a shot. All leads are worth following. Do it. I take it we still have no idea who the ringleader is. The guy who calls himself Ace?"

"Nope. His firewall is airtight" said Dickson miserably.

"And his talk about something bigger?"

"No clue. Could be anything."

"Diamonds," said Madison suddenly. Simpson thought she was sulking or on a period or something, so was surprised when she spoke again.

"His challenge was to steal diamonds," she said. "It would make sense that it's diamonds again. I read an article in a magazine the other day. There's a real valuable diamond coming into the country at the end of the month. Worth about fifty million it said."

"Jesus" whistled Dickson. "Fifty mill?"

"Look into it" barked Simpson. "Find out where and when. Could be a red herring, but if it comes in and they take it, we're gonna look like bloody idiots. At least we can warn them if we think there's a threat."

"Will do boss," said Madison.

"Anything on the Sparkles diamond?"

"I interviewed Felix Radcliffe, the guy from the courier company who collected the diamond," said Madison. "He's been a personal friend of Colin Rhames the director at SJH for years. Rhames doesn't believe for a second that it's him. Radcliffe had his IT guys check out their systems, and they believe they were hacked. Whoever it was was good though as they didn't leave a trace. He can't prove it. He was adamant that he had an email from Rhames to move the diamond. He collected the diamond from the museum - that much we definitely know as Ray Boyden, the manager at Sparkles, confirmed that Radcliffe took it away. It all seems legit. It's just that the diamond has disappeared from EZ-Store where he claimed he dropped it."

"And EZ-Store?"

"They have no record of it in their system or their CCTV. They still claim that Radcliffe was never there."

Simpson sighed. "It's not looking good for him is it?"

"He has no proof, but unless we search his place and find the diamond, we can't prove it either. To make things worse, Rhames won't press charges against him. He's going down the insurance route."

"I'd imagine that the insurance company might have some tricky questions for him," said Simpson. "OK. We could try for a warrant and search his premises, but we won't find it. If it was him, he'll have it squirreled away somewhere. Let's just keep an eye on the insurance company and see if they dig any further. With no diamond, no evidence, and a guy who doesn't want to press charges, I'm not gonna waste resources on it."

"Yes boss. I'll dig out that magazine and concentrate on the other diamond."

"Good. Thanks." Even with a hangover, at least she was still on the ball.

"There is one more thing," said Dickson. "We've finished sorting through the garbage from the coffee shop. Got about forty different prints after we take the staff's dabs out. Nothing jumping out of the system, but we might get a match if we can fingerprint Mr. Zachery on Friday night."

"Now wouldn't that be nice," said Simpson. "If we can match prints and the GreySpider account to him, then we'll have no trouble bringing him in and getting his place searched. OK, keep at it. Let's see what Friday night brings us."

Chapter 34 – "Loose Ends"

Thursday 27th February

Buddy had watched the bank video half a dozen times but couldn't be sure. Briars – the bank manager had appeared out of his office holding the swipe card in his hand hanging from a lanyard. After he had opened the vault, he had shaken Buddy's hand and gone back into his office. Buddy was turning towards the vault, but there were a few frames where Briars could be seen through the glass partition window. He had entered his office with the card in his right hand. The door had closed, and as Buddy had turned away, he got a glimpse of Briars hand. The swipe card was gone. Had he stuck it in his pocket or was it hanging somewhere in the office for easy access? Maybe he switched it to his left hand that was out of view. Another half a second and he would've been more confident, but the video had cut away.

Damn.

He would have to go back with his fake ID. Would he be able to get a meeting with Briars at short notice? The new deadline had taken luxuries like that away from him. He called the bank anyway and requested a meeting with the bank manager regarding a substantial business loan.

"I'm afraid Mr. Briars is not available until Thursday 19th March. We have an appointment available with one of our loan specialists though who could see you on the 2nd."

He thanked the girl and hung up. If Briars was so busy, how was it that he could jump up and open the vault at the drop of a hat? Maybe there was someone else with another card?

Time to go back to his safety deposit box. This time he would watch Briars all the way back into his office. He dressed in his Douglas Iford-King disguise and headed out to the bank.

****

"Mr. King. Good to see you again. I understand you need to access your safety deposit box again." Marsden looked exactly the same as he had a fortnight ago, right down to the inch-thick glasses and the gaudy tie which looked like someone had vomited on it.

"I have some more papers that I wish to add to the box in the vault," said Buddy pompously. "I shall only require a few moments."

His button camera was already running as they descended in the lift and along the already familiar corridor. A corridor he was looking at just a couple of hours ago repeatedly.

The big security guard was sat by the vault sending a message on his phone. He hurriedly put the phone in his pocket when he saw them approaching.

"Morning Aseem," said Marsden. "Is Steve not here yet?"

Buddy had a sense of deja-vu sweep over him.

"Morning Bob," said Aseem. "I think he's in a meeting."

Marsden glanced towards the office and saw that Briars had someone with him. He turned to Buddy. "Sorry. I won't be a moment."

He walked towards the office and knocked on the door as Buddy watched like a hawk. A second later, he pushed the door open and said something. Briars glanced out of the window towards Buddy and gave him a nod. The door closed a fraction and then opened again and Marsden appeared with the swipe card.

Back of the door, thought Buddy. It must be. That meant that he wouldn't get a chance to clone it, but they could just use the real one when they came into the bank.

The swipe cards were swiped, and Aseem used the code that was sent to his phone. The vault swung open.

****

Ace,

I have attached a video of another trip to the bank. As you can clearly see, Stephen Briars' swipe card is kept on a hook on the back of his office door next to the vault. This makes it impossible for me to get hold of a copy. However, I don't see any issue with accessing this room and using the real swipe card when it is needed.

Also, I have downloaded and installed the requested software on Briars' mobile phone.

Please confirm all is OK and let me know my next task.

Budster

****

Ace read Budster's message with mixed feelings. The swipe card concerned him. They would only get one shot at the bank and if the card wasn't there, then they might as well pack up and go home.

On the other hand, Budster had somehow managed to get the bank manager's phone and load the software, something that he thought would be a massive challenge. He fired a one-liner off to Pandora.

Pandora,

Briars' phone has your software installed. Please confirm that you can access it and commandeer his messages.

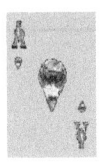

He rubbed his forehead with the back of his hand. If Budster was right, then getting their hands on the swipe card before Ozzy went in was going to be very difficult. Unless...

They had access to the cameras and the bank's door security. The plan was to override this to get in to steal the diamond. Why not have a dry run to get to the card and clone it? Going in an extra time would increase the risks of being caught, but it would also allow them to overcome any potential unforeseen issues.

He got off his chair and paced the room

"One, two, three, four, five, six, seven, eight, nine." Turn.

"One, two, three, four, five, six, seven, eight, nine." He sat down again and straightened a pen.

Was it worth the extra risk? Would the card be there when Ozzy went in anyway? It might be an unnecessary journey. He spun around in his chair contemplating the problem, considering the different angles, worrying over the potential outcomes. He decided that they had no choice. If he did nothing, then there was a chance that the swipe card would not be there, and the diamond would be unobtainable. That was an unacceptable outcome. Should he send Budster in or do it himself? Budster was familiar with the area so it made sense to give the task back to him.

He composed two new messages, one to Budster, another to Pandora, requesting that they access the bank over the weekend and get the card copied. They would have to be in contact with one another for the first time, and he reluctantly posted their GreySpider details in the message.

After a lot more pacing, he finally sent the messages, and then spent fifteen minutes on a pencil sharpening spree as he had a near panic attack over what he had done. He knew that Pandora would have to talk to Ozzy when he went into the bank, but now he had connected her to Budster too, and he still had the problem of who was going to assist Ozzy on the day. His golden rule of keeping them separate was falling apart fast.

His breathing finally settled, and he realized that his pencils were no more. He threw the remains into the bin and opened up a drawer that was stacked full of small boxes; blue pens on the left, black pens in the middle, pencils on the right. He removed four pencils from a box and placed them carefully in front of him. His computer pinged as a message arrived.

Ace,

I'm good to go and will touch base with Budster. I have accessed Briars' phone without a problem. His dog-sitter has just messaged him to tell him that they're OK.

Pandora

Pandora again was proving to be the most reliable member of the team. GreenZero was a liability who had not come through yet, Budster had given up on the swipe card and Ozzy kept whining about who was going to help him on the day, something that he still hadn't decided on. His first choice would be Pandora, but she would be needed to override the security, and she didn't want to leave the house. He had considered going in himself, but he had promised the team that he wouldn't be the one to enter the bank. Also, he preferred to stay anonymous as long as possible.

A crease appeared on his brow as he considered his options. He reached for a pencil, but stopped himself, hauled himself out the chair, and chose to pace instead.

"One, two, three, four, five, six, seven, eight, nine." Turn.

****

Friday 28th February

Oscar canceled his show at the Mirage feigning illness. He put on an "ill voice" that any fourteen-year-old kid would have been proud of.

"I'm really sorry Micky. I feel like shit. I'm gonna spend the day in bed. I'll do you a twenty percent discount next month."

"Fuck Oz. That's really left me in the brown stuff. I'll never get a decent replacement on a Friday night at short notice."

He apologized profusely and hung up feeling bad but pleased that Micky considered him a "decent" act. The phone call to Brandy would be a little more difficult. He needed to put her off all weekend so that he could crack on with the build. He wasn't sure that pretending to be ill would fly, so he made up a story about his brother Ed needing to see him urgently. He had told her previously that Ed had tried to get in touch, so it was almost believable.

"I'll come wiv ya," said Brandy. "Is he as cute as you?"

"Well, we're twins, so I guess so."

"Twins. Fuck me. I've only done it wiv twins once before" she cackled.

He managed to put her off, but only by promising to see her on Sunday night. At least he would have the weekend. He wasn't sure what state he'd be in on Monday though.

****

"Hey brother. It's Aseem. It's 4pm on Friday. We're short of a dealer on Monday night. Manda's got shingles. I hope she didn't cough over us the other day. I don't suppose you know anyone who can step in? Free pizza and forty quid plus tips for the night. Let me know."

Owen didn't pick up the message until he was sat in the casino losing his wages on the roulette table and slowly getting inebriated.

"Are you working on Monday night?" he asked Estelle as she swept away another two chips.

She looked alarmed. Was he asking her out?

"What did you have in mind?" she said cautiously.

He told her about the poker night. "Easy money and a bit livelier than this place."

She twitched. "Noodles" she barked and looked away embarrassed.

Owen cracked up, spilling his beer over his chips. "Fuck" he said, wiping them down with his shirt. "I could request noodles, but they normally do pizza."

"Forty pounds you say?"

He stuck two chips on black. "Yeh, but it won't feel like working. It's more like a night down the pub with your mates. The winners tend to chuck a bit more your way too."

She spun the wheel and considered it. It wasn't far from her flat and it was her day off. She had no other plans.

"Why not," she said. "Can you meet me outside at 7:30? I don't like going into strange places alone."

"It's a date," said Owen brightly.

"It's not a date. I'll be working" she said smiling.

"Worth a try. Fuck." The ball had landed in red. His chips were diminishing rapidly. He handed her four chips. "Pick a bet for me. You got to be luckier than me at the moment."

"You know I'm not allowed to do that," she said, and then whispered "Evens."

He dropped the chips on "Evens", and she spun the wheel.

"Twenty-two. Winner." She added to his chips.

"There you go. Hopefully, you can bring that luck with you on Monday night" he said. "Let 'em ride." He drained his beer.

"You really should quit while you're ahead," she said twitching. "Bastard loser."

He laughed but it turned to a groan as the ball dropped into number seven.

"I'm gonna go practice at poker. See if I can lose the rest over there. Take care, Estelle. I'll see you Monday."

Chapter 35 – "Return to Larkins"

"What the fuck are you wearing Dickson?"

Simpson stared at Dickson's "casual" shirt for the night at the Mirage with distaste. It was a very tight-fitting, short sweatshirt that almost showed off his midriff. Coupled with the skinny ripped jeans and some guyliner, it wasn't what Simpson was expecting.

Dickson laughed. "This is me when I'm not in the office," he said. "What's the problem?"

Simpson muttered something that sounded like "I'm walking into a club with a fucking queer boy" but was striding through the door and it was lost by the noise coming out of the club.

They grabbed a drink and found a table near the front.

The lights dimmed and a barrel of a man walked to the middle of the stage. The microphone was about a foot above his head, and he struggled for half a minute trying to lower it, to much amusement from the gathering crowds.

"Ladies and Gentlemen. Thank you for joining us at the Mirage Lounge tonight, winner of the best entertainment venue in Paddington three years in a row. We have a packed show for you this evening. Not one but two acts. First, we have the lovely Ky-Lee, the number one oriental Kylie Minogue tribute act in the country. If you've never seen her before then you're in for a treat. You should be so lucky."

His weak attempt at a joke was met with silence, and he moved on quickly.

"And at 9pm, we have a change to the advertised program. Unfortunately, our resident magician – the Wizard of Oz can't be with us this evening, but we have an amazing act to replace him. We've been fortunate enough to get hold of Fabba – An Abba tribute act with a twist. They come highly recommended, so we've taken a chance on them. They will have you dancing like a queen and we hope that you will stay with us for the evening spending your money money money."

Simpson groaned. "You got to be kidding me."

"So, get your dancing shoes on and give a warm welcome to the fabulous Ky-Leeeeee."

"Come on," said Simpson. "Let's go and talk to the guy. I'm not sitting through fucking Ky-Lee."

A disappointed Dickson followed as Ky-Lee hit the stage dressed in a feather boa and not much else. She was being carried on by her four muscular male backing dancers dressed in outfits not dissimilar to what Dickson was currently wearing.

"Can I have a word?" said Simpson flashing his badge to Micky.

Micky looked the detective up and down and checked the credentials.

"What can I do for you detective?"

"I was hoping to have a word with Oscar Zachery tonight. You say he's not coming?"

"No. he's not well. Let me down this morning. You'll love Fabba though." He leaned in and whispered "The twist is they're all men. Very funny, in a camp way if you like that kind of thing." He gave Simpson a wink

"Do I look like...."

Dickson interrupted Simpson who had gone from naught to full-on-furious in about half a second.

"It sounds amazing. Can't wait" he said. "Do you know how we can get hold of Mr. Zachery? Do you have an address?"

"Just a phone number," said Micky cautiously. "He's not in any trouble is he?"

"Just following up on inquiries. Nothing to worry about" said Dickson.

"It'll be up in the office. I'll see if I can dig it out in the interval" said Micky. "I need to see the sound and lighting guy and check on Fabba. I've only got forty-five minutes. Have a drink. Enjoy the show and I'll come find you in a bit."

Simpson was getting agitated. He reluctantly returned to his seat and spent the best part of an hour watching Dickson sing along to Kylie's greatest hits and even joining in some of the dance moves. He escaped to the loo when Ky-Lee started a conga for the locomotion. He wouldn't be seen dead involved in anything like that.

The final number, "Especially for you" was a duet with the aptly named Jay Son Donvan and Simpson got up.

"I can't take any more of this. I'm going for a smoke. If he gets you that number, come and find me." He stormed off.

It was another half an hour before Micky appeared with a phone number, and Fabba had taken to the stage. Simpson was back and getting grumpier by the second.

"Sorry to keep you. The Bjorn lookalike from Fabba had a major diva meltdown and insisted that he wanted a bigger dressing room. He was threatening to walk. I couldn't have two canceled acts in one night. This business can be a nightmare sometimes."

Fabba were in the process of murdering Mamma Mia, but they seemed to be whipping the crowd up nicely, including Dickson who was dancing in front of his table and getting admiring glances from two of Ky-Lee's dancers who had hit the nearby dancefloor.

"Let's go," said Simpson. "We can call Zachery from the car."

"Oh. I was planning on meeting someone here later" said Dickson. "Do you mind if I stay?"

"Suit yourself. I'd rather gouge my eyes out with a spoon than listen to any more of this shit. Enjoy. I'll see you on Monday."

Dickson moved on to the dancefloor as Simpson strode out of the building as fast as he could.

Micky was frantically texting Oscar.

"Oz. Police have been here looking for you. I've not given them your address but had to give up your phone number. Trust it's nothing to worry about but thought I should let you know. You may get a call".

****

Saturday 29th February

It was nearly midnight and Buddy was sat in a car opposite Larkins bank, fiddling with a miniature earpiece. It connected to his phone, which was running some software that Pandora had sent him. It allowed them to talk on a secure channel over the internet.

"Hello. Can you hear me?"

Nothing. He had been trying to get the device working for nearly fifteen minutes and failing miserably.

He sent her a message via GreySpider on his phone.

Earpiece not working. Is there a backup plan?

Have you put it in your ear? was the reply he got back. Was she for real?

He typed No. I've just stuck it up my arse. What do you think? but deleted it again.

Yes. It's not connecting. I've reset the Bluetooth but still no good

A minute passed.

Try turning it off and on again

He sighed. He wasn't happy about entering the bank in the first place, but Ace had insisted that they needed the card. He was intrigued to talk to another member of the team though, so had agreed.

He pushed the little button on the earpiece and held it for a few seconds and it beeped as it was turned off. A few seconds later, he switched it on, and the device finally connected to his phone.

"Hello," he said holding it near his ear.

"Hallelujah. I thought I was working with a dickhead" said Amy Ross - Pandora. "It's not rocket science, you muppet."

"Ah Pandora? Hi. Good to meet you" said Buddy timidly, stuffing the earpiece in his ear. "It was just being temperamental I think."

"Was working perfectly when I dropped it off" she said moodily. She had shipped it to EZ-Store and he had collected it earlier that day. "Where are you?"

"I'm sat outside the bank," he said. "It seems quiet. What can you see?"

"I've got eyes inside the bank and full access to all their systems except the vault. This will be a doddle if you don't fuck it up."

"I'm ready. You said you can open the car parking lot."

Pandora had messaged Buddy earlier in the day with her plan to get him inside the bank. She had come across pleasant and easy-going when chatting via the computer but talking to her was a different matter.

"I will if you stop jabbering," she said shortly.

Buddy heard her tapping away on a keyboard. A minute later, he saw the large shutter that secured the bank's car park slowly lifting.

"Looks like it's opening," he said.

"Of course it's opening. I just opened it" she said sarcastically. "Get in there. I need to shut it behind you."

"You're shutting me in?" said Buddy, alarmed.

"Unless you want every passer-by, tramp, stray dog, and local fucking policeman to join you, then yes – I'm shutting you in."

"OK. OK. I'm moving Jeez."

"Sorry," said Amy bluntly. "I don't like people."

Buddy locked the car and swiftly crossed the road, ducking under the still rising shutter.

"OK. I'm in."

The shutter stopped and reversed.

"If you go down the slope and to the left, there's a couple of large bins. Behind the bins, there's a door."

Buddy flicked on a torch and headed down into the underground car park. The shadows bounced around the deserted lot making him feel uneasy.

"I hope there's no one down here" he muttered.

"Who are you expecting behind a locked shutter at midnight?" she said. "Stop being a wimp and find that door. Ah – There you are."

"You can see me?"

"I can see some fat bloke with a torch approaching the bins," she said.

Buddy was far from fat, but in his current predicament, he thought it best to let it go. If he annoyed her then she might leave him trapped, although her default setting seemed to be bordering on angry already. The torch beam picked out a red door with a keypad entry next to it.

"OK. I'm at the door."

"I know. I can see you."

"What now?"

"Wait a minute."

Buddy heard lots of keyboard tapping, a frustrated sigh, a fizz sound as if a coke can had been opened, some more tapping, and then she came back.

"215567C," she said briskly.

"Sorry. What's that?"

"The code for the door. 215567C."

He shone his torch on the keypad and started typing.

"What's after the one?"

"Jesus Christ. Do you want me to come down there and type the fucker for you? 215567C."

He keyed in the number, but nothing happened.

"OK. Didn't work."

"Did you press enter?"

He shone the torch again and saw there was an "Enter" key. He pressed it and the door clicked open.

"You didn't press enter did you?" she said sarcastically.

"You didn't tell me to," said Buddy meekly. "Which way?"

He found himself in a pitch-black loading bay area that was stacked with old filing cabinets, a kitchen area with a sink and some cups and saucers, a microwave, and a chest freezer. Must double up as some kind of lunch area he thought as he shone the torch around.

"I don't know. There's no camera in there" she said. There should be another shutter that takes us into the bank. I need to deactivate the alarm before I open it though. See if you can do something useful and find it while I work."

He shone the torch about, and his heart leaped as he heard a scurrying sound.

"What the fuck was that?"

She ignored him, focused on the job at hand. His torch beam scanned the wall where he heard the sound and he saw a large rat frozen like a deer in headlights. He squealed and the rat scarpered.

"Will you shut up. I'm trying to concentrate here."

"There's a fucking rat as big as a dog in here with me." Buddy had backed up to the wall, as far away as possible from where he'd seen the rat, but another scurried along behind him making him squeal again.

"Jesus and you managed to steal a diamond?" said Amy under her breath.

Buddy was frantically shining the torch around. "I don't like rats," he said. "Get me out of this place."

"Yeh, Yeh. I'm trying here" she said exasperated.

It seemed like an eternity to Buddy, but a minute later he heard a shutter open up in front of him and he scurried through it.

"I'm in," he said breathlessly. He found himself in the corridor near the vault that he had walked down twice before. "I know where I am."

"Bully for you."

Buddy made his way along to Briars' office with Amy watching him all the way.

"OK. I'm at the office. I'll try the door."

"I know," she said bored. "I don't need a running commentary."

"It's locked," he said alarmed. His hand was probably a foot from the swipe card, but he couldn't get to it.

"Not for long." A flurry of keys and the door made a click sound.

"Good job." He pushed the door open and sure enough, on the back of the door was a hook with the vault swipe card hanging from the lanyard. He retrieved his card cloner from his pocket, inserted the card, checked that it read OK and returned it to the back of the door, and closed it behind him.

"Done," he said. "You can lock the door again. I'm on my way out."

Buddy was a few steps from the metal shutter when the rat appeared in the doorway and stared him down. He stopped.

"What's up?" said Amy. "Why have you stopped?"

"It's the rat" whispered Buddy. "He's blocking the door."

Amy rolled her eyes. "He's eight inches long. He's hardly blocking an eight-foot shutter. Just keep moving. I'd like to get some sleep at some point tonight."

Buddy took a tentative step towards the rat, but it stood its ground. He held his breath and ran at it. The rat scarpered, startled but unfortunately for Buddy, it ran forwards, down the corridor and towards Briars' office making Buddy leap to the side with a yelp.

"Shit." He swung around following the retreating rat with the torch.

"What's wrong?"

"It's in the bank. The bastard rat's in the bank."

Amy laughed. A sound he didn't think she was capable of. "Well you're gonna have to catch it. If the staff find it, they'll know that someone's opened the door."

"I can't" wailed Buddy. "I hate them. I got trapped in a shed when I was younger with two rats."

"Stop being a wuss and go after that rat. Do you really want to fuck this up because of a rodent?"

Buddy ran down the hall after the rat.

"I can't find him. Shit. This corridor is long. He could be anywhere."

He ran up and down the corridor, Amy watching him from the bank's cameras. She pushed a button to record his antics. This was priceless. She watched as he cornered the rat, but then jumped out the way as it ran at him.

"Stop playing with it and catch the little fucker" said Amy, trying to suppress another laugh.

"It's too quick. How the fuck am I supposed to stop a runaway rat?"

It took another ten minutes before he finally chased the rat back into the loading bay, puffing and frantic. He leaped after it and yelled "It's out. Shut the door. Shut the fucking door."

Amy was crying with laughter as she sealed the bank back up, reset the alarms, and wiped the cameras, although she would have loved to have left it on the system so she could see the look on the bank manager's face as he watched what had happened in his bank in the early hours of the morning.

"Well that went well," she said when he was back in the car. "I hope you got what you needed."

He patted his pocket. "Job done," he said smiling wearily. "Piece of cake."

Chapter 36 – "Poker Night #2"

Monday 2nd March

"I'm not sure about this Owen."

Estelle was anxious as they opened the door to the Royal Oak. In the casino, everyone knew about her outbursts and she felt far more in her comfort zone.

"You know my tics are worse when I'm nervous."

Owen smiled at her. "Trust me," he said. "They're a friendly bunch. You might even get a regular gig out of this."

They walked into the lounge area and there was a hearty cheer.

"He's back."

"Might get my money back from him."

"He just wants a piece of Annie."

"Hey brother. Good to see you."

The last comment was from Aseem and he waddled over and gave Owen a bear hug.

"Hi guys. I figured it was easy money last week, so I'm back to take more from you" said Owen, releasing himself from the big man's massive arms. "This is Estelle. She's here to help out. Please be gentle."

Aseem took her hand, gave a small bow, and kissed it. "It's a pleasure to meet you, Estelle. Thanks for coming down at short notice. Owen here has good things to say about you."

Estelle smiled, aware that there were about a dozen pairs of eyes on her, twitched and blurted "Arse muncher."

She went bright red as the pub fell into stunned silence, which was broken by Aseem breaking into a deep booming laugh.

"Honey, you're gonna fit right in here," he said, taking her hand. Let me buy you a drink. What you having Owen?"

"Coke, lots of ice," said Owen. "Thanks."

He knew that he had to be focused tonight. With the new deadline, it was going to be his last poker night before the 9th, and he had to get both the phone and swipe card from Aseem. After handing his wallet back in a drunken stupor last week, he knew he couldn't make the same mistake twice.

Aseem wasn't having any of it though and looked at him in disgust. "You ain't playing cards with me drinking coke my man. I'll get you a beer."

Owen protested, but when they returned from the bar, a beer was placed in front of him. He'd have to pace himself.

"So, how do you know this reprobate anyway?" said Aseem to Estelle when they were seated. Owen had managed to sit next to Aseem again, and Estelle was opposite.

"He literally lives in the casino I work at," she said, sipping a glass of cheap wine. "I think he knows the dealers there better than his own family." She pulled a face at the bitter taste, sniffed it, and uttered "Bellend" a little bit louder than she would have liked.

Aseem choked in his beer, spraying it all over Roley, and started crying with laughter.

"For fuck's sake, not again," said Roley. "Can I sit somewhere else? This fucker sprays me every week."

Owen ignored the outburst and was nodding. "True story, but to be fair, I'd rather be sat with Estelle giving my money away than spending time with my rellies. Bellend is about right for most of them."

Estelle was wishing that she hadn't let Owen talk her into coming. The unfamiliar faces and new surroundings were unsettling her. She took a large gulp of her wine and tried to relax. She needed a distraction and was relieved when the bell rang at 8pm and the game started.

"Let's play," said Aseem, clapping his hands together. "I'm feeling lucky after last week. Deal me some Aces sweetheart."

The first half-hour was pretty uneventful, with money passing back and forth with no clear leader. Estelle had settled, glad to be doing something that was so familiar to her and she had only had one more outburst. It was about 8:45 when things started to get interesting. Owen, still on his first drink and racking his brain to work out how he would get to Aseem, pulled a pair of Aces. Roley had a pair of queens and had bet big before even seeing the Flop. The rest of the table had folded. Owen raised by ten, and Aseem whistled.

"You trying to get home early tonight brother?"

Roley matched the bid and Estelle flipped the cards.

QC, AH, 4D

Owen didn't flinch, but he'd just pulled three Aces and his hand was looking strong. Roley took a sip of his drink and pushed ten chips forwards. Owen matched it, aware that Roley was likely to have an ace, queen, or maybe two queens, not as good as Owen's hand.

Estelle added the 5H to the table, no help for either of them. Roley tapped the table, but it was Owen's turn to put the pressure on. He bet another ten and Aseem let out a whoop.

"What ya gonna do now Roley Poly? He's after your money."

"Do you really have to jabber on all the time?" said Roley annoyed, pushing his chips forwards. "Every week it's the same. It's like verbal fucking diarrhea with you. Give it a fucking rest."

"Hey. Just shooting the breeze my man" said Aseem, holding his hands up defensively. "It's what I do."

"Gets on my tits" muttered Roley. "We're here to play, not listen to you talking shit."

"Pipe down brother. It's all harmless fun."

Roley was getting agitated, and Estelle, picking up on the vibe twitched violently and yelled "Piss flaps."

Aseem's laughter boomed again and tears ran down his face as he banged the table with his fist, trying to get under control but sending chips flying everywhere. Roley grabbed at his drink that was wobbling precariously and threw himself back in his chair to get away from the big guy. Unfortunately, Annie was passing with a tray of drinks, and the back of his head caught her arm. She screamed, wobbled, and the whole tray came crashing down on Roley's head.

"Fucking idiot" screamed Annie as everyone stopped what they were doing and looked around.

Roley's scream was even louder as three pints of beer, two vodkas, a wine, and the tray landed on him.

Aseem who was already crying from Estelle's latest outburst thought this was the funniest thing he'd seen all year. He threw his head back and laughed even harder.

"You got a bit of drink on you, my man," he said, gasping for breath. "Fuck me. Look at the state of him?" He leaned forward holding on to the table, and then threw his head back and laughed again.

His twenty-stone bulk and the constant rocking back and forth proved too much for his chair, and it gave up suddenly, causing him to collapse backward on the floor, sending his own drink flying over Owen.

Owen leaped up, wiping himself down, and reached down to help Aseem up who's laughter had turned to a groan.

"Fuck. You OK man?" said Owen alarmed. He'd gone down pretty hard.

He tried to pull him up, but Aseem was huge and he just rocked back and forth a bit. Roley had disappeared into the bathroom to clean himself up and the others around the table were making space so Annie could clear away the remains of the glasses. Estelle went to help, and they got him a few inches off the ground, but he was too heavy, and he fell back again with a groan, his wallet slipping out of his pocket in the process.

Owen clocked it straight away and put his foot on it.

The next few minutes were chaos as Aseem was helped to his feet and onto a stool while Annie was sweeping up glass and the broken chair was removed and replaced. Owen took the distraction to scoop the wallet up and disappeared into the toilets to clean the beer off his shirt.

He locked himself into a cubicle and removed the card cloning device from his pocket. He silently prayed that the card was in the wallet and heaved a sigh of relief when he spotted it – "Property of Larkins Bank" stamped in small neat letters across it. He slipped it into the machine, pushed a button and the card was scanned.

Five minutes later he was back in the bar.

"You OK? That looked nasty" said Owen clapping Aseem on the back.

"Don't worry about him. Look at the state of me" said Roley, who had returned, his hair askew and shirt and jeans still wringing wet.

"It'll ache like a bitch tomorrow, but it was worth it," said Aseem still chuckling. "Sorry man, but from here that was pretty damn funny."

"Hey, you dropped this," said Owen, handing him the wallet.

"Again? Shit, thanks." He pocketed it and looked at Estelle. "You need to come back every week honey. This has been the best night ever and it's not even nine o'clock."

They resumed the game and Estelle turned the River card – The ace of clubs. Roley went all in with his full house. He had an idea that Owen might have the aces and if he did, then at least he could go home and clean himself up properly.

Owen pushed his chips forward and revealed his cards.

"Sorry man. Not the best night for you" he said.

Roley grunted and got up, still dripping "Thanks, guys. I'm off home to get changed."

"You know your problem Roley boy? You've had too many drinks" said Aseem with a grin. He got up and clapped him on the back. "No hard feelings brother. See you next week."

At 9:30, the remaining players from the other tables joined them. Both Aseem and Owen were doing well, but no one was going to beat Julius tonight. He was a long way ahead, and he bided his time, picking off the players with small pots until he was down to the last three with Owen and Dave Two. Aseem had bowed out in fifth, losing to Julius with a badly timed bluff. He ordered another beer and watched the climax of the game.

"In the money again brother," he said as Owen took another hand.

"Estelle's my lucky charm," he said, smiling at her. "I think you're right. We should get her back every week."

"It's been an eventful night," said Estelle dragging the cards off the table. "I never see this kind of stuff at the casino." Following all the excitement, she'd relaxed into the game and her tics had subsided.

Dave Two went out just after 10pm and Owen grabbed a second-place pocketing over a hundred pounds. He slipped some extra money to Estelle and they sat with Aseem and Julius, finishing their drinks.

Owen was inwardly panicking. He had copied the swipe card but was running out of time to get the phone. Fifteen minutes later when the last orders bell rang, he still had no clue how he was going to do it. Julius said his goodbyes and Estelle went to the ladies' room as they walked out, leaving him alone with Aseem.

"You coming, next week brother?"

"Hopefully. It's turning into quite a lucrative evening" said Owen with a grin. "You know, I might even treat Estelle to a taxi ride home."

"Lovely girl," said Aseem. "Are you two an item?"

"Sadly not. We had dinner once, but you know..." he trailed off, thinking back to the once chance that he'd had with Estelle and had blown it by getting stupidly drunk and making an embarrassing pass at her.

"I do know," said Aseem. "Women." He rolled his eyes knowingly.

Owen took his phone out and frowned, pushing a few buttons.

"What's up?"

"Fucking phone's dead," said Owen miserably. "I was gonna call a cab. Looks like it's the tube again."

Aseem tossed his phone to him. "There's a couple of taxi numbers in there. I need a piss. Feels like the beer is trying to escape without my help.

He lumbered off leaving a stunned Owen staring at the phone in his hand.

A few seconds passed before he leaped into action, firing up the browser and downloading Pandora's app. Estelle appeared and he called a taxi company, only to be told that there would be a forty-five-minute wait. He hung up as the download finished, and he closed the browser and installed the software.

"What are you doing?" said Estelle.

"Trying to get us a cab," said Owen smiling. "Thought I'd treat you with my winnings. Not having much luck though."

"Don't worry. It's a nice evening. Let's walk" she said. "Thanks for bringing me down here tonight. It's been fun, and I made some good money with the tips." Julius had taken quite a shine to her and given her a twenty as he'd left.

Aseem appeared and Owen handed him his phone.

"Looks like you've got to put up with us a bit longer," he said. "Taxi's are rammed. Lead the way."

Chapter 37 – "Paranoia"

Wednesday 4th March

Oscar was getting paranoid after the message from Micky a few days earlier and had spent most of his time working in the lock-up. How had they found him? It had been weeks since the close call at the tube station and he thought that the trail had gone cold. That and the fact that they got their diamond back, led him to believe they would give up on him and concentrate on the others. Seems like he was wrong.

His phone had rung from an unknown number just after Micky had messaged him, and he had switched it off immediately, concerned that they may be able to trace him through it. He had picked up a cheap phone and sim card so he could make calls, and even packed a suitcase and moved out of his apartment, choosing to sleep in the office space at the back of the lock-up where there was a sofa and a kitchen area with a microwave and sink.

He had taken Brandy out to dinner on Sunday night and picked a restaurant far from his home that he'd never visited before but still spent the evening looking over his shoulder, jumping at the sound of a passing police car, and nearly having a heart attack when a policewoman came in. It turned out she was visiting her sister who worked in the kitchen, but Oscar had gone white and slid down in his chair. Brandy had asked him repeatedly if he was OK and he had smiled and said he was just tired, even managing to convince her not to spend the evening with him. He appeased her by talking about going to Paris at the end of the month and showing her hotels that he'd found.

If he could just lie low and get through the next week, then he'd be able to reassess his living situation. Maybe he'd take his show to Vegas as he'd always dreamed. He was sure he could convince Brandy to join him and figured it was far enough away to keep the police off his trail until the heat was off.

It was Wednesday afternoon when his paranoia turned to outright fear. He had rigged up a small television in the office and was flipping through the channels on a break from his build when he saw himself on the news.

"Police are interested in interviewing Mr. Oscar Zachery, a local magician, in connection with the theft of the Four Feathers diamond from the Monument Museum. Zachery is not considered dangerous, but it is believed that he may be able to help with their inquiries. Anyone who has seen him can call Inspector Adrian Simpson on..."

He stared at the screen in shock. They had his name, picture, and phone number and had linked him to the Monument theft. He got up and checked the lock-up was secure and spent fifteen minutes pacing, running his fingers through his hair. The stress bought on an attack, and the voice in his head came rushing back.

"They're on to you Oscar. Call them. Hand yourself in. It's all over".

He shook his head, forcing the voice away, and found that he'd lost a few seconds, coming around slumped on the sofa. His hands were shaking as he took another tablet, noticing that he was running out. What if Dr. Pullman had seen the news bulletin? How was he going to get more?

He ran himself a glass of water from the sink and picked his phone up to call Pullman. Maybe he'd be able to get some more before the whole world saw him on the news. He was just about to push the green phone symbol when it rang in his hand, making him jump and dropping it. It bounced on the hard floor with a loud crack, and slid across it, coming to rest face down against the office door.

He scurried after the phone, grabbed it, and found that the screen was obliterated. He couldn't see who was trying to call him but assumed it was Brandy as she was the only person he'd given the number to. She must've seen the news report. Should he answer? If he ignored her all week, then she'd never trust him again. Better to talk to her now and claim that there must be a mix-up and that he was going to call the police. He jabbed at the screen, but the damage was too severe. He tried several times until it rang off.

"Shit" he exclaimed.

He threw the phone across the room in frustration and it hit the wall finishing it off for good.

He turned to his laptop and sent Brandy a message, telling her that the new phone was playing up and that she could call him via the computer. He had public wi-fi in the lock-up, but it was a bit intermittent. He waited five minutes, but there was no call, so he turned back to the build. Concentrate on the plan he thought to himself. One more week and he could go into hiding with enough money to set himself up for life. He was nearly done and was now confident that it would be finished well before the weekend.

"One more week" he mumbled to himself as he worked. "I can do this."

****

GreenZero,

Congratulations on completing your task. One of our team has confirmed that they can connect to Aseem's phone, and another is currently creating a clone of the card that you swiped.

Good job.

I have another task for you. I will be connecting you to one of our team called Ozzy. Ozzy is going to need some help in the bank on Monday evening, setting up in the vault. The equipment that he is installing is too heavy for him to do on his own. Please wear a face covering as staying anonymous is still a key security protocol for this plan. Ozzy will be in full charge while in the bank, so please follow his instructions. You are to meet him at the car park shutter just before midnight.

Good Luck

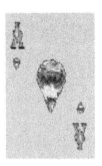

****

Thursday 5th March

"Monroe" bellowed Simpson. "Car. Now. We've got a hit on a casino." He was striding towards the door with the address of the casino in his hand.

"She's called in sick boss." Dickson looked up from his computer.

Simpson stopped mid-stride. "What the fuck is wrong with this team?" he said exasperated. "No one seems to do a full week's work anymore. Can *you* join me or are you finishing early to wax your legs or something?"

Dickson jumped up.

"I'm in. Let's go."

Dickson had checked through a list of casinos within a five-mile radius of the Tempest. He thought they would be able to visit them all, but it turned out there were eighty-one of them. He ended up emailing them all with a picture of the drunken guy who had hit the Tempest. It had taken a week, but they'd got a hit.

Dickson strapped himself into the passenger seat and said a silent prayer as Simpson screeched out of the station car park.

"So, tell me more about this guy. What did he say?" said Simpson

"John Nolan - known as Jonno," said Dickson consulting his notes. "He's a security guard. Seems that the guy in the picture is a regular there. Likes to have a drink or three. Owen someone or other. Didn't know his second name, but one of the dealers there knows him a bit better. She may be able to help. Should only take us fifteen minutes with you driving."

Dickson hadn't experienced Simpson's white-knuckle driving as often as Madison had, but he knew enough to be pleased that this would be a short trip.

He squealed like a girl as Simpson overtook a lorry, accelerated into a roundabout, and exited into a bus lane, cursing in frustration at the bus in front of him that was actually sticking to the speed limit.

"Come on slow-arse" he yelled beeping his horn.

"It's a bus in a bus lane," said Dickson, stating the obvious. "I think he's allowed."

Simpson grunted, swerved around the bus and found an open road in front of him, and floored the accelerator.

"Any news on Zachery? Surely someone must recognize the bastard. He plays the circuit."

"We've had a few calls, but no one who knows where he lives. One of them even passed his phone number on to us, so we know that it's genuine. At least we know that the guy at the Mirage – Micky, gave you the right number."

"Have we traced it?"

It's gone dark. Looks like he saw the news bulletin and turned it off before the paperwork went through.

"Shit. Why does everything take so long and have to be signed in triplicate? We could've tracked his phone and brought him in days ago."

Dickson shrugged. Nothing ever happened overnight.

They pulled up in front of a grubby casino and Simpson dragged his pipe out, having a few puffs before they went in.

He flashed his badge to the guy on the door. "Are you Jonno?"

"Yes Sir," said Jonno. He was military trained, and the "Sir" came out of habit.

"Thanks for calling us," said Simpson dragging out the photo "What can you tell us about this guy?"

"Owen. I've just found out that his surname is Kelly. He's a bit of a liability. Always in here, always drinking. Gets a bit lairy after a few – especially if he's losing. He got banned once after an incident, but the boss always lets him back in. He puts a lot of money our way."

"Have you got an address or a phone number?"

"No idea, sorry. I guess he lives nearby though as he's a regular. People who visit two or three times a week and drop money like he does don't tend to come far."

"I don't suppose you know if you saw him on or around 24th January?" said Dickson.

Jonno shrugged. "All the days roll into one working here," he said. "We have a camera that you could look at, but I don't know if we keep copies that far back. You could check with the boss."

"When did you last see him?" said Dickson.

"He was here last Friday. Sat with Estelle on the roulette. He always sits with Estelle. I think he's got a thing for her. He's probably been back since, but I've had a couple of days off."

"Is Estelle here?" said Simpson. "I'd like a word with her too."

"No. It's her day off. The boss will have a number for her though."

"Ok. Thanks. Can you call your boss? Is he in today?"

"Yes. He'll be in the office upstairs."

Jonno grabbed a phone, pushed a button, and said a few words.

"Go on up," said Jonno, indicating a door with a sign that said "Private". "He'll meet you at the top of the stairs."

They thanked him, opened the door, and found a corridor with a flight of stairs that led to a large room with a bank of monitors. A guy was sat watching and controlling the cameras, scrutinizing the punters and making sure that no one was counting cards or trying to cheat any of the games.

"It's sad that we have to do it, but you'll be surprised how many people try to bend the rules when money is involved," said a voice behind them.

A guy in a smart suit stuck out his hand. "I'm Paul Tarrant, the manager. I understand that you are interested in one of our customers."

"Hi Mr. Tarrant. Sorry to bother you" said Simpson. "Yes, we're interested in the whereabouts of a Mr. Owen Kelly. Mr. Nolan on security recognized him but doesn't know much more. We were hoping to get an address or phone number for him."

"Yes. We all know Owen. Bit of a character that one. He's harmless but can overstep the mark when he's got a few drinks in him. We keep a close eye on his drink intake from up here when he's in. Make sure he has water now and then to keep him on the straight and narrow."

"I don't suppose you keep contact details of your regulars?"

"No. No need to" said, Tarrant. "We're not a members club or anything. People come and go. Estelle might know though."

"Yes. Mr. Nolan suggested that too. Do you have a number for her? I'd like to catch up with her today if possible. What's her full name?"

"Let me call her," said Tarrant. "It's Estelle Rose-Price. I'm sure she'll be happy to talk to you. Word of warning. She has a condition. Tourettes. It tends to be worse when she's nervous.

Dickson jotted down her name while Tarrant looked up her number, grabbed a phone, and called her.

"Hi Estelle. It's Paul. No, don't worry. I don't need you in today. I have a police officer with me who would like a word. He's trying to track down Owen Kelly."

"Owen? I'm not sure I can help but put him on." Estelle was worried. What's Owen got himself into now, she thought.

Tarrant passed the phone to Simpson.

"Good afternoon Miss Price. My name's Inspector Simpson from the Metropolitan police. I was hoping that you may be able to help us locate the whereabouts of a Mr. Owen Kelly."

"I know Owen," said Estelle. "He's a regular. Likes to come and chat me up at the roulette table. Nice guy. When he's sober" she added.

"I don't suppose you have an address or phone number for him?"

"I think he's local, but no. No idea. I have a phone number for him, but it might be an old one."

"I'd like to take that please if that's OK. When did you last call him?"

Estelle was getting nervous. She didn't like to lie to the police, but at the same time, she didn't want to drop Owen in it. Her mind was wrestling with whether or not to give up the number or use his old one. He'd updated his phone last year and she'd only got the new one last week when they'd gone out. She decided to protect Owen and call him later to find out what it was all about.

"Oh, probably a year ago," she said. "I'll text it to Paul when I hang up. I need to look it up." There was a pause, she stuttered, tried to stop herself, but it came out anyway "Pig wanker."

"Ah. OK. Right. Sure" Simpson was flustered, unsure on whether to acknowledge the outburst or move on. He chose to ignore it. "Thanks for your help, Miss Price. Have a good day."

****

Back in the car, Simpson called the number, but it was dead.

"Shit. We take one step forward and before we know it, we're back to square one" he said miserably.

"I'll get on to the network," said Dickson. "If it was a contract phone, they should have an address for him. We'll get him."

Simpson sighed and screeched away from the curb in front of a dustcart. The dustcart driver hit his brakes but was moving too fast. The impact caught the back of the police car hard, and the weight of the dustcart span it ninety degrees. They collided with a bollard and Dickson got catapulted through the windscreen.

He had been reaching for his seatbelt.

Chapter 38 – "Set-up"

Monday 9th March

Oscar had had a busy week. He had tried his best to lie low, and other than a visit to EZ-Store to pick up some things for the bank, he had been tied to the lock-up working. Brandy had been messaging him regularly on the computer, asking about the police and when he was going to get his phone replaced. He had managed to convince her that it was all a misunderstanding and that he had sorted it out with them, and that he would get a phone when he got a spare hour, although he wasn't sure when that would be.

She surprised him on Saturday evening by taking advantage of the video calling and gave him an impromptu striptease that culminated in her pouring whipped cream over her nipples and spanking herself with a copy of Heat magazine.

"It's the only fing I could find" she cackled after.

He realized he missed her and was pleased with the pleasant distraction from the police and the stress of the work he was doing. The fact it was pain-free was an added bonus.

The time in the lock-up had allowed him to complete his build and he had just finished loading up a rental van with everything. He checked the items that he had picked up from the storage facility - two swipe cards to get into the outer vault, an earpiece, a miniature camera with a built-in microphone, and a six-digit passcode that would open box number six.

Ace had told him that one of their team – Pandora, would be talking to him on the earpiece and would connect to him just before midnight. Apparently, she had the means to get him inside the bank, but he was given no further information other than to await her instructions. Also, another member – GreenZero, would be meeting him outside the bank at 11:50pm to help him get the gear inside and install it.

It seemed that Ace's plan of keeping us all separate has fallen a bit by the wayside, thought Oscar as he slammed the van door and made his way to the driver's seat. Ace was still keeping things close to his chest, but tonight he would be meeting one of the team and talking to another. He checked his watch - just after 11pm. It would take him forty-five minutes to reach the bank and he didn't want to be late.

****

11:55, Oscar was sat opposite the bank looking out for GreenZero, when a voice from the earpiece made him jump. For a split second, he thought it was the voice in his head again. He had run out of tablets the day before and wasn't feeling his best, certainly not as sharp as usual. Something was just a little off.

"Hello. Ozzy? Are you there?"

"Shit. Hi. Yes. Is that Pandora?"

"Well, who else would it be? Are you at the bank?"

"Yes. I'm sat outside. I'm waiting for GreenZero though. He's not here yet."

He heard a loud sigh.

"Fucking amateurs" she muttered.

"Are you connected to him too? Can you talk to him?" said Ozzy, slightly shocked by her aggressive tone.

"I'm trying. Jesus. Give me a second."

He heard her thumping away on a keyboard and then she said "GreenZero. Where the fuck are you?"

"Erm. It's still me" said Ozzy.

"I know it's fucking still you. I've patched his earpiece into the call."

"OK. OK Just checking" said Oscar defensively.

"GreenZero. Are you there?" she yelled again.

Nothing.

"We can start without him," said Ozzy. "I can unload. I just need help inside to fix everything up."

"I'll get you in, but if he doesn't turn up, we might as well all pack up and go home," she said tetchily. "What are you building anyway? Ace hasn't told me anything. Just to get you guys in."

"I have been told to tell you everything once the build is complete. I think Ace is a bit power crazy. I feel like a pawn being pushed around a board."

The shutter by the bank started to open making Oscar look up.

"I don't know why he feels the need for all the secrecy," she said. "Mind you. Suits me. I'd rather keep my distance. People piss me off. Is the shutter opening?"

"Yes," said Oscar. So, not a people person then, he thought. No shit.

"OK. Head into the car park. I'll close it behind you. Drive down to the bottom. There's a door by the bins. That's your way in. I'll start working on the code."

"What's the code for?"

"Just drive" she yelled. "Let me worry about it."

Oscar rolled his eyes, followed her instructions and reversed up to the door, and killed the engine.

"GreenZero. Can you hear me? What's going on? We need you at the bank?" he said.

Still nothing.

"Have you spoken to him before?" he asked Pandora.

"No. I've only spoken to the other guy – Budster. What a twat he was. You're not scared of rats are you?"

"Rats? No why?"

"Long story. Maybe I'll share the video one day. OK – Looks like the door code hasn't changed. It's 215567C."

Oscar tapped in the number and pressed "Enter" and the door clicked open.

"OK. I'm in. You have a video of him?"

"Would probably go viral if I released it." She tapped some more, and a shutter began to open inside the loading bay that he found himself in.

"The inner door will take you to the corridor by the vault," she said. "I've disabled the alarms. Start getting the gear in. I'll message GreenZero on GreySpider. See if I can get him that way."

****

Half an hour later, Oscar was sat outside the vault with the gear piled around him, sweating and taking a rest. GreenZero hadn't shown up, and Pandora had given up trying. She had even messaged Ace, but he seemed to be offline. How could he not be available on the night they were going in?

"You're gonna have to come help me," said Oscar for the third time. "I've not come this far to abandon."

"No fucking way," said Pandora. "I told you. I don't do people. I barely leave my apartment."

Oscar sighed wearily. This girl may be a tech wizard, but she was pissing him off.

"Look. The diamond is already in transit" said Oscar getting agitated. "It hits the bank tomorrow. If I can't set this up tonight, then we're screwed. Do you want to tell Ace that the whole plan is off because you didn't get off your arse and help out when we hit a problem? I get it. GreenZero's the one at fault, but it's nearly one o'clock in the fucking morning and you're the only one available, so get yourself down here pronto."

He let out a breath. He rarely swore, but the stress of the last week was really getting to him and a headache was forming over his left eye.

Pandora was shocked. No one talked to her like that, mainly because no one talked to her period. She was a hermit. The thought of leaving the safety of her apartment and traveling to the bank horrified her and she had an immediate impulse to shut off the comms to Ozzy and leave him stranded in the bank. Ace had promised her that she could assist from home. This is not what she signed up for.

"GreenZero" she yelled desperately. "Where are you? We need you now."

"Pandora," said Oscar gently. "Come to the bank. It will only be a couple of hours and then you'll be safely back inside your apartment. Please. I need your help."

She could feel the pressure building up inside her head. The feeling of being backed into a corner. She only really had one choice but didn't like the choice that was presented to her.

"I'll be thirty minutes," she said sullenly.

"Thank you," said Oscar, massaging his temples.

****

He was dozing gently when he heard the shutter opening. He had a moment of panic before he realized that it was likely to be Pandora. He grabbed at the mask; a plain white featureless model that made him look quite spooky. Ace had asked him to wear one when he met GreenZero. It seems that he still didn't want them to be able to identify each other. He stood up as Pandora came in.

She wore her own mask – something that looked like it had been used in a masquerade ball.

"Don't even mention the mask" she said as she walked towards him. "It's all I could find at short notice."

What use she had for a masked-ball mask when she never went out was beyond Oscar, but he refrained from asking.

She carried a laptop with her and set it down on a small side table near the entrance to the vault.

"Thanks for coming," said Oscar. "I'll be sure to let Ace know that you saved the day."

She grunted. "Let's just get this over with," she said moodily.

He handed her one of the swipe cards. They'd both seen Budster's video so knew the protocol. Pandora opened her laptop and launched a program. A few key presses later and she was done.

"The two mobile phones have been locked down," she said. "Let's do this."

They counted to three and swiped together. One of two things would now happen. Either, the copied cards would be rejected, and the alarms would start ringing, or Pandora's mobile phone would pick up two texts - one from the bank manager's phone and one from Aseem's. There was an agonizing ten-second delay when nothing happened, and then her phoned pinged twice in quick succession. Oscar hadn't realized he was holding his breath until they arrived, and he let it out in a rush.

Pandora entered the code from the phone into the keypad by the vault. There was a loud click and it swung open.

Oscar whistled. "Good job," he said. "How did that just happen?"

"Ace tasked the other guys to install a program to the phones," said Pandora. "I wrote the program. The texts won't get through to them. I had them re-routed to here." She indicated the phone she held and stuck it into her pocket. "So now it's over to you. What exactly is all this stuff?"

"Let's get the inner door open and I'll show you," said Oscar. They stepped into the vault and Oscar approached the terminal that controlled the safety deposit boxes. The software was simple. Twenty-five boxes were displayed on the screen. Pandora's device had been placed in box number six a few weeks earlier by Budster, and Oscar had the code. He pressed number six on the screen, entered the code and the door to the safety deposit room clicked open. They went in.

Box number six was open.

"So now what?" she said "Are we putting something else in the box?"

Oscar closed box number six again.

"Nope. That was just our way into here. Now we replace the boxes."

She gaped at him. "That's the plan?" she said sarcastically. "How the hell can we do that? They're bolted to the wall."

"Maybe I should have said "disguise"" said Oscar. "I've built a replica. It will sit in front of these boxes and look identical. I've got some plasterboard too. We create a new wall above. Once it's complete, this whole side of the room will look exactly the same to anyone coming in."

"But the room will be smaller. What if someone notices?"

"Have you watched the video?" said Oscar.

"Several times," she said impatiently.

"And who comes in?"

She suddenly got it. None of the bank staff entered the room. The only people coming in would be the security team dropping off the diamond. They would never have seen it before.

"We could almost stick any array of twenty-five boxes in here," said Oscar. "As long as it looks good. It's only for a day. The diamond will be dropped into one of our boxes and we can come back and get it tomorrow night." He headed back to the outer vault. "Let's get working. It all bolts together. Should only take us an hour or so."

Pandora followed him numbly, focusing on just one sentence of what he'd just told her. "You mean I've got to fucking come back tomorrow?"

****

It took then just over an hour to rig up the boxes. He spent another half an hour building a stud wall frame above the boxes and Pandora helped him in with a large sheet of painted plasterboard that he clipped into place. It wasn't the strongest structure in the world, but it looked the part. The table in the middle of the room was pulled back a foot so that it was in the center of the new area. He stood back and admired his work.

"What do you think?"

"I think I'm ready to get out of here," said Pandora yawning. "Are we done?"

"Just the camera. Oh. And we need to check that you can connect to the new box array we've just installed. Can you try it?" The boxes and the camera had a Bluetooth connection and Pandora grabbed her laptop and quickly paired them both to her laptop. Oscar returned to the terminal that opened the inner door and mounted the tiny spy camera in the corner of the room above it.

"Can you connect to these remotely?" he said.

"Of course I can," she said scornfully. They're all part of the bank network now, and I'm already into that."

"Good. The diamond will be hitting Heathrow airport at 8am this morning" said Oscar. "It should be arriving at the bank just after 10am. The security team will be bringing it down to this room. The bank's vault system will select a box number, and they will use their own system, to open the box. Of course, that box is behind ours now, so it will open but they won't be able to get to it. You need to listen in and watch on the camera and open up the corresponding box in my setup at the same time."

They had a couple of tests to confirm all was working OK, and Pandora opened box eleven and twenty on request.

"Perfect," said Oscar. "When the box is pushed closed there is a sensor that triggers a device on the back of it that flips up and pushes on the matching door behind it at the same time. This will close the bank's deposit box so they won't get suspicious. As far as they are concerned, they've opened their box, deposited the diamond, and closed it again.

"So tomorrow we come back, open it up, and grab the diamond?" said Pandora. "Are you taking all this down again?"

"That's the plan. Cover our tracks. If the police find the replica vault, they'll know what happened and start a nationwide search for us. If we can remove everything, then the first place they will start looking is the security team who dropped it off. If no one else has come into the vault, and the CCTV backs that up, then all fingers will point to them. There will be no evidence." He looked at her. "Ace tells me you're on top of the CCTV."

"Yep. It's easy. I can splice previous recordings together to make it look like no one has been here, and also fool the operating system into thinking that the files haven't been tampered with."

"Then we're good to go," said Oscar with a smile that she couldn't see under the mask. "Twenty-four hours from now, we'll be collecting the diamond."

Chapter 39 – "The Diamond"

Tuesday 10th March

"Yes Sir. We landed fifteen minutes ago. We've just got to the car and are heading to Larkins."

Chuck Delallio was the head of Seth Rayman's personal bodyguard team and had been given the unenviable task of ensuring Mr. Rayman's diamond got safely to the bank. He had a briefcase handcuffed to his wrist and had spent over fourteen hours sat in the luxury of Rayman's private jet with the diamond tied to him at all times. He was looking forward to completing his mission and handing it over. Now he was on the ground, he had his other hand hovering near the Glock G19 pistol that was strapped to a holster under his jacket. His eyes were darting left and right, taking in the surroundings and keeping a watchful eye on anyone who came within ten feet of the security team. Chuck had his own security of three who had encircled him as he left the plane and they had all shuffled together like a bizarre dance troupe to the bullet-proof limo that had been waiting for them.

"Very good," said Rayman. "Let me know when it's safely in their vault. We are only responsible until then." He hung up swiftly, no time for chit-chat or pleasantries.

"Let's go" ordered Delallio. I want to be in my hotel room sleeping before midday, and then back on the plane tomorrow. This British weather sucks balls."

The car moved away and started its journey through London's rush hour traffic, heading to Chelsea. Delallio was on edge all the way. He had felt relatively safe in the air in familiar surroundings, but the last leg of this epic journey was always going to be the weak link.

He needn't have worried. Other than a painfully slow end-to-end crawl up the M4 due to an overturned lorry, the journey went without incident, and he and the security team entered the vault at Larkins at 9:45am.

Briars was gushing about the security of their "state of the art" vault and accompanied him into the outer room. He selected box number eight, and Delallio entered a code and then re-entered to confirm. The door clicked open.

"The door to box number eight should be open," said Briars, gesturing him towards the room. "Please take as much time as you need."

****

Several miles away, Amy Ross was watching and listening. The big guy was walking towards the safety deposit boxes with a briefcase handcuffed to his wrist. She had remotely opened box number eight of Ozzy's array of boxes, but as they hadn't left a camera in the vault itself, she had a nerve-jangling five-minute wait watching the closed door for him to appear again. What was he doing in there? Surely it would only take thirty seconds to open the briefcase and maybe another thirty to drop the diamond off and close the door to the safety deposit box. Perhaps he was admiring the diamond but surely, he should be out by now?

When the door finally opened, she held her breath. Had Ozzy's device closed the real box number eight? If not, the bank manager would surely go in and check and they might be rumbled.

"Many thanks for your assistance" she heard the guy with the briefcase say. "I will pass my personal code back to Mr. Rayman so he can in turn pass it on to the new owner."

They all shook hands, exited the room and the vault door swung shut.

Amy punched the air. She fired a message off to Ace and Ozzy telling them that the Queen of Diamonds had safely been delivered and was sat in box number eight in the vault.

****

"Feels like déjà vu," said Oscar as Pandora came in through the shutter wearing her gaudy mask.

"I can't believe I'm here again," she said irritated. "It seems that GreenZero has disappeared off the face of the Earth."

"I think he was the one who stole the Tempest diamond," said Oscar. "I presume you saw the footage on tv. He was out of his head. Maybe he's on a bender?"

"I don't care. He's let us down. I know he's done other work on this job, but I'm going to recommend that he gets a reduced share. It's a piss-take."

"You're not wrong," said Ozzy. He shook his head as a pain shot from his temple and down the left side to his ear.

"You OK?"

He breathed for a few seconds as the pain subsided.

"Yeh. Let's get on with this."

He passed her one of the swipe cards and she did her magic with the laptop.

They stood with their cards at the ready and she counted down.

"3. 2. 1. Swipe."

She swiped down, but Oscar had held on to the wall for support and had fallen to his knees. The voice screamed at him from inside.

"You're going to get caught. You're all going to get caught. Trust no one".

"Ozzy? Ozzy? What the fuck are you doing?"

The world swam back into focus and Ozzy found himself on the floor, Pandora looking over at him.

He sat for a second as his head cleared.

"Shit. Sorry. On-going medical issue. It's passed. Let's try again."

"Are you sure you're ready? I don't know how many goes we get at this?"

As she said it, her phone pinged and she glanced at it. A message from the Vault's security system.

"VAULT ENTRY FAILURE: 2 ATTEMPTS REMAINING"

"Fuck. We get two more goes. You better do the counting" said Pandora.

"OK. I'm fine now. Really. Ready?"

They tried again, and this time a pleasant beep sound informed them that all was good. The vault code arrived on her phone and Pandora entered the code.

Oscar's head was swimming as he entered the vault. Pandora used her laptop to open box number eight and they both peered in. Inside was a small box, similar in size to the box that Buddy had brought into the bank several weeks ago. Pandora lifted it up, surprised by its weight, and clicked it open.

The diamond was huge. The light from Oscar's torch bounced off it and it reflected stars all around the small room. Pandora's eyes sparkled as she gazed at it.

"Wow. That's stunning" said Oscar.

"It really is" she whispered, hypnotized for a second. The blue diamond was mesmerizing. The cut and quality were like no other and it was too large to conceal in a hand. As Ace had promised, it made the Four Feathers diamonds look like tat in comparison.

"Come on. Let's tidy up and get out of here?" said Oscar. "I'm not feeling too great."

She blinked, looked away from the diamond, and became all business-like.

"Right. Yes. Grab the tools. Let's get this thing apart."

It only took them thirty minutes; dismantling the boxes proved much easier than putting them together. Oscar grabbed a broom from the van and swept the area to ensure they hadn't left any dust from the plasterboard wall. They returned the table to its former position and inspected the room.

"Looks good to me," said Pandora. "Shall we leave the camera? It will give us an early alert if they find anything."

Oscar pondered it for a moment.

"Would be nice" he said. "But no. We need to make it look like we weren't here. The camera is evidence. It all needs to go."

He reluctantly grabbed the stepladder they had been using and climbed up to take it down. As he put his hand on it, his head felt like it was going to explode. He grabbed at it, wobbled, and went crashing to the floor, sending the ladder sprawling.

"TRUST NO ONE OSCAR. YOU'RE NOT SAFE".

The voice was all-consuming as he lay on the floor holding his head. He could hear Pandora shouting at him as if from a distance.

"Ozzy? Get up, Ozzy. Come on. We've finished. We've got to get out the fuck of here."

She was shaking him when the pain subsided, and his vision came back into focus.

"Shit. That was a bad one" he moaned.

"Jesus Christ. You scared me. Go and sit outside. I've got this. I'll help you back to the van in a minute."

Oscar crawled out of the vault on his hands and knees and leaned up against the wall breathing deeply.

A few minutes later, Pandora was back with the camera and the ladder. She pulled the vault closed.

"You dropped this when you fell," she said, handing him his wallet. "Everything fell out. Cards, coins. The fucking lot. I've been scrambling around on the floor for the last few minutes trying to get it all."

"Thanks," he said. "At least we're done. Let's go."

"You're not going to have a brain hemorrhage on the way home and die with that diamond on you, are you?" she said pointedly.

"Thanks for the vote of sympathy," he said. "No. I'm fine."

"I'm serious. We've come too far to lose it because you pegged out on us."

"I'm fine," he said again, more forcefully. "I need to take it to EZ-Store for Ace."

She stared at him. "You're putting a fifty-million-pound diamond in EZ-Store?" she asked incredulously.

"Safer than the bank," he said. "Besides, you can keep an eye on it."

"I'm coming with you," she said. "I'm not letting that out of my sight until it's secure."

"And I thought you didn't like me. Fine, whatever. Let's just go so I can get some sleep."

****

Wednesday 11th March

It was 9:25am when Briars got a call from Aseem.

"Mr. Briars. Can you come out to the vault? I've got something that I'd like you to look at."

"What is it Aseem? I have a meeting in five minutes."

"Maybe nothing Sir, but I think you should check."

"OK. On my way."

Aseem was looking troubled when Briars joined him outside the vault.

"What's up?"

"I found this," said Aseem, handing him a card. It was sticking out under the door of the vault.

Briars turned the business card over.

"So, someone dropped a card. What's the big deal."

"It wasn't here yesterday. I was here till 6:30pm last night. I walked the floor like I always do. Everyone was gone except for you. This morning, I was first here, and that card was sticking out from under the door. I would've seen it yesterday. It definitely wasn't there."

Briars frowned. "Check the cameras," he said. "There's no way anyone got in there without me and you though."

"I already did. There's nothing. But I'm telling you. That card was not there yesterday. Someone's been in the bank since last night."

Briars looked at the business card again. It was for a Dr. Aaron Pullman – "Private Psychiatrist".

He thought about the diamond that had just been delivered to the bank. He was confident that no one could possibly get in, but due to the contents of the vault, he thought it best to follow up.

"OK. It's probably nothing, but you're right to bring it up. Let me make some calls. We need to check that the vault hasn't been compromised, and especially the contents. Good job Aseem."

****

Chuck Delallio was not happy at being back at the bank. He was scheduled to be on the private plane and heading home within the hour, but it seemed there was a security issue that he was required for. Not my problem was his first thought. The diamond had been handed over and was now the responsibility of the bank. My Rayman had insisted though and he met the manager at the entrance to the vault.

"Thanks for coming back," said Briars. "I apologize for having to drag you back down here, but we had a security anomaly and due to the rather special item that you dropped off yesterday, I'm just being extra cautious."

"It's not a problem Sir. What do you want from me?"

"I'd like you to open your safety deposit box and check that the contents are..." he paused struggling to find the right words "...intact."

"Are you suggesting that someone has managed to break your unbreakable 'state of the art' security?" said Delallio amazed.

"Not at all. It's just a precaution. The vault cannot be opened externally, and the cameras show no activity, but an item was found on the floor that wasn't there before." He showed Delallio the card. "I don't suppose you recognize it do you?"

"Sir, I live in Tahiti," said Delallio, inspecting the card. "And I can assure you I have no requirement for a psychiatrist, especially one across the other side of the world."

"Of course Sir. Sorry." Briars went red. "Let's get this over with so you can be on your way. I don't want to take up too much of your time."

They went through the process of opening the vault, and Delallio entered his code for box number eight. He disappeared into the room.

A moment later, he appeared at the door looking pale.

"I think you need to call the police," he said.

Chapter 40 – "Closing In"

Simpson hobbled into the incident room using his crutches for support.

"You OK boss?" said Madison. "You shouldn't be here. I thought you'd been signed off."

"I heard about the diamond," he said, wincing at a stab of pain in his foot. I'm not sitting this one out. How's Dickson? Any news?"

"He's stable, but they're worried about his head injury. Something about pressure pushing on his brain."

Simpson winced again. He'd got off lightly with a broken bone in his ankle and some cuts and bruises. Dickson wasn't so lucky.

"Poor kid" he muttered. He felt guilty. He'd seen Dickson reaching for the seatbelt and hadn't considered what might have happened when he pulled out. It was over so quickly that he still couldn't quite believe that he'd caused it. The truck driver was unscathed. Driving a vehicle that weighed six times more than Simpson's car and was built like a tank hadn't even left a dent.

Simpson lowered himself gently into a chair as Madison passed him a coffee.

"Right," he said. "What do you know?"

"The Queen of Diamonds. This is the one that I was telling you about. It got delivered to Larkins bank yesterday morning just before 10am by a Chuck Delallio – head of the security team in charge of the diamond. This morning, a security guard at the bank found a business card sticking out from under the vault. He convinced the bank manager that it wasn't there when he left the night before. They called Chuck back in as a precaution, opened the safety deposit box where the diamond was stored, and it was gone."

"Wait. Back up a second" said Simpson. "Weren't you going to warn them that our diamond thieves might be targeting them?"

"I was going to," said Madison. "But they moved the date up. It was supposed to be the end of the month. It's on my to-do list."

"Shit. We could've prevented this" said Simpson angrily. "For Christ's sake, don't let it slip that we suspected this. Our heads will be on the block." He paused to take a sip of his coffee. "We better get down there. How the hell did someone get in and out of a bank vault without them even knowing? If they hadn't dropped the business card, they'd never have known until it was collected."

"Unless the card is a decoy," said Madison. "Maybe they never actually put the diamond in."

"Yes. We'll need to talk to Mr. Delallio" said Simpson grimly. "Let's go. I'll let you drive today."

****

Simpson settled in a chair in Briars' office and was introduced to Chuck Delallio. Delallio relayed his steps from the day before, informing them that the diamond was indeed dropped into box number eight and that the door was securely closed after.

"Did you pass the safety deposit box code on to anyone else?" asked Simpson.

"Just my boss - Mr. Rayman. He was going to pass it on to the buyer so that it could be collected tomorrow. It's going to the

Tower of London, but they insisted on using their own security team. Mr. Rayman spoke to Larkins who assured us it would be safe here for forty-eight hours." He looked pointedly at Briars as he said it.

"The vault is impenetrable," said Briars holding his hands up. "Jesus. There are two swipe cards to get in, and then a text is sent to my phone with a new number every time. There's no other way in. Check my phone. There are no texts. That door has not been opened since we let Mr. Delallio in yesterday, and – even if someone did get in, they would need the code to the box. It's impossible".

"But the diamond isn't there Mr. Briars," said Simpson impatiently.

"Maybe it never was," he said, looking at Delallio.

"What are you suggesting?" said Chuck getting to his feet angrily.

Briars looked at him levelly. "We have alarms and CCTV. I've checked both. Nothing was triggered and nobody has been anywhere near that door. The swipe cards are secure, and I or our head of security never received a text with a vault code. I am saying categorically that nobody has been through that door since you did yesterday."

"Well I'm sorry to have to inform you but clearly someone has" yelled Chuck. "The diamond was there yesterday. As agreed, the responsibility of its security was passed to you as soon as we closed the door."

"OK. OK" said Simpson impatiently. "Sit down Mr. Delallio. Let's assume for the moment that the diamond was indeed dropped off as you say." He turned to Briars. "If the vault is impenetrable how do you explain the business card? Can I see it?"

Briars had had the forethought to put it in a plastic bag, one of the many coin bags that the bank used daily.

"It was found by our security guard Aseem, sticking out from under the vault door," he said. "It could have been there for months though and got dislodged when it was last opened."

"But you've already said that the last person to enter the vault was Mr. Delallio here," said Simpson. "So, the card would've been in full view all day yesterday, yet it wasn't spotted until today. Is that what you're suggesting?"

Briars looked flustered but didn't have an answer.

Simpson studied the card thoughtfully. From the outside looking in, Delallio would be looking guilty as hell right now, but Simpson knew something that he didn't want to divulge. The fact that they had diamond thieves operating in the area and had suspected that this diamond might be targeted. He wanted to throw his resources at following up on the business card.

"I'd like to talk to your head of security," he said to Briars. "And I need the number for Mr. Rayman," he said, turning to Delallio. "I need to find out who else knows this code. Also, I'd like a private word with my officer. Do you mind?"

"Of course," said Briars." I'll go and find Aseem for you.

"Can I leave?" said Delallio, scribbling his boss's phone number on the back of his business card. "I have a plane to catch."

"Mr. Delallio I suggest that leaving the country in a hurry would not look good for you," said Simpson sharply. "I may have some more questions for you later today. Please let me know where you are staying and leave me a number so I can contact you."

The two men got up and left Simpson and Madison alone.

"I want you to visit Dr. Pullman," said Simpson when the door had closed. "It's not too far from here. Find out if he recognizes any of the names that we've established for the diamond thieves - Owen Kelly and Oscar Zachery. Show him the pictures too. If we get a hit, then we might be able to find an address for one of them. If not, we'll focus on Delallio. Come back here after. I'll talk to security and Rayman, check the cameras, and look at the vault."

Madison nodded, left, and headed for the car.

Five minutes later, Aseem lumbered in.

"Tell me about this business card," said Simpson.

****

"Dr. Pullman's office. Elena speaking. How I help you?"

"Oh, good afternoon," said Madison. "It's Constable Madison Monroe calling from the Metropolitan police. I'd like to talk to Dr. Pullman regarding a case we are working on."

"I'm sorry Constable, Dr. Pullman has taken some time off and is not expected back for a couple of weeks. Is it something I can help with?"

"Possibly," said Madison. "I'm not far away. I'll come to the office if that's OK."

"Of course. I'll be here."

Madison started the car and drove twenty minutes to a quiet road in a tree-lined avenue. The address she had on the card was for an upmarket Georgian building that had been converted into business units. Dr. Pullman's office was on the first floor and she entered to find a middle-aged lady sat at a reception desk in front of a small office.

Crikey. This place is tiny, she thought. She introduced herself to Elena and they sat down in the office.

"It's not much," said Elena, "but it works. Dr. Pullman works from home a lot, and it's only him and me. The office is a bit cramped, but he likes to see his patients one on one. He does a lot of telephone appointments too, so doesn't really need anything bigger."

Madison explained about the business card and how it was found at the scene of a crime.

"We have a couple of suspects, and we'd like to know if any of them are on Dr. Pullman's books," she said. "A Mr. Owen Kelly and Mr. Oscar Zachery."

"Zachery," said Elena. "I know that name." She spun around in her chair and pulled open a filing cabinet, reaching for the back.

"Williams, Young, Zachery" she mumbled. "Here we are." She pulled the file out and opened it.

"Yes. Oscar Zachery is one of Dr. Pullman's patients. Has been for a couple of years by the looks of it."

"Do you have an address for him?" said Madison holding her breath.

"I do," said Elena, but promptly closed the file. "Unfortunately. That falls under doctor-patient privilege. I cannot divulge it without a warrant."

Madison sighed. "Can you tell me why Mr. Zachery was seeing the doctor?"

"Same answer I'm afraid. Sorry."

"Can you get hold of Dr. Pullman? Maybe I can ask him directly?"

"Even if I could, his answer will be the same," said Elena. "He takes privacy very seriously. It's imperative in this kind of work. Anyway, he's not available. Told me to take messages and make appointments. I can release these notes with a warrant, but I've probably said too much already."

She thanked her and returned to the car and called Simpson.

"Bingo," he said. "We need that file. Call it in and get that warrant ready, then come get me. We'll have the file within the next couple of hours and hopefully, have Zachery by the end of the day. Good job."

****

Oscar had slept at the lock-up and woken to a killer headache. The diamond was safely secured in EZ-Store and he had messaged Ace when he had got in with the good news. Pandora had waited in the car when he'd dropped it off, and unbeknown to her, he had rented a different box at the storage facility at Ace's request. He was the only one who knew the code.

Ace had suggested that he would be in touch within twenty-four hours so they could arrange to meet up with the whole team and the buyer.

With nothing to do, the lock-up was depressing as hell. He was still feeling rough, and he decided to take a chance and head home. He was long overdue for a shower, and he hoped he might be able to find some old pills lying around to overcome the hollow feeling in his head.

Back at the apartment, he pulled out a suitcase and started to pack the essentials. If he got his pay-out within the next few days, then he wouldn't be returning. He grabbed his phone too. He wanted to talk to Brandy later but had run out of money. Buying a new phone was out of the question.

An hour later, after a shower, some breakfast, and a fruitless search for some tablets, he had loaded up his old Volkswagen and was about to get in when two police cars screeched to a halt in front of him and two burly officers got out.

"Mr. Oscar Zachery. I am arresting you on the suspicion of diamond theft. Anything you say….."

He didn't hear the rest as he was handcuffed and pushed into the back of the car.

Chapter 41 – "Oscar"

"I don't feel good. I need my tablets" said Oscar. "I'm not talking to anyone until I've got my medication."

"We'll get your tablets when you answer my questions," said Simpson impatiently. "Where's the diamond, Zachery?"

He'd asked the question a dozen times in the last forty-five minutes. Oscar had been fingerprinted and led to a cell where they left him for an hour before they pulled him to the room and started questioning him. An hour later and Oscar was like a broken record. It had started with "No comment" to everything that was asked of him, and as time went on, he grew more agitated and restless and started demanding his tablets.

"Monroe, where's the copy of that doctor's file? What tablets does he need? Maybe we can get him some and get him talking."

The warrant had gained them the doctor's file, but they hadn't read all the notes yet and she flipped through to a page headed "Medication".

"I'll get back on to the doc's office. He's away, but Elena, his receptionist might be able to sign for a repeat prescription" she said reaching for her phone.

Simpson took the notes from her and started to read when he was interrupted by officer Jones.

"Sir. I think we've got a hit on Owen Kelly."

Simpson looked up, his eyebrows shooting up.

"Talk," he said, putting the file aside.

"I've been following up on the phone number that you picked up from the girl at the casino. The network has finally come through, traced the old number, and given me an address."

"Excellent. We might be able to pick up another one of the bastards" said Simpson with delight. "Take Jackson and see if you can find him."

"There's a problem with that Sir. The address is bogus. 220 Park Drive. Trouble is, there's only ever been eighty-four houses in Park Drive."

Simpson's face dropped. "Why are you wasting my time with this Jones?" he said, picking up Zachery's file again.

"Well, the phone company has another number on file. New contract taken out last year. It must be his new one" said Jones.

"Have you called it?"

"Yes. No answer. Goes to answerphone."

"Keep on it. Let me know if you get anywhere." Simpson returned to the file.

"Yes Sir."

****

Oscar was kicking himself. Why did he have to go home? All he had to do was sit tight until Ace contacted him and he'd have been OK. A couple of days of boredom followed by a lifetime of luxury. He racked his brain trying to work out how they'd got to him; what evidence they had to link him to Larkins bank, but couldn't work out where he had slipped up. Even the bank shouldn't know that the diamond was missing yet. He had been arrested for diamond theft, so maybe it was just the Monument diamond they were holding him for. If that was the case, they definitely had no concrete proof as the diamond had been returned. He planned to stick to his "No comment" strategy, at least until they showed their hand.

After two nights working in the bank, the stress of the previous week, and attempting to sleep on a lumpy sofa, he was tired to the bone and his head was hurting like a bitch. The voice hadn't returned, but he had experienced the rush of air that normally preceded it three times when he was locked in the cell.

He was still in the interview room having been grilled for nearly an hour by the detective with the broken foot. Simpson his name was, permanently angry and reeked of tobacco. That hadn't helped with how he was feeling, and his stomach was churning.

"Hello" he called. "Can someone get me a bucket? I think I'm going to be...."

He didn't finish the sentence as he vomited his breakfast all over the interview room table.

An officer rushed in.

"Oh shit he said. "What a mess. You OK?" He disappeared and returned a moment later with some paper towels for Oscar to clean himself up. Simpson limped in behind him.

"Put him back in the cell," said Simpson in disgust. "And for God's sake, find him a bucket or something. We better seal this room off until we can get it cleaned up."

"Yes, Sir," said the officer.

Oscar was helped back to his cell, demanding his tablets all the way. Ten minutes later the officer returned with a jug of water, a bucket, and some tablets to settle his stomach which he took gratefully. He laid down on the bed, closed his eyes, and slept for over twelve hours, the previous week finally catching up with him.

****

Thursday 12th March

"Dickson has stabilized," said Madison as she walked into the precinct. "I've just come from the hospital and they've relieved the pressure on his brain. He was sitting up talking when I left."

Simpson let out a long, relieved sigh. "Thank God," he said. "Thanks, Monroe. That will at least help me focus a bit today. I'll go see him later."

"How's our prisoner?"

"Slept for England. We left him to it after the mess he made of the interview room. I was about to go and get him and have another go. There's some weird shit in that medical file. Did you read it?"

"Only the medication. I'm getting nowhere with the doctor. I swear the receptionist was born with a stick up her arse. Keeps citing protocol and doctor-patient privilege. She can't or won't release any more tablets."

"Shit. He's not being very cooperative. Can we give him something that looks the same? Maybe he'll talk."

"I'm not sure that's particularly ethical Sir."

Simpson grunted. "I'll meet you in the interview room. Can you bring him up?" He indicated his leg.

"Sure. I'll probably get there before you" she said with a grin.

Madison headed down to the cells and heard the commotion halfway down the stairs.

"Mr. Zachery. Please calm down. I don't want to have to restrain you."

"My name is not Zachery" he screamed. "Why am I here? How did I get here? I demand to see my lawyer."

"Sir. That is your right, and if you calm down, I will see what I can do" said the young officer. He glanced up as Madison approached, looking relieved to see her.

"He woke up like a man possessed. I think he's got short-term memory problems or something."

"Let me talk to him," said Madison. "Thanks, Matt. Don't run off. You may have to help me escort him upstairs."

She approached the bars of the cell and stood calmly, looking at the angry man a few steps in front of her.

"Mr. Zachery, detective Simpson would like to talk to you," she said as if addressing a small child. "I can take you out of your cell and lead you quietly to the interview room, or we can handcuff you and drag you there kicking and screaming. I know which one I'd rather do."

"I'm not Zachery. I keep telling you people" he screamed.

"OK. OK. Tell it to the detective. Are you going to come quietly?"

He seemed to compose himself and took a breath.

"Yes. Sure. OK. I want some answers though. Why am I here? What are you holding me for?"

"Just come with me and we'll have a chat," she said, unlocking the cell. "You're not going to give me any trouble are you?"

"No. I just want to know what the hell is going on."

Madison led him upstairs and joined Simpson who had just reached the interview room. She sat him down and whispered in Simpson's ear.

"I think he's pushing for an insanity plea. Tread carefully."

"Mr. Zachery," said Simpson. "I hope you're feeling a little better. I was hoping you would be a bit more cooperative today. We need to ask you some questions."

"My name is not Zachery" repeated the man angrily for the third time. "My name is Horace-Harvey Willis and I demand to know why I am here. I don't remember how I got here. I woke up and found myself in your cells."

Simpson paused and sat back thinking.

"Mr. Willis. Please tell me what you do remember. Where were you yesterday?"

"I don't remember," said the man rubbing his hand back and forth on his forehead in frustration. "I have blackouts. I forget things. My doctor tells me to write stuff down. It helps me to remember."

Simpson was thinking back to what he'd read in the medical file.

"Mr. Willis. I'd like to talk to my constable alone" he said. He removed a pen from his jacket and pushed his pad towards him.

"Please write down what you do remember. We'll be back in ten minutes."

"I'm not writing anything until I see my lawyer."

"So write down your lawyer's number too," said Simpson angrily. He lifted himself up on his crutches. "Monroe. With me" he said.

They left the room and Simpson led her to an office with a one-way mirror that looked in on the interview room.

"What do you think?" said Madison. "Is he trying to play us?"

"I'm not sure," said Simpson. He passed her the medical file. "You need to read that though. Take a look. He's got a condition. Some identity disorder or something. The notes suggest that he can alternate between multiple personalities."

"Your shitting me." Madison picked up the file and flipped through it until she came to the diagnosis. In small, neat handwriting, the doctor had written some notes.

"It is my opinion that Mr. Zachery is experiencing Dissociative Identity Disorder (DID) and will alternate between two or more distinct personality states or experiences. These might have their own names, voices, and characteristics. These personalities might seem like they're trying to take control in a person's head. With 'DID' a person may have memory gaps of daily events, personal information, and trauma that they have experienced..."

"So he thinks he's someone else?" said Madison skeptically looking up from the file.

Simpson shrugged. "That's what the file suggests. If he does, then we're going to struggle to talk to him about a robbery that he has no knowledge of. We'll need to wait until Oscar Zachery returns."

They looked up and saw the man they thought was Zachery pacing the room, mumbling to himself. Simpson flicked a switch so they could hear what he was saying."

"One, two, three, four, five, six." He stopped and turned and repeated the process, walking the other way.

"One, two, three." He stopped again, pausing at the desk in the center of the room. He reached down and straightened the pen.

****

Four hours later Simpson was getting frustrated. Monroe had gone back to see Dr. Pullman's secretary to discuss Oscar's condition and insist that she contact the doctor. In the meantime, he had told "Horace" that his lawyer was not available and that he was trying his hardest to contact him. He was playing for time, looking for a change, hoping to get Oscar back.

At just after 1pm, the change came, but it wasn't what he'd hoped for.

The man he still knew as Zachery had sunk to the interview room floor, clutching his head, and had started rocking back and forth, mumbling incoherently. Simpson had set up a video in the adjoining room so that they could record his actions. Suddenly the rocking stopped, and a new personality emerged. An angry one.

He started hammering on the locked door and screaming.

"Where the fuck am I? Let me out. Who's there?"

Two officers bundled in and restrained him, and Simpson followed dropping into the chair.

"Who are you, people? Why are you holding me?"

"Mr. Zachery, Horace. Whatever your name is" said Simpson impatiently. "Please sit down. You are in a police interview room and you're under arrest. We are not going to hurt you, but we need you to calm down."

"Under arrest? What the fuck for? I've done nothing wrong. Get the fuck off me."

He was pushed down forcefully into his chair and the two officers stepped back but hovered menacingly nearby.

Simpson looked at him and spoke calmly. "I understand you have a medical condition and we are trying hard to contact your doctor. In the meantime, I have a few questions for you. Can we start with your name?"

The man settled, looked confused, and folded his arms defiantly.

"I need a drink," he said angrily.

"Get him some water," said Simpson, not looking away.

"No. A drink drink. Whiskey."

"I'm afraid that won't be possible. We cannot allow you to have alcohol while in custody."

"Fuck's sake. Why should I answer your fucking questions if you're not going to help me?"

"Sir. Your name please" Simpson persisted.

"Kelly," he said sullenly. "My name is Owen Kelly."

Simpson's eyebrows shot up so far that he lost them in his hairline.

****

"Monroe. What's happening? We need to speak to that doctor."

"She's trying," said Madison between mouthfuls, tucking the phone under her ear as she ate a sandwich. "The doctor's not answering. He's on vacation apparently and is proving difficult to trace."

"Shit. Keep at it and keep me posted."

"Any sign of Zachery or do we still have Horace?"

Simpson laughed. "No, but you won't believe it. We've got another one…and it's fucking Kelly. Owen Kelly."

Madison choked on her sandwich.

"You're shitting me."

"He's not talking either. Angry bastard. At least he's not screaming for his lawyer. Just wants a drink"

"We need to get something out of one of them," said Madison. "We've got to charge him or let him go soon. Clock's ticking. Our twenty-four hours are nearly up."

"There's no way I'm letting that fucker go until I get some answers," said Simpson angrily. "He doesn't know how long we've held him. As far as he's concerned, he's only been there an hour."

He hung up.

"Jones" he yelled. "Did Zachery have a phone?"

Jones scurried over. "Yes. It was bagged and locked away" he said. "Why?"

"Get it. I think I know why Kelly's not been answering your calls."

They grabbed the phone, and sure enough, there were over twenty missed calls, fourteen of them originating from the police station.

"You mean I've been calling him, and he's been here all the time?" said Jones in disbelief.

"Yep. The evidence is stacking up" said Simpson with a gleam in his eye. "Check out that partial fingerprint we've got for Kelly too. The one from the phone of the woman that he shot. I'll bet a tenner that it matches Zachery."

Jones sat at his desk and pulled up the fingerprinting software while Simpson returned to the phone and the other six calls. There was a bunch of voicemails.

"First message received today at 1:15 pm. Hi, Dr. Pullman. It's Elena. I'm really sorry to bother you on your holidays, but I have a police constable with me who needs to talk to you urgently about a patient. Please can you call me back as soon as you get this message"?

"You got to by fucking kidding me," said Simpson.

Jones looked up "What's up?"

"He's the doctor too. He's his own fucking doctor."

****

Two more personalities emerged that evening. One of them – Buddy Barnes had clammed up and refused to say a word. Simpson was convinced it was one of the other Four Feathers robbers but couldn't pin anything concrete on him. The other one was a quiet, confused guy who revealed that his name was Ed and said nothing more.

Simpson and Madison had been to his house with a warrant and turned it upside down. They didn't find any diamonds but grabbed his laptop in the hope that they could find something incriminating on it. Simpson wished they had Dickson to look over it. They had other techies, but none of them were as good as Dickson. If any files had been deleted, then Dickson could weave his magic and get them back. Nothing really got deleted unless you knew what you were doing.

"So where's the diamond?" said Simpson exasperated, slumping onto Oscar's sofa. "It must've been him. We've got the names from the Greyspider website, and Jones matched his fingerprints to the Tempest and the coffee shop as Owen and Oscar. The business card in the bank is linked to him too. He must've been the one that took the diamond."

"If that's true, then three of the Four Feathers diamonds should be here too," said Madison. "Did you say they were two other personas? I'm struggling to keep up."

"Buddy and Ed," said Simpson. "I'd bet good money that they stole the other two diamonds."

"And then there's Dr. Pullman," said Madison "Oh, and Horace?"

"Shit. I forgot about him" said Simpson throwing his hands in the air. "This case is frying my brain. I'm too old for this shit."

He started to get up. "Let's get back to the station and start on the laptop. We could…." He stopped.

"Horace," he said thoughtfully.

Madison looked over. "Horace. Yes. What about him?"

"Hor-Ace. It's Ace. The man with the plan who started all this."

"Are you saying that he set a challenge, put it out on Greyspider, and then completed it himself?" said Madison. "As four different personalities. That's pretty far out."

"Fucking case gets weirder by the minute," said Simpson. "Nothing surprises me anymore. Come on. Let's get out of here."

Chapter 42 – "The Queen of Diamonds"

Saturday 13th June

Madison Monroe woke up to the sun streaming through the window. She stretched, yawned and crawled out of bed, and headed to the kitchen to make herself a coffee and some bagels, turning the television on as she passed to catch the news. She recognized the picture on the screen instantly and stopped what she was doing to listen.

"Oscar Zachery, the man arrested in March of this year for the theft of two of the Four Feathers diamonds was released today following a lack of evidence. Embarrassed police officials suggested that key information regarding the case had been misplaced, and what was left was circumstantial at best. Members of an underground website called GreySpider also speculated that Zachery was responsible for the theft of the fifty-million-pound "Queen of Diamonds" that went missing around the same time from Larkins bank. Only one of the Four Feathers diamonds was retrieved, and the Queen of Diamonds is still missing. Investigations are ongoing. Mr. Zachery has been referred to a psychiatric ward in a private clinic where he will be treated for a rare personality disorder."

The report went on to show a frightened Oscar outside the police station with reporters clambering around, shouting questions at him, and thrusting microphones in his direction. He ducked into a waiting car and it sped off.

The video cut to Detective Simpson leaving the police station. He was down to one crutch and still walked with a limp.

"Our investigations are continuing," he said to the waiting throng. "We have a number of leads that we are still following up on and we hope to have an arrest in the coming weeks. Thank you."

Madison smiled. She was glad she was out of it. Two weeks after they'd arrested Zachery, she'd handed in her notice, and was gone by the end of April. She loved her police work, but things had changed. Things would never be the same again.

She poured water from the kettle into her coffee mug and took it into a large walk-in dressing room where she had rows of clothes, shoes, and even wigs. She put her coffee down and ran her fingers over the wigs.

Who shall I be today? she thought. Her fingers stopped at the blonde wig. Brandy? No. Too brash, but always good fun. She hoped that Brandy and Oscar would meet again soon. She had a new vibrating rabbit cock ring that she'd not had a chance to use yet. Oscar would love it.

She stopped at the red wig. Shanice? Now she always enjoyed being the redhead, the soft Irish accent and the striking look always turned heads. It might work for her meeting today. She smiled to herself as she thought of poor Buddy struggling to get to second base. Maybe that day would come sometime soon.

The jet-black wig that Estelle had worn was her favorite, but she quickly moved on. The shock value that came with Estelle wouldn't work. There was always a time and a place for her, but today wasn't it.

She hovered on the short blonde spiky wig. Amy Ross, the loner, the quiet one, the people hater. What she lacked in charisma she made up for in technical skills. Amy could've probably stolen the diamond on her own, but where's the fun in that, she thought.

She decided on the red wig and stood in front of the mirror to put it on. Hang on, why not just be Madison? She looked back at the girl that had started it all. The cute sensible one, the one that had the career, the fiancé, the lifestyle. The one that was engaged to Aaron Pullman.

Two years ago, Dr. Pullman and young officer Monroe had been the perfect couple. All their friends were envious of what they had. The nice clothes, the cars, the apartment. They were going places. Aaron's private psychiatry business was taking off, and her move to the Metropolitan police working with Simpson had put her on a fast track that would see her make junior detective in five years.

She still remembered the day when things had begun to go wrong. Aaron's behavior had started to become erratic - the headaches, the voices, the personality changes. Back then, the characters that he would later develop had not fully emerged, but some of the traits did. She had come home one night to find her fiancé drunk and feisty, and after a heated argument, he had hit her. She took him down instantly, bending his arm behind his back until he apologized and pleaded with her to stop. He'd promised to get help but ended up prescribing himself various tablets which did little to no good. Eventually, he found one that suppressed many of the symptoms, but by then their relationship was in tatters.

She left in tears, vying to never go back, but never stopped loving him. She'd made good friends with Kate in the apartment upstairs and a few months later, hid a small device at the back of Kate's wardrobe that allowed her access into the building's wi-fi, so she could keep tabs on him.

The personalities that would later become Oscar, Buddy, Horace, Owen, and Ed slowly materialized in the coming months and she watched them evolve, unbeknown to him via his laptop camera. As time went on, Dr. Aaron Pullman seemed to have less and less control as the illness progressed.

It was nearly a year later when she decided that she needed this man in her life in some form or other. She missed him. She wanted to be near him. She had to ensure that distance could be kept and that she was always in control of the relationship though, so when Oscar advertised for an assistant, she invented Brandy. Brandy, the strong one. The loud one. The one always in control.

The others quickly followed.

Horace was the last personality to emerge from the man she loved, and from the beginning, he had a fascination with diamonds. She watched his plans evolving, spending many hours working at the computer, coming up with a plan of her own. She saw his many attempts at composing his "challenge" and knew that this was her chance to join in and take control. He caught her unawares when he posted it on New Year's Eve, and the whole thing was nearly scuppered as she didn't get a chance to override the message board for twenty-four hours. What if someone else stole one of the diamonds? She wanted a team that she could watch. A team that she knew. She'd given a little nudge to Buddy and was watching when Oscar and Owen both read about the diamonds. With the GreySpider post blocked from everyone else, the odds were good that her "boys" would come through. She kept up the façade of the website, painstakingly adding hundreds of comments a day so that they would think they had competition.

Somehow it had worked. With the team completed, she saw that she had a real shot at stealing the diamond and disappearing without anyone having any knowledge of her. Oscar's arrest was part of the plan. No one would be looking for her while they had someone in the frame. He was never going to go down for it. She'd made sure of that when she hid the diamonds from Simpson when they searched his apartment, and more recently when she'd destroyed the fingerprint evidence they had from the Tempest and the coffee shop.

She had a mild panic attack when she went to collect the diamond from EZ-Store and found that it wasn't there, but a trace through their system quickly turned up the real box. She had made contact with the buyer that she had found long ago on Ace's computer - the buyer that Ace claimed would give him twenty million for it. After some hard negotiating, he had agreed on fifteen and transferred her the money. The diamond was now somewhere in Africa. She didn't know where and didn't care. She had started tracing the buyer's computer activity and transactions though. She'd find a way to get that extra five million one day.

Her thoughts returned to Aaron, to Oscar, to Buddy, and to Owen. It was her who had organized and paid for the private clinic for him under the pseudonym "Rubato Feather". She wasn't sure whether he'd pick up on the Italian reference or not, but she'd planned on seeing him soon anyway. She didn't know in what capacity and how it would work, but she knew she needed to be with him.

Her outfit and wig chosen, Madison opened the bedroom door and stepped out onto the deck of her Sunseeker Predator 74 private yacht. She was moored off the south coast of Sicily and the sun was beating down a glorious twenty-nine degrees. She had some time before the meeting with "Ivan", the handsome Russian billionaire who wanted her skills for something that wasn't particularly ethical, but she could do with her eyes closed. The fact that he was willing to pay her a quarter of a million was a bonus.

She stripped off her silk dressing gown and dived naked into the Mediterranean, the cool water making her gasp, but she always loved the feeling of it on her bare skin. She did two laps around the boat, before returning for a shower.

The message waiting for her on the laptop on GreySpider was from Ivan.

Ivan_11:   Still OK for midday? Usual place?

She smiled. Today was going to be a good day.

QueenOfDiamonds: Looking forward to it

Afterword

Oscar and Brandy took their show to Vegas and gained a supporting slot for Penn & Teller at the Rio for six months. People from all over the world were wowed by "The Wizard of Oz" and his beautiful assistant. Their loofer illusion is legendary.

Buddy and Shanice got married at the Graceland Wedding Chapel by an Elvis lookalike. Buddy finally got to use his condoms.

Owen found a tiny casino on the outskirts of the golden mile, where he fritters away large chunks of money. Estelle is a hit with the punters and has adopted a southern American drawl when calling them all "Yankee motherfuckers." Unknown to Owen, Estelle owns the casino and makes a tidy profit, and keeps a careful eye on his drinking.

Dickson recovered from his head injury, and while lying in the hospital bed, proposed to his boyfriend Tony. The wedding reception took place at the Mirage Lounge, and Dickson persuaded Simpson to be his best man – something that his guilt would not allow him to refuse. He is still recovering from what he called "The gayest fucking event I've ever been to in my entire life".

Ace is completely enthralled by Vegas and spends a lot of time pacing the seven and a half thousand steps of the Vegas Strip, mumbling to himself.

"One, two, three, four..."

He's heard about a diamond owned by a Vegas entrepreneur known as the "King of Diamonds". His plan is coming together. If only he could find a team….

The End

Authors Note

Some of my favorite stories are those that you finish and want to read again immediately as some plot twist gets revealed at the end that changes everything. When I started to think about this book, the idea of one guy playing all the parts was appealing. Trying to write it and keep the reader unaware was a challenge. I really hope it worked and you were fooled right up to the big reveal.

The bigger challenge was the timeline. I'd written a few chapters when I found that Oscar was doing a show with Brandy while Buddy was on a con. I soon realized that I would need to keep a tight rein on the timeline for all the main characters so that they couldn't overlap. It was actually worse than that. The girls - including Madison, couldn't meet up with any of the other guys in case she was recognized. This timeline has allowed me to keep them all separate and I am confident that there are no gaping flaws in the plot.

If you have enjoyed this book, I would appreciate it if you could leave a review on Amazon using the link/website below:-

https://www.amazon.com/review/create-review/ref=cm_cr_othr_d_wr_but_top?ie=UTF8&channel=glance-detail&asin=B088Q2JTL5

Also, for more information about my books, short stories, news & events, etc, please visit my website and sign up to my mailing list:-

https://jdiggle69.wixsite.com/jmdiggle/contact

As a final note, all of the characters, places, and names in this book are completely fictional and not based on real people or events.

If anyone I know recognizes themselves – oops !!!

Printed in Great Britain
by Amazon